e-Book ISBN: 978-1-969444-12-8

Paperback ISBN: 978-1-969444-13-5

Cover design by Designs by Charly

Interior design and formatting by Brianna Cooper

Editing by Hannah G. Scheffer-Wentz, English Proper Editing Services
Proofreading by Zee, English Proper Editing Services

Internal art by Giovanna Capel

A
MASQUERAVE
NOVEL

CODED IN CONTROL

KL HILL

To anyone brave enough to follow the masked stranger down a dark hallway and risk it all, this one's for you.

PLAYLIST

If We Ever Meet Again (Feat. Katy Perry) – Timbaland

Talking Body – Tove Lo

someday, someone – Kenzie Cait

Unholy (feat. Kim Petras) – Sam Smith

Close To You – Gracie Abrams

Dirty Thoughts – Chloe Adams

Good For You – Selena Gomez, A$AP Rocky

What a Feeling – Alex D'Rosso, Yusuf Alev, Kelly Matejcic

Sports car – Tate McRae

Can't Help Falling In Love (DARK) – Tommee Profitt, brooke

Greener (Acoustic) – Taylor Acorn

Latch – Disclosure, Sam Smith

Ordinary – Alex Warren

We Go Down Together (with Khalid) – Dove Cameron

Toxic – 2WEI

Heaven – Julia Michaels

Beautiful Things – Benson Boone

You Don't Own Me (feat. G-Eazy) – SAYGRACE

I Think I'm in Love – Taylor Acorn

Iris – The Goo Goo Dolls

2 hands – Tate McRae

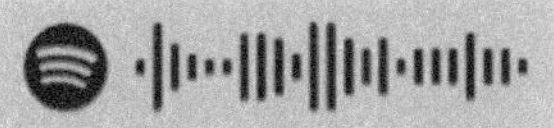

"We loved with a love that was more than love."

-Edgar Allan Poe, Annabel Lee

AUTHOR'S NOTE

Hello, Little Hillion,

Coded in Control is the first book in the *Masquerave* series and contains mature, graphic content. This novel includes sexually explicit scenes, dark themes, and intense emotional and physical elements, including non-consensual situations, violence, and explicit sexual content. It is not suitable for all audiences and is recommended for readers 18+.

Reader discretion is strongly advised.

While I prefer you to go into the story blind, a full list of detailed trigger warnings is available on **www.klhillauthor.com**. This is a work of fiction, but if you are sensitive to such material, please proceed with caution.

Please note that Coded in Control is the first book in the series and ends on a cliffhanger. What may seem like plot holes will be filled, one way or another, I promise. For the full experi- ence, it is recommended that you read the series in order.

Join KL Hill's Little Hillions Hang Out Facebook Group to chat while you read!

Lastly, in honor of all those that Lena represents, if you or someone you know is seeking support or a path to safety, please visit https://www.thehotline.org/ for the resources and guid- ance you deserve. You are not alone.

xoxo, KL Hill

PROLOGUE

I'M a shark waiting for my prey, hidden among the waves of people on the dance floor, blending in with all the masked faces. The game of hidden identity makes this game even more fun, because behind every one of those masks is a sinner. Their secrets are passed around like a drug, and their sinister deeds are worn like badges of honor.

Reaching up, I tap my finger against my mask, the metal cool against my skin. The gold is molded to my face and sparkles in the light as a reminder of who I am. This club oozes with powerful and conniving monsters dressed in their designer clothes. They pay high dollar for their fucks and for their secrets to remain mere whispers inside these walls.

Those whispers remind me that I'm not the only predator in the room, but our masks make us one and the same. The only difference is that mine lets me hide in plain sight as the new-age golden boy with a thirst for blood. Particularly, the blood of the men who have made my life a hell of a lot harder than necessary. I want to drag them all down together to drown in their own blood, watch as they fight and claw for their lives while they turn on each other.

But I don't.

Like a shark, I wait in the dark depths, keeping my urges pushed down and building pressure. The pressure that, when it finally releases, will spring me up and I'll crush them between my teeth. Shredding them and letting their blood coat my tongue, painting everything in crimson.

Even as my beast lurks under the surface of my skin, begging me to let him take a bite, I keep a casual air about me. A smile graces my lips as I pass by people, giving them a false sense of comfort as my eyes scan the floor, looking for my target. I clutch my soda water, my palms itching as I curl my fingers around the glass. The fingers of my free hand curl into a fist, and I let my nails press into my skin. The need to draw blood, even my own, is nearly overwhelming.

As much as I enjoy stalking my prey and being on the front lines, I have eyes and ears all over this club. The whispers that flow through this place find their way to me and are saved for later. Tonight, though, I'm out for blood, and this take-down is personal.

While I could keep my hands clean and let one of my trusted people have the hits, I want to coat my hands with their blood. Stain my skin red. I've been on the hunt for a while now, and I'm ready to make the kill of a lifetime and finally let my inner beast sink its teeth into the flesh of my enemies.

I'm too distracted in my thoughts as I turn to cross the club, just as another body crashes into mine. My first instinct is to grip the woman's arms to keep her steady, the smell of her sweet perfume flooding my nose. She gasps, her phone clattering to the ground, the screen bright against the dark floor.

"Oh my gosh." The voice is as sweet as her scent, with a hint of surprise. "I am so sorry. I—"

Her wide eyes meet mine, stopping her sentence short as if the breath was stolen from her lungs. Even from behind her mask, I can see how fucking beautiful she is. Her long, brown hair cascades over her shoulders in waves. Her black dress is just revealing enough to make my mouth water as it hugs her body, accentuating her curves. Her amber eyes shine bright in the disco lights, ones that I could get lost in.

I let my eyes rove over her before they halt on her hand pressed to her chest. A black stone ring sits on her left hand. One that is made to look like a fucking wedding ring, but with even deeper ties. I keep my face neutral, because that ring can only mean one thing.

Obsidian.

Only men of power have rings like this for their women—and usually, their women are just as fucked up as their men are. This one, though, doesn't give off the same vibes as the other women I've met. The ones who stand next to their men like docile creatures, only to have a knife at their backs, ready to strike. They're loyal to a fault because they have ultimately picked the wrong side.

She stiffens, as if ready for a blow. "It's all right, love," I croon, taking in her delicate features behind her black, lace mask. "If I wasn't so far up my own ass, then I wouldn't have *unintentionally* bumped into you."

She lets out a polite giggle, covering her mouth with the same hand that her infernal ring sits upon. I watch as it glints in the light, nearly igniting my blood. We stand here for a moment, my grip on her arms loosening enough that if she wanted to step away, she could. However, she holds my gaze, electricity buzzing between us.

Who the fuck does she belong to? Whoever they are, they're careless for letting her wander away like this. Usually, they're shackled to their men when they're out in public, not free to roam around in a club like this.

"You have beautiful blue eyes." Her voice is barely above a whisper, but it echoes through me, filling me.

With a smirk, I say, "A gift from my mother." It sounds like a cheesy line, and it is, but there's truth laced in it when they're one of the only things my mother ever gave me. They got me both in and out of trouble in a blink.

She gives me another smile, and even though this woman could be dangerous, a ticking time bomb, I want to pull the pin and see how long it takes for her to detonate.

I loosen my grip a little more, and this time, she takes a small step back. Not far but enough to require me to let go of her. She doesn't move anymore, though, as her eyes lock on my face, as if she wants to take in every inch. The electricity between us makes the hair on my arms stand on end, my fingertips tingling with the need to keep touching her. If I didn't know better, I'd think this little vixen has drugged my drink and is plotting her own takedown.

She fiddles with the fucking ring as she says, "A very impressive present." Her voice is low this time, thick, as if the words were sticking to her throat. It's how I would imagine her voice would be after she was mouth-fucked by my cock, my cum coating her throat. I nearly groan at the vulgar thought, my cock already twitching.

A piece of her thick, brown hair falls over her masked face, blocking her amber eye from view. I reach up and brush it behind her ear, catching her intake of breath as I feel an electric zap prick my fingers. My touch lingers, her gaze holding for a beat before drifting down to where her phone lies on the floor. I reluctantly drop my hand, my fingers instantly going cold, as I bend for her phone. My fingers brush against the screen, lighting it up again, and displaying her background photo.

What I was hoping would be a photo of her and her *betrothed*, was nothing more than a photo of the sunset over the city. A perfect depiction of this fucking place with the light shining over the tops of the buildings that leave shadows over the rest of it, permanently cloaked in darkness.

I hold it out for her as her delicate fingers brush against mine, her nails gently scraping my skin. The image of those same nails clawing at my back as I fuck her hits me so hard that it nearly topples me over, releasing the beast that lurks in the darkness.

Get it the fuck together.

"Thank you." Her voice is breathless as if she could read my mind and the filthy thoughts that plague it. "And I'm sorry again."

She seems so innocent, almost embarrassed to be here. She's so sweet that my teeth ache to take a bite. I let the corners of my mouth curve, showing those teeth. "It's an honor to have a woman as beautiful as you plow into me."

A blush crawls up her neck as she lets out a laugh that has my heart racing. It's full and velvety to my ears. A laugh that hits me in the chest and tries to pierce my heart. "You're very clever." The chuckle lingers in her voice.

I give her a wink, working my charm on her, just as a male voice cuts through the crowd.

"Lena. *Lena!*"

The woman flinches slightly as she turns toward the dance floor and takes a step away from me, her long legs creating distance, as a man exits the crowd that seems to part for him. He's on her in a few steps, gripping her arm and tugging her to his side. His eyes are bright with a fiery rage that could burn you alive.

"Lena, what the *hell* is taking you so long? You've kept us waiting," he growls, and she immediately shrinks an inch. My fingers curl into a fist as I take this fucker in.

He's average height, but his massive, broad shoulders make him seem even larger. He's dressed casually in jeans and a black tee that cuts into his biceps. His hazel blue eyes are a contrast to his plain, black mask that gives too much of his face away. If he's trying to be discreet, like most are in this club, then he's clearly an amateur.

But that's not the case, is it? He likes it this way. This

fucker wants to be seen and believes that he's the top dog here. *Untouchable*. But he couldn't be more wrong.

I know this man and he's exactly who I've been looking for, even hiding behind the scrap of cloth he calls a mask. What I find interesting is that he's ballsy enough to let his woman off leash in a place like this. Men in his position want their women at their side and to remain quiet, hanging on every word they say, or they want them to become quiet killers, ready and willing to shed the blood of their enemies.

The urge to knock his teeth out and shove them down his throat one by one has my nails biting into my palm. This fucker hangs out like *he* owns the place. He prances in with his entourage, slides into his private booths, and fucks whatever woman looks his way. He normally doesn't show up with a woman, only wanting to play the field, but he's been bringing this same one around more. Flaunting her like a prized dog. She's nothing more than his little bitch that he feels like he needs to keep on a tight leash. And I have a feeling after tonight, she won't get this far away from her master again.

Her shoulders stiffen, even as her legs tremble. It's like she doesn't know what to do. Run and risk being hunted down by him and his dogs or staying and taking his punishment up front. But I know that if she knew what kind of shit he was up to around here, the things that have been whispered about him, she'd be running as fast and as far as she could.

More dark thoughts fill my mind as I imagine her running right here where I tie her up and keep her in a room beneath our feet. I'd gag her so no one could hear her scream my name as I fucked her senseless, her muffled cries begging me for more.

Her amber eyes have a darkness to them, the kind that comes with being with a man like this piece of shit. The ones where her own demons press against her and try to claw their way from the inside out. It's clear that she's been worn down and finds solace in her own mind, crawling to the dark corners of it and letting those demons consume her. I can tell that we're not that different and maybe she wouldn't mind being leashed by me, barking my name as I pound into her. My cock twitches again, and I resist the urge to palm myself right here and now.

"Who the fuck is *this*?" His words yank me back from my thoughts, his lips curled in disgust, his eyes committing me to memory.

This woman, Lena, is nearly groveling at his feet, her eyes looking at the floor as she answers him. "I accidentally ran into him on my way back from the bathroom." Her eyes discreetly slide to me, the look almost begging for me not to say anything incriminating. "I'm sorry, Matt."

Matt.

She sounds so pathetic as she says his name, in a pleading way, as if he has his hand wrapped around her throat and she's begging him to let go. That at any moment he'll squeeze tighter and tighter, choking the air from her lungs, just to watch as more of the light leaves her eyes.

I'm a sadist and occasionally a masochist. A thrill seeker. But even I couldn't find the pleasure he does by sucking the life out of her, dimming those beautiful amber eyes until the light finally goes out.

"Are you sure?" He grips her tighter, his eyes darkening as he looms over her, forcing her to crane her neck to look up at him. "You looked like you were having a grand time chatting him up." His words are smooth, but there's a sharp edge to them, intended to slice her up. "Like you were about to make a deal like one of the whores who slum this place."

Motherfucker.

She starts to shake, her eyes dropping to her feet. Her hands are fisted at her sides, her lip nearly trembling as she fights back tears. He truly is a fucking piece of shit to have a woman this afraid of him instead of bowing down at her feet and pleasuring her while he's down there.

I take a step between them, giving my award-winning smile to ease the tension and get an even better look at this fucker. "It was an honest mistake." I gesture to her. "The lady got turned around and I was pointing her back in the right direction." I give him the same edge in my voice that he gave to her.

Anger rolls off of him at my response, not pleased about me standing up for her or for getting in his space. His entire demeanor changes as he finally takes me in, realizing the power I hold around here and that he's in my territory. He flips a switch and the charming community leader persona comes to the forefront. His shoulders relax and his face forms an eerily pleasant grin, as if he's in front of a boardroom or a camera. His too white teeth gleam in the club lights like a predator's in the moonlight.

"Women, am I right?" His voice is light as he lets out a chuckle, reaching out to grip my shoulder as if we're old friends. My skin crawls where he touches me and I have to refrain from shrugging him off.

My eyes flicker to Lena, and her entire body vibrates. Her arms are stiff as she presses them to her sides, holding herself together.

Her eyes flick back up from the floor, forcing a smile and blinking rapidly as if to hold back the tears that are shining in her eyes. It's practiced behavior and it makes me see fucking red.

I hold his stare, keeping my face neutral. "I'm not sure what you mean, *Matt*." I try to hold back the snarl in my voice as I take a step toward him, crowding his space and putting more distance between him and Lena. He can tell what I'm doing and sidesteps me, his hand falling from my shoulder, but making sure to keep his eyes on her at all times.

Interesting.

He's fucking threatened. Good—because he doesn't have a fucking clue who he's fucking with.

His eyes darken more as if in a challenge. "I mean that they're clumsy as fuck and always playing the fucking damsel in distress." He lets out another chuckle as he waves his hand in nonchalance, but I don't miss the way his eyes flash to Lena. Controlling.

Possessive.

I shrug, turning to give her a soft smile. "If anyone is clumsy as fuck, it would have to be me." My eyes shift to where he holds her arm, his fingers pressing into her skin, red marks already forming. I want to saw his hands off one at a time, shoving one in his ass and the other down his throat.

She looks up at me, desperation swirling in her eyes. She gives me a soft smile, dropping it just as quickly as she made it. I also don't miss the way her eyes keep looking to the exit as if she's trying to build up the courage to run from this bastard. I wouldn't be surprised if he didn't have a GPS embedded in her somewhere and he would get off on the chase.

Matt scoffs. "Well, thank you for your *assistance*, but we have a booth to return to." He steps away from me, yanking her with him. Her face is flushed red with embarrassment and something else. Fear, maybe?

My fingers twitch with the urge to reach out and grip his hair, yanking it from his scalp for dismissing me like that. If she thinks that her little boyfriend is bad, she has no idea what kinds of things I can get into. The blood that's forever stained on my hands.

She gives me a polite smile as he pulls her away, trying her best to be the dutiful woman of a criminal. I can almost hear her whimper as the leash tightens more and they disappear into the crowd.

My heart is pounding in my ears, drowning out the music, and I narrow my gaze on where they disappeared. Pulling out my phone, I type out a quick text with very specific instructions. In less than a minute, I get a response, moving my plans forward. Letting that piece of shit walk away from me without pummeling his face has my muscles aching as I lie in wait for the chance to pounce.

Before I can pocket my phone, I get another text, one that pulls up the corners of my mouth into a dark smile. I give the dance floor one last sweep, seeing if I can catch one more glimpse of them, of *her*, but they're lost in the waves. *Until next time, Lena.*

Turning on my heel to head toward the back stairs, I slip into the dim hallway. The music drowns out behind me as I slide the door close. I pass the other lacquer, black doors as I move to the end of the hall, letting myself through the more discreet one. My shoes quietly click against the metal steps as I make my way down, hearing moans of pleasure through the door at the landing. Tonight, though, I'm not here for pleasure.

I'm here to inflict pain.

With my fob, I unlock the door that hides in plain sight behind an erotic painting. It slides open with a quiet whoosh and I'm met with another descent. Each step down lowers the temperature another degree as I head even further underground, the walls aging from smooth concrete to exposed brick. At the last step, I'm met with a large metal door, sealed tight by all the security measures I've taken over the years, that includes the elevator doors that are shut tight to my left. Very few are allowed this far down, and fewer have permission to leave. One misstep and this could be the last place you see.

As I scan my thumb, the door unlocks and I push my way in. The lights are off, the only light coming in from the threshold as the door swings wide open. My shadow casts itself across the concrete floor like the monster in me is reaching out, searching for its next victim.

I step in, closing the door behind me, letting the darkness cloak me. Before my eyes fully adjust, I flick on the light switch next to me. The single bulb hanging down burns bright, casting its light onto a figure in the middle of the room.

I keep myself in the shadows as the man whose arms and legs are strapped to an anchored metal chair squeezes his eyes shut, his moans filling the quiet space. His head is still lolling from the drug-induced haze he was put in not too long ago.

I clear my throat and his head snaps up, eyes flying open, trying to see who is beyond the light and lurking in the shadows. Blood trickles from his temple and nose, his one eye already swollen shut. He put up a fight not to be dragged down here, but not enough of one to spare his measly life. People like him deserve to be brought down a few notches and see what it's like to have their life in someone else's hands.

I take a few steps toward the light, my steps echoing through the room as the shadows cast across my face. He furiously shakes his head, trying to clear his mind from the drugs that are flowing through him. "W-who the fuck are you?" His breaths are heavy as he fights at the leather straps holding him in place. "Let me fucking go."

I chuckle as I examine the table of tools that was left out for me, tapping my fingers on each one. "Why the rush?" I croon. Something like desire flows through my words, but not for his cock—for his blood. He fights harder as I pick up a blade, the chair rattling against him. I let the metal shine in the light, my body still coated in shadows, as I tap the sharp point with my finger, letting it nick my skin. The pain nearly makes me hard as ruby red liquid wells up before trailing down my finger. Just call me a fucking masochist.

I catch the blood on my tongue as I step into the light, making a show of dragging the tip up my finger before licking it clean. With slow, predatory steps, I close the distance between me and the man floundering in the chair.

I let him fight, his veins bulging as adrenaline pumps through his body. I lower the blade, pressing it against the base of his neck, and he freezes. I press the blade in more, tearing open his skin, the metallic smell of his blood flooding my nose.

It wells over the blade, running down his chest as if it's trying to escape the inevitable.

"P-please," he begs, his eyes going glassy with tears. "I-I'll do whatever you want."

Fucking pathetic.

I roll my eyes at his pleas, pressing the blade further into his skin. He lets out a pained groan, but he's already shown his cards. He only made himself look tough, but deep down, he's a pathetic piece of shit. He found his way down here by trying to touch what didn't belong to him and giving out one too many secrets of his own.

"Anything, huh?" I keep my voice low, my words purring through my chest. I lean over him and press my nose to his, making his eyes cross as I move the blade to his collarbone, letting it bite into the skin. He sucks in a sharp breath and I can't help the smile that pulls up my lips. "Then let's play a game."

His screams fill the air as he sings his confessions like a bird, his blood painting the gray floor crimson as more than words spill out of him.

CHAPTER ONE
3 MONTHS LATER

Lena

THE FAMILIAR SMELL of sweat and expensive cologne permeates through the club. With a drink in hand, I make my way back from the bar to one of the tall tables that sit around the dance floor's perimeter. There must be hundreds of people in here and more waiting outside to get in. The line is more than wrapped around the building of the hottest club in town, Masquerave. The requirement to get in is simple: you *must* wear a mask.

The building takes up an entire city block and is at least five, maybe six stories. Even in the light of day, it's a looming presence in the middle of the city. While it's a place to come and let loose from your regular life, I've also heard whispers of sinful debauchery that happens behind closed doors. But I've never been close enough to the action to see for myself.

To get in, we showed the bouncer our masks and IDs, who were definitely judging on more than the fact that you have a mask to put on. I'm extremely thankful for the girl we made friends in line with, because without her flashing her impeccable tits and all of us slipping that bastard an extra twenty, I don't think we would have gotten in this time. Fucking men.

Looking over the edge of my drink as I take a sip, I watch

the people in front of me on the dance floor and savor a moment to take in the club around me. The atrium of Masquerave is like walking into a cathedral of sin and debauchery. Up the three stories, the club lights glitter off the balcony railings like stained glass in the sunlight, their colors lighting up the club from floor to ceiling and shining a light on the crowded dance floor. People are dancing like they're worshiping the music and the other bodies around them. I let my gaze float across the dance floor to the club's dark, more private corners. There's not much to see from this distance because I'm making it a point to stay away. I'm not sure who I'd run into tonight, but I'm well aware of what happens in the shadows when the monsters come out to play.

The few times I've been here, I was surrounded by power hungry public figures and their equally hungry gazes as they watched the people who worked at this club. It wasn't lost on me that they looked down their noses at the staff, only giving them their cheapest smiles when they were passing the non-discrete bills to pay for their experience behind the door of a private room.

Those people see themselves as gods on Earth and expect to be worshiped as such. They usually get off on bringing people to their knees, sometimes looking for their own pleasure and other times looking to cause pain. The latter brings them the most joy and erects their egos as much as their cocks.

The view from here gives me a better look at the exclusive booths at the back, blocked from everyone else behind velvet ropes, with staff waiting on them hand and foot. Now that I'm free from the watchful eyes from behind those ropes that might as well be chains, I finally get a view of the dancers in the cages that are suspended from the ceiling while others are on platforms that are level with the balconies on the higher floors. They are strategically placed so no one misses out on the show. They move to the music, enticing onlookers and the sea of masked people who are all grinding together on the dance floor.

The DJ booth sits high above our heads. A metal staircase leads up to one of the VIP balconies, and security guards flank both sides, ensuring that no one who isn't permitted steps near it.

Adjusting my mask, made of face-formed black lace and a satin ribbon tied around my head, I look through the sea of sweaty bodies to find my friends, Bri and Kate. I see them grinding up on two men. Both are ripped and seemingly handsome, even from this distance.

Bri catches my stare through her scarlet red mask that's almost identical to mine. She waves and starts blowing kisses at me, drawing Kate's eyes in my direction. Her eyes light up through her plum-colored mask, gesturing for me to join them.

I raise my drink, saluting a carefree night. I add a reassuring smile and let them continue their fun.

My therapist claims that socializing will help with my previous traumas and assist me back into a normal routine within society. Whatever the fuck that means.

I write in my journal like the good patient I am, satisfying her just enough that she doesn't press and clock the evenings out with my friends.

I'm done with people controlling me and telling me what to do. I give her just enough to make her feel like we're getting somewhere, but never the whole truth. That could open up a can of worms that I worked too hard to seal shut.

I take a sip of my drink and I feel my phone buzz on the table, the screen face down. I ignore it, taking another sip, only for it to buzz again. It's like I can feel his eyes on me, watching me. I look at my phone to be greeted by an unknown number sending multiple messages.

Taking another deep breath, I unlock my phone to see

what it could possibly be now. What could I possibly be doing wrong, even though I'm single and away from him?

I read the first message.

UNKNOWN

Lena, baby. I miss you

Well, that's a new one.

But then, we're followed by:

UNKNOWN

Where the fuck are you?

And:

UNKNOWN

I know you're not at home.

A shiver runs down my spine as I reread the last message. The image of the crowd parting and his broad shoulders casting large shadows under a spotlight, staring at me, has my heart racing. I've had this feeling of being watched ever since I left. The sensation of someone watching through the windows or following me on the street has weighed heavily on me. I feel fucking insane, because every time I look, no one is there.

Even with my growing paranoia, how could he possibly know that I'm not home? I've checked all my settings and apps to see if he has access to my location and there's nothing. Anything else that he might have had access to was left behind when I finally got the fuck out of there.

I squeeze my eyes shut and place the phone back on the table, trying to calm my racing heart. He's just fucking with me, that's all. He probably paid someone to access my new number and wants to make me feel like a crazy person. And unfortunately, it's working.

Opening my eyes, I trail across the mass of people to one of the pole dancers. I watch her move gracefully up and down the pole, completely mesmerized by her. She's a great distraction in her red lace lingerie and delicate high heels. Her mask glitters in the disco lights and I'm fully entranced by her movements. I'm so engulfed in her show that I don't even realize someone is walking behind me as I shift my weight back, bumping right into them.

I yelp, my heart jumping into my throat as I pull myself as close to the table as humanly possible. The table rocks forward and I grip the edges, so it doesn't topple, which causes my drink to slosh over the edge, half of it spilling out. Embarrassment heats my cheeks, but a deep voice cuts through the music before I can blurt out an involuntary, *I'm sorry.*

"Excuse me, love."

I nearly shudder with relief at the voice because it's different from the one that plagues my nightmares. I stand up straight and turn to see a man in a black and silver mask shielding the top of his face, the intricate design shining in the dance floor lights. His thick, dirty blond hair is mussed like he's been running his hands through it. His chiseled jaw frames a charming smile.

"I'm so sorry," I blurt out. My nerves are nearly shot because, of course, I would bump into a handsome man and make a fool out of myself. I only had one sip of this drink and someone might think I was already hammered.

Our eyes meet, and I hold his gaze for a moment, taken aback by his striking blue eyes. They're stunning and I have the sense that I've looked into them before, but I can't seem to put my finger on where. More than likely here at one time, in passing, because it wasn't like I was permitted to go anywhere that another man this handsome would also be.

He's wearing dark jeans, dark dress shoes, and a white button-up shirt with the top few buttons undone, showing off part of his *very* chiseled chest. His sleeves are rolled up to his elbows, showing off forearms that mirror a Greek god's. He's built, yet on the leaner side, but there's nothing short of *power* that rolls off this man.

He nods in the direction of the dance floor as he says, "She's good, isn't she?" His deep, husky voice rises over the thump of the music, pulling me back from my thoughts.

My brow furrows. "Excuse me?"

"Tasha." He nods again, this time toward the dancer I had been watching. "The dancer. She's good, isn't she?"

I look toward her just as she drops down into a split, before going hand over hand on the pole, bringing herself back up. Her moves are fluid, almost effortless. My mouth gapes open at her. "She's…uh…amazing." I watch her as she twirls around the pole and imagine the freedom she must feel being able to express herself like that, being a confident woman. She's wearing lingerie, but she might as well be naked in the see through lace. "I could watch her all night." The words slip from my lips, and I snap them shut, the heat of embarrassment crawling up my neck.

I look back at him and see a smile pull on his lips. "She is one of the best dancers we have here. A true artist." He watches me like a wolf would watch a lamb, his bright blue eyes burning into me. I try to imagine what he looks like behind his mask, trying to place him. This place and their fucking rule. "Can I offer to buy you another drink?" he asks, gesturing to the mess on the table.

My face goes flush as I take in the mess I made, the cocktail napkin already drenched. I nervously giggle, because I don't know the last time I've been asked by someone if they wanted to buy me a drink. I really don't remember the last time a man offered anything to me where I actually had an option. Which makes me feel like this could be a trap set by my ex, that this guy could be here to lure me to wherever he is. *God, Lena, you're fucking paranoid.* The man just wants to buy you a drink.

He watches me intently, his hands casually placed in his pockets. "I-I'm good, thank you." I'm a fucking mess and need to get my shit together in front of this extremely attractive man. I can feel my face flushing even more, my racing heartbeat filling my ears. This stranger already has me flustered and I can't figure out why, like there's already a connection between us that I just can't place.

He leans in, his breath smelling like a mix of whiskey and mint. "Are you sure?" His eyes lock with mine. "It's on me." I feel the curl of heat in my lower abdomen, because I feel like he's offering me more than just a drink. I'm lost in his eyes and croak out the only two words my tongue can form. "I-I'm sure." He smirks, as if sensing the pull he has on me. Without a word, he turns on his heel and walks toward the bar.

The heat that was curling in me snuffs out as I watch him walk away. Fucking great. I just offended this man, who is clearly someone of status in this club, by declining a drink. I let out a quiet, frustrated groan. Way to fucking go, Lena. You come out with your friends for a good time and act like you've never interacted with anyone before.

I slump onto the high-top table and let my eyes drift back toward the dancer, Tasha. She's climbing up the pole and twirling down with grace. She really is an artist, the kind that makes you feel something deep and makes you want more of their work.

I would see videos of dancers on my social media and always wanted to take a pole dancing class. I brought it up one time to Matt, thinking he would find it sexy, but instead, he accused me of being a whore. He went on a whole tangent about how I would be out cheating on him in this class, that I would be learning how to whore myself out. He was absolutely furious that I would even suggest it, and the next day, I couldn't find my car keys. I had to get an Uber to take me to work and bring me home, because he was giving me the cold shoulder and acted as though I didn't even exist. I cried myself to sleep that night as he lay next to me, disgusted at myself for wanting to do something so erotic. I went through my phone and blocked all the accounts with any suggestive content, because the only thing I needed to be was the woman that he wanted me to be.

The next morning, my keys magically appeared on the hook by the door, as if they had been there the entire time. He made me coffee, and when I got home that night, he fucked me, actually taking the time to get me off first. I allowed the orgasm to wash away my hidden desires and we never spoke of the incident again.

I pick up my glass, sipping on what's left of my drink and watching her a while longer. I'm lost in her movements as the song comes to an end. She does one last twirl around the pole, sticking out her flawless ass as she looks over her shoulder to the crowd, giving them one last look before she exits the stage.

I throw back the last of my drink, trying to wipe away the spill with the small cocktail napkin to no avail, and scan the crowd for my friends. A hand catches my elbow as I step away, causing my heart to speed up as fear pulses through my veins. I turn and am once again met with striking blue eyes and a black and silver mask.

It's clear he doesn't miss my overreaction and lets his hand slip away, my skin tingling where his fingers were. "I see that you're ready for another round." He smiles, looking at the empty glass on the table. "So I let the bartender know that all of your drinks are on the house tonight."

My mouth opens and closes like a fish out of water. I take in the hard line of his jaw, his lush lips, and his blond, tousled hair. "Thank you," I barely manage to squeak out. How has this man left me so speechless? It's like he has me by the throat.

He reaches out and gently brushes a stray piece of hair away from my face. "Of course, love. Enjoy your evening."

I'm left standing there, my skin tingling from his touch, as he saunters past and heads toward an open doorway behind me. It's dark except for a faint glow, making it seem very exclusive and not for regular patrons like me. He crosses the threshold and stops, turning back in my direction. His lips curl up into a Cheshire smile, seeing that he still has my attention. He holds my gaze for a beat longer before turning and disappearing into the dark.

Am I having an out of body experience or is this man attempting to lure me down a dark and mysterious hallway? I look back in the direction of my friends, who seem to be having the time of their lives on the dance floor. Bri is now turned around and is practically dry humping the guy she was grinding on earlier, while Kate has her arms wrapped around a new guy, her tongue shoved down his throat. He grabs her ass and hoists her up. Her legs wrap around his waist as he starts walking them toward the back wall where the private rooms are.

My mouth gapes at the sight, but I'm not surprised at their ability to be so carefree. I know we didn't pregame that hard, but it's been years since I've been out with the two of them. Maybe this is their normal now. Which is fine because, apparently, the urge to follow a stranger down a dark hallway is my new normal. I walk past a few people as I slowly make my way to the doorway he passed through. A part of my brain is screaming at me that this is a bad idea, but this is the same part of my brain that stayed quiet all those years. I don't think its voice is valid anymore.

I brace my hands on the framing, leaning in to take a look around. It's dimly lit by sconces on the walls, but there's not a soul down it. I pass the threshold, and it's almost as if the club on the other side is non-existent, as the music is drowned out.

As I walk into the long hall, I feel like I've walked into a completely different world. It's lined on one side with doors, each with a gold number and a small red light next to it.

My heels click on the floor as I brave a few steps in, just as a door unlocks ahead. I freeze in place like a deer caught in headlights, watching as one of the doors down the hall opens slowly. Two women walk out, holding hands. Even from this distance, they look stunning, dressed in only black bras, thongs, and strappy, black heels. They're both wearing black masks with bunny ears popping up past their hairline.

They both turn to face the door and I see that they have matching cuffs on their wrists and choker necklaces. Their lips turn up into dazzling smiles as a man walks out, cupping their faces and lifting their chins up. His upper body is bare, with tattoos covering both arms in full sleeves. He's wearing black jogger pants and black sneakers, giving off a gym rat vibe. I've seen a lot of masks tonight, but not one like his. Its form is fitted to his head, like a ski mask, with a large zipper up the back. Only his eyes and mouth are exposed.

Still in my frozen state, I watch as he turns and stares right at me. His eyes light up as I stare back, his hand slipping into his pocket, pulling something out. My eyes flick down to see that he's gripping two ropes—no, fucking *leashes*—and runs them through his hands until the metal clips hit his palm. Without breaking eye contact with me, he clasps the leashes onto each of the chokers and gives them a light tug to ensure they're secure.

My eyes widen as realization hits me that those aren't just chokers, but fucking dog collars. After another tug, chuckling, he breaks eye contact. He runs his hands down their necks to their breasts, running his thumbs over their nearly exposed nipples. I hear their soft moans, which seem to make his eyes twinkle with delight before he leads the women to a door at the other end of the hall. The clicks of their heels are almost in perfect sync with each other, the sway of their hips mesmerizing.

They stop in front of the door as he reaches out for the handle, but stops as his fingers wrap around it. He clears his throat, the sound traveling down the hall. I watch in amazement as both women clasps their hands in front of them and tilt their heads down in submission. He nods and grunts at them approvingly as he swings open the door, letting them through. He looks back at me one more time, letting his eyes run up and down my body. He gives me a grin that sends heat right down to my core before he passes through the door, closing it with a click behind him.

Once again alone, I stare at the door they went through, hardly believing what I just witnessed. Did I just walk into a sex club? I've been to this club a dozen times before and knew about the private rooms that people could use, but it didn't even occur to me that there could be more happening behind the scenes. Has this always been here?

Clearly, I'm out of my fucking league here and just need to see myself back out to the club. I have no idea where the masked stranger went as he's nowhere to be seen. I was out of my mind to think that he was flirting with me and encouraging me to follow him. Why would he when there are dozens of women here who would be a much better catch than me? Even though those dark thoughts would crowd my mind when I spent nights alone while Matt was out doing business, I'm too vanilla for this place.

I feel and definitely look like an idiot just standing here. Alone. I need to get the fuck out of here and find my friends. I turn to head back, but there's someone leaning against the doorframe of the exit. The lights from the club behind him cast a shadow across him, blacking him out. I can barely make them out as a deep voice says, "Well, love, I didn't expect to see you down here." My heart races and the flame that had flickered out earlier burns bright again as he carries on. "Have you come to join the real fun?"

CHAPTER TWO

Lena

THE MYSTERY MAN straightens from the doorframe, standing at his full height. He's now fully blocking my only exit out of here. My heart races, but I can't decide if it's from panic or thrill.

Why is it that I can't find it in myself to run past him back out to the club, or better yet, to even fucking move? A stranger has me trapped in this hallway. Granted, he's extremely handsome and very muscular, but a fucking stranger, nonetheless. He takes a few predatory steps down the hall and slides the door closed, trapping us in.

What in the actual fuck have I gotten myself into? There's a reason this is considered an exclusive club, and if I make it out of this hallway alive, Bri and Kate will never believe this. Hell, I can't believe what I'm seeing. These private rooms must be soundproof, because all of the red lights are on except for the door that the threesome came out of, and I can't hear anything from the club or any of the other rooms. The silence down this hall is almost deafening. There's no way in hell that anyone would hear me scream if this man tried to attack me.

"Relax, love," he says, as if he could hear my screaming thoughts. He slowly closes the distance between us and it's like my body automatically wants to relax at the sound of his voice, but I know better and resist.

"Um, I think I should go back out there," I say, trying to hide the rising panic in my voice and doing my best to sidestep him.

"Is that really what you want?" he asks, stepping into my path and drawing closer.

"My friends will be worried about me," I say with only a small tremor in my voice. He looks down at me and doesn't take another step. His bright blue eyes are practically glowing in this low light.

"Will they?" He asks me in a voice that makes me want to drop my panties right here.

"Yes," I answer, the heat rising from my neck to my cheeks. "They'll be *very* worried about me."

I want to smack that smirk off his handsome face as he says, "Well, the last I saw of your friends, they were *very* preoccupied with their dance partners." He takes another step toward me, saying, "One of them has even found herself in one of the private rooms." He flashes me another grin. "And I don't think that she'll be coming out anytime soon."

My breath catches in my throat as I take another step away from him, my back bumping into a door. I curl my hand around the handle, trying to give it a turn, but it doesn't budge an inch. Has he been *watching* me?

Regardless, I walked right into this spider's web and now I'm tangled in it. Trapped.

"Shit," I mutter under my breath as he takes the opportunity to close the last of the distance between us. He leans in and braces his hands against the door on either side of my head.

He lowers his lips to the crest of my ear, his breath warm, but it still sends a shiver up my spine. "There's no need to run, love," he says in a low voice, almost like he's trying not to startle me. "I'm not going to hurt you." He pulls back, his eyes meeting mine and gives me a wink. Is he *flirting* with me?

The silver design on his mask almost shines in the dim lighting. His shirt clings to his biceps as he keeps his arms on either side of me, and dear God, he smells delicious. He's so close that I immediately think of running my tongue up the column of his neck to see if he tastes as delicious as he smells.

What the fuck is wrong with me?

The smirk that has been plastered on his face turns into a grin as he says, "Go ahead and take a bite, love. I know you want to."

I almost choke on my breath with embarrassment, as if he can read my mind and has called me out for my dirty thoughts. I grip the door handle harder, hanging on for dear life.

We stare into each other's eyes, his flashing with delight as electricity forms between us. His eyes move to where my hand grips the handle, narrowing slightly before they move back up over my body. His gaze burns into me, scorching my skin.

Even in this low light, it's clear to see just how strikingly handsome he is. His blond hair falls delicately over his brows. It's longer than most men keep it, giving him the look of a man who doesn't give a shit what you think. The kind of man who could cut anyone down with a single look. Power pulses from him, causing my own heart to quicken and thunder in my ears.

His breath smells faintly like whiskey and mint as it mingles with mine. I run my tongue across my lips, wanting a taste of him. He watches the movement like a cat watches a mouse, waiting to pounce and devour its prey whole. But even as distracting as he might be, there's a feeling that I just can't shake. One that I've been wondering about since I bumped into him out by the dance floor. "Have we met before?" The question tumbles from my lips.

He pulls back a little more. "Have we?" He watches me for

a moment, his eyes scanning my face as if he's comparing it to memory. "I have been told that I'm unforgettable."

Cocky bastard.

But still, he has me down this dark hallway. And while I should be terrified to be trapped here with a stranger, one that has me begging for his touch, tension rising between us, I'm not. He's a powerful man. From the way he carries himself to the smooth tone of his voice that I'm sure he uses to persuade whoever he needs information from. Not to mention his ability to have me pinned to a door, me ready to drop to my knees for him without a second thought. And I would know better than anyone, because I have spent the last five years surrounded by men just like this.

And with that knowledge and experience, I should be running the other way, but there's something different about him. He's effortlessly drawing me in, his claws so sharp, that I don't even notice as he latches onto me.

He has the first few buttons of his shirt undone, exposing his sculpted chest. My hand drifts up and I let my fingers dance across the bare skin. He stiffens slightly under my touch and I swear that he's holding his breath. He looks down at where my hand is, his eyes flaring and his grin growing wider. All teeth, ready to take a bite out of me.

His arms flex as his hands press harder into the door behind me. "Do you want to play a game, love?" His voice is smooth as silk. Spider's silk. "Can I propose a touch for a touch?" he asks.

A game. He wants to play a game before spinning me tighter into his web and feasting on me. I should say no. I should leave, but the hungry look in his eyes has me in a trance as the blood rushes to other parts of me, making me lightheaded.

I'm lost for words as his eyes meet mine again, waiting for my answer. I let all the thoughts of why this is a bad idea run through my mind. He could be a serial killer, or someone sent in to kidnap me and sell me to the highest bidder. But, even with all the alarm bells going off in my head, I still nod.

The need to be wanted and touched by a man, even one who seems as dangerous as he does, takes over. But maybe my wires are crossed and I'm more fucked in the head than I thought I was. After all, I stayed with a man for years who would have raised a million red flags to any other human with a pulse, but not to me. Maybe these aren't alarm bells going off, but they're the sounds that play at the end of a game as they raise the curtain, showing the elaborate prize to the winner.

I'm willing to put myself out there and find out because I was held down since I was twenty-six years old by a man who only saw me as his property. And now that I can spread my battered wings, I'm going to attempt to fly. If I fall, well, at least I gave it a chance. I'm already broken, with so many pieces of myself lost with time.

He shifts his body, his hand sliding away from the wall, and places it over my neck, gently brushing his thumb over my exposed collarbone. His touch is electric, and I feel my eyes go wide as heat curls into my lower abdomen, my clit throbbing as I try to keep my breathing steady.

He leans in, running his nose up my jaw, his lip trailing to my ear. The light caress sends a shiver down my spine, drawing goosebumps in its wake. His mouth hovers over my ear again, his whispers making me weak in the knees. "I've been wanting to take a bite out of you all night."

His words are like a sweet caress across my skin, sending a shiver up my spine. I listen to his slow and steady inhale of breath over my thundering heart. His teeth gently scrape my earlobe, yanking on my earring, eliciting a gasp from me. He chuckles into my ear, his fingers twitching around my throat like he wants to squeeze the breath from me.

The image of him squeezing my throat, cutting off my air as he thrusts his cock into my needy pussy has me letting out a small whimper. Heat spreads throughout my body as the need grows between my legs. He runs his nose back down my jaw, the touch so light I would miss it if I wasn't already on pins and needles with anticipation.

His lips hover over mine, our breaths mingling. My hand still on his chest, I let my nails gently prick into his skin. His pupils flare as he angles his mouth over mine, our lips almost touching.

The sound of a lock clicking pulls me from the trance, and my eyes cut over as one of the doors opens. A man steps out, wearing dark slacks, dress shoes, and a white button-down shirt that screams "money." His sleeves are rolled up to his elbows, and his black, leather-gloved hands match his simple mask.

Reaching out his hand, he guides a woman out. She's in a black corset that pushes up her exposed breasts, her nipples budding, with a black thong that doesn't leave much to the imagination. Her stilettos click lightly on the floor as they approach us. The man gives the stranger caging me against the door a curt nod, barely acknowledging me before they disappear behind the door at the end of the hall.

His gaze drinks them in before cutting back to me. Heat swirls in his bright blue eyes as he takes in my face, making me feel like he can see straight through my mask. Right into my soul.

He brushes his knuckles across my jaw, trailing them down the column of my throat and brushing my collarbones. His other hand takes my fingers as he takes a step toward the end of the hall, to the door the couple just went through. "So, love, are you up for some real fun?"

My limbs freeze in place as my heart thunders in my ears. *What the fuck are you doing, Lena?* You just fucking followed a stranger down a dark hallway and have watched people disappear behind a strange door. A door that this man just suggested you go through.

With him.

Alone.

Am I fucking insane?

He holds my gaze for a moment, his voice going low and gravelly, sensing my hesitation. "Well? What do you say?" He looks over his shoulder toward the door, and when he looks back, he licks his lips, like a wolf ready to devour their prey. To sink his teeth in and eat me alive.

And maybe I'll let him.

I'd been trapped in a glass house for far too long that I forgot what it's like to throw stones. To cause a scene. To be myself. The old Lena wouldn't have thought twice about running off into the night with a stranger and would have relished in it.

He gently tugs at my hand as he takes a step, and I follow him right up to the door, leaving my worries behind. He pulls it open, stepping back to let me through. "Ladies first," he says, that grin still taking over his face. It's as if he didn't even hear my request, but the notion is lost on me as I stand at the threshold of what looks like the stairs to hell.

Against my every instinct, I step through the door. We're on a small landing; the steps are lit up by red, neon, dim lights that make them glow but show each edge so no one trips. The masked man steps past me, holding his hand out for me again.

He leads us down the stairs, the light growing dimmer, hues of red casting on the wall from the open doorway at the bottom. I step down and my stomach does a flip as he leads me into a room full of people in every position. Their moans of pleasure fill the room along with soft, sensual music.

I dig my heels into the ground, almost yanking him back. He turns, that grin still on his face. He leans in, his warm breath caressing my ear. "Welcome to the Underground." His eyes flash as he pulls away like he just shared a dark secret.

He takes another step, extending our arms between us. I look around and see people bound and gagged on the floor, being fucked from behind, squealing in time to the sound of skin slapping. A man is cuffed to a wooden X on the wall, a woman flogging his ass as he moans, "Yes, Mistress."

I take a few steps and stop again because before me, a woman hangs from ropes that are so intricately wrapped that it's like a work of art. Chained clamps pinch her nipples as her partner tongue-fucks her from behind, holding a vibrator to her clit. Her moans of pleasure are like a song.

Panic starts to build in my chest. "I-I can't be here," I croak out, lightly tugging back on his hand as the masked man tries to lead me into another room. He doesn't even acknowledge my words as we pass through another doorway. I watch as an orgy plays out on a bed of pillows. The sound of skin slapping together, moans of pleasure, and carnal fucking has my pussy throbbing.

I shouldn't be turned on by any of this. I should be disgusted, running for the hills. But instead, I'm fully infatuated with the sights and sounds around me. The idea that this has gone on under my feet every time I've been here has me in utter disbelief. If Matt knew this was happening, he would have never allowed me to come to this club with him. He would have taken his business elsewhere.

The masked man leads us to another room where a woman has a man in a full latex body suit, his face completely covered, strapped to a table. "You think you're going to come, big guy?" she croons before snapping a flogger over his erect cock. His muffled screams push through the full mask. She has complete control of him, and I pause to watch, the masked man's fingers almost slipping from mine. She taunts and edges him, making him scream in pain until she finally lets him come. The raw power she emits is hot as fuck.

A switch flips in me, and this time, *I* lead the masked man into the next room where a woman is cuffed to a bench and is being fucked from behind by men taking turns, while another man fucks her mouth. Every room is like another dark corner of my mind playing out in front of me. My mouth is water-ing, and my pussy is dripping at every scene that's in front of me.

I'm lost in a trance as the masked man pulls me to him, lowering me down on his lap to face the scene. His lips lightly touch the crook of my neck. "Relax, love. Enjoy the show." I lean back against him and watch this woman being dominated by these men, the lustful look in her eyes mixing with her tears as she gags on the man's cock. The sound is so erotic that it causes more heat to flood between my legs.

"Spread your legs. Hands on your thighs," the masked man says to me as his hand skims over my stomach. I know I shouldn't, because this is insane. He's a fucking stranger who lured me down a dark hallway and convinced me to come with him to an underground sex club. No one would ever believe me if I tried to tell them about this. If I wasn't so entranced by the scene in front of me, I wouldn't believe any of this either.

I let my legs drift apart as his hand runs up my inner thigh, his knuckles brushing at my core. "You're already so wet." His fingers graze along the edge of my panties and I almost start panting. His free hand cups my breast, pinching my nipple through the fabric of my dress. I let out a gasp and let my eyes close, the pain causing pleasure to pool between my legs.

"Eyes on them." The command in his voice has my eyes flying open. One of the men drops to his knees and eats the woman out, while a different man fucks her mouth. "Don't look away," he whispers in my ear. "It's just getting good."

His fingers push my panties to the side, and he circles my entrance with one of his fingers while he continues to pinch my nipple. As he slides one finger into me, a moan slips from between my lips. He slowly pumps his finger in and out before adding a second one. He curls his fingers, hitting my G-spot and nearly making me come on command. He tsks in my ear before his rough voice says, "No coming yet, love. Not until I say so."

His hand comes up from my breast and wraps around my throat. His fingers gently press into the column of my neck, pulling me back to him. He pumps his fingers into me faster, his palm pressing into my clit. "Oh, fuck," I bite out. Heat starts to build in my core, spreading down between my thighs, curling around me like a snake.

This man is playing me like a stringed instrument, his touch so methodical. He swirls his fingers around my clit as he tightens his hand around my throat, limiting my air supply. The woman in front of me squirms and I watch as her own pleasure builds like mine.

The edges of my vision start to blur as my pulse thunders in my ears. The sound is deafening before his voice cuts in. "I want you to go over the edge with her." Before I even have time to react, he lightens his hold on my throat and pinches my clit. A wave of pleasure crashes over me, nearly drowning me in its intensity.

The sound of our moans mingles in the room as I come at the same time as the other woman. The masked man presses into my clit, his fingers riding out my orgasm. Sounds I've never made before escape me as the intense orgasm rocks my body. My head falls back on his shoulder as I let out another moan, my sensitive clit throbbing as he releases it.

His thumb strokes over my throat, still holding me in place. He brings his other hand up to my face, his fingers hovering at my lips. "Open," he commands, and I do, my orgasm making my mind hazy. He slides his fingers into my mouth as I swirl my tongue over them, tasting myself. "Such a good fucking girl," he rasps as he nips my earlobe. His deep, commanding voice almost sends me over the edge again.

This man has done to me what no other man ever has, and I don't even know his fucking name. Even if I never see him again after tonight, he unlocked a part of me and let it loose into the world. No matter how desperately I would want to, I don't think I'll ever be able to lock this new side of me back up. This rush is intoxicating. Like a new party drug.

He readjusts my panties and guides my legs closed, resting his hand on my waist. He kisses the spot right below my ear, his hand never leaving my throat. He says nothing as we continue to watch the scene before us, the men coming in her and on her, making a beautiful mess of her. Even with tears running down her face, she has a gleam in her eyes telling anyone who's watching that the scene went exactly how she wanted it to.

We stay seated as they each slap her ass before they dive headfirst into the aftercare. Even this part is insanely hot as they dote on her and each other, their kisses turning soft and sensual.

"Are you ready?" The masked man's voice is barely a whisper in my ear, as if he doesn't want to disturb the scene. "Unless you want to stay for round two?" He chuckles darkly in my ear and I can't imagine another round after that, so I slowly stand. My legs are wobbly from the intense orgasm and he grips my waist to hold me steady.

We stand for a moment so I can regain my balance before heading back the way we came, scenes still playing out in each room. The smell of sex and leather is even stronger, the taste of my own orgasm still on my tongue.

We reach the top of the stairs, and he lets me through first. I stop just on the other side and turn to him. He hasn't said much, but his eyes are bright with desire. I would have to be blind not to notice the large bulge he's been sporting, the same one that was pressing into my ass downstairs.

He catches me looking at his crotch and closes the space between us, backing me up against the wall. His lips hover over mine again, our warm breaths mingling. "Next time, I'm going to devour your pussy and have you come on my tongue."

I whimper as he tightens his grip on my hip, his other hand snaking around the back of my neck. My pussy is still wet, and I feel the heat curling in my abdomen again as the ache between my legs pulses. I wrap my leg around him, letting his hard cock press into me. This man, this *stranger*, shouldn't have this kind of hold on me, but he does. The thought of him fucking me against this wall, out in this open hall, where anyone can see, sends a thrill through my core.

I grind my pussy against him, and he growls as his grip tightens to nearly bruising.

My mind is still hazy from the events that happened downstairs as my gaze moves to his mouth. I curl my fingers into his shirt, pulling him to me as his lips crash into mine, his tongue sweeping into my mouth. He groans against my lips, "Fucking delicious."

He nips at my bottom lip, his hands pushing the skirt of my dress toward my hips. I grind myself harder against his bulge, my clit throbbing and my pussy aching.

The sound of our heavy breaths and quiet moans fills the hallway as my hand snakes between us and I grip the waistband of his pants. Just as my fingers grip his belt, the door to the club slides open, slamming inside the threshold.

We both jump at the sudden intrusion, our attention on the figure that now fills the open doorway. "What the actual *fuck* is going on here?" shouts a far too familiar voice.

CHAPTER THREE

Lena

THE VOICE that's the muse to my nightmares breaks me from my trance. Our heads jerk toward the door in sync, the only movement I make as fear turns my once boiling blood to ice. The figure in the doorway takes a step in, his broad shoulders blocking out the light from the club behind him like an eclipse.

"*What the fuck* is going on?" Matt's voice is almost a roar as it rings out down the hall.

The masked man's hands slide down my body, the last bit of warmth against my skin leaving me exposed. He slowly turns toward the door, blocking me from view. He adjusts the sleeves that are rolled to his elbows nonchalantly before his once smooth voice shatters, the edges now jagged and sharp. "Can I *help* you?"

Matt takes another step in, his hand tucked behind his back. "You can help me by getting your hands off of *my* fucking woman." He closes the distance more, his eyes narrowing in the blue neon lights. "Come here, Lena. *Now.*"

My body involuntarily flinches at his command. My legs ache with the need to run, either to him or as far away from him as I can. I force myself to take a step away from the wall, then another, one at a time until I am in the middle of the hall looking at Matt head on, the masked stranger still standing between us. Matt's eyes flash, his pupils nearly swallowing up all the color from his irises like a black hole.

"What are you doing here, Matt?" As hard as I try to keep my voice steady, it still wavers, giving away my fear.

He takes another step toward us, the arm that's bent behind his back tensing, the muscles bulging as if he's holding something heavy. "This little game of yours is over. You had your fun and now it's time to come the fuck home." The masked man shifts, his hands moving to his pockets as he attempts to relax his stance, but the tension continues to grow. "Let's go."

I keep expecting this stranger to intervene, but he doesn't. However, he doesn't move from between us, his muscles tense as if he's waiting for the other shoe to drop. Matt's movements are jerky as if he's fighting off someone. The vein that runs through his forehead bulges and I swear I can hear his teeth grinding from here.

"I'm not going with you." I nearly choke the words out as fear grips my throat. "We're done."

His eyes flash again and it might as well be his hand wrapped around my throat. He looks me up and down, his face darkening. "We're done when I say we're done." He snaps his fingers as if he's commanding a dog. "I'm not going to tell you again."

The masked man takes a slow, nearly feline step in Matt's direction. "If she says she's done, then she's *done*." His voice is still sharp. "I think you need to leave while you still can."

Matt's arm drops from behind his back, his fingers curled around his gun as it hangs at his side. His eyes flash again, anger swirling through the dark depths of his pupils. "Do you know who the fuck I am?" His fingers tighten around the grip, his knuckles going white.

The masked man takes another step, his hands still casually placed in his pockets, but I don't miss the tic in his jaw. "I think the real question is, *Matt*, do you know who *I* am?" His voice is low, the edge in it growing sharper, nearly drawing blood.

Matt scoffs. "I know you're the man who's been seen with his hands on what belongs to me." His steps are slow, his eyes turning predatory. "So, be a *good boy* and get the fuck out of the way."

The masked man's mouth curls into a cruel smile as he takes a step in Matt's direction, the heel of his shoe clicking loudly on the floor. He makes a show of straightening his rolled sleeves and collar before running a hand through his hair. It's almost as if he's put on a whole new layer of skin, it even seems like he's grown taller and filling the room.

He glides his hand in and out of his pocket, the light gleaming off a blade as he flips it open, never taking his eyes off of Matt. "Oh, she's not going anywhere with you," he says darkly, his finger running up and down the side of the blade. "In fact, I think both of you are going to come with *me* and have a little talk."

Matt shifts, his eyes darkening as he watches the masked man. He doesn't bother to look at me as I tremble behind the masked man like a fawn. "Lena..." His voice crawls across my skin. "Get the fuck over here. *Now*." He bites out the words, but I don't make a move.

"I-I'm not going with you. I told you we're done." I try my fucking hardest to keep my voice steady, but my trembling body makes my voice shake, the words losing their luster.

Matt's growl echoes down the hall as his large body lunges forward, barreling toward me. I let out a scream, but before he can tackle me, the masked man throws himself between us. Their bodies slam into each other and I don't know how I don't hear the sound of bones breaking as they fall to the floor.

Matt's gun goes skidding across the floor to my feet, right in my reach, but I don't make a move for it. I just watch in frozen horror as they roll, grappling at each other. The masked man manages to grip his arm around Matt's neck, pinning him to the ground. The muscles in his arms nearly bulge out of his shirt as his free hand grips Matt's hair, yanking his head back.

"Get your fucking hands off me, you motherfucker!" Matt roars. He tries to free himself of the masked man's grip, but he doesn't make much progress.

"All I've wanted is to get my hands on you, *Matt*," the masked man growls into his ear. "I've been waiting patiently, and now, I finally fucking have you."

He picks the knife up that had fallen from his grip and presses it to Matt's throat. His eyes grow wide with panic and fear, a foreign expression for me to see on his face. Matt never showed fear to anyone. He was always the one being feared, by me, by the people around him, and by anyone who crossed him. Seeing him in such a state sends a small thrill through me.

"Lena, baby. Help me, baby. Please," he begs.

There's a small voice in my head, one trying to remind me that he was my fiancé and he provided for me and kept me safe from the dark corners of the city and the world. That everything he did was for the best.

But there's another one, a voice I don't recognize, that snaps for me to let him suffer. To let him feel the pain that was inflicted on me. That *he* inflicted on me. He kept me as a prisoner, locked away in his high tower over the city, and loved watching me become nothing more than a shell of a woman. One who wouldn't talk back or act out. One who would hang on his arm and his every word.

But enough is enough.

I don't want him to die tonight; I just want him to fucking go away. To finally leave me alone.

He struggles as the tip of the blade presses into his throat, a trickle of blood rolling down his skin. The masked man tightens his grip even more, and I swear I can hear Matt's hair ripping out at the roots as he struggles against the masked man.

Against my better judgment, I take a step toward them. The two voices in my head screaming. Completely at war with one another. I suck in a breath, one that rattles my ribs with the force, and silence one of the voices. Shutting it out.

"Please, let him go," I said, my voice wavering slightly, the familiar voice the victor, rising above the other. The masked man's head jerks in my direction, his blue eyes going cold. *Malicious*.

These weren't the same eyes that I was looking into mere minutes ago, and for the first time this evening, I feel a tinge of fear looking into them. A chill runs up my spine, the temperature seeming to plummet around me.

His whole demeanor shifts as he looks between Matt and me. His look is murderous as he holds my gaze, his eyes darkening even more. There's a flicker of emotion, one that I can't seem to put my finger on.

Disappointment? No...*betrayal*.

Seizing the moment, Matt jerks his body, throwing the masked man off kilter. He loosens his grip enough for Matt to turn on him, flipping and throwing his fist right into the side of the masked man's head. Matt jumps to his feet as the masked man shakes his head and tries to get up, seemingly dazed from the impact. Matt kicks out, slamming his foot into the masked man's stomach. He groans and bends over just as Matt kicks again. His foot slams into the man's ribs and he falls to the ground as Matt repeatedly kicks him.

"Stop!" I yell, my voice bouncing off the walls. He freezes, mid kick, his eyes wild with a look I know all too well as he turns toward me.

He gives the masked man a smirk as he curls in on himself. He turns to me fully, his chest rising and falling with deep breaths. "Come on, Lena, let's fucking go," he says between breaths. He reaches out his hand, but I take a step back, trying to make as much room as possible between us. "I've had about enough of this bullshit."

My mouth gapes open as I take him in, because how the hell did he find me? Just when I felt like I was loose from him, he comes back trying to leash me again. My eyes flick to the masked man on the floor as he lifts himself onto his hands and knees, holding his side where Matt kicked him. His breathing is ragged and I see the blood drip from his mouth, splattering on the floor beneath him.

I take in a deep breath and straighten my spine. The other voice in my mind rises up and comes forward to take command of the situation. "No." My voice echoes down the hall, the defiance blowing a hole through Matt's plan.

Matt stares at me. His eyes darken with anger, and his jaw tics. I do my best to push my fear of him down, but it slowly crawls back up. My body starts to tremble as we face each other off.

For the first time, I'm going to use the fact that someone else saw him slip, someone outside of his circle, to my advantage. "Fuck *off*, Matt," I spit at him. "We're done. We've *been* done. Now leave me the hell alone."

His eyes go wide with shock, and anger flickers across his face, but only for a moment, and then he conjures up his look of despair.

"Lena…" His voice is soft, almost a plea. I was never granted that voice unless he was worried I'd really run off or he was at risk of someone seeing him slip. "I'm sorry, please, baby."

He reaches out his hand and takes a step toward me. The masked man gets to his feet, stumbling slightly, sliding his free hand into his pocket.

I'm shaking now, because I realize that I've been brainwashed for years to just go back to him all those times. To think that he was the only one for me and that I *needed* him. I feel the flush of anger rising up my chest and neck. Squaring my shoulders, I let the anger ooze into my voice. "Leave, Matt. *Now*. I fucking mean it."

His eyes go hard, anger screwing up his face. His hands curl into fists at his sides as he takes a step toward me, his boot stomping the ground. As if he's stomping at a dog who misbehaved, ready to raise his voice and reprimand it. Remind it who its master is.

"So, you're whoring around now, Lena? Finding men at this sleazy club and luring them into dark hallways for a quick fuck?" His voice is breathless, but his words strike me hard. So hard that I take a step back from him and fight down a sob. "I always knew you were a fucking whore. Anytime I brought you here, I saw the way you fucking looked at other people."

The pounding of my pulse roars in my ears as my anger mixes with fear, unease curling in my gut.

"You're a fucking, ungrateful, *whore*," he grits out. "And after all I've done for you. Everything I gave you. This is how you treat me? *Fucking bitch.*"

His eyes are wild, and his face is beet red as his anger rises. Before he can take another step, the masked man steps behind him, throwing a punch to the back of Matt's head, causing him to stumble forward.

He turns on the man and starts throwing more punches as they square off. Matt's a stocky man, barely hitting six feet, giving this man a few inches on him. But Matt has never been one to back down from a fight and has come home with the cuts and bruises to prove it. I've had to call the doctor a few times to come in and stitch him up after a few bar fights, with no one ever asking any questions about the incident. They were in and out with hardly a word, making only passing glances in my direction.

Blood splatters as they hit each other. I take a step toward them and my foot bumps into something on the floor.

The gun.

My eyes widen and my heart thunders as I bend down to pick it up, hands shaking as I curl my fingers around the grip. I've never held one before, and it feels like a cool metal brick in my hands. I raise it and point at the men as they continue their assault on one another.

"Stop!" I screech, my grip tightening on the handle, my finger hovering above the trigger. My finger twitches and I take an erratic breath. Narrowing my gaze, I swallow down the bile that's rising in my throat, gritting out the next words. "Stop or I'll shoot."

They both freeze, their heads turning in my direction, eyes locked on the gun. The masked man takes a step away from Matt, as if to politely give me a clear shot. My hands continue to tremble and my heart thunders in my ears. It's deafening, drowning out their words. I can see Matt's mouth moving, but I don't hear a thing he's saying. He raises his hands in surrender, slowly taking a step toward me.

"Lena." His voice is low and muffled, but it finally reaches me, cutting through the pounding that thrums through me. "Give me the gun."

He lifts his hand, but I press my finger on the trigger more. "No," I choke out as a sob works its way up my throat. "Leave *now*."

He chuckles softly. "Lena, Lena, Lena," he croons. "You won't shoot me, sweetheart." He takes another step toward me. This time, I take a step back, not letting him close the space between us. He slides his hand into his pocket and pulls out a second gun. My heart plummets into my stomach at the sight of it. "You don't have the fucking guts to." He lifts the gun, pointing it right at my head. "But I do."

His finger presses on the trigger, and a shot rings out. I squeeze my eyes shut and scream, the sound tearing at my throat. I wait for the pain to fill my body, but it never does. My eyes fly open and I see the masked man gripping Matt's wrist, the gun pointed at the ceiling. His other hand is wrapped around Matt's throat, squeezing the air from his lungs.

I try to let out another scream, but my voice lodges in my throat. Before I can raise the gun again, the sound of boots fills the hallway as four large men rush in right toward Matt.

Another shot rings out, and this time, I drop to a crouch, covering my ears and squeezing my eyes closed. The sound of grunts and curses is chaotic, along with the sound of bodies slamming into one another. I look over, trying to gauge the danger around me, and see Matt pinned to the floor by one of the men just as three more figures enter the hallway from the club.

There's more shouting and the sounds of punches hitting their marks as more people join in on the fight. I try to back away from the chaos in front of me, but bump into something hard. I turn and see the biggest man I've ever seen in my life, his steely gray eyes staring down at me.

CHAPTER FOUR

Lena

THOSE STEELY GRAY eyes sweep over me, taking in every inch of me. He towers over me at well over six feet, with shoulders almost as wide as a doorframe. He's dressed in all black with a slotted, dark-colored, tactical mask that covers the entire bottom half of his face. His black hood is pulled forward, almost completely shadowing his features.

His eyes flick up again, darkening as he takes in the scene that's unfolded behind me. I pull my gaze from him and see that one of the men who came from the club has taken the masked man to the floor. He's fighting against his hold as a knife hovers inches from his throat.

The giant rushes past me, making it to them in a few strides. Grabbing the man around the waist, he hoists him off his friend. Yanking the knife out of his hand, he doesn't hesitate to slice the blade across the assailant's neck, his gags bubbling as the crimson blood falls across his chest.

The giant drops him like a sack of potatoes, blood pooling around his now lifeless body. Turning on the group of men, his eyes narrow as he zones in on Matt.

The giant takes a step toward him, but hesitates. I follow his line of sight as two more men enter the hall, running straight for us. One of the men beelines toward the giant, a knife glinting in his hand. They crash together before the giant grips the man by his head, snapping his neck like it was a twig. I choke on a gasp as he throws the body to the side as if he was nothing more than a rag doll.

I don't see the masked man anywhere now, but I catch sight of one of the club's men falling to the ground, gripping his side and moaning in pain, just as the two new men grab Matt and drag him away. He steadies his footing as he swings an arm around one of the men's necks, then limps toward the door, blood running down his leg. It drips on the floor like he's leaving a trail of breadcrumbs.

Just as they hit the threshold, he looks back, his cold eyes landing on mine. My pulse races at everything that look could mean and every intention he has for me. The words he mouths send a chill down my spine. *You're fucking mine.*

His gaze is cut from mine as the men drag him through the threshold, disappearing into the crowd of people on the other side.

I'm frozen in place and the world is slowly fading around me. The commotion has become muffled and my vision is tunneling as my knees grow weak. The knot in my stomach has moved up to my throat as panic starts to take over, because all of this is too much.

I stumble back against the wall, barely holding myself up as my knees buckle. What the fuck just happened? I look down at my trembling hands, my vision blurring on the edges as panic wraps itself around my throat, trying to squeeze the air from my lungs.

The murmur of voices around me seems to turn into a roar as the events begin to replay in my mind. I can hear his voice saying *you're fucking mine* over and over, as if it's a war chant. A hot tear escapes and rolls down my cheek.

What have I done?

Why didn't I just go with him and make things easier for

everyone? Why did I think I could escape him and go on to live a normal life? I endangered everyone in this club tonight, and now, their blood is on my hands. If it wasn't for me, none of this would have happened. I should just go. Follow him out the door and hand myself over, make it easier for everyone in the end. I'll suffer the consequences of my actions and take the hits that I deserve.

A voice whispers my name, but I don't register who and just keep staring at my shaking hands, trying to will them to stop. Trying to find the strength in my legs to carry me from this place. To save anyone else from their downfall by just being in the same room as me while Matt is on his war path.

"Lena." The whisper grows louder, cutting through my thoughts.

A hand brushes my hair away from my face before a finger hooks under my chin, forcing me to look up. I'm met with sharp blue eyes that glitter behind a silver and black mask. His thumb rests on my chin, keeping me locked in on him. "Lena, are you okay?" he asks, his voice low.

I try to shake my head, to snap myself out of this panic attack that's trying to take over, but he keeps his grip on me. I focus on his breaths as they fill the space between us, the smell of whiskey and mint filling my nose. My skin tingles where his fingers are, heat spreading along my cheeks. I take deep breaths, letting his scent fill my lungs, but they're still too fast and my head is spinning.

"Say something," he whispers. I part my lips, trying to find words that just won't come. My mind is still reeling from the fight and my eyes flicker from his to the pools of blood on the floor. Bile crawls up my throat and I swallow thickly, my panic rising higher.

He tugs my chin. "Eyes on me, love." He brings his face closer to mine, blocking my view of the men moving around behind him.

I squeeze my eyes shut, blinking several times, trying to

bring things back into focus. The tunnel vision starts to turn back into blurry edges, the spinning room slows, and my breaths steady. His face becomes clearer, his features turning sharp again as I take a deep, steadying breath. "There you are." The gentle praise in his voice sends my heart into overdrive.

"I-I'm fine now," I murmur. My cheeks heat from embarrassment as I try to shake his grip from my chin. His hand falls away, and I press myself harder against the wall as he takes a small step back, giving me some space. I look him over and see that his face is already swollen and bruised from where he was punched, along with splatters of blood across his shirt.

"Oh God." My hand claps over my mouth at the realization of seeing a man's throat be slit. Nausea roils in my stomach and I gag into my hand. I bend over, coughing as the image of the knife cleaving his throat fills my head, searing itself into my memory.

He places his hand on the small of my back, the warmth of his touch spreading across my now clammy skin. I brace my hands on my knees and suck in deep breaths, working to push down the urge to vomit across his designer shoes.

Another pair of designer shoes joins him, these paired with a rough voice. "Boss, we have to remove the bodies, so we'll have to keep the rooms locked a little while longer."

I keep my head down as the masked man answers quietly, "Fine. Do whatever needs to be done." He rubs his thumb back and forth across my back in a soothing rhythm. "Are any of them still breathing?"

"Yeah, boss. He's been stabbed and knocked out, but he's more alive than dead," the rough voice answers, amusement lacing his words.

"Good. I want him taken to the basement." His thumb switches to small circles, his other fingers pressing into my skin. "I'll deal with him later."

The man leaves us, and I attempt to stand back up

straight, but still being lightheaded, I stumble. The masked man grips my arm to hold me steady. "Easy, love. Take as long as you need."

I look past him and see the lifeless bodies laid out on the floor. Men dressed in all black start dragging them toward the far door, throwing them down without a care. Men move in and out of the space, dragging bodies out and coming back empty-handed. There must be an elevator or something on the other side of that door, because they're not gone for very long with each trip. And I don't even want to think about how they're going to dispose of them.

More men come in. This time, they're wearing rubber boots and dragging cleanup equipment behind them, right over to the pools of blood that have been left behind from the carnage, and begin their cleanup efforts.

Body bags are laid out and the few bodies left are lifted with more care and placed inside of the bags. They zip them up to their necks, leaving their faces exposed. They must be men who worked here and will be properly handled, unlike the others who were with Matt.

My heart breaks for these men and their families, because they were caught up in a fight that started over me. One that should have never happened if Matt would just fucking let me go.

"You're coming upstairs with me," the masked man says, his voice low and rough. His grip on my arm tightens, as if he expects me to fight him. What he doesn't realize is that I want to be anywhere but here right now. I already followed him down to a sex dungeon, what's the harm in following him up?

I'm still in a state of shock, so I know that I should just walk out of this hallway, back to my friends, and fucking leave. But, in my stupor, I just keep letting him lead me away from all the blood and bodies. I try to form the words to ask about my friends, but they fall silent on my tongue. I don't even bother to look at my phone that's tucked away in my dress, because how do I even explain what the fuck has happened tonight?

I slow my steps and yank us to a stop. "I need to check on my friends." My voice is monotone, the emotion almost drained out of me completely. But that voice in my head is screaming to make sure he remembers that other people are here with me tonight, to remind him that someone will be looking for me eventually. I don't try to fight his hold, but I find just enough strength in me to hold my ground. "I need to make sure they're not in danger, too. That he didn't get to them."

My body is numb as I try to pull him back the other way, moving on autopilot as I step back toward the club, but we don't budge.

He looks past me and nods, but I can't find it in me to care who he is communicating with, because I just need to lay eyes on Bri and Kate. I just need to know that they're safe. "We'll keep an eye on them tonight and make sure that they're in good hands." He gives me a reassuring smile. "I promise."

This man is dangerous. His ability to shift his demeanor and fit his personality to whoever he's talking to gives me a false sense of security.

Fuck, this man is probably a sociopath, because he doesn't seem to give a shit about all the blood around us and the lives that were lost tonight. And the way he's looking at me, as if I'm his next fucking meal, has the hair on the back of my neck rising.

I should fight him, run away screaming for my life, but I don't. Instead, I nod and let his hand slip back around my arm, his fingers gripping me firmly. The warmth of his touch spreads up my arm, giving me a sense of security. I hear boots on the ground as the giant man approaches us.

I watch him as his fingers tap away on his phone, the glow on his face makes his gray eyes bright. He looks up at the masked man, giving him an affirmative nod like a solider to their commander.

Who the fuck is this man?

He watches me for a moment, his brows knitting under his hood as if he's looking at something repulsive. He's a calculated killer, one who will remember every detail of their target and will be ready to strike when the time is right.

Both of these men, whoever they are, are going to ruin my life. I can already tell.

"We've just confirmed that your friends are safe, and they won't be going anywhere anytime soon. They're none the wiser to what's happened here." His words are smooth, like he's speaking to a room full of important people. He nods toward the door. "Come with me."

"How do you know which ones are my friends?" I ask sharply because, of course, I'm more worried about my friends and their safety than my own.

He looks to the giant who once again gives him a nod, their silent conversation continuing, leaving me in the dark. "We have eyes watching every person in the building, love. Your friends included." He leans down to me, his breath warm on my ear. "You think we didn't already know who you were the minute you walked into this place?"

My heart thunders in my chest and my eyes go wide as dread crawls across my skin. Fuck, they've probably been watching me since the first time I came here with Matt. My legs ache with the need to run, but I stay put, because there's a question hanging in the air. "So, you only tried to fuck me because of my ex-fiancé, right? You wanted to get under his skin?"

He pulls back from me, his eyes narrowing on me before a sly smile pulls at his lips. "Oh, love. If only he was that important to me to think that far ahead." His voice drips with a condescending tone as he pulls me closer to him, our chests pressing together. He looks down at me and presses his hips into me. I swear I feel his erection growing between us as he uses his finger to hook under my chin, pulling my face up to look at him. "All I saw tonight was a fucking beautiful woman who looked like she hadn't been properly fucked in a long time, and I wanted to give her that. You being that fucker's fiancée was just an added bonus."

I should pull away and slap him. Grab those words and shove them back down his throat, but I'm too stunned to do anything. If his words are true, then he didn't care who I was, he was genuinely interested in me. Which sounds insane because no man has looked at me twice in the last five years. So, if it wasn't for Matt, then what was it?

He takes a slight step back, his hand still wrapped around my arm. He gives the giant man one more silent nod before forcing my legs to move again. I don't know where he's taking me, but he leads me to a door that's hidden behind a large, full-length painting.

It's an odd sensation to follow this strange man farther into the building and not be afraid of him hurting me, or hell, killing me to send a message to Matt. If that was what he wanted to do, he would have taken the chance while Matt was here in the flesh. Took his knife and sliced my throat open right and paint the club crimson with my blood.

I have no doubt that I'll be part of some plan, but for now, I'm going to accept any help I can get.

Part of me knows better than to blindly follow this stranger, but the other part of me just watched them not only disarm my ex-fiancé, but made sure to keep me safe during the whole attack. I'm not looking for a knight in shining armor, but after that debacle, I clearly need some allies. And this man and his people seem to be my best bet at the moment.

His grip loosens to a casual hold as we get closer to the door. He looks down at me, a smile tugging at his lips. "I owe you a drink on the house. Are you still interested?"

I stare at him, my mouth agape at this casual suggestion, but he's right. I could definitely use a drink after all of that. So, I give him my best smile, which isn't much at this point, and slowly nod. "How's your amaretto sour?"

He leans down, his lips brushing the shell of my ear as his words nearly send a chill down my spine. "To die for."

I FIND myself on an elevator heading up several floors of the building after he gained access with his fob, showing me just how secure this place can be.

"Where are we going?" My anxiety is slowly starting to rise with the elevator.

He looks at me and smiles. "To the safest place in this building."

"Which would be?" Apprehension fills my voice.

"The penthouse, of course."

My eyes widen, but he just smiles at me, only looking away to check his phone before typing a message and pocketing it again.

The elevator slows to a stop, the doors sliding open to a short hallway.

He steps out first, turning to hold the door for me. "This way, love."

Leading me to the single door at the end of the hall, which is decorated with the same dimly lit sconces and lacquer-painted, black door, he scans us in with the same fob as before.

We cross the threshold, and I take in the space. It's open-concept, with the living room, which has two black sofas and two black, high-back chairs, and the kitchen, with its shiny, black cabinets and the largest white marble-topped island I've ever seen, on one side. The ceilings are high and adorned with skylights, which complement the whole wall of windows that look out onto the city.

On the other side, two large wooden desks face each other, each with multiple computer screens. An obscenely large flatscreen TV hangs between them and hangs over an electric fireplace framed by dark wooden bookshelves.

On the back wall are three doors painted the same lacquer black, which I assume are all bedrooms. Everything here is so pristine that either he's sleeping with his housekeeper or pays them incredibly well.

The masked man takes my hand and leads me over to one of the sofas. I take a seat, letting myself sink into the soft leather.

I lean my head back and stare up at the skylights, my muscles aching from the mix of adrenaline and these high heels. I listen as he moves around in the kitchen, the clinking of glasses and bottles almost hypnotic. It fills the silence, which is strangely comfortable. If he has plans to kill me up here, he's good at making me feel at home before he does so.

He comes around, a clear, fizzy drink in one hand and an amber colored one in the other. He hands me the clear drink as he takes a sip of the amber liquid.

"Thank you," I say, my voice just above a whisper.

He raises his glass to me before taking another sip, attempting to be graceful as he sits in one of the high back chairs, but I don't miss the wince. The light of the city gives him a glow, making him look almost angelic with the golden mask on his face.

I take a sip of my drink, expecting a vodka and soda, and almost giggle about being served lemon-lime soda in a fancy glass.

The masked man catches my smile and takes another sip, not even trying to mask his own.

The silence between us is electric, prickling across my skin as he watches me take another sip. "This is the worst amaretto sour I've ever had."

He nearly chokes on his whiskey, his laugh mixing in with a cough. He grabs his ribs, wincing.

"I'm sorry!" I yell out, sitting forward and cutting off my own laugh.

"Oh, love." He chuckles as he wheezes in a breath. "That one was worth the pain." He readjusts in the chair, running his free hand through his hair, his pained face smoothing out again.

"I'm sorry," I say again, this time, my tone is softer.

"About?"

My brows furrow at his response. "About the fight and you getting hurt. About Matt." I look down at my drink, watching the bubbles float to the top. "People died tonight."

"And how was that your fault?" His voice is laced with curiosity, his head cocking to the side.

"Because he——"

"Broke into our club and attempted to kidnap you?" He leans forward in the chair, watching me carefully.

I gape at him, every explanation that I could come up with falling silent. I guess I hadn't considered that.

"No one would have been hurt if he hadn't slithered into the club like the fucking snake that he is." Anger flashes through his eyes, but he does a long blink and it's out of his gaze in a matter of seconds. "You did nothing wrong, love. Leaving that piece of shit was the best decision you made. Hell, it probably saved your life."

My eyes widen as his words sink in. The story clearly told itself earlier, but the way he's talking about Matt, it's almost like he knows him. Like he's been waiting for the day that Matt stepped a foot back into the club. I thought the masked man was just taunting him, but I'm beginning to believe that none of this was a coincidence.

The question sits heavy on my tongue, the one where I ask

what they know about Matt, but before I can ask them, the door beeps and swings open, the giant stomping through the door.

I feel this pull to look him over, like a hand pressing against my cheek and forcing my head in his direction. I don't fight the instinct; instead, I drink in the sight of him. He's rugged, and based on the size of his muscles, he's seen the inside of a gym a time or two. His broad chest pulls his black tee tight across his body, and when he shifts, his pecs flex, and I imagine they're hard as stone. He's wearing fitted, black cargo pants that taper down into very large black combat boots. He has a bandage wrapped around his left thigh, his blood turning the stark white fabric crimson. He limps past us without saying a word and disappears behind one of the bedroom doors.

"Is he…is he alright?"

The masked man looks toward the closed door and then back to me. "He will be. He's just pissed he got stabbed."

I feel my panic rising. "Stabbed?"

The masked man waves off my panic, scoffing a little. "It's not the first time. Besides, he's had worse done to him. He's just sulking about the fact that he might be losing his touch. He's fine."

My mouth falls open at this man's nonchalance about the whole situation, but I watch an emotion cross his face as he sips on his drink, one that I can't quite place from under his mask.

I let silence fall between us as I look out at the city, replaying tonight's events in my mind. He was here. After months of being away, he came here to drag me back to that miserable life. To *him*.

It feels like an eternity of silence but can only last about ten minutes. I finish off my soda and thunk the empty glass on the coffee table, the masked man's eyes drawing up from his phone to meet mine.

I've had plenty of time to calm down and now I want answers. I take a deep breath, steadying my nerves. "Who are you?"

He chuckles, cocking his head to the side. "Not one for small talk, are we, love?"

"I think after everything that's happened tonight, we can go ahead and skip the small talk, can't we?"

He chuckles again while leaning forward, placing his now empty glass on the coffee table, mimicking the sound of my glass. I watch as his breath catches and winces, his hand lightly touching his side again.

I let my frustration disappear because this man helped me when he didn't have to and was injured. "Are you okay?" I scoot forward, closer to the edge of my seat, trying to get a better look at him. "I think you need a doctor."

He waves his hand, trying to air away my concern. "I told him to come see me last. I need him to take care of my men, especially the careless assholes who get themselves stabbed." His eyes cut to the door that the giant went through and his brow furrows.

"I can take a look at it." His eyes cut back to me, wariness creeps over his features. "I'm not a doctor, but I've helped with minor injuries a time or two."

He cocks his head again, his eyes sweeping over me. Reading me. "Is that so?" His lips pull up into a smirk. "Or are you just trying to get me naked?"

My mouth drops and I start to stammer. "No…I…"

What the fuck is wrong with me? Get your shit together, Lena. He's trying to throw you off your game.

He chuckles, the sound light as it cuts through my hodge-podge of words that never seem to form a complete sentence.

A quiet hiss cuts between his teeth as he scoots forward in the chair. He's silent for a beat, before he goes on. "Your ex get into a scuffle a time or two? Like the one tonight?"

I stiffen at the mention of Matt and my pulse quickens,

anxiety pulsing through my veins. "It's…it's complicated." He watches me for a moment, letting the silence weigh down on me, as if he's waiting for more from me. For me to crack. I hold his gaze, but shift the subject, because I'd rather not discuss him right now. "Besides, you've yet to tell me who you are."

"Persistent. I like that in a woman."

I stare him down, my face heating as a curious smile pulls up the corners of his lips. Even with a bruised face, that smile is dazzling and even more dangerous.

"Fine. I guess since I swept you off your feet and up to my home, I should at least give you the honor of knowing my name." His voice is playful, but I catch a few whispers of darkness.

The audacity of this man to have the fucking nerve to compare offering to help me as sweeping me off my feet. Anger and frustration begin to fill me, coursing through my veins with every beat of my thundering heart. My fingers curl into fists in my lap and his eyes flick down to them, curiosity filling them again.

He stands from the chair to sit on the coffee table in front of me. Even sitting, his tall, lean body towers above me. He holds out his hand as if he wants to shake mine. I stare at it for a long moment before undoing my fist, finger by finger, and placing my trembling hand in his. His grip is firm but oddly gentle as he shakes my hand up and down.

"Lena, I'm Devin Green." His voice is smooth and almost seductive as his name rolls off his tongue. When I look up from his hand, I see his eyes have softened and are almost twinkling with delight.

"Green?" Why does that name sound so familiar?

His smile falters slightly before he smooths back out again. "It's a fairly common last name, Lena *Taylor*." He says my name with a bite that nearly sinks into my skin.

I curl my fingers tighter around our still linked hands as he grips mine back. "Have you been stalking me?" I ask.

His grin turns devious. "I wouldn't call it stalking when you're the one who came into *my* club, but yes, I have been keeping an eye on you while you've been here tonight. And a few fingers in you, as well."

My cheeks heat at his words, the thought of his fingers fucking my pussy has me clenching my thighs. As if he can sense it, his eyes light up, his smile turning wolfish. I pull my hand from him and fist them in my lap, breaking eye contact. The longer I look into them, the more I feel like he can see right into my mind. That he can read my every thought.

"It's not the first time I've watched you come into this club, but it was the first time I finally got the taste of you I've been dying to have."

My head jerks up at his words, but all I can think about is the way he touched me, like he had been starving and was ready to devour me whole. My body tingles at the memory of a few hours ago, the sight of the orgy happening before, and the powerful orgasm I had from his hand.

Even as heat curls between my legs, I can't forget that this man is dangerous and has clearly had his fair share of scenes in the sex club that remain hidden underground.

He leans down, his breath warm on my skin, the smell of whiskey filling the space between us. "Have I left you speechless, love?"

I cross my legs, trying my best to seem casual, even as my pussy throbs. "No, Mr. Green. Just thinking about all the other women you've lured down to your sex club and taken advantage of just to feel like a *man*."

His head jerks back slightly, like I've slapped him, and his eyes widen before they narrow on me. He leans down farther, placing his hands on either side of my head. "It's just Devin," he says with a growl. "And if you think your little jabs will cut through me, you're sorely mistaken." He leans in more, his nose brushing against the side of my face, his metal mask cool against my skin. "Unless you want to cut me, then I can certainly arrange that, love."

I stiffen at his words, his dark chuckle echoing in my ears. A shiver crawls across my skin at the thought of this man sliding a blade across my skin and his, getting off on the pain. His tongue lapping up our blood as he fucks me to the edge, both of us falling to our deaths.

What the fuck, Lena?

I've never had thoughts like that before and I nearly jump out of my skin as his fingers brush my jaw. "Where'd you go, love?" His voice is thick and the tension between us is nearly suffocating me.

My eyes flutter as I try to blink the images from my mind or at least lock them away. Those thoughts can never be acted on. *Never.*

I clear my throat, desperate to change the subject.

"So, Devin, what do you do here?" I gesture around the room. "Do you own the club?" I clarify.

He opens his mouth to answer, but the door behind him opens, hitting the wall with a bang. The giant walks—or, more accurately, limps—through, his mask and hood still intact. I hear him scoff in our direction, probably at Devin's close proximity to me, the sound deep and slightly muffled.

Devin rolls his eyes, giving his own scoff in response. He props his elbows on his knees, his eyes level with mine. "I'm what some might call *security*." The giant sits down at one of the desks on the other side of the room and starts pressing buttons on his keyboard. The TV comes to life, filled with smaller screens showing different areas of the club. "The owner doesn't come around much. He's bravely put us in charge of keeping the club safe and keeping people like Matt on a tight leash. Apparently, we aren't doing a good enough job and one of us should be fired." He cuts a look to the giant, who continues to ignore us.

I stare at the giant as he clicks on his keyboard. There's an edge to him, the way he keeps himself distanced and acts as though no one else is in the room with him. He's fascinating and seemingly different from Devin. Which makes me wonder even more how they function under the same roof.

"Love, this is Tony Fox." He gestures toward the giant. "Tony, this is Lena Taylor."

Tony glances up at me and then goes right back to the screen as if I'm nothing more than a fly buzzing past him. His air of indifference snuffs out the electricity that was running between Devin and me, along with the air in my lungs.

I watch him as he works and feel Devin's gaze burning into me. His bright blue eyes light up like fire when my gaze collides with his, drawing me in like a moth.

The room recharges, and I feel like I can breathe again.

What is this man doing to me?

This large man has piqued my interest, and I want to know more. "What exactly do you do here then, Tony?" I try to keep my question light, but something about him makes everything seem heavier. That at any moment he will take me in his hands and crush me, turning me into nothing more than bone dust, only to scatter me in the wind.

"We run security *together*." Devin's short answer makes it seem like I shouldn't press Tony on the matter. But why? Who is he, and what do they have to hide?

"Now, enough about us; tell us about you, Lena."

I don't want to fucking talk about me. I don't want to rehash my messy past, but what Matt did downstairs was terrifying. The look in his eyes was like none I'd ever seen before, at least not while looking at me. I rarely stepped out of line to justify a look like that. But I guess I'm the girl who got away and he's not too pleased about that.

"Listen, you've hardly told me anything. Just your names and a *very* vague job description. For all I know, I could be sitting in a room with two serial killers."

Tony's eyes cut from his screen, boring into me, as I feel the heat from Devin's gaze burning into me even more. I should be afraid because it seems like I just cracked a code, and they don't seem too pleased about it.

"That didn't seem to be a problem for you over the last five years, why would that scare you now?" Devin's voice is sharp and his words hit me square in the gut.

"Why would you say something like that?" What do they know that I don't?

Tony scoffs as Devin leans in. "You can cut the innocent act, love. We're well aware of the circle you ran in, so you don't have to play pretend anymore."

My pulse races and my stomach lurches, working its way up to my throat, making my face turn hot. "Pretend? Pretend what?" My fear morphs into anger at these men. "I don't know exactly what you're accusing me of, but I have never laid a finger on anyone."

Another scoff from Tony and the pair's disbelief in me sends fire scorching through my veins.

"Yeah, he would come home and have gotten in a bar fight or two, or I would have to patch up one of his friends because they got into a scuffle, but it wasn't anything more than that. So you can shove any of your accusations up your asses."

The room goes still, and the men watch me closely. My whole body is trembling, and I close my eyes, squeezing them as I try to take a deep breath. I can't let them see me come undone or what kind of mess I was left in. I've been working so hard over the last few months to heal and find my inner peace, and I can't let a few harsh words dismantle the progress that I've made.

"Is that what you believe happened to him?" Devin's question breaks the silence, disbelief still lacing his words. I blink my eyes open to look at him, expecting to see a hard gaze, but to my surprise, his eyes have softened. "That he was just getting into bar fights?"

"Yes," I snap, the anger rising higher in my voice. "He would come home and be covered in blood. I would have to help clean him up and occasionally wrap his knuckles. Maybe give him a few stitches." Both men are still as stone while I talk. "Sometimes he'd bring home a friend, sometimes it was a guy I recognized, other times it wasn't, who would need some assistance. But it was never anything more than a few cuts and bruises. Less damage than what happened downstairs."

Devin and Tony watch me, their eyes widening. "And you never thought to ask questions about this?" Devin's voice is still soft as if he can't decide if he's supposed to be the good cop or the bad cop. I look down, picking at the seam on the couch cushion, refusing to give them the satisfaction of seeing the tears flood my eyes.

The strength falls from my voice as flashes of those nights play through my mind. "I wasn't allowed to ask questions. I just did what I was told to do because that was the easiest thing to do."

I squeeze my eyes shut, trying my damnedest to shove the tears back as my skin turns hot. I take a stuttering breath and feel Devin lean in closer. His fingers brush the hair from my face, and I let the warmth of his touch flow through me, the electricity between us wrapping around my bones.

"How do you know about him?" The words tumble from my lips, curiosity giving me the ability to push the tears back down. "You acted as if you knew who he was and I want to know what you know. I *deserve* to know if he has some secret life."

I open my eyes to see Devin staring toward the TV. The screen is still split into multiple squares, showing the packed club below us.

He looks back at me, his face neutral. "How long has he been texting you?"

Wait… how does he know about my text messages?

His finger traces along my knee, leaving goosebumps in his wake, which is the only thing keeping me grounded. "And are you also aware that he's been tracking you?"

"Tracking?" I think back to all the messages that I've received. No matter how many times I changed my number, he always manages to figure out my new one, seeming to know when I was out. My stomach rolls with nausea and I cover my face with my hands as the reality of it all hits me like a ton of bricks. I fight back the urge to vomit, and instead, a sob escapes me.

"How could I be so fucking stupid?" The words come out muffled from behind my hands, tears slipping through my fingers. "He's been watching me this entire time. He's been waiting for the chance to force me back with him. How did I not fucking figure it out?"

"He was going to get to you no matter what," he says, his voice low but gentle.

"Who do you think your ex is, Lena?" His words remain gentle, but have an edge to them. "Tell me what you know about Matt Chase?"

"Chase?" I stop at the name. "His name isn't Matt Chase. It's Matt Gibson."

Devin and Tony look at one another from across the room as Tony's fingers fly across the keyboard. Devin stands and walks to Tony's desk just as a picture of Matt comes up on the screen.

"You think that this man's name is Matt Gibson? Executive for…" He looks at one of Tony's screens. "Nexus Gen Solutions?"

Tony once again scoffs, the sound prickling my skin as another tear glides down my face. Insensitive bastard.

A wave of heat washes over me, my face feeling flushed. "Yes," I push the word out. While it's the truth of what I know, it feels like I'm failing a very important test. Like I had all the tools the study and was too fucking stupid to use them.

"So, you had no idea about his real identity." His head cocks to the side, watching my every move. "What was he really doing outside of your home?"

"Why would I lie about this? You literally just dropped a bomb on me." The words are almost a screech, my throat tightening around them. "I always felt like there was something else going on, but I never had enough proof. So I turned my head to a lot of things because it was easier than him turning it for me." The words come out as dead as I feel inside.

I stare at the photo of the man I spent the last five years with. Who proposed to me on that rooftop, claiming to want forever with me. I want to claw my skin from my bones as I think about his hands on me, the lies he spoke into my ears, the fucking promises he made that he never intended to keep. He played me like a fool.

My hand slowly reaches up and presses against my chest, feeling for a heartbeat to make sure that something in me is still ticking, because otherwise, I'd think that I'm just a shell of myself.

I ran. I took the chance I was given and ran as far away from him as possible, still believing in the lies he told me. But I should have known that I wouldn't have been able to run far without him hot on my trail. Breathing down my neck. I should have realized that I was fated to be trapped in his clutches and locked away in his high tower for the rest of my life.

The man who posed as my prince charming was not all that he seemed and was actually the villain in disguise. And because of that, I need to come to terms that I'm not destined for a happily ever after.

"Lena?" Devin's voice cuts through my thoughts, and I look back at him. He's now sitting in front of me again, holding out a fresh soda. The bubbles are clinking against the glass, filling the silence. I didn't even notice that he got up and decided to be the good cop.

My fingers wrap around the glass, bumping into his as the electricity that's crackling between us tries to break through my skin. I pull the glass away and take a tiny sip. My mouth has gone bone dry, and I refrain from chugging the whole glass in one go.

I cling to the glass with both hands, cradling it in my lap. I stare out the massive windows, taking in the cityscape, trying to corral the hundreds of questions running rampant through my mind. I lasso the most important one. "Who is he, then? Who *is* Matt?"

The photo of Matt on the screen minimizes and text starts filling up the blank spaces. I see words like assassin, hacker, and dark web multiple times, but one word that stands out is *OBSIDIAN*.

I watch as the text continues rolling down the screen like credits at the end of a movie. I see dates well before we even started dating, and other names I don't recognize continue filling the screen. My heart begins to race again, the roaring filling my ears as I become hypnotized by the string of information on the screen.

Devin's now leaning against what I assume is his desk, sipping on his whiskey as he starts rattling off information from the screen. "Matt Chase is one of the leaders of a group called Obsidian. A secret society of very powerful people who are set on controlling every aspect of this godforsaken city. They're all interconnected and some of them are influential across the world. Since money isn't an object to them, they deal in favors and blackmail. Deals that not only put people into powerful positions but take out those who oppose them in any way they deem necessary."

Devin's jaw tics as emotion flashes through his eyes like lightning, his words hanging in the air. His fingers curl into fists at his sides before he uncurls them and crosses his arms. "He frequented the club *a lot* but went MIA in the last three months. We had men working on tracking him down, and even had some men going undercover to get answers and piece together their next move. Little did we know that he was off tracking someone of his own." Devin's body shifts so he's facing me. "The night you ran was the last hit we had from him…" I look away from the screen and straight into his cold, blue eyes as he continues, "Until tonight when he came stomping into Masquerave, looking for you."

My hands tremble so hard that I feel the soda splash onto my skin, but I can barely register the cool liquid as my world crashes. I lived under the same roof as this monster for five years. A monster in disguise. One who lied to me in every way imaginable and had me believing he was someone else completely.

I knew he was powerful, but I didn't have a fucking clue just how powerful he is. How influential he is to other people in this city.

I shudder, nausea roiling through me as I think about every time he came home bloody. Whose blood was really on his hands and why?

And like a fucking idiot, I truly believed that I had escaped him. That my best friends would be able to keep me safe. But this was just a game of cat and mouse for him. I'm sure he got off every time I looked over my shoulder after he sent me an unsolicited text.

Hot tears roll down my face as I stare at his face on the screen. The face of a man I thought I loved and loved back, but all he wanted was to keep me at his side to play the part of his little, innocent fiancée.

The screen splits, showing more cameras throughout the city and even inside of private residences. "He has been very good about covering his tracks, so much so that we thought he wasn't even in the city anymore, but he was just tucking himself away in the shadows waiting for his own opportunity."

A shiver runs down my spine as I think about all the parking garages I walked through and the dark corners I passed by where he could have been waiting for me.

"What does he want from me?" My tongue sticks to the roof of my mouth since it ran dry, causing my question to sound slurred.

"That's the million-dollar question, isn't it, love?" He crosses to me and slowly takes the drink from my hand, placing it on the coffee table as he sits. "Tell me the truth, Lena. Did you have any idea that he was part of this group or are you playing the part of the innocent fiancée to be the wildcard in his games?"

I cut my eyes away from him and look at the image of Matt's face still on the screen. Anger pulses through my veins, and I press my fingers to my temples, my head pounding. "He wasn't always bad," I start. "He was very sweet in the beginning." I shrug. "But aren't they all?"

I keep my eyes on his face. It morphs in front of me, shadows curling around him as his dark parts come to light.

"Then it all started to go downhill after about six months of being together. It was slow, the changes, or maybe I was too close to the situation to see it for what it was. He did what any abusive boyfriend would do when their girlfriend starts to pull away: he proposed."

The energy in the room shifts. Both men's eyes are on me, watching me as I lean forward, gripping the seat cushions.

"He told me that he got a new job and was being transferred about two hours away. At this point, we'd been together for almost two years. Isn't that what you do with someone you've been in a relationship with for that long? Follow them, especially when you don't have anyone else to hang around for?"

Devin shrugs. "Can't say I would know from experience."

I let out a dry laugh, throwing back my head and letting it rest on the back of the couch. "So, as I'm sure you can guess, I followed him. He put us in a beautiful apartment and made sure that I had everything I needed so I never needed to leave."

"And what about *your* job?" Devin asks casually, but I don't miss the darkening of his tone.

I raise my head and stare at him, because I can't believe I'm admitting these things, saying these hard truths out loud to strangers. Especially to strangers who more than likely believe me to be the enemy and could very well kill me at any time without a second thought.

However, the mood in the room is heavy, but not in a way that has me worried about my life. I can tell they're listening and taking note of everything I say. I'm sure it's all being recorded and could more than likely be used for quality assurance at some point.

I take a deep breath, finding the strength for the next words that are still hard for me to say out loud. "He encouraged me to quit, even though they offered for me to be remote. He claimed that I didn't need it; all I needed was him."

Tony's brow furrows and I can see the judgment in his eyes. He's actually the first one to look at me that way instead of with pity, and I want to be mad at him for passing judgment on me, but I think he's the first one to give me the response that I need. The real one. "He promised that I would want for nothing and didn't need to work another day in my life. I was to be the woman who stood by him as he climbed the ladder. That when he got to the top and sat on his throne, I would have my own right there beside him."

Devin nods as if in understanding, but stays silent, giving me the chance to decide what I want to tell them. What do I need to tell them? They're giving me a chance to tell my story, something that no one else has done because it either didn't matter to them or they were afraid of me pulling away. Of course, Bri and Kate listened when I needed to talk after I left, but they never pushed. I would hear them whisper-yell at each other because Bri wanted to push for answers, but Kate insisted they let me tell them on my own.

A part of me was thankful for Kate, but the other part of me wished that Bri would have ripped open the wound and made me bleed. Ripped it open wide and let the poison in my veins spill out, finally giving me relief from the years of being spoon fed the toxins that had started to destroy me. Killing me slowly.

A knot starts to form in my chest. "I had a schedule. One that he set for me. And if I ever strayed from it and he found out, which he always did, I knew I was in for it when he got home." My leg bounces as my anxiety builds. "One night, I was tired of his outbursts and always needing to be in control, so I stood up to him."

I subconsciously raise my hand to my cheek and hold my fingers there, the phantom sting prickling my skin. "He didn't appreciate me trying to stand up to him, so he took me down a few notches." As the words leave my lips, guilt hits me in the gut and I wince. "He reminded me that I was nothing without him and that I was lucky he didn't just throw me out to the street."

Devin stands from where he was leaning on his desk, the muscles in his jaw bulging, his nostrils flaring. A noise comes from Tony's direction, almost like a growl as his hand nearly crushes his mouse.

Tension begins to build in the room and the silence is deafening as they look at each other. I wait for the look of pity, but it never comes. Instead, Devin crosses back to me and sits down on the coffee table, his knees bumping mine. "What made you finally leave?" His question is soft, but not like he's trying to console me. No, it's as if it's a secret. That whatever I say won't be used against me and that my words will stay safely in this room. His knees press into mine as if to hold me in place.

I stare at Devin for a long moment and his eyes soften as realization hangs heavy in the room.

"I stayed for another three years." My voice is quiet, the confession tasting like ash on my tongue. "Of course, after I dropped to the floor from the impact and the dust settled, he flipped a switch and apologized. The next day, he bought me a new computer and diamond earrings to make up for it.

"He didn't lay a hand on me again until a few months ago and then that's when I ran." A tear rolls down my cheek, stinging my skin.

Devin reaches up and catches it on the side of his finger, then puts it to his lips, licking it away.

I suck in a shuddering breath, but the tears I had worked so hard to push down spring from my eyes, blurring my vision. The memories of that night play through my mind and I get lost in them. Before I can get too lost, though, a large hand cups my chin. The pads of Devin's fingers press into my skin, pulling me back to reality.

I sniff and wipe the still cascading tears from my face, not caring if I smudge my makeup. Devin watches me carefully and that's when I notice that he's removed his mask. While it didn't do much to hide his identity, it's still a shock to see him sitting bare-faced in front of me.

I let my hand float up and touch the side of his face. My voice cracks as I say, "Your mask. You took it off."

He grins, the smile reaching his eyes. "You're *wildly* observant, aren't you, love?"

"I think tonight has proven otherwise, don't you?" I give him a little chuckle, trying to keep the mood light, but it doesn't work.

His smile falls, but his eyes stay soft. "Hindsight is always 20/20." His hand slips from my face and I feel the absence of his warmth. He stands and heads over to his desk, dropping into his computer chair where he leans back and props his feet up, lacing his fingers behind his head.

I notice that Matt's photo is no longer on the screen, but instead it's back to the security cameras focused on the club. Tony is standing in front of them, watching one screen in particular, arms crossed, his head cocked to the side. I watch as his hands flex, his fingers pressing into the hard muscles of his upper arms.

From here, the screen is just a series of people, dancing and having a lot better night than I am. But I can't complain about the view. Tony's black tee is pulled tight over hard muscles that would make any man reconsider crossing paths with him. I follow the veins that bulge out as they disappear under his shirt sleeves.

I slide my gaze over to Devin, whose broad chest is pushed out from being leaned back. The buttons on his shirt pull against his rigid pecks. His biceps push the limits of his white shirt, and his rolled sleeves expose those corded forearms and golden skin.

"You believe me, don't you?" I watch them and wonder if I would still be sitting here, unscathed, if they didn't.

Devin drops his feet to the ground, sitting a little straighter as he looks at me. "You're a survivor, Lena." He curls his hand into a fist and presses the side of it against the top of the desk. "That's what we are here: *survivors*. I think you'll fit right in."

I open my mouth to press on what he means, but I think better of it. While I am curious, I don't want them to think I told them my story just to pry information from them, because I actually don't know why I told them any of it. It was so easy to let the words tumble from my tongue as if they gave me some sort of truth serum. Maybe there was something in my glass, but I highly doubt it. Was it because this man gave me one of the best orgasms of my life in front of a group of strangers or is he just that good at what he does?

My cheeks heat and I'm desperate to look anywhere but at

him. I avert my eyes to the screens that have switched onto the hallway where all hell broke loose. It's empty now, and even from here, I can see that every drop of blood has been cleaned up. No one would have any idea what transpired there tonight.

"The people in those rooms…could they hear what was going on tonight?"

Devin's eyes flash and my cheeks heat at the devilish grin that pulls at his face. "No," Devin says lightly. "The rooms are completely soundproof. No sounds make it in and no sounds make it out."

"What if they would have come out during the fight?" The knot in my chest tightens more, because that would have put more innocent people in danger all because of me. I press my palm to my chest, trying to loosen the knot that's pressing my chest and stealing the breath from my lungs.

"Tony secured all the rooms before he came down and everyone in that hall was sent an alert to stay in their current room until further notice."

I watch him as he flicks his hand in nonchalance, as if it's not a big deal for there to be an all-out brawl in the club. "How often do these lockdowns happen?"

He quirks a brow. "Not as often as you would think, love, but they happen occasionally." He shrugs. "The occasional lovers' quarrel that needs to be dealt with." He leans his elbows on the desk. "Sometimes the drama outside of the doors heightens the experience behind it." He winks at me before averting his attention back to the screen, flicking back and forth between the people on it and Tony.

"So, who are the people behind those doors? Are they important?"

Tony turns his head from the screen, looking at Devin, the hood blocking part of his face, making it difficult to get a read on him. They're having a silent conversation, the kind that only close friends or lovers can have. Their dynamic seems interesting, and I wonder which one of those options they are. Perhaps both.

Tony shrugs before turning away, giving what I assume is the go ahead, and Devin continues, "This hallway has a series of private rooms for exclusive guests to the club." Devin pulls his phone out, typing out a message before continuing. "They pay a premium and can use them anytime they want with their access card. The red light lets us know that they're in use and keeps everyone accounted for. The more you pay, the higher up in the club you can go for even more debauchery."

He shoots me a sly grin. "And like I said, every private room is soundproof because we don't want to hear what's going on behind those closed doors, and they certainly don't want mundane noises from the hallway to interrupt their pleasures." I feel my cheeks warm as I think back to our interaction and what could have possibly happened if he'd pulled me into one of those rooms before Matt interrupted that moment with us.

I can still hear my own moans echoing through my mind, the intoxicating smell of his whiskey and mint as he spoke dirty words in my ear, eliciting a shiver from me.

My blood heats through my veins and I tighten my thighs together as the warm curl of desire swirls in my lower abdomen. I shouldn't be attracted to two men who could just kill me right now or, worse, turn me back over to Matt at any moment. I pull myself back to reality from my dirty thoughts, only to find that both of them are watching me, their eyes swirling with heat, and I think I'm in more trouble than I realized.

CHAPTER FIVE

DEVIN

I WATCH as she squirms on the couch, trying her best to hide the clenching of her thighs. The blush on her cheeks brightens, which is a much better look for her than the flush from her tears.

This woman has seen some shit, and while she may not bear any physical scars—at least any that I can see—the trauma that she's endured mentally and emotionally makes my hackles rise.

I can tell she's trying to remember me, and that's okay if she doesn't, because it doesn't diminish the way she took my breath away all those months ago. Little does she know that I was looking for her just as much as I was looking for him. She doesn't even realize that she caught the attention of the devil.

My phone buzzes from a text from Tony.

TONY

Her phone. Now.

I roll my eyes at him because, of course, he would choose to keep his brooding, tortured soul persona and not say anything to her. Fucking prick. And it's not like he hasn't already hacked into her phone and has been going through her information this entire time.

I give her a lopsided smile, because I have a feeling that she's going to resist my next request. "Lena, love, we need to have a look at your phone."

Her eyes sharpen at me, her brow furrowing as she clutches her phone from her back pocket. "Why?" Just as I expected.

"We need to run some diagnostics on it, pull some data—"

"Why should I trust you?" Her question rings out and stops me dead in my tracks. The room falls silent, and even Tony's typing ceases. "How do I know that you won't just use me as a bargaining chip and turn me back over to him?" Well, shit.

She clutches her phone even tighter, crossing her arms across her chest, pushing her breasts up. I can't help but let my eyes fall on them, but I'm doing my best to play it off like I'm looking at the phone in her hand.

I'm actually surprised at her reaction given the way she freely talked about her trauma to us. But she was just handed some alarming information about the fact that her little fiancé wasn't the man she actually thought he was. I can only imagine how hard that is to fucking process.

I would love to know how he orchestrated it. How he led her on for so long believing he was someone else. He must have done one hell of a job censoring her internet access and her phone usage. And while that shit makes me see red, it's important that we figure out what kind of access he has and for Tony to get as much information as he can. For her safety and ours.

However, if I'm going to get her to pick the right side, then I can't be gentle about it. "Love, if we were going to turn you over to that piece of shit, we would have just let him have you downstairs. Besides, we have bigger plans to take down Obsidian."

She furrows her brow, her gaze flicking between me and Tony. "So, I'm just a pawn for you?" She drops her arms, her body stiff. "I escape one man and fall into the hands of two more?"

I stiffen at the accusation, and I watch her as she begins to spiral, her body tightening up, her cheeks reddening. She looks like she's planning on bolting, but since she can't go to her default flight mode, she's trying out some fight. Fuck, if that's not hot.

I keep my body relaxed and talk her off this ledge. "You are free to walk out of this club at any time you want, but I wouldn't recommend it."

Her body shifts. "Why? Because I'll have three stalkers now instead of just one?"

"We want you to be free of him, love, but that's only possible if you help us take him down. Help us take down Obsidian from the inside out."

"And what happens if I refuse?" Her body is almost vibrating as she looks between me and the door. "He was my fiancé, after all."

Well, fuck, she's feisty when she feels threatened. I knew I liked this woman. "You can choose to leave, but just know that there are people out there who would kill to get their hands on you and turn you over to him." Her eyes widen as I keep going. "You're the one who got away…literally. And now he has something to prove by getting you back."

"If I just keep ignoring him—"

"He won't go away, Lena." I let my voice raise, cutting her off, because I need her to understand the severity of all of this. I take a few steps toward her, and I watch her freeze in place, but I keep going until we're inches apart, and her perfume floods my nose. A sweet floral scent mixed with berries.

Peonies.

"He's been watching you from afar this entire time. He's

had eyes on you and has been waiting for the perfect opportunity to pounce." She looks down her nose at me, her eyes blazing. "He took the leap tonight and he's going to be even madder that it didn't play out like he thought it would. He's pissed."

"And how, *Devin*, do you know all of this?" she snaps my name out, letting her pearly white teeth show as her maroon stained lips curl back.

"Because we've been watching him for a while and letting him think this is a safe place to conduct his meetings. Letting him get laid by our girls while they collected information on him and his cronies."

I watch as my words hit her, her head snapping back as if I had just slapped her. "Watch him get laid? But…" Her eyes instantly become glassy. "…we never had sex here." Her voice softens with each word. Her delicate fingers wrap around her neck, fingertips pressing into the skin as if searching for her pulse.

Well, *fuck*.

I run my hand through my hair and grip it at the roots, letting the tingle of pain keep me rooted in place instead of running to her side. She's been telling the truth this entire time and really didn't have a fucking clue about this guy. That he's a lying, cheating, piece of shit.

I look over to Tony for backup, but that fucker refuses to look over here and just keeps typing away at his keyboard as if he's none the wiser to the bomb that I just dropped on her.

I let her mull over my words as I take a step back, giving her space. "He was in here a lot more than you realize, love." A tear escapes and rolls down her face, the track shining like a beacon. The urge to reach out and wipe it away has me flexing my hands at my side. "We clocked you quite a few times, but he was here multiple times a week, with different women on his arm almost every other night."

Her eyes flick up to mine. "That doesn't mean he was

fucking them." Her voice is still quiet, but the words are clipped, her sadness beginning to morph into anger. "You're just trying to fuck with me and get me riled up. Like I said, I don't fucking know anything about this Obsidian or Matt's involvement in it." She throws her arms up and slams them down on her thighs. She's being a brat by throwing this tantrum, and if it was any other time than now, I would bend her over this couch and fuck the brat right out of her.

"No, love." I keep my words soft, because as much as my mind wanders into dark corners of my mind, I need to stay levelheaded. Otherwise, I'll make a reckless decision that could blow our entire plan. "We have transactional receipts where he paid for private rooms off the dance floor. Some nights, he was with the women he brought with him, and other nights, he paid extra to be with one of our girls."

Her shoulders slump and the look of defeat settles onto her beautiful face. I look back at Tony, who's staring at his phone, avoiding this entire interaction. I'm going to fucking rip that phone from his hand and shove it so far up his ass that the only thing he can contact is his past fucking life.

"You're just trying to hurt me," she grits through her teeth, more tears collecting in the corner of her eyes.

"I'm sorry, Lena." And for once in my life, I am. I've seen people doing horrible things, but in this world, they usually deserve it. But her? She was as loyal as they come and gave her whole life up for someone who couldn't give a shit about her. Who was too busy using our club for his dirty deeds while she waited for him at home. All that makes the pain that radiates through my face that much worse, because I let a fucking coward get a swing on me. *Never again.*

She sniffs and roughly wipes the tears from her face, her breathing starting to get erratic as her eyes widen. "I...I need to get tested." Her head whips up to me, fear dilating her pupils. "I have to go to the clinic and get tested." She goes to stand, but I grab her knee, holding her in place.

"Fuck," I mutter. This time, when I look back at Tony, his eyes are on mine. I can't read his expression, but his gray eyes are turning molten with rage.

I meet her wild eyes, the panic and fear swirling through them. "We can help you with that." Her breaths are erratic and are only getting faster. "We can have someone come in tonight. Have answers long before the sun rises." I squeeze her thigh, trying to keep her grounded. "Would you want that, Lena?" Her breaths rattle through her as she wipes at her face, nodding to give me her consent.

The pressure of my own monster pushes against my skin, sharpening its claws and teeth. It's out for blood after tonight and this isn't helping me stay calm. I keep my words steady and try my best to reassure her. "Tony will have someone down here in no time. He's one of the best doctors in the city."

My hands itch as the image of Matt tied up, blood running down his neck after I slice it open, floods my mind. Pressure builds under my skin at the thought of that piece of shit and the fact that he fucked around with other women, then came home and to fuck his fiancée makes me nearly feral for blood. *His* blood.

I'm not worried about our girls, because they frequently get tested, but the other ones that he would bring into the club? No fucking clue. She had no idea about any of them and he was recklessly gambling with her health and wellbeing like the selfish prick that he is. I'm doing my best to hold back my rage, but I can feel my hands begin to tremble. I shove them in my pockets and try my fucking best to remain calm, curling my fingers around my knife. I run my thumb along the handle to remind myself what I'm capable of.

She reaches up and grabs my elbow before I can turn away. I look down at her, and if I thought I was going to be able to stay calm, I was fucking kidding myself. The tear tracks down her face might as well be slices across my chest. Even in her current state, she's undeniably beautiful. And after what I did to her in the Underground, she must be a good fuck, too. That piece of shit couldn't have had a clue about the woman he worked so hard to control.

And that's the difference between me and him. I *want* to know about the woman underneath. I want to know what makes her tick. What gets her off. I want to be the person who pulls her out of her comfort zone and lets her run wild. Be free to be herself. She deserves that much.

She shoves her phone at me, her lips pulled into a thin line. I curl my fingers around it, careful to make sure that they brush against hers. She doesn't pull away as the electricity runs between us, the charge sending my monster into a frenzy.

"Use whatever you need to take that cheating mother-fucker down." Anger flashes across her face before she turns her gaze away, looking out to the cityscape. He's royally fucked.

IT'S BEEN about an hour since our private doctor came in and took her blood sample, which he promised we would have the test results back any minute. I set a timer on my phone. He will get a call from me for the results as soon as it goes off, because I won't make her wait a second longer than necessary.

I'm settled into my desk chair, admiring Lena as she sits restlessly on the sofa. She's been going between watching the feed on the screen and staring out at the cityscape, all while constantly wringing her hands in her lap. She finally took off her heels and curled up under a throw blanket that I gave her, making sure to tuck it around her, letting my fingers graze across her exposed skin as I went. And they say chivalry is dead.

I take a sip from my whiskey, letting it burn across my tongue before swallowing it, trying my best to feel anything else but the rage that's coursing through my veins. Tony's phone buzzes constantly on his desk as reports from the girls come in. It's been a busy night since our run in with Obsidian. We called for all hands on deck to sniff out anyone involved with them still in the club, and clearly, several of them have been apprehended. Good, because I need some fresh fucking meat.

My phone buzzes on my desk, rolling my eyes when I see that it's from Tony. This prick can speak clearly through his mask, he just chooses to stay fucking silent except for the occasional grunt. People have always found him to be intimidating or a mystery waiting to be solved. The latter has gotten him laid more times than not, even though he would never admit that out loud.

I see his message and look directly at Lena, who is now blankly watching the feed of people dancing in the club. I stand, crossing the room to her, her eyes widening at my approach as I hand her my phone. "Click the link for the results." I take a step back, because she doesn't need me hovering over the top of her. She stares at the screen, her thumb hovering over the link. "Take your time, love."

I sit down on the coffee table as she clicks the link, the screen filling with the results. Her eyes scan quickly over the words before her hand claps over her mouth, stifling a sob. I stiffen as fresh tears cascade down her face as she hands me back the phone. I hear Tony shift behind me, his energy bouncing off me as I look at the results.

NEGATIVE.

Relief loosens the knot in my chest, and I watch as she takes in the news that she's clear of any STIs. I lean forward, placing my hand on her knee, giving it a squeeze.

"I thought I was doing everything right. I have an IUD, and I haven't slept with anyone except him in *years*." Her eyes cut to mine and while I made her come all over my fingers, I didn't fuck her, even though I desperately wanted to. So, regardless of our little rendezvous, it's a statement she can still stand behind. She must come to the same realization, because she takes a steadying breath and keeps going. "I used protection in college for any hookups and would get tested if I had any suspicions. And now, I just had a scare because my fucking fiancé"—she sucks in a breath—"*ex-fiancé*, who has been fucking around on me for God knows how long." She lets out a defeated sound. "Fuck, I'm so fucking pathetic." She drops her head into her hands and sniffs, pressing her fingers into her eyes as if that will stop the tears that are threatening to fall.

"You're not pathetic, love. He's just a fucking piece of shit who has no issue with laying his hands on women." I look over at Tony who's avoiding my gaze. He can't handle other people's emotions, just like I can't handle my own. Two peas in a fucking pod.

Her voice is rough as she tries to clear her throat. "Where are my friends?"

Goddammit, she looks so fucking defeated. I look to Tony who switches the screen to show the feed from some of the private rooms at the back of the dance floor. "They're still in there, love." I give her leg another squeeze, trying my best to reassure her that they're safe.

She scoffs. "Of course, they're still getting fucked while I thought I was getting fucked over with an STI."

As hard as I try to hold it back, a chuckle tumbles from my lips, a mere echo of the one that comes from Tony, I can't help myself. Her brows furrow, but I see the tug at the corner of her lips, the tension in the room crumbling.

"We're finishing up with your phone." I nod toward the screen. "We can end their night whenever you want. All we have to do is make a call." I rest my head on my fist and reach over to brush her hair from her face. I fight the urge to run it through my fingers as other thoughts creep into my mind. Now is not the time to imagine what her long locks would look like wrapped around my fist as I yank her head back while I pound my cock into her pussy. Now is the time to get it the fuck together.

She watches the screen for a few moments, her eyes squinting like she is staring into the sun. "Make a call?"

I smirk, surprised that she hasn't caught on to the fact that we're a little more than security around this fucking place. "The men that they're with are on our payroll, love." Her eyes go wide, and her hand drifts up to cover her mouth, which has popped open from a gasp.

She's a fucking tease with that mouth and doesn't even have a clue.

"Your friends are actually having a lustful romp in those rooms, just with men who work for us." I waggle my finger between Tony and me, giving her my slyest smile. "Not only are they safe from Matt, but anything else that might come with a one-night stand."

I love the surprised look she gives me, the look of innocence on the face of a woman who is far from it. My fingers tingle at the thought of how her pussy clenched around them while I finger-fucked her, my other hand pulsing like it's still wrapped around her neck, her thundering pulse pressing against it with every beat.

"But…but how?" She looks at me, the innocence on her face morphing into accusation, her eyes narrowing on me. "Did you…Did you plan for this to happen?"

I shrug. "Once I realized it was you, I wanted to make sure I could have you all to myself."

Her face reddens. "Excuse me? What the fuck does that mean?" Her voice is low, a growl rumbling in the back of her throat. The things I imagine that throat could do has my head spinning and my fucking cock thickening.

She pushes my hand off her leg as she goes to stand, but

before she can storm away, I grip her wrist. She stares at my fingers that are wrapped around her delicate wrist, her eyes burning with rage.

"Love, listen." I loosen my grip on her slightly, giving her the chance to step away, but she doesn't move. "You hadn't been seen in months and Matt had stopped showing up completely." I stand up, still not letting her go. "But tonight, when I heard word that you were possibly in my club and that you weren't with that piece of shit, I had to know if it was true."

She watches me as her eyes simmer with rage. If only she knew that I wasn't the only one watching her tonight and that she's lucky I was the one to get to her first. I was well aware of every set of eyes that watched her from the moment she stepped foot in here, with every sway of her hips while she danced, the way her dark, perfect lips looked as she sipped on her cocktail. She has no idea the men who were drooling over her and the ones who were looking to cash her in for whatever fucking prize Matt put on her head.

The former makes my fist curl that they got a free show, but the latter makes my pulse race and my hands itch. The roaring in my ears becomes so loud that it's nearly deafening, while pressure builds under my skin, my monster begging to come out. To pluck out every set of eyes that dared to fucking look at her.

"Who told you I was here?" She finally pulls her wrist from my grip, crossing her arms over her chest.

I take another step to her, my lips curling into a smile that would send grown men running, but she just glares at me. That look has me nearly falling to my fucking knees, begging for her to take her anger out on me. "We have eyes and ears all over this club, love. If anyone of interest makes their way through the door, we know about it."

Her arms tighten around her, keeping me from getting any closer to her. "So, you separated me from my friends and then lured me down a dark hallway? Then had your way with me and expected to fuck information out of me?"

Well, fuck. "No. Believe it or not, that wasn't the plan at all." I have to rectify this situation, because if she shuts this down and walks out of this building, he will have her in no time and she'll be a fucking goner.

I can tell by the way she's looking at me that she doesn't believe a word that's coming out of my mouth, which if the tables were turned, I wouldn't believe me, either. "Yes, we sent two of our men to distract your friends, but I just wanted to get close enough to see if it *was* you and be able to keep an eye on you tonight."

She pushes her hip out, the disbelief rolling off her. Fuck, the way I want to reach out and brush my fingers across that hip. How does she already have me so fucking infatuated with her? She's practically the enemy, and here I am, lusting after her. I need to get it the fuck together before I end up doing something that will jeopardize everything we've been working toward.

She cocks her head to the side, her eyes narrowing on me even more. "Did you know Matt was here? Is that why you lured me away from the dance floor?"

My face heats, because I didn't have a fucking clue that he was here. We're trying to track down why the fuck none of us were notified that our enemy number one was back in the club.

Also, I can't tell her about the way she's had my mind in a fucking vice for the last three months or that I forced Tony to run scans of all the CCTVs in town to see if there was any sight of her. She consumed my every thought and now that she's here, standing in my living room, I don't want to let her out of my sight.

"Pure coincidence." I give her my best smirk and try to keep my demeanor relaxed.

Her phone buzzes on Tony's desk and the room falls silent,

tension filling the room. The backlight glows on Tony's hooded face as he picks it up and stares at it, reading whatever is on the screen. He flashes me a look before sitting it back down on the desk, typing furiously on his computer. His gray eyes have gone steely and I know that look. It's never fucking good when he gives that look.

"What?" The snap in Lena's voice echoes in the room. "It's him, isn't it?" She nods her head at the phone, her long hair falling over her shoulder.

Goddamn, she looks good when she's worked up, but *I* want to be the one who does it. Not that piece of shit.

As if in answer, Tony flips the screen over from the security footage to the messages on her phone. A slew of message bubbles fill the screen, all from unknown numbers. They range from desperate pleas to rage-induced slandering, calling her every name known to man.

That motherfucker was trying every tactic in the book on her to get her to break.

While Tony scrolls, I notice a few threats and some photos that seem to be from outside of her apartment building. I look at her and see that her face has paled, and her hands are fisted at her side. Her eyes widen in panic, and her body starts to tremble like a fawn as they stare down the face of a wolf.

Anger begins to course through my veins at the reaction he's caused her to have and the voice in my head is starting to egg me on. Seeing the threats he's sent to her and the names he's called her makes me want to cut off his fingers one by one, for every letter he's pressed. Then I'd cut out his tongue for all the things I know he's said to her, including tonight, and watch as he chokes on it. I imagine the feeling of his blood, warm and sticky on my fingers, as the life drains from him, finally freeing her from his clutches.

She lets out a gasp, her hand comes up to cover her mouth as Tony finally scrolls down to view the newest messages. First is a photo of a brightly lit hallway with doors down each side.

My eyes widen at the realization that this photo is inside her apartment building. The text under it has my blood plummeting to ice, nearly sending a shiver up my spine.

UNKNOWN

Knock, knock, bitch.

She takes a sharp breath before slowly backing away as if he's here in the flesh, closing in on her. Legs bumping into the sofa, she tries to lower herself, but ends up falling into the seat. She starts mumbling into her palm that's still covering her mouth, incoherent words spilling out from between her fingers.

Her eyes cut from the screen back to me, terror filling them, and I see the tears that are collecting on her lashes as she lets out a near silent sob.

"Call in a team to sweep the area and secure the apartment building." My words are sharp as I bark at Tony, my instincts kicking in. I imagine he's already on it, but it gives me a sense of purpose and power to try and take command of the situation. "I want the whole block covered and someone checking every fucking inch of that place."

Minutes pass, none of us saying a word as Tony works through his list to notify our best people to hit the streets and prepare for a take down if necessary. I would prefer to have every motherfucker in this building who had some connection to Obsidian dragged down to the basement and locked up until I could get answers out of them, but if they're here, then they're not directly involved in this stunt. Which means I have to play it cool...for now. But no one is going to threaten her, *especially* that piece of shit. If he lays a finger on her or her friends, he will pay in blood.

Even though I haven't proved it yet, I just know that it's his blood I'm owed.

"If he finds me, I don't know what he'll do." Her voice is soft, her gaze stuck to the coffee table. She scoffs. "He won't kill me, because that would be too easy. But that doesn't mean he won't make me pay for all of this."

She's not talking to anyone in particular, but her words ring true. He won't kill her, at least not at first. He thinks that she's his property, that he has some claim on her, and I won't fucking stand for that. He can have her back over my dead fucking body. I shove my hands in my pockets to hide the shaking and curl my fingers around my knife. I rub my thumb along the handle, caressing the smooth grip. The image of using it to carve out his heart, his blood running down my arm, oddly soothes me

"We're going to protect you, love." I nod to the screen as Tony switches it back to video surveillance. "You and your friends."

Her head slowly turns, her gaze sweeping over me as if she's remembering that she's in the room with us. "He was so close to taking me tonight, what makes you think he wouldn't be able to get that close again?"

I cross the room and cup her face, letting my thumb lightly rub her cheek. Her eyes widen at the contact, but she doesn't pull away. Her skin is hot and tear tracks stripe her face, making her look like a warrior in their war paint. Even like this, she's no less stunning. "If he tries to pull anything again, we'll be fucking ready for him." And next time, he won't fucking get out alive.

CHAPTER SIX

Lena

MY CHEEK TINGLES from his touch as his thumb wipes away a rogue tear. The urge to press my face into his rough hand is overwhelming. He's so intoxicating that he almost takes my breath away. How can I already be this infatuated with this man after only a few hours? Even if he did finger-fuck me in a sex club, in front of strangers, nonetheless, I shouldn't feel the need for such an intimate touch.

I'm obviously under a lot of stress tonight and that must be the reason my body seems to be aching for his touch.

Fucking stress.

Admittedly, the knot in my chest loosens slightly at his reassurance that he's not going to turn me back over to Matt and that he's on the top of their shit list. A list I don't think I would ever want to find myself on, because the rage that is rolling off them is suffocating.

My eyes drift back to the security footage, and I scan the mass of masked people who are crammed into the club. I wonder how many of those people were aware of who I was and wanted to grab me for themselves. "How did he even get in here?" The question comes out so quietly that I don't even know if I actually said anything out loud.

"That's what we're trying to figure out." Devin stands up straighter and crosses his arms, causing his biceps to bulge through his shirt. I can only imagine the kind of carnage those arms could commit if he was given the chance. "If someone freely lets him in, then we'll know in no time." He looks at Tony, grinning like a fool. "It helps when you have the best at your disposal."

Tony lifts a middle finger at Devin, not even looking away from his screen. Devin lets out a laugh as he turns to the TV screen on the wall, pulling out his phone and typing away. I watch them as both of their expressions turn steely while they work. They occasionally look at one another, nod or shake their heads, and then go back to what they were doing.

I lean back into the couch and chew on my bottom lip. These strangers have made a vow to keep me and my best friends safe. But, why? What do they get out of this? Men like them don't do things out of the goodness of their hearts, there's always a fucking catch.

Tony makes a huffing sound, causing Devin's head to snap in his direction, his eyes flashing to the footage playing on the screen. The knot in my chest tightens as Devin jerks his phone up to his ear. He doesn't bother to turn around and look at me as he bites out, "Bring me Vince. *Now.*" His words are low but sharp. They could cut a man off at the knees. "Find a replacement for his post immediately. He *won't* be coming back."

He drops the phone away, ending the call. He takes in a breath as he scrubs his hand over his face. The tension in the room shifts as Devin flashes Tony another look, his eyes filled with rage. It presses down on my chest, making it hard to breathe, and my panic starts to rise up my throat.

"Who's Vince?" I push the words out, nearly gagging as anxiety attempts to close up my throat.

"Someone who has made a huge mistake." Devin's voice drips with disdain as he growls out the words. "Someone who needs to be reminded of what we're capable of."

He glides across the room to the bar, pouring himself a finger of whiskey. He throws it back in one gulp and pours another without hesitation. He looks as though he's about to throw it back, too, but Tony clears his throat. The sound rings out in the room as the glass stops at Devin's lips, hovering there as if he's contemplating whether to ignore him or not. He lowers the glass slightly, a slight sense of calm coming over him as he takes a small sip.

Tony's eyes are glued on the screen, his hands alternating between clicking his mouse and his fingers flying across the keyboard. The room goes silent, the only sounds being Devin swirling his glass and Tony's clicking.

I want to speak and ask them more questions, but the look in Devin's eyes tells me to keep my mouth shut. The power that he exudes swirls through the room, seeming to hold me in place. I watch as he scans his eyes between his phone, the security footage, and me. I'm used to being under a watchful eye, but somehow this feels different.

The difference is that he's watching me like a mother would watch their child. With a sense of care and adoration. It's a strange feeling, because I've only ever been used to being under scrutiny as someone waits for me to fuck up. Waiting for me to step out of line and to be struck down by punishment.

The comfortable silence is cut off by someone pounding at the door, making me jump. The door clicks open and two men enter the room, dragging a third. They grip him under the arms, his hands tied behind his back, his mouth covered with duct tape.

The man is struggling, his large body thrashing as they let him drop to the ground with a heavy thud. I gasp, because I recognize this man as the bouncer who let us into the club.

Vince.

He lands face first onto the floor, rolling himself onto his side, a groan of pain muffled by the tape across his mouth.

Vince looks up at Devin, panic swirling in his eyes. Devin

closes the distance between them and, without any warning, kicks the man in the face. A muffled scream sounds from under the tape, blood gushing from his now crooked nose. His eyes are already swollen, and it looks like he took a beating before Devin's foot connected with his face.

I'm frozen in place on the couch with my fingers digging into the cushion like an anchor. The two guards take a large step back, as if they already know what could happen if they get too close. Get caught in the crossfire.

Devin reaches down, his large hands wrapping around the nape of Vince's neck, wrenching his head back. "Look at me, Vinny." The growl in his voice sends a shiver across my skin. The man whimpers as Devin wrenches his head back farther, the man's labored breathing rushing through his crushed nose, spraying blood across the floor. "I said look at me, you fucking piece of shit." Vince's eyes widen, nearly bulging out of his head. His pleas press against the tape, begging to be let out to no avail. "Nothing you say will save you now. You fucking did this to yourself."

Devin pulls Vince where he holds him by the nape of his neck, forcing him onto his knees. Tears run down the bouncer's face, mixing with the blood that now drips onto his white shirt.

Blood usually makes me queasy, but for whatever reason, I can't take my eyes off the scene in front of me. The *man* in front of me. The way he has taken command of the room and grabbed another man by the nape like a dog nearly sends a thrill through me.

What the hell is wrong with me?

Devin wrenches his arm back, his fist connecting with Vince's face, splattering more blood. His head flies back and he screams in pain. Devin's bloody hand wraps around Vince's throat, pulling him closer as he punches him again and again. Blood coats Devin's knuckles, and while every part of my brain is screaming at me to look away, I just can't. Devin's eyes have nearly gone blank as he grits his teeth through every blow.

I didn't even notice Tony until he was right next to Devin. He reaches out and grips his shoulder, keeping an arm's length away as Devin throws another punch. The veins on the back of his hand that is wrapped around Vince's throat bulge, his grip tight around his neck, completely cutting off his air supply. His fist is cocked and ready for another hit, the blank look masking his face. Tony's large hand squeezes Devin's shoulder and he immediately freezes, halting his punch midair.

As if Tony's touch brought Devin back, he slowly lowers his fist, his breaths heavy, and removes his hand from the bouncer's throat, his body falling to the floor in a heap. Blood flows from Vince's nose and mouth as he lies on the floor, whimpering. Devin looks in my direction, his eyes still vacant.

Soulless.

Tony hasn't let go of his shoulder yet, his grip is still just as tight, like he's holding back a rabid dog. Devin heaves in deep breaths, his blond hair falling over his face that's now speckled with blood.

"Take him downstairs," Devin commands, his voice hollow. "I'll deal with him later."

The two guards grab Vince under his arms and haul him up. He grunts as they drag him across the floor, back toward the door, leaving a bloody trail. His head drops, chin pressed to his chest, as he fights for consciousness. All three disappear through the doorway, leaving us in complete silence.

Devin straightens himself, running his clean fingers through his hair, pushing it away from his face. He rolls his shoulders back, trying to ease the tension from his body as Tony's hand falls away. My eyes are wide at the scene that unfolded in front of me, nearly as violent as the one that happened downstairs.

I should be running and screaming at the violence that has

surrounded me this evening, but I stay seated on the sofa, my body full of lead. Both men stare at the door for a long moment, as if they're anticipating someone else to be drug through the door, before turning their full attention to me.

The tension fills the room, nearly drowning me, as they watch me. They're waiting for a reaction that I don't think I can give them. I should be cowering in fear, but I just watched a man beat another man within an inch of his life, and all I can do is think about the way I came all over those same hands tonight.

Tony breaks his gaze from me, huffing out a breath as he stalks back to his desk, continuing his work as if nothing even happened. Devin flexes his hands at his sides, Vinny's blood still dripping from them.

He looks like a monster, splattered in blood, with a smile so sharp that it could rip me to shreds. His eyes are cold and calculating as he watches me, making note of every breath I take. Like a wolf watching its prey, ready to rip open its throat.

My tongue darts over my lips and his cold gaze heats, a spark lighting behind them. He chuckles darkly and I know what I'm doing is insane, but my skin heats and all I want are his hands on me. I want him to smear the blood that's on them across my skin.

Marking me.

My senses awaken and my heart thunders at the thought of those powerful hands on me, the pulse between my legs has me nearly squirming in my seat.

Tony clears his throat, causing Devin's eyes to soften, his body relaxing slightly as he comes back to reality. He gives me a once over, and even though the life is coming back in his eye, they're still burning hot. He moves to the kitchen, washing the blood from his hands and face, washing the evidence away.

He stalks to the bar cart and pours himself another finger of whiskey. He throws his back with even more ease than earlier, pouring himself another, but this one stays in the glass.

"What did he do that was so terrible?" I ask quietly, trying to gauge the entirety of the situation I've found myself in.

He watches me over the rim of his glass, his bright blue eyes flashing from hot to cold. "He broke rules. Rules that are made to protect everyone in this club." He takes a tentative sip, dragging his tongue across his lips, licking them clean. "And now he must pay the consequences for his actions."

I gulp, thinking about the way he so easily flipped a switch from a charismatic gentleman to a wild-eyed assailant. "Did he hurt someone?" I can picture the way Vince looked when we entered the club, taking in each woman from head to toe. Sizing each of us up. He had a friendly demeanor, but there was something dark about his eyes. A look that not everyone would notice unless they were looking for it, or used to having one just like it, looking back at them.

"He might as well have," he grits out.

"What's going to happen to him?" I already know the answer, but part of me wants to hear it from him.

"He will no longer be employed here after tonight," he replies, his shoulders tensing as he raises the glass to his lips. "And you're not safe to leave on your own."

Fear courses through my veins, my body stiffening at his words. "What the fuck do you mean by that? Are you going to do something to me?" My words are sharp, and I shift myself to the edge of the sofa, my body on high alert.

"What I *mean* is you can't leave here on your own."

My eyes widen and my cheeks flush with anger from this man's sheer audacity. Who does he think he fucking is? My hackles rise and my legs twitch with the need to run. I curl my toes in the rug, ready to gain traction, as if I would make it far before one of them caught me. I know damn well that I wouldn't even make it to the door.

He rolls his eyes at me, but not with sincere agitation, because a smile hints at the corner of his lips. He leans against the island, sitting his whiskey down on the marble. "What I mean is, you can't leave here without an escort and some security measures."

I open my mouth to protest, because I refuse to become someone's prisoner again. But before I can say anything, he raises his hand as if to silence me. "Love, we're not going to let anyone hurt you and we're not going to trap you here. Okay?" His voice is soft, but there's an edge to it, like he's trying to talk someone off a ledge and won't accept 'no' for an answer.

"Then *what* exactly is the plan, if not to trap me?" My words are clipped. I don't mean for them to be so sharp, but for some strange reason, I feel comfortable enough to throw them at him. He's coming off stern, but there's something about the way he looks at me that is throwing me off.

He lifts his glass again, taking a long drink before answering me. "We're going to escort you home tonight, because we see that you took an Uber here." His eyes flash to the TV, which is now showing the CCTV outside of my apartment building. How the hell do they—

"Then we're going to have our men stake out in front of your apartment building to ensure your safety while we investigate this entire situation."

I stare at the screen as other views of my apartment building fill the other squares in it. I watch as a black car pulls up on the opposite side of the street and parks. My face goes hot as the anger starts to build, pulsing through my veins. "You don't even know me, so why the fuck are you helping me? Is this some kind of trap?"

Devin closes the distance between us, crowding me and forcing me to lean back onto the sofa. He cages me in with a hand on either side of my head, hovering over me and forcing me to look up at him. The smell of the whiskey on his breath floods my nose, along with the tinge of copper from the blood that is splattered across his shirt. "If I wanted to trap you, love, I would have dragged you down to the basement and left you to rot in one of the cells."

I suck in a breath as he continues. "And you think I haven't been following your every move since the last time I laid eyes on you, just hoping that you would make your way back here?" I stiffen as the memory floods my mind, realization of why he seems so familiar finally hitting me. His sharp, blue eyes looking down at me all those months ago, the way he made me feel like I was the only woman in the room.

I've thought about this place since the night I left Matt, because running into Devin that night was what drove the final nail in the coffin for my relationship. I had looked up the club a few times online and mentioned briefly to the girls how much I like the atmosphere, but didn't know if I could ever go back. But, just last week, I received an email from Masquer-ave, like I had signed up for their newsletter or something. I thought it was just a coincidence, but now, I'm not sure I believe that.

My eyes widen as I connect another dot. "You sent me the email." He smirks, and I so badly want to slap it from his perfect face. "You *wanted* me to come here, didn't you?"

He leans in closer, his nose nearly touching mine. "It had been over three months since I last saw you, love, and I had to make sure you were okay."

My mouth gapes at his words. Make sure I was okay? We were strangers that night, and I still considered us as such tonight, but he apparently had a different idea. I should be worried about that, but oddly enough, I'm not.

I watch him closely, his predatory eyes burning into me. "But why?"

He pulls back, a puzzled look on his face as if I missed the punchline of a joke. "Because your fiancé is the leader of one of the groups filled with elite criminals. You showed up on his arm, sporting their ring."

"What does my ring have to do with this?" I feel as though

I am standing on the ledge again and one slight breeze will have me tumbling over it.

He stands up, his tall, powerful body casting a shadow over me. I fight the urge to curl in on myself, because I feel like I just failed a test. His brows furrow at me and this time I look over to Tony, who is also staring at me with disbelief in his gray eyes. I look down at my now empty ring finger, the thin line etched in my skin where my unique engagement ring used to sit.

"You really don't know, do you?" Curiosity fills his voice as his question hangs heavy in the air. I avert my gaze, refusing to look at him.

I try my best to think back. All I can think is the rooftop dinner over the city, Matt going down on one knee and asking me to be his wife. It was romantic and extremely out of character for him. The giant, four-carat, black diamond ring left me speechless, not only for its size, but the uniqueness of it. The oval cut diamond glittered in the moonlight; the black diamonds crusted the band like little black stars. It was everything I didn't know I wanted in a ring.

The next night, I found myself in this very club, perched on Matt's lap, flashing the ring for all to see. That was nearly two years ago, and after the newness of our engagement wore off, so did my frequency at the club, only letting me come every so often so I wouldn't be suspicious.

I press my palm to my chest as even more realization pounds into it, my heart nearly breaking all over again. It was all for show. For fucking status. I see now that the ring wasn't unique, especially by the way that Devin mentioned it. My neck flushes with heat as tears prick at my eyes.

I was nothing more to him than the cost of that ring and the status boost it brought him. He paraded me around like a prized pony. How could I have been so blind? So fucking stupid?

Devin's finger crooks under my chin, slowly lifting my now

pounding head. His expression doesn't change, but his eyes are filled with understanding.

"I was nothing but a pawn for him," I croak around the lump in my throat. "He kept me around for his image, not because he loved me." My chest grows heavy, the weight of my own words trying to suffocate me.

I was willing to look the other way, to ignore all the red flags, because I thought that was what I was supposed to do. What a good future wife would do—all for love.

But his love was nothing but smoke and mirrors. A devious lie. One I believed until the rose-colored glasses were shattered from my face, and I saw everything for what it was. Bleak and bruised.

Devin presses his thumb into my chin, keeping my head up and forcing me to look at him. "You're worth more than that, Lena." His eyes flash to Tony, who is still staring at me, his expression once again unreadable. "Let us help you and we'll all get what we want."

My brows knit. "And what's that?"

He raises his brow. "Revenge, of course."

CHAPTER SEVEN

Lena

REVENGE. I never thought about taking revenge on the man who locked me away from the world, because all I ever thought about was finding a way out. He kept me locked away in his high tower and only brought me out for his image, but I was blind to all of that. I was *starved* for his attention and would devour whatever he would give me.

All I wanted was for the world to see how in love we were. For someone to notice the sacrifices that I had made for him to climb the ladder. Every ounce of me I poured into our relationship, only for him to feed off my desperation. His goal was to drain the life from me until there was nothing left but a shell of myself.

I pull my chin from Devin's fingers as tears start to fall, burying my face in my hands. They splash against my palms and hang heavy on my lashes. "He's a fucking asshole." My voice is muffled against my skin.

Devin's hand brushes my hair back, tucking it behind my ear. "He's worse than that, love." The coffee table creaks as he sits down on it, resting his hands on my knees. The warmth of his touch soaks into my skin, sending heat snaking up my thighs. "He's a monster in disguise."

His words slide over me as I look up at him, his knees pressing into mine. I take in the sight before me: the blood still covering his clothes, the dark look in his eyes, the way he nearly beat a man to death. "What makes you any different from him?"

He hooks his finger under my chin again, running his thumb over my lips. His touch causes heat to curl in my lower abdomen and my heart to race. His smile is all teeth as he brings his face closer to mine, our breaths mingling. "Besides the fact that the only pain I would ever inflict on you would send you over the edge with pleasure"—his voice is gravelly, his words sending goosebumps across my skin—"I'm worse."

He lowers his mouth to mine; the words that were on the tip of my tongue devoured by his. I melt into his touch as his hand slides up my legs, stopping right at the apex of my thighs. I think about how his hands felt earlier tonight as they inched up to my center, the hold he had on my throat as his fingers took me over the edge harder and faster than I ever had before.

He pulls back, his kiss leaving me breathless and desperate for more. His eyes are bright, as if the monster that was lurking beneath had receded, and the man was back in front of me.

Dr. Jekyll and Mr. Hyde.

"Can I trust you?" My brain is foggy, and I can't seem to trust my own instincts being in the same room with these two men. I should leave, run from the danger they present, but I want to stay to see if they'll light a match and burn me alive.

"You trusted him, didn't you?"

I gape at him, embarrassment warming my cheeks as my heart thunders in my chest. "You see where that got me," I whisper, the knot in my chest tightening again.

He runs his fingers across my collarbone, his touch sending a shiver through me, leaving more goosebumps in their wake. Heat continues to curl in my lower abdomen and the urge to reach over and haul his mouth back to mine is almost unbearable. He smirks, clearly seeing the effect his touch has on me and relishing in it.

"It got you here, didn't it?" He looks over his shoulder toward Tony whose heated, gray eyes are watching our every move. "Right here to us."

"And *who* exactly are you, Devin Green? You never have told me." My eyes trace over his face, the purpling bruises from tonight's fight, the small cut above his brow, the slight wince whenever he turns his torso wrong. But he seems as though he could care less about those things as his hungry eyes devour me.

He leans back slightly, and I catch the wince that pulls at his mouth. I reach my hand out and brush it along the buttons of his shirt, tracing the pattern of blood that's splattered across his chest. *Vince's blood.* He drops his eyes to my hand and all I can imagine is running it down the plane of his abs to the top of his pants.

Tony clears his throat, pulling me from my thoughts as I yank my hand back like I'd just been caught in a devious act. The smile on Devin's face is pure lust, but he doesn't answer me.

"If you aren't the owners, then who exactly are you?" I ask.

He lets out a chuckle, the sound rumbling through his chest. "I told you, love, consider us security. We do our job, keep the place clean of fucking scum, and stay in the owner's good graces."

I look around the apartment, noting the three doors on the back wall. "Where is he, then? The owner?"

Tony lets out an annoyed huff, causing Devin's sharp eyes to cut to him, the lust that had filled them draining out before they cut back to me. "He's too busy jetting around the world, but will occasionally pop in to check on the place." He leans in, cupping his hand next to his mouth and whispers, "But between us, he's just the name on the mortgage because we're the ones who are actually in charge around here." He leans back and gives me a wink.

"So, why the two of you, then?" I look between the two men, and even though power radiates from them, I'm still curious what their skill sets are to be left in charge of a place like this. Where evil lurks in the shadows, waiting to apprehend you around every corner.

"The owner and I go way back—" He looks over his shoulder, his eyes twinkling at Tony as he says, "And Tony's hands were tied, so he really had no choice in the matter when he was brought on board."

Tony cuts his gaze to me, his eyes darkening as if I had just overheard something incredibly damning. He looks as though he's about to pounce on Devin, sink his claws into his skin, and devour him. It's almost unsettling to feel this strange tension rise between them, especially since Devin seems completely unfazed by it as he goes on. "The owner was having trouble with the reputation of the club and decided that I might be a good fit to make it a little more exclusive, attracting powerful people with a lot of money."

Watching the screen and all I can think about is all the booths that are oozing with money and power, I say, "Looks like you did a good job."

His eyes darken slightly. "Maybe *too* good of a job."

The club is filled to the brim with dangerous people, people that I once associated with, but who were only keeping me around because I was a pawn for Matt. It makes me so angry to think about the women I trusted, who I thought were my friends, who were more than likely waiting for me to fuck up and ready to watch me burn.

I absentmindedly rub my thumb over my ring finger. That ring had more weight than the four carats attached to it, and even though he is still watching me, I felt that weight lift when I finally had the strength to take it off. It still sits in my jewelry box at the apartment I share with Bri and Kate, not because I can't give it up, but in case I ever need some fast cash.

I had a small lump of savings in a secret account. A nice little nest egg that I had spent the first part of my adult life saving. But I hadn't been able to touch it in years, because I couldn't attract attention to the fact that I had money that he couldn't keep account of.

It's been enough to keep me on my feet these last few months and will hold up while I figure my life out. But the minute I walked—no, ran—so did my seemingly endless cash flow. But thankfully, I have the friends I do, who didn't think twice when I called them all those months ago, whispering into the phone from a coffee shop bathroom, begging for them to save me. If anything would ever happen to them, I don't know what I would do, because they pulled me from the waves that were attempting to drown me.

If it wasn't for them, I would still be trapped.

"Love," Devin's voice cuts through my thoughts, snapping me back, "we want to talk to you about some terms of protection."

Crossing my arms, I lean back against the sofa. "What else is there to talk about? You're going to escort us out to the car, take us home, watch us for a few days to make sure he's not coming back, and then it's done."

Tony lets out a low grunt and leans forward, his elbows resting on his knees, lacing his fingers together. Devin stays relaxed back as he goes on, "Oh, no, we're going to have eyes on you until we can get our hands on whoever sent you that message and they're properly disposed of. We already have someone working on tracking down your ex." My eyebrows raise at this, and he keeps going, "He should have never left this club alive." His voice lowers to a growl. A muscle in his jaw tics, his nostrils flaring as if he's disgusted with himself.

I hold up my hand and take a deep breath. "I don't want to be involved with his shit anymore. I'm done. You do whatever you need to do, but please, leave me out of it. I just want to live my life in peace."

Tony huffs and the sound of his annoyance prickles against my skin. Devin pays him no mind as he unlocks his jaw and smooths out his voice. "If it were that easy, love, we'd already have you back at your apartment tonight, sleeping soundly." He grips my knee harder, causing me to jump. "But unfortunately, this plan for revenge has only just begun."

CHAPTER EIGHT

DEVIN

I SIT PERCHED on the stool in the corner of the basement, watching the unconscious man who's currently strapped to my table. My boiling hot blood pumps through my veins as I look at this motherfucker, his head lolled to the side, drool and blood collecting on the table beneath him.

This is going to be fun.

I palm my half-hard cock as I play out all the ways that this night could end and the retribution I'll gain for Lena. I think about how I want to show her the underbelly of the club and exactly how we use those private rooms that she seemed all too curious about. The things that I could do to her has me groaning under my breath. But there's plenty of time for that after I make her fall in love with me. *With us.*

Until then, I have this piece of shit to deal with.

I left Tony on duty to get Lena and her friends home safely, and to post people up outside for the foreseeable future. Knowing that she's safe and not alone tonight puts me slightly at ease; however, I will finally be able to relax once I have my eyes and hands on her again when she comes back tomorrow evening. She thinks staying away is the smart choice, but after some persuading, I finally changed her mind and convinced her the safest place she can be is here with all our security.

And by security, I mean me.

But for now, I'm sitting in this dank basement, listening to the drip of a leaky pipe. I can nearly see my breath as the chill night sinks into the earth, making this level even colder since we're so far underground. The single lightbulb that's hanging from the middle of the room gives off an ominous glow as my breath fills the air around my mouth.

Of course, I could turn up the heat, but it's more fun to watch them shiver.

My phone vibrates in my pocket, and I shift on the stool to pull it out, seeing a message from Tony informing me that he's heading back. That all three women are locked up tight and under full surveillance. No one is going in or out of that building without us knowing.

Pulling up the feed, I watch the empty hallway inside her building before flipping to the street view, making sure our men are in the right place to stake out. The tension in my chest eases slightly, knowing we have the best watching over her. That she's safe in her bed.

It would be even better if she were in mine… but that time will come eventually. She's going to fall for me, whether she realizes it now or not. She doesn't have a choice, because she's fucking mine. And if someone would stop being such a fucking prick, she might want to be his, too.

I quickly reply to Tony, telling him not to look for me for a while. It's better if only one of us is triggered by what's about to unfold down here.

A moan comes from the body that's strapped to the metal table in the middle of the room, gaining my full attention. Standing, I pocket my phone as our old pal Vince starts to stir. I watch in delight as his eyes open and he takes in his surroundings, realizing exactly where he is and the severity of his crimes.

I can feel his panic rising as he jerks at the restraints, grunting like a caged animal. The rattle of the table sends a thrill through me, knowing that he can't get away. He looks around, trying to see who, if anyone, is here with him. But for a little extra fun, I stick to the shadows, just out of sight, watching him squirm like the fucking worm he is.

"Help! Help, please! Somebody!" His restraints continue to clang, and he keeps screaming for help. He tires himself out faster than I expected, and his voice becomes hoarse. "Please, please God, help me. Save me. Please."

It's funny how people who have inflicted pain on others for so long seem to forget all of the sins they've committed and pray to their god like he's going to fucking do anything.

He didn't do shit for me, no matter how much I prayed. I figured out at a young age that I had to save myself. Eventually, through a stroke of pure luck and not divine intervention, I found the few people I can trust. Ones who have proven time and time again that they've got my back. This piece of shit, though, isn't so lucky. He won't find a savior on the path he's paved for himself. The one-way path that's sending him straight to Hell.

And I'm the devil incarnate.

Vince's breaths are erratic, and his head drops back with a metallic thud against the metal table, his eyes closing as he lets out a whimper.

A fucking whimper.

I tug on the leather gloves burning a hole in my pocket as I close the distance between us, taking quiet, calculated steps. The last thing I want to do is ruin the element of surprise that the shadows have granted me. A sheen of sweat coats his skin, and droplets drip from his bald head.

Standing right behind him, I lean over to take in his battered face, blood still oozing from his broken nose. It felt good to beat the living shit out of him. I plan to keep him alive just long enough to confess everything he knows. I check the clock on the wall in front of me and figure that Tony will be back soon, and I really don't need him to come looking for me, because he will, despite my instructions not to.

I cock my head to the side as I watch Vince's breathing even out and his body relax, exhaustion taking over, along with his false sense of security. I tsk softly while I adjust my gloves, pulling them tight against my fingers. His eyes fly open, wild with panic, exactly how I wanted them to look. My voice is low as I say, "Hello, Vinny. Welcome back to the basement."

Craning his head back to look at me, he immediately starts begging for forgiveness. I plant my hands on the side of his head, caging his face between them, holding his head in place. At my touch, his eyes go even wider as I bring my face closer to his. "Oh Vinny, Vinny, Vinny. It's a little late to apologize now, isn't it?" I feel the tug of a smile on my lips as I continue. "You weren't sorry for all the money you hocked off women at the door when you know that those women are supposed to get in for free. You *definitely* weren't sorry for the ones you took favors from; what was it you told them?" His eyes goes wide as I come even closer to his face. "Oh yes, it was your *'special VIP treatment'*."

"I was just trying to make some money on the side and give the women here a good time, boss. I know how much you want the ladies to have a good time." The fucking bullshit this fucker is spewing has me pressing my gloved hands even harder into his skull.

Anger courses through my veins, and without thinking, I pick up his head and slam it against the table. He lets out a cry from the impact and his breathing goes erratic, blood spraying from his nose and mouth as he forces his breaths. I peel my hands off his head, the pressure under my skin feeling like it's nearly tearing it open. I stalk around the table, this time letting my shoes click against the concrete floor as I head to a cart just out of reach of the light.

His hands are fisted as he yanks on the restraints holding

him in place. The smell of his anxiety fills the room, making me twitchy. It's the kind of tension that makes my heart race with my own anticipation as the voice in my head whispers devious things. Things it claims will help settle our bloodlust. The same lies it's been telling me for years.

I casually walk over to a table, letting the shadows cloak me as I grab a coiled wad of cash. I turn slowly, letting my hand back into the light as I toss it in the air like I'm getting ready to play fucking catch with my old man. I stalk back toward him, and he yanks his limbs against the restraints even harder, as if he can free himself.

Leaning against the table, I let him watch the cash float up and down in my hand. He sputters as he tries to string together a sentence of pleas, his words falling on deaf ears. I throw the wad up high this time, snatching it just as it comes back down, about to hit his face. He flinches like a little fucking bitch. I smirk down at him, watching the beads of sweat as they roll down his face, mixing with the blood that's dripping from his nose.

"Please, Devin. I-I won't do it again. *Please.*"

Anger rolls through me at the sound of his incessant lies. I take the wad of cash and smash it into his mouth, cutting off his pleas mid-sentence. I shove it as far back as I can, pressing it in until he gags, his teeth pressing into the leather of my gloves. "You're right, Vinny. You won't."

His eyes widen as I turn around, grabbing the roll of duct tape off the other cart of toys. I make a show of pulling a long strip from the roll, tearing it with my teeth, and slap it over his mouth. His eyes widen and he lets out a muffled scream as I clamp his busted nose, cutting off all his air supply.

He struggles under my grip, trying to wrench his face from my hand, but it only makes me press his nose tighter. I give him a smile, showing all my teeth. "This money isn't going to save you now, is it, Vinny?"

A long whistle comes from behind me, and I spin toward

the door, my hand going to the gun that is wedged into my waistband. The bright light of the single bulb makes it hard to make out who is standing in the shadows and has interrupted my fun. "I didn't know we were having fun like this tonight, Dev. You should have called," a feminine voice muses with a hint of amusement.

I look back at Vince, who is now unconscious. All because I couldn't fucking help myself and was distracted by the intruder.

"Dammit," I mutter under my breath, because I really don't have time to wait around for him to wake up since the clock is ticking. I know he has fucking information about Obsidian and I want to know exactly what it is.

"Why don't you let me take over?" the feminine voice croons as Tasha materializes into the light. She's wearing nothing but a black, see-through lace bra, matching thong, and her signature stilettos. She must have followed me down here or been tipped off that one of the bouncers was being permanently removed.

Her eyes are like mesmerizing pools of black, contrasting her smooth, porcelain skin. The true embodiment of a woman of the night. She commands the crowd with her long limbs, thick, flowing, black hair, and her impeccable body. She keeps the dancers in line, with her own crew as the eyes and ears of the club, reporting on the happenings behind the closed doors of the elite levels of the club. She's smart, cunning, and one hell of a Dominatrix. You could almost call her the Queen of the club, if that seat wasn't now reserved for Lena.

"You don't need to get your hands dirty, Tash. He's not worth the notch in your belt and if Tony—"

She cuts me off. "Don't worry your pretty blond head. I intercepted Tony when I caught him questioning one of the girls about your whereabouts." Her lips pull up into a malicious smile. "I told him I would come put a stop to your little game and he's now occupied with watching over the security team. The one that you placed outside of your mystery girl's home." Her eyes flash to Vince. "And besides, I think it will be very poetic if *his* woman finishes the job."

"You actually just wanted this job for yourself, didn't you?" My tone is light, because I'm good at making things hurt and ending things a little too abruptly for Tony's liking. He likes to inflict just enough pain so people will be willing to talk and once he's finished, he'll put a bullet right into their skull. But Tasha, she will hang you on the brink of death, give you a look into the depths of Hell, bring you back, and then do it all over again. She's like a predator playing with her food. She'll carry on until she's bored and even then, she'll keep edging them to their death.

She laughs, the sound like dark, black velvet. "I think you and Tony just need to jerk each other off to the security footage of your girl sleeping and call it a night."

I chuckle. "He doesn't seem too into her, so maybe I'll just get to keep her for myself. Also, with as much as he disappears, I'm pretty sure he gets laid more in a week than I have in months."

What she doesn't realize is that I haven't indulged in sex with another person since the night that I got my hands on Lena. The thought of another woman's body beneath my fingers just hasn't sat right with me. It's just been me and my hand like I'm a fucking teenager again.

She cuts me a look. "He hasn't fucked anyone in the club for nearly three months, Dev." She runs her fingers down Vince's face, holding them there, her nails pressing into his skin. "He's obviously been holding out for someone." Drawing back her hand, she slaps Vince so hard his neck audibly cracks, but he's still out cold.

My eyes narrow at her words, because I've seen him go to

his favorite room on multiple occasions, but never stuck around to see who he met up with in there. Tony has never been picky with who he fucks, preferring to keep his kinks in the private rooms and not out in the open in the Underground. Well, except for one specific kink that I've played a part in a few times—and casually pretend like I don't know about it.

"Tell your spies to mind their own fucking business, Tash." I cross my arms, my eyes drifting down to Vince's still unconscious body.

Tasha smirks, her eyes giving me a once-over. "Testy tonight, aren't we?" She pops open a button on Vince's shirt. "Heard you tried to fuck the leader of Obsidian's little fiancée and got into a little bit of trouble tonight." Her fingers deftly undo another button.

"I fucking handled it."

She rolls her eyes as she pops another button open. "Is a few of your men dying, you getting the shit kicked out of you, and Tony being stabbed your way of 'handling it'?" She puts the last two words in air quotes just before she pops open another button.

I scoff at her. "I said I handled it, not that it was handled *well.*"

She cuts me another look. "Tell me something, Dev. Is she worth all of that?"

I stiffen, narrowing my eyes at her. But before I can say anything, Vince lets out a groan, his eyes drifting open. As he stirs, Tasha hops on the table and straddles his chest. She rests her hands on her thighs and watches as he comes to.

Vince's breathing is labored from the hits he took, and he raises his head to meet Tasha's eyes. He tries to speak around the wad of cash and the tape that's covering his mouth, but it's no more than muffled screams. She slaps him hard across the face, his head jerking to the side.

"Shut the fuck up, you piece of shit," she spits the words

like venom. She grabs his face, letting her nails dig into his cheeks as she forces him to look at her. "All those years I spent swooning over you and letting you lead me along." She leans down, a breath from him. "Let me think that you were interested in me, telling me that we had to stay a secret, so it didn't jeopardize our operations. And I was stupid enough to believe your bullshit, when the only thing you were interested in was shoving your cock in me on the nights you couldn't get pussy from the poor girls you targeted at the door."

Her anger is building along with my own, her milky skin turning flushed. "You owe a *very* large debt for the services you received from me." He tries to pull out of her grip, but her fingers become a vice, drawing blood with her sharp, red talons. "Most men would sell their *souls* for a night with me," she says through gritted teeth, "but I think I'll take my payment from you, right here, right now," he lets out another pathetic whimper, "in blood."

My mouth gapes as her words filter through, the pieces falling into place. I wondered how he had gotten away with this for as long as he did, but how he got past her eyes and ears makes more sense. Even though they were secretly sleeping together, that doesn't mean that he wasn't telling other people, persuading her girls to turn a blind eye and feeding them lies to cover his own ass. I wouldn't doubt that he even blackmailed some of the girls to keep them quiet about what was really going on.

I can't blame Tasha for any of this, though. While Vince is charming and handsome, I have a feeling that he won't be for much longer after she's through with him.

I start to back away as he attempts to snarl, his last-ditch effort to go out like the monster that he is, but her nails only dig further into his skin, slicing through as she squeezes his cheeks in her grip; Tasha seemingly transforms before my eyes, her own monster showing up to play.

"Need anything from me before I go, darling?" I say teasingly, because I know fucking well that she doesn't need shit from me.

She looks my way, her dark eyes seem to be glowing with her own bloodlust. "First, don't call me darling, you know I fucking hate that." That makes my lips quirk. "And second, if you'd be a good little boy, roll that table over here. I'm comfortable where I am." She runs her nail down Vince's now exposed chest, leaving a red line in its wake. "Little Vinny carved up my heart and put my friends in danger, so in return, I'm going to carve up his dick." Her smile is that of a Cheshire cat as he starts screaming, the sounds still muted, as he tries to buck her off.

She laughs darkly. "Quit trying to show off, Vinny. It's not that big, anyways." She puts her hand up to her mouth as if she doesn't want him to see her mouth as she whispers, "Too many steroids."

I let out a chuckle as I roll the table to her, the different tools and their sharp edges shining under the light. I gently pat her on the leg before heading toward the door. "Have fun and let me know when you're through playing with your food. I'll call in the vulture to clean up the scraps."

"I can't guarantee there'll be anything left when I'm done, but I'll still let you know." Her voice is cruel as she reaches over to pick up a scalpel and examines it in the light. "Besides, I might be here awhile."

She runs the tip of the blade across his chest, blood swelling from the thin line. He starts screaming louder, the muffled sounds like the howling wind as she presses the scalpel to his throat, blood welling as the tip slices into his skin. She throws her head back, a maniacal laugh filling the room.

"If you need more after you're through with him, you can take your pick from the cells down either hall. It's about time to clean house, anyways."

She looks playfully in my direction, giving me a curt salute just as I turn to leave. "You got it, boss," she says, her voice low. She moves down his torso to his hips and begins to unbuckle his pants, the blade now pressing against his inner thigh. His muffled screams are silenced as the thick, metal door slams shut behind me.

CHAPTER NINE

DEVIN

"ARE you sure it's a good idea to get involved in this shit?" Tony's sharp voice cuts through the silence of the room, pulling me from my thoughts. Even from behind his mask, his words are sharp.

I lounge on the couch, continuing to swirl my whiskey out of habit. I don't rush to look his way, because even though the rest of the world only sees him and barely hears him, he's a constant nag in my ear about one thing or another. "We're already in this shit. Maybe she can unknowingly give us some insight into their inner workings."

He scoffs, clearly not buying it. "I highly doubt that. She seems fucking oblivious. She just stared out the window the whole ride back to her place while her friends carried on in the backseat. I can tell you that I did *not* need to hear about the size of our men's dicks and how they compare to different fucking vegetables."

I take a long sip of my whiskey, still not bothering to look his way as a rush of anger floods my veins. "Don't undermine her like that." I try my best to keep it together and not snap at him, but there's still an edge to my voice that I know he can hear. "I can only imagine the toll everything had on her tonight. So, don't be a fucking prick."

His gaze is just as hot as mine and it burns into me. I avert my eyes and watch the security cameras. The crowd is still thick in the club, and it makes me wonder who the fuck is still down there. Who is in the booths at the back, what information are they gathering, or who the fuck are they planting into our ranks?

Crossing my ankle over my knee, I slouch more into the soft couch as my thoughts drift right to Lena. Who is she to him and why is he so keen on trying to take her back? She was clearly nothing more than someone to keep locked up in a high tower somewhere, showing her off when it was appropriate for his image, and wetting his dick with on occasion.

My fingers curl tighter around my glass, the pressure on my fingertips keeping me grounded as I think about the way she was sitting at home, while that piece of shit brought other women here and more than likely fucked them before going home to her. I need to make a mental note to check the footage and find out for sure. Tally every time he fucked around on her and mark him for every single time.

"Her connection to him is a fucking liability, Devin. We can't risk having her around and putting even bigger targets on our backs." I let Tony's words go in one ear and out the other. He's skittish, and rightfully so, given his past, but my gut is telling me differently.

There's just something about her that tells me she didn't have a single fucking clue of what that piece of shit was up to. He pulled her in, probably in the way that all pieces of shit like that do, with niceties and full glamor. Then, as time went on, he let the mask slip and showed his true self, but she just passed it off as his ego.

A single moment in time that she convinced herself was a one-time thing. I mean, fuck, she was in her mid-twenties when they met and I'm sure that the promise of marriage was on his lips. Empty promises filled to the brim with lies.

Yes, I'm well aware that she puts a target on us. That having her around will shine a spotlight on our checkered pasts, and we risk them catching up to us. But I saw the look of fear in her eyes as he entered the hallway. I saw the woman behind the mask, both literally and figuratively, right through to the pain and suffering she endured at his hand. One that I fully intend to remove.

I can't even imagine the kind of damage he's done to her during the years they were together, but tonight confirmed that he hadn't broken her. It was so goddamn heroic the way she stood up to him. Her defiance shook him, and you can bet your ass that I'm going to keep the footage of tonight for myself and watch that moment on repeat.

Maybe, if she sticks around long enough, I'll show her what a fucking badass she is for that. But I know that with it shaking him up put an even bigger target on her back. He will be coming back, and he will be after her. He thinks that she belongs to him and wants her back, no matter what it takes.

For men like him, it's all about status. Sure, he can sleep with however many women he wants, bring women to wherever else he rests his head at night—I know they have another hideout somewhere around this fucking town—but all in all it's about the woman who stands at his side for pictures. His show woman, the one who everyone sees in the limelight. The tabloids. The one who makes him look like he has life together, makes people think he's a fucking god.

I'm sure if I searched online, I would see them all dressed up at some gala, looking like the happiest couple on the planet —wholly in love with one another. And I would make sure that Tony figured out a way to erase every single one of them —scrub them from the internet for good.

"Maybe…" I say, my lips pressed against my glass. "Maybe, if we keep her close, it'll draw the mice out from the hole. She can be the cheese, and we'll finally have them where we want them."

My eyes float up to Tony and he's just watching me with those steely gray eyes. They're cold to everyone but me, and even though I've been looking at them for years, they keep me guessing what he's really thinking. There's a connection between us that I can't fucking deny. Simmering.

"I think that's a fucking terrible idea and will get us all killed," he quips. "We've been discovering moles left and right and we'll eventually get the answers we need from them."

A laugh rushes up my throat and comes out as almost a bark. I drop my foot to the floor and lean forward, my elbows resting on my knees, clutching my drink with both hands. "They're all fucking idiots who don't know fucking shit, thinking they can fuck whoever they want and come out ahead. None of them that are here are worth fucking anything to us."

Tony just continues to stare at me, analyzing my reaction, and I can tell he thinks I'm fucking insane.

And he's right.

This whole thing is fucking insane, but the minute I laid eyes on her, I knew that she was something special. She deserves so much better than to be around that piece of shit and his posse of miscreants. It makes my blood boil that he ever laid a hand on her, let alone just being able to touch her when he fucking felt like it.

I stare at the screen, watching the feed of the empty hall-way, her apartment door closed tight at the end. I don't fucking want her there, out in the open to be taken back to him at any time. Her friends would have no way of fending them off if they chose to bust down that door.

I clench my jaw at the thought of them being in the line of fire, making my hands itch. It's been a few weeks since I've had this urge. I'm trying to keep my shit together because when I get this worked up, I either need to fight or make someone bleed. I try to keep my calm demeanor about me, because when I get worked up, Tony usually follows suit or will put an end to whatever has me on edge.

I see him out of the corner of my eye as he leans back, his muscular arms crossing over his hard chest. He seems like he's putting some distance between us, reminding me that my energy can also drive him to that dark place in his mind.

I think back on the timeline, since the last time that we saw Lena and how everything went dark. But did it?

"We thought that they had disappeared because Matt wasn't coming around, but in reality, he was sending his people in and hiding in plain sight." I scrub a hand over my face, letting out a breath into my hand.

Tony's voice is rough, with a sharp edge to it. "I have proof that Vince let Matt in tonight." My eyes snap from the screen to his. "He was wearing a full face mask. When he approached Vince, they shook hands and he walked right in. No ID check or anything." My blood boils and if I thought I could, I could haul ass down to the basement and finish that fucker in one go. But he's either already dead, or Tasha won't let me anywhere near him while she's unleashing her pent-up rage. "He ditched it right before he entered the hallway and started this whole fucking mess."

Tony clicks the screen, showing the footage of Matt approaching the hallway entrance and disappearing through it. It's not long until his backup crew starts filtering in. It's like entering the Twilight Zone as I watch the scene begin to unfold from a different perspective, but I'm more relaxed at the thought that a majority of those men are dead or locked up in one of my cells. Only a couple made it out unscathed and those were the ones who dragged Matt to safety.

The reality of the situation slams into me. "There's no way that Vince did this alone, T." Tony's eyes darken at my words. "This runs deeper than we thought."

Fuck this shit. I get to my feet, my blood pumping so fast

as anger roars through my veins that I get lightheaded. "We need to figure out who is the fucking snake in the hen house." I take a deep breath to try and steady myself, but it's not working. "I don't fucking care who it is. I want answers ripped from their lips and their blood on my hands." I curl the fingers of my free hand into my palm, pressing in my nails and raking them over my skin.

The anger that's pumping through my veins is making me see red. My hand twitches, and I chuck the glass at the wall without another thought. "Motherfuckers!" I roar as the glass shatters all over the floor, pieces flying through the apartment.

My breaths are erratic, and my vision is blurring at the edges. I'm fucking losing it and I feel like the heathen in me is trying to claw his way out. The need to inflict pain on someone, draw blood from their veins, break their bones, and end their life is almost unbearable.

I feel large hands grip my shoulders and I tense, not wanting anyone to get in my way if I let my rage fully take over. I look up into gray eyes and I try my best to focus on them, but my mind is reeling as they go from gray to black voids.

Maybe he's right, because he usually is, and maybe she will be a liability for us, but I don't fucking care. I may not have a hero complex, because I know from experience that those people rarely make it out alive, but I sure as fuck have a god complex. And this club is my realm, and I will do anything to protect what's mine, and that now includes her.

Tony's fingers dig into the muscles of my shoulders, his grip almost bruising against my skin. He watches me, not letting me slip from his grip or get lost in the dark corners of my own fucked up mind. His fingers press even harder, and I relax into his hold, letting him sink in deeper.

Finally, my shoulders relax and so do his. I listen to his steady breathing as it comes out from the slits in his mask, and I do my best to match them. He doesn't normally get this close to me, but his hold is hot on my skin, and I can't help but see the man behind the mask.

His hands slowly slide down my arms, leaving a trail of fire in their wake, letting them drop to his side as he takes a tentative step back. He gives me a heated once-over before turning on his heel and crossing to the kitchen.

He yanks off his mask as if he's suffocating behind it and I take in the sharp lines of his jaw, the slight stubble across his face. He pours a finger into a glass and throws it back, his Adam's apple bobbing as he swallows. He sits the glass down with a thunk before pouring himself another. He braces himself on the countertop with an almost defeated look on his face.

Heaviness pulls at my bones as the last drops of anger leave my body. I come up behind him, the muscles in his back tensing slightly and the air grows thick again.

"We have to help her, T." I can hear the exhaustion creeping into my voice as it turns low and rough. "We need her just as much as she needs us." I lean against the counter, pressing my hip into the cool stone, running my hand through my hair for the umpteenth time.

He eyes me, his brow furrowing with frustration. "You can help her and I'll just follow your lead." His voice is flat with disdain and he might as well have slapped me. A minute ago he had his hands on me, making me feel like he was raising me up, but now? Well, now I feel like it was a persuasion tactic, and this conversation didn't go the way he wanted it to. "She's a liability to our cause, and if she puts you or Tash in danger—"

I hold up a hand, cutting him off. Maybe I do have a hero complex, because I just can't give her up.

No, not a fucking hero. *Vigilante.*

What I don't understand is why he can't see how this will all play out in our favor. Having her here will keep people coming into the club who can give us valuable information one way or another. I guess his stubborn ass will have to figure that out on his own.

"Nothing is going to happen to anyone, okay? We will tighten security and have her here as much as possible. That way, if she's being followed by him, he'll send someone in for her. They'll be flies in the spider's web." I try my best to smile at him, but his lack of faith in my plan has taken me down a few notches, turning it into a grimace at best.

"This doesn't have anything to do with—" he starts, but I hold up my hand again, silencing him. He's lucky it wasn't my fucking fist this time.

"This has everything to do with *Lena*," I bite out, showing my teeth. "Anything else that comes from it is only an added bonus."

Tony lets the room go silent, not bothering to take his eyes off me. He's so fucking calculated and looks at everything under a microscopic lens, when all I want is to have the pound of flesh I'm fucking owed. His piercing gray eyes hold mine and I let the electricity of the room prickle across my skin, causing the hair on my arms to stand on end, but I refuse to let him see the effect it has on me.

After another long moment, he's the one to finally break the silence, breaking the tension along with it. "Go to bed, I'll clean up your fucking mess," he gruffs out.

A condescending smirk pulls up on my lips. "Don't you always?" And even though my words are laced with the same condescending attitude as the smile on my face, it's not lost on me how true it is. He has taken care of me as much as I've tried to take care of him through our years together. He's let me see some of the darkest parts of him and I've shown him my most deranged. The monsters that live beneath us mingle, as though they have waited lifetimes to be reunited.

But honestly, if he thinks I'm going to let him clean up this particular mess, he's mistaken. Yes, I grew up with a silver spoon in my mouth, but my father paid more attention to my brother, who he proudly claimed as his son. And as the not-so-golden child, I was usually left with a nanny or other staff members, because even my own mother didn't have the bandwidth to deal with a child me.

So, instead of just letting the staff do the work for me, I had them teach me everything they knew. Cooking, cleaning, minor maintenance, and most importantly—how to snoop around. That one was an unintentional skill, but I caught on fast that the walls saw and heard everything. I use that skill to my advantage every night with the fuckers who frequent this place as I hide in plain sight, only this time, I have the help of one of my many masks giving me full advantage of the anonymity they create.

I grab the broom and vacuum from the closet and begin to clean up the shards of broken glass. I can feel his heated gaze on me as I work. I find myself occasionally looking up and meeting those haunting gray eyes. Eyes like molten metal as they watch me, and if it was anyone else, I would probably tell them to take a fucking picture, but not Tony. Never him.

I switch out the broom and sweep up the glass I missed, obsessively going over the hard floors until I feel like I would walk around this place barefoot and not risk a shard of glass making a new home in the bottom of my foot.

I chuck everything back in the closet, exaggeratedly wiping my brow, giving him a smirk. I leave the room without another word and close the bedroom door behind me with a soft click.

I never lock my door, and I know he doesn't either. Even when he first moved in and we were complete strangers, I never felt the need to lock it. I've always tried my best to keep everyone out at arm's length, but I've only ever wanted to let him in. Show him what's behind the magic curtain that is the legend of Devin Green.

After a shower to finally wash the remaining blood off my body, I crawl into bed, always choosing to sleep naked. I stare up at the ceiling and hear the subtle clicks of his keyboard through the crack under the door. He's quiet, but my ears can pick up his mundane sounds like he's crashing cymbals through the apartment. He works too much, and I know when he can't sleep, he gets up and works at all hours of the night as if he can never truly relax. Like I have a lot of fucking room to talk.

I know damn well that I won't be going to sleep anytime soon. I could go back down in the basement and yank my newest victim out of their cell and use them to burn off some of this pent-up energy, but Tony would never let me out the door. Instead, I pull up Lena's apartment feed on my phone, watching the black and white footage of the empty hall like a silent movie.

It's odd, but I feel like someone else is also watching this channel. I can just assume it's Tony, because I'm sure that if I walked out of this room now, we would be watching the same thing. However, if we could easily get into it, that means anyone else can, too.

I scrub my hand over my face, because I know that if I asked him to, Tony would be able to pull up anything from inside of that apartment. He's a fucking hacker by trade and once he figures out how to get in somewhere, they'll never be able to get him out.

As fucked up as it is, I *need* to see what's going on inside of there, see what Lena is doing. Goddammit, this woman already has me wrapped around her fucking finger and she doesn't have a fucking clue about it.

My cock twitches at the thought of my fingers running over her body, and at the thought of how easy it was to get her to come on my fingers. I roughly grip the base of my cock, fighting back a groan as I pump my hand over my hard erection. I was so fucking close to having her tonight, but that piece of shit had to come and ruin my chance. If he thinks that he can have her back, he's dead fucking wrong.

She's been on my radar for a while and I've finally homed in on her. I will remove the hand of anyone who dares to try and touch her.

I grip my cock even harder at the thought of slicing through skin, watching the blood pour out, their screams of pain as she watches me remove anyone who has ever attempted to hurt her, because she's fucking mine.

Mine. Mine. Mine. I chant under my breath as my strokes gain speed. My balls constrict, heat building through me as I get off to the thought of her screaming my name as I pound into her, my blood-soaked hand wrapped around her throat, painting her in crimson. I bury my face into the crook of my arm to suppress my moan as I come across my abs.

I lie breathless, my hand still gripping my cock as I stroke through the orgasm, staring at the ceiling. I've been waiting for her to show up here for months after having my eyes on her for nearly a year. If I could track her down again that easily, with all the resources at his disposal, so can he. And that just doesn't fucking work for me.

All of this is fucking dangerous, and it's been a while since I've felt this out of control. My skin itches and my hands ache with the need to destroy every person who has ever wronged her. Who stood by idly as she was manhandled and mistreated. They'll all be sent to an early grave one way or another.

I let my eyes drift closed, my cock twitching in my hand as I think about all the ways to show her what she was missing while she was trapped by that piece of shit. She deserves to know what it's like to have the attention of a real man, one who not only destroys our enemies but will light the fucking world on fire for her.

The gasoline is poured and I'm holding the match. All she has to do is say the word, and I'll strike it because I'm ready to watch it all go up in flames.

CHAPTER TEN

NO MATTER how hard I try, I can't seem to keep my eyes closed. Sleep is miles away from me as my mind reels from tonight's events. This was supposed to be a fun night out with my girls, and it turned into being rescued from my ex by masked strangers, offered their protection, and given the chance to help enact revenge on him. On an entire organization that I didn't even know existed. It all happened so fucking fast that I don't even really know if I'm processing everything correctly.

Tony escorted us out of the club, into a blacked-out SUV, and back to our apartment. Bri and Kate were so caught up in their good time, going on about the men they ended up in private rooms with, that they hardly noticed that our Uber wasn't an Uber at all. They nearly fell out of the vehicle when he parked in front of our building, hung onto each other as we rode the elevator, and then walked us to our door. They didn't even question that he was still wearing an ominous hood and adorning his mask.

To live in their world of sweet oblivion.

Even after we deadbolted the door, the distinct feeling of being watched pressed in on me. So much so, I kept looking out the peephole to see if he was still standing there, protecting us like a watchdog. Lurking in the shadows, waiting to intercept any danger that might be coming our way. But the hallway was empty every time I checked, not a soul to be seen.

"Spill, Lena." Bri's slurring voice startles me, and I yank my head away from the door.

I turn to find them both standing in their pajamas, clutching bottles of water as if it's their only lifeline. "Spill what?" I ask, false innocence lacing my tone.

"Don't play coy, Lele," Kate says, giving me her signature disapproving look before she hiccups. "You disappeared into the crowd after we saw you talking to some fuckin' blond guy, and now we're being escorted home by what seems like your personal, masked bodyguard. So, fucking *spill*."

Well shit, maybe they were more aware of their surroundings than I thought. But, instead of giving in, I roll my eyes. "Oh please, Kate, you didn't notice anything when your tongues were down those guy's throats." They look at one another, their cheeks turning red. *Checkmate.*

Obviously, I can't tell them the truth, because even I don't believe it. Plus, they would completely lose their shit knowing that Matt showed up, and knowing Bri, she would do something out of rage and could get herself into trouble. So, I do what any friend would do and I lie out my ass. "I was in a private room with that guy, and he showed me a really, really good time." I break eye contact, because the image of us in the Underground floods my mind and I can't look at my best friends with such dirty thoughts filtering through me.

They look at each other, eyes going wide with delight, and then like banshees in the night, they scream. Their squeals of excitement ring through my head.

How am I going to explain all of this to them? Probably about as vaguely as I can. I'll give them just enough to not worry about me and I definitely won't divulge the details. I don't need them prodding me with questions and concerns, because they already have enough of those with me as it is. Right now, the less they know, the better off we all are.

They are my two best friends, after all. Bri and I have known each other since freshman year of college, and Kate came around when Bri desperately needed a roommate after I moved in with Matt. I got to know her during that first year that Matt and I were together, that is, until Matt started becoming a wedge in our friendship. He put a lot of distance between us, and while I'd like to come clean about everything that's gone down over these last few years, I'd rather just pick up where we left off.

Staring at the ceiling, the glow of the city outlining the curtains, I listen to Bri's steady breathing as she sleeps next to me. Her deep breaths are causing my eyelids to get heavy and I'm beginning to feel the pull of sleep. I snuggle deeper under the duvet, rolling onto my side. My eyes slowly start to drift shut, but they snap open at the sound of my phone buzzing on the nightstand. Anxiety rushes through me, the feeling nearly choking me as I reach for my phone.

All I can think about is the middle of the night phone calls after the driver would give his report on where he'd taken me, who I'd seen, or if I asked for him to keep this trip to himself. I was such a fool to continue to think that he would eventually come onto my side. That he would see the desperation in my eyes and turn a blind eye just once. He never did.

Those calls always turned into Matt screaming, calling me a whore or a slew of other names, and telling me to prepare myself for when he got home. I would beg for his forgiveness until he would hang up on me, leaving me spiraling. I would lay in bed, my heart racing, as I listened for the sounds of him coming home. His footsteps pounding down the hallway, like a bull charging forward, before he would slam into the room and make me pay for misbehaving.

A shiver runs through me as I think of nights like those, the knot in my chest tightening to where I can't breathe. I tell myself that it's not him, that I'm safe with the security that's watching over the building. I'm hanging on to Devin's promises, fingers barely gripping the edge, and I can't let myself fall now.

My fingers slowly curl around the phone, lifting it from my nightstand in my now shaking hand. The backlight nearly blinds me as I'm met with a message from an unknown number. I hold my breath as my finger swipes across the screen to open it, anxiety yanking the knot tighter, choking the air from my lungs.

UNKNOWN

Eyes on your building. Don't leave until we say so. -T

Relief rushes through me, releasing my breath, and with it comes a huff of a laugh. The knot in my chest eases, the anxiety receding like the tide as I save Tony's number into my phone. I crawl out of bed, careful not to disturb Bri, and pull back the curtain to look out the window to the street eight stories down. I catch sight of a car on the street that I don't recognize, but I know exactly who sent it. They kept their word and for the first time in a long time, I have a real sense of security.

Even so, my eyes roll as I realize that I left one possessive asshole for what seems like two more. But this isn't the same kind of possessiveness, is it? No, this is protection at the highest level.

I'm the ex-fiancée of enemy number one, and not to mention the fact that they could have easily turned me back over to him for anything they wanted, but they didn't. Instead, they offered me protection far beyond anything I could have imagined someone would ever offer me.

There's still a slight sense of unease about the whole thing, because why? Yes, Devin and I seem to have a connection, and I was more than willing to go a step further with him tonight, but it can't just be that…can it? No one falls that hard at first sight, do they?

Snuggling back into the bed, I lay the phone back down on the nightstand and roll on my side toward Bri. I snuggle into her, smelling the mix of her sweet perfume and the faint scent of cigarettes. The anxiety that had filled my chest is now a forgotten feeling as my eyes drift shut. My breathing slows and my heart rate steadies before I find myself dreaming of nightclubs, secret underground rooms, and mysterious, masked men.

THE SUN FILTERS through the crack in the curtain that I didn't close properly after last night. My body is curled around Bri's, her head stuffed under her pillow. Peeling myself away from her, I crawl out of the bed. Standing, I clutch my throbbing head that's making me dizzy as the smell of bacon fills my nose. Of fucking course, Kate would already be awake and making breakfast.

I tiptoe out of the room, gently closing the door behind me. I lived with Bri long enough to learn not to wake her up, especially after a night out. You might as well be waking a bear from hibernation, one that will claw your face off the moment it opens its eyes. I'm a believer that the phrase 'don't poke the bear' was inspired by her.

The sound of sizzling bacon is like music to my ears as I round the corner into the kitchen. My eyes squint from the bright sun filtering through the kitchen window, again blinded by this sunny day. Kate is sitting at the kitchen table holding a cup of coffee, eyes wide with alarm as she stares toward the stove.

I stop dead in my tracks when I finally notice the man

that's standing there, his eyes glued to the sizzling skillet. I watch as his muscled back flexes under his black tee, the spatula flipping each piece as if he's a professional chef. My mouth gapes, because this truly can't be happening. "What the *fuck* are you doing here?"

Devin turns around and his eyes go wide with delight. "Lena, love." His voice is gravelly, probably due to lack of sleep, but he still flashes me a shit-eating grin as he says, "Just in time for breakfast." The bruises on his face shine out in the sunlight, the cut on his lip swollen, but he still looks like a Greek god.

Kate's watching him warily, her eyes narrowing on him like she's watching a bug crawl across the floor. I gesture to Devin. "Did you let him in?"

Her eyes snap to mine, looking at me over the rim of her coffee mug. "I had just started making coffee when he knocked on the door." She looks at him suspiciously as she says, "He introduced himself, telling me that he was the man you were with last night, and then strolled right in. He had grocery bags on his arms and just started cooking as if he does it here every day. His timing was *impeccable*."

I feel my cheeks heat. It dawns on me that he probably had a way to figure out that Kate was up. My eyes roam around the apartment looking for a hidden camera or mic, before they settle on the microwave clock: *11:47 a.m.* Holy shit, we slept late.

Granted, Tony didn't drop us off until well after two, but I'm still shocked that I let myself sleep that long. I have half a mind to think that Devin was going to come and cook for us regardless of what time it was. I'm sure it would have been a cakewalk for him to just let himself in, but he seemed to take the more gentlemanly route.

"It *was* impeccable, wasn't it?" Devin turns from the stove, giving me a wink. My heart races and heat crawls across my abdomen. "Just like my cooking."

I take him with his fitted black tee, perfectly tailored black jeans, and shiny black shoes. He manages to make a relaxed outfit look regal and entirely too sexy for eleven a.m.

His eyes follow the line of my body, a wolfish grin pulling at the corners of his mouth. I look down and take in the sight of me in an oversized, ratty T-shirt and skimpy shorts, which makes it look like I'm wearing nothing under it. My cheeks heat even more as my neck flushes with embarrassment.

Kate's glare could turn him to stone, especially as he looks over his shoulder at her, giving her his million-dollar smile. I pry open my mouth to say something, anything, to break the tension that is growing in the room, just as Bri stumbles into the kitchen. She rubs her eyes, cursing the sun, before taking a deep inhale through her nose. "Oh my God," she groans, "there's fucking bacon."

She walks right up to Devin and peers over his shoulder at the skillet, the bacon sizzling as he scoots it across the pan. "A man who can pleasure our girl *and* cooks?" She reaches past him to grab a mug, careful not to touch him, as if he's a priceless work of art. "Dinner is usually at six if you want to come back for round two."

Devin's grin grows bigger as his eyes flash to me, causing heat to creep up my neck again. "You'll have to excuse her, I think she's still drunk," I say, giving Bri a classic *go to fucking hell* look.

"Fuck you, Lele." She chuckles as she fills her coffee cup, drinking it straight black. She likes to compare it to her soul, but I know her better than that. She might be rough around the edges, but she has a heart of gold. Except for maybe when men are involved and then she becomes a feral animal with teeth as sharp as knives.

Devin carefully removes the bacon from the pan as he says, "Unfortunately, I won't be able to stay for dinner, ladies, but I'll write an IOU before I leave." His eyes meet mine. "And Lena won't be home for dinner, tonight, either."

Kate's mug thumps onto the table, the liquid nearly spilling over the edge. "And where, exactly, is she going to be, *Devin?*" Kate snaps.

Bri gives her an incredulous look, but she doesn't seem to notice.

Devin starts cracking eggs against the pan, completely unaware of the icy stare at his back, the sizzle filling the silence before he says, "At the club with me, of course."

Kate's eyes flash with anger as her face seems to redden. Even though Bri and I have more of a history, Kate has always acted as the mother of the three of us. She was the one to send the most texts, checking in on me, and letting me know that they were there. Her nose scrunches, her teeth flashing like a mother bear's who's ready to protect her cub. I cut in before she can unleash herself on him. "I agreed to go back to the club with him tonight." Kate's glare shoots through me like pointed arrows, trying to pin me in a lie. "I… I want to see more of what the club has to offer."

My choice of words was a mistake as the daggers from Kate's glare slices me open, exposing me for the liar that I am. Before Kate can retort, Bri's laugh breaks the silence. "Ooo, girl. You get it." She nestles into one of the chairs at the kitchen table next to Kate, pulling her knee to her chest. "You deserve to have all the fun after the last five years of bullshit you endured." Her smile is so bright as she looks at Kate. "*Right*, Kate?" I can hear the edge in Bri's voice, her tough girl persona front and center.

The steel slowly melts from Kate's demeanor as she takes me in, her eyes softening as she looks down at her coffee mug. "Yeah, I guess you're right." Her wary eyes cut to Devin. "I'm just thrown off by this stranger barging into our home at first light, cooking fucking breakfast."

He laughs and turns to her. "First light? How late do you ladies sleep around here?" He gestures to the apartment and turns back to start plating the eggs.

Bri laughs again. "Kate works her own hours because she runs her own e-commerce business, and *I* bartend, so I'm always out late. By the way, I could put those bartenders to shame last night. Whoever taught them how to mix a drink needs to be bitch slapped."

I nearly choke as Devin's brows raise as if he's considering her words. With a plate in each hand, he delivers plates full of bacon, eggs, and toast to them at the table. "Business owner? Bartender? What can't you ladies do?" He gives Bri a dazzling smile as he goes on. "If you ever want a change of scenery, or to bitch slap someone, I'm always looking for bartenders at the club."

She pauses, her fork hovering midair as his offer hits her. "Are you serious? I would make so much fucking money at that place."

Devin chuckles as he pulls his wallet out of his back pocket, pulling out a matte, black card. Handing it to Bri, he says, "Call this number and ask for Tasha, tell her I told you to call." She stares blankly at the card in her hand. "She'll love having you on staff. She *loves* a challenge."

Bri's eyes narrow on the card, flipping it over in her hand. "I can make a mean margarita on the rocks and lemon drops that'll make your panties fall right to the floor."

She keeps her eyes on the card as Devin chuckles. "You're hired." He looks in my direction for a moment, his expression unreadable, before turning and setting another plate down at the table. "Eat, love. I'm sure you're starving."

I cross the kitchen and take my seat just as he sits a coffee mug in front of me. I take a sip and nearly choke on the hot liquid. It's exactly how I like it, three sweeteners and a splash of creamer. My eyes cut up, his handsome face watching me as if he's waiting for my reaction. There's no way in Hell he could know this; it must just be a coincidence.

I tentatively take a bite of the food and nearly groan at how perfectly cooked everything is. The bacon is crispy, and the eggs are perfectly sunny side up. With those hands, this man is proving to be a jack of all trades.

"Thanks for breakfast," Bri says around a mouthful of bacon. "Who knew a man could perform so well in the kitchen?"

I kick out my foot, connecting with Bri's knee. She lets out a surprised yelp and giggles, shoving more bacon into her mouth to shut herself up.

"You should see what I can do in other rooms," Devin says darkly as he rounds the table to me, lifting my free hand into his. His words and the gentle scrape of callouses against my skin sends a curl of desire through my abdomen, the thought of those hands on me again nearly makes me fall out of my chair.

He lightly kisses my knuckles, holding his lips to my skin. His lips are soft, and I don't miss the swipe of his tongue, as if he's trying to sneak a taste of me. "I'll see you this evening, love," he says around my knuckles, his voice low, his eyes heated.

My eyes widen and my head bobs, the only answer I can conjure up, considering all my words are lodged in my throat. The ghost of his lips makes my skin tingle, heat spreading throughout my body like wildfire.

He backs away from the table with a smug look as he heads to the door. Hand on the knob, he pauses and looks over his shoulder at us. "Lock this behind me, ladies. We don't need any strange men coming in now, do we?" His voice is light, but I don't miss the flash of warning in his blue eyes.

As soon as the door clicks shut, Kate jumps up, swiftly crosses the apartment, and snaps the deadbolt into place. She takes a step back from the door, watching it as if Devin will come back and bust it down. I want to check the peephole because even though I can't see him, I can sense he's still on the other side, waiting to see if I'll take the bait.

The tension in the room grows as we all stay silent but

eventually pops when Kate throws me a glare and I audibly gulp. "Lena, what. The fuck. Was that?"

I shrink back in my seat, the pressure of guilt building in my chest.

"Uh…he's…I—"

"Oh Kate, don't be such a bitch," Bri interjects before shoving another piece of bacon into her mouth. "Let Lena live," she says around the food. She looks at me and gives me a once-over before looking back at Kate. If looks could kill, then Kate would be six feet under with the way Bri's glare cuts through her. "She wasn't allowed to do shit for years and she doesn't need you reprimanding her about getting laid by a hot blond, with the body of a god, who can also fucking cook."

"If she invited this man to our apartment for breakfast, then she could have warned us," she retorts, crossing her arms. "Plus, we don't know anything about this man. He could be just as bad as Matt or fucking worse. He obviously had no qualms about showing up here *unannounced*."

Anger surges through me, my neck and face flushing. "I didn't invite him, *Kate*," I bite out. Her body stiffens, her eyes going wide at my tone. "He came on his own accord, and honestly, it's the nicest thing a man has ever done for me. So, until he proves to be a dangerous stalker, just let it be, okay?"

She looks between Bri and me, seeing that she isn't going to win this argument, and takes her seat at the table. Sipping her coffee, she picks up her phone and starts scrolling her social media feed. After a few moments, she looks up at me, her voice calm again. "He seems like a nice guy, Lele, and he's hot as hell. His cooking is a bonus."

A soft smile pulls up at the corners of my mouth. "He does seem nice. So does the other one." As soon as the words leave my mouth, Bri's fork clatters the table and she leans forward, grabbing for my hand.

"There's *another* one?" Her voice holds a level of wonderment. "My God, Lele, and I thought I had a good fuck last night, but you were shacking up with *two*!"

"Nothing actually happened with him, Bri, but there's some strange tension between us." His piercing gray eyes and giant body pressed against me in the hallway floods my memory. "And he's actually the one who brought us home last night," I say casually, trying my best to get her to calm the fuck down and stop making this a big deal in front of Kate.

Kate cuts me another glare. "Then why was he the one to bring us home, not Devin?" She leans on her elbows. "It's also not normal for a man to not only escort us home, but to do a full sweep of our apartment before we're allowed to come in. What the fuck was that about?"

Fuck. I'd completely forgotten about the extra measures that Tony silently insisted he take before finally leaving last night. Did he bug the place while we weren't looking, and if so, how much can he hear and see right now?

As if she can hear my thoughts, Kate does a scan of our apartment, her eyes wary. While I've always appreciated her motherly nature, the way she hones in things is a little unnerving. Bri is the wild child, one who got me into a whole mess of trouble at times, but Kate has been a grounding source for her. She's the one who has kept Bri alive these last few years, and I guess I could be a little more grateful for her often overbearing tendencies.

"Listen," Bri says, breaking the tension, "I thought it was super fucking hot and if you're not interested in him, I'll take him for a spin."

Kate nearly spews her coffee and starts to cough. My cheeks heat and I let out a girlish giggle. "I'm not sharing my new toys, Bri. Get your own." I give her a wink as she cackles, giving Kate a smack on the back as she continues to cough.

"Then I better find someone if I'm going to go and work at this club, preferably one like what you snagged."

I just shake my head, because I don't know what it is I

have with those two. It's almost too early to tell. But I do know that they'll have their hands full the minute Bri is added to their payroll.

Kate and Bri start to bicker about what kind of man Bri should go after, and their differing opinions provide me with some comedic relief until the image of Matt looming in that hallway, gun pointed at me, filters into my mind. Fuck, Lena. You just had the man who finger-fucked you last night show up to your apartment, I need to think about anything but that.

As Bri and Kate slip in and out of conversation, I let my mind wander while I sip on my coffee, their conversation shifting to last night, going into great detail about their hookups. I see flashes of red neon lights, leather, people bound and gagged, and the man who pushed me over the edge takes over in my mind, pushing the image of Matt aside.

I let myself think about what these two men could do to me and how crazy it sounds to be attracted to both. Lustful attraction, Lena, and nothing more. Except for the part about revenge and protection rings out, their actions already follow suit with Devin's promises. Because, why else would he show up here other than to make good on his word?

My skin prickles with anxiety as I constantly check the clock, waiting for it to be six. Devin texted me not long after he left that I was to be in the lobby at six sharp and that someone would be there to pick me up.

So, like any reasonable woman, I start ripping through my closet. I try for the sluttiest thing I own, and when that doesn't feel up to par, I rifle through Bri's closet.

And without much looking, I find the perfect thing that will leave both of their jaws on the fucking floor.

CHAPTER ELEVEN

DEVIN

"HAVE YOU LOST YOUR *GODDAMN* MIND?"

I'm barely over the threshold of our apartment before Tony's voice cuts through me.

Oh, he is *pissed*.

I knew he would be, that's why I left while he was in the gym and wouldn't be able to try and stop me. I'm positive that he was alerted when I left the parking garage, just like I am when he tries to sneak off to his little coffee shop across town for his expensive-ass coffee beans, because he's above the shit that we import in.

But I know the minute my car was within fifty yards of the club, he was made aware of my arrival. And like the fucking creep he is, he's been sitting here, waiting to bite my head off.

"Is that any way to greet me, T?" I lean against the door-frame, flexing my muscles as I cross my arms, giving him my award-winning smile.

Of course, he doesn't buy my charm like any other person on this fucking planet. He knows the monster that lurks underneath. The one that would lure you in with this exact smile, before swallowing you whole.

"What the fuck we're you thinking, Devin?" His voice is

gruff, his eyes molten. I don't miss that he has the screen showing footage outside Lena's apartment, along with the hallway, and even in her fucking kitchen and living room. My blood heats at the fucking audacity that he had to put cameras in their apartment, even though it was a genius move and gives us the chance to check on them at any time.

I cross the threshold, kicking the door closed behind me, doing my best to be as dramatic as possible. I point to the screen as I approach his desk. "And what the fuck were *you* thinking putting cameras in her fucking apartment?" I throw my arms wide. "Do they know, or did you just take it upon your fucking self to do that?"

His silence is damning, which has my hackles raising even more.

"Besides," I bite out, "I wanted to have a look at her living situation *myself*, and it sure looks a lot like three women sharing an apartment. Nothing of a man in sight, except for me." Tony rolls his eyes and huffs out a long breath. "And the ladies *loved* my cooking by the way."

He watches me intently. "Were you actually checking on her or were you just dangling the carrot in Obsidian's face? Because I know that you fucking know they have someone parked a block away. *Watching*."

While I'd like to say that I was just there for Lena, he's right. It couldn't have been more obvious that I was showing off my presence. I hope that they took photos and are showing little Matty as we speak. I *dare* him to show up there and try to put his hands on what's mine.

I take a seat in my desk chair, propping my feet up, crossing my ankles. "They're quite the trio," I say with a smile, ignoring his question and ruffling his feathers.

"I can't fucking believe that you just showed up unannounced and she didn't go running for the hills." He pulls his vape out of his pocket, pulling his mask up to take a long drawl, the sweet smell filling the air. "She must really be fucked in the head."

My fingers curl into fists in my crossed arms, but I take in a deep breath through my nose, letting it out slowly to calm myself. "We're all fucked in the head around here," I say slyly. "Some of us a little more than others." His gray eyes narrow at me, but they don't lose their shine.

"Oh, and I think I have us a new bartender." I wave my hand nonchalantly.

Tony raises his brow at me. "Is it her friend, Brianna?" I don't let the surprise show on my face, because of course he already looked the women up. I'm sure he could recite their fucking social security numbers and who their first grade teachers were. Like I said, a fucking creep.

"Don't be such a know it all, T. It's unbecoming of you." He rolls his eyes again, his fingers flipping his vape. "Besides, it'll help us keep a closer eye on them and let us find out if she knows anything. See what company she attracts during her shifts."

He shakes his head. "Tasha is going to kill you for doing that. She's already not exactly thrilled that we brought Matt Chase's ex-fiancée to the penthouse last night."

I drop my feet to the floor and lean forward, resting my elbows on my thighs. "Did you happen to tell her where else I took her last night or are you keeping that little detail to yourself?"

He says nothing, his eyes nearly going blank before he seems to check himself, coming right back to reality. I pop the bubble of tension by retorting, "She'll be fine with it. Plus, she likes a little fresh meat every once in a while." I give him a shrug. "And it seems like Bri will be able to handle herself here. And the more of her inner circle that's here, the more she'll trust us."

He crosses his arms, his bulging muscles flexing, pulling his shirt tight across his triceps. "What's gotten into you?" His voice is nearly a growl, the sound vibrating across my skin. "You've never been after a woman like this. Never mind that it's a woman who was part of Obsidian. What is it about her that you're willing to blow everything for?"

I sit up, my spine straightening. "Because she needs our fucking help, Tony. She was with Matt-fucking-Chase for five goddamn years. I saw the way he looked at her in that hallway, like she was his private property. His bitch that ran away."

And by having her around, maybe, just maybe, she can help me uncover answers to my own shit while I help her through hers.

He watches me and I know he's reading my fucking mind. He's always been able to see past my walls, making note of every twitch of my jaw, flex of my hands, and narrowing of my eyes. His attention to detail borders on insane and drives me damn near to it sometimes. As smart as I know I am, he's smarter. Too fucking smart for me.

"Quit staring at me." My voice is sharp. "I know it sounds ridiculous, but there's a fucking connection here. She's been plaguing my fucking mind for months and I've had my eyes on her for even longer. She's not like the other women in fucking Obsidian, who will lure you in with one hand, while they hide a knife behind their back in the other. But she's not fucking innocent, either."

I feel the push under my skin, because even though I have decent intentions in my pursuit of Lena, my monster is right here, reminding me of exactly who I am. Like I'd ever be able to fucking forget. "Oh, and I let Tasha kill Vince."

His eyes blaze, heating my skin as if I was right next to a flame. "You let her *kill* Vince?" His voice is quiet. Lethal. He goes still as stone, the light in his eyes darkening.

"He was a liability to the club and was clearly working both sides." His eyes go even darker, disdain swirling through them. "And she followed me down. It was justice for her, especially since he was leading her along and lying to her. I simply offered her some closure from that piece of shit."

His hand flexes around his vape, his knuckles turning white as the plastic cracks in his hold. "And you thought that was a good idea," he growls, "to just let her be a part of your killing spree? To let her fall back on old ways?"

Pressing my teeth together, I tighten my jaw, because as badly as I want to lash out at him, he's fucking right. She's worked so hard to maintain control, but last night wasn't mindless. No, it was retribution.

"She walked out of there looking better than she has in a long time, T. And if you know what's good, then you won't say a fucking thing to her." I grit the words out, my jaw tightening with each one. "Do you hear me?"

His eyes cut up to mine, unreadable emotions swirling in them. He lifts his mask, taking another long pull, exhaling the cloud slowly out of his nose. He relaxes his muscles, and I watch the tension slowly leave his body. "So, how did she do it? Or are you going to make me guess?"

A smile tugs at the corners of my mouth at the carnage she had left in her wake. "I watched the footage and she's gotten more creative in her methods." I lean back in the chair, cupping my hands behind my head. "Never underestimate the power of a scorned woman."

He shakes his head. "He manipulated her and flew under her radar; I can only imagine the things she came up with to settle the score." If I didn't fucking know better, I'd say there was a smile hiding under that mask of his, the one he rarely removes.

"Gotta thank my brother for setting her loose in here." I chuckle, trying not to take a walk down memory lane. "What I witnessed will make even *your* soulless dick ache."

Tony huffs a laugh. "Maybe you should give her a raise, so our dicks stay on her good side and remain attached to our bodies."

Waving a hand at him, I say, "Already done. She'll see it in the morning."

Tony shifts in his chair, slowly cracking his knuckles, releasing more of his tension. "So, you already fucking watched it, huh? *Without me*?"

This time, a real laugh escapes me, and I jump to my feet. "Go ahead and pull it up, I'll make some fucking popcorn, and we'll make a date out of it."

He groans. "You fucking psychopath."

I hold up a finger to him, letting a Cheshire smile pull the corners of my mouth up, and tsk. "*Sociopath* and you fucking know it." I turn toward the kitchen. "Now, how much butter do you want, or are you worried about your figure?"

I look over my shoulder to see him simply shaking his head as if *this* is the most insane thing I've ever suggested. "Fine. A fuck ton of butter it is."

A few minutes and a whole stick of butter later, I lounge back in my chair, popcorn bowl in hand. I gesture to the TV. "Now, get that shit pulled up, because we're going to need time to prepare for our date with Lena tonight."

Tony's eyes widen as his head snaps toward me. "What did you just fucking say?"

I throw a few kernels in my mouth as I grab the remote, turning up the sound of Vinny's screams to drown out the sound of Tony unleashing on me. I put my finger to my lips and shush him. "Quiet down, you're going to miss the best parts." I throw another kernel into my mouth. "Or well, *Vinny's* best parts. Because, if you blink, you'll miss them."

Tony glares at me, not fazed by me at all. However, he knows better than to try and steer me away from my already made plans. He will just have to pout from behind his mask, because there's no way he's going to want to miss out on what I have in store for us tonight.

CHAPTER TWELVE

Lena

THE ELEVATOR SLIDES OPEN, revealing the crisp, white lobby, where I'm met with a beast of a man holding a notecard with my name on it like I'm being picked up at the airport. He's dressed in a black suit, has to be at least 6' 3", and looks like he could crush my skull between his finger and thumb. I slow my pace. "Um, hi." I point to the sign in his hands. "*I'm* Lena."

"I know, miss." His voice is deep with a slight hint of a Russian accent. "But the boss required me to hold this up." He holds the card up and waggles it toward the security camera, as if insinuating that we're being watched. I hold my gaze to the camera, my brows furrowing. I should be upset that I'm being watched, but for some reason, I can't find it in me. It's almost comforting to know that they have their eyes on me. "Come now, Ms. Taylor. I'm to escort you to the club tonight."

He holds the door open for me, and that's when I notice the other man standing at the open car door. He's dressed in a similar suit, slightly shorter than the other man, but still dangerously handsome. What is in the water at this fucking club for all the men to look this good?

My heels click on the sidewalk as I approach the open car door. The man takes my hand, helping me into the backseat. "Thank you," I murmur, trying to give him my best smile.

"My pleasure, Ms. Taylor. You look lovely tonight," the second escort says in his very thick Russian accent. "Mr. Green will be very pleased."

I feel myself blush at what seems like a genuine compliment as he closes the door. The windows of the car are blacked out, the seats are soft black leather, and there's a window between the front and back seats. Alternative rock floats through the speakers as we pull away from the curb. There's no way that they could have known it was my preferred music. This must be the product of Devin and his ability to find out information about anyone.

A smile tugs at the corners of my mouth. Even if it should be a huge red flag that he not only showed up at the apartment unannounced this morning to make us breakfast, but that he also managed to find my favorite playlist. Somehow, I feel like there could be even redder flags and I'm going to choose to ignore this one. I let myself relax back and watch out the window as we make our way through the city.

The escort in the passenger seat turns around, handing me a sleek black box. "This is for you, miss. A gift from Mr. Green."

My cheeks heat as I open the box and find a metal mask that's cut to look like lace. It's beautiful. Small crystals glimmer around the edges. It's light in my hand and seems as if it would be nearly weightless on my face. I sit it gently back into the box and place it on the seat next to me, so it's ready for me to put on when we get closer to the club.

The two men are watching me in the rearview mirror, as if they're waiting for my approval. "It's perfect, thank you," I say with a smile. They both nod and then avert their eyes back to the road, more than likely already informing Devin of my reaction.

The silence in the vehicle is comfortable, and even though I have no idea who these two men are, it's as if we have been doing this together for years. I've had drivers and escorts before, mainly when I wanted to leave the apartment for anything, but they always made me feel like a burden. However, these two casually watch me through the rearview mirror, not to spy on me, but as if they're genuinely checking on me.

We approach the club and drive right past the front entrance, going around the corner. I feel a slight sense of panic as we drive down the side street. "Um, excuse me, but where are we going?" I try to dampen my rising panic, the familiar knot in my chest tightening.

"We were instructed by Mr. Green to bring you through the private entrance, miss," the driver says casually.

We turn again onto another street that runs parallel to the back of the massive building, where we're greeted by a large metal garage door. It's subtle and almost blends into the building as we slow to a stop in front of it. The door slides open, and we drive into the underground garage.

We slowly descend, expensive vehicles parked in spots on every level. The bright white walls contrast against the dark gray floors, with LED lights that make the garage look like a showroom. I don't know shit about cars, but I know that every single one of these are high end. Maybe even a few are one of a kind.

We start to slow and approach a set of black elevator doors. Just as we stop, they slide open, revealing Devin, and my mouth nearly starts to water.

He looks hot as hell in his golden mask, cream button-up shirt with the top buttons undone to show off his collarbones and chiseled chest, and his tailored, black dress pants with his shiny shoes. His sleeves are rolled up, showing off his corded forearms as he slides his hand into his pocket. There's not a doubt in my mind that women will be clawing at each other to get to him tonight.

I look down at my black satin midi dress with the slit nearly to the top of my thigh. It has a slight sweetheart top, but the real show is the open back. Bri screamed when I stepped out, going on about how it's about time I got back into my party girl phase. She just kept fluffing my hair and twirling me, as if she was showing me off to the empty room.

Kate helped me with my makeup, going for a darker lip than I'm used to and giving me a smokey eye. Bri nearly threw her strappy heels at me, telling me that they were the only shoes that would work with a dress like this. She slapped my ass on the way out the door and was continuously catcalling me, while Kate gave me a hug and a weary smile. She didn't say much about him the rest of the day, but I know that she doesn't trust Devin and will probably worry herself sick while I'm out with him tonight.

I grab my mask off the seat and adorn it to my face, careful not to mess up the face of makeup that Kate worked so hard on. The cool metal is molded to my face, fitting me like a glove.

Both men exit the car, opening the door wide. Devin stands right outside of it, his teeth flashing with a devious smile as he holds a hand out for me. His fingers curl around mine, warm against my skin as he guides me out of the SUV. He holds me at arm's length, his bright, blue eyes sweeping over me. Heat curls in my abdomen as his eyes meet mine, licking his lips like a wolf hungry with desire.

"Stunning," he purrs.

My cheeks warm, heating the metal of my mask. I let my eyes sweep over him, imaging what every muscle looks like underneath his clothes as the feeling of phantom fingers brush against my center. "You don't look half bad yourself."

His lips curl into a devilish grin and he brings my hand to his lips, his warm breath ghosting over my skin before he gently kisses my knuckles. The simple touch has heat flooding my core. He holds my gaze, lips caressing my skin as he continues to brush them back and forth. This bastard knows exactly what he's doing, and who I am to stop him?

Some sick part of me wants him to sink his teeth into my skin and devour me piece by piece as desire burns in his eyes. He lowers our hands but doesn't let my hand go, linking his fingers through mine. He guides us into the elevator as I watch the two men get back into the car and slowly start backing away, leaving me wholly alone with Devin.

The smell of his cologne is so intoxicating in the small space, with his body only inches from mine, that I would let myself drown in it. My blood heats as anticipation floods my veins. I keep my face straight ahead but let my eyes drift side-long, only to see him looking right at me. The same wolfish grin on his face, the same hunger in his eyes. If I'm not care-ful, he might actually take a bite and mark me.

Claim me.

"I can't wait to see your face when I show you what I have planned for us." His warm breath curls around the shell of my ear, nearly melting me. His fingers tighten in mine. "I also can't wait to hear those sweet moans again. Utter music to my ears, love."

I hitch a breath and turn to look at him. His eyes have darkened from behind his mask, and he rounds on me, his free hand on the wall next to my head. His hard body cages me as he presses against me. My heart pounds against my ribs as he loosens his grip on my hand, trailing his fingers up my arm. Goosebumps rise in their wake, sending a shiver up my spine as heat pools between my legs.

He lowers his head, his lips next to my ear. "So, fucking beautiful," he whispers. "The things I want to do to you for wearing a fucking dress like this tonight." His fingers follow over my shoulders, hooking under the strap of my dress. "How easily I could tear this off of you." His lips brush across the sensitive spot under my ear like a phantom kiss. "And do all of the things I wanted to do last night before we were *interrupted*."

My pussy clenches, and I lean back against the wall, trying to hold myself together as he continues to run his fingers across my skin. He traces the line of my collarbone up my neck, my skin burning from his touch with delicious heat. His fingers wrap around my neck as I lean into his hand, and he presses his palm against my throat.

I clench my thighs together as his other hand drops from the wall, gliding down to my breasts. His fingers brush over my already sensitive nipple, circling his thumb around the peak. He watches as my body reacts to his touch, his hand holding me against the wall. He continues to slide his fingers down, brushing against the seam of the slit running up my thigh, sliding them across my exposed skin. His eyes flick down, a growl vibrating through his chest. His fingers slip further under, caressing the edge of my panties. "Are you wet for me, love?" His question causes even more heat to flood, desire swirling through me.

I nod as a quiet moan slips past my lips as his fingers trail down the edge of my panties to my core. His hand cups my pussy, and he groans just as I let out a gasp. "So *fucking* wet." His hand tightens around my neck, forcing me to take in shallow breaths as he slides his fingers past my panty line. I gasp and buck my hips as need floods through me. "I can't wait to taste you, Lena, and feast on you like the starved man I am."

I whimper as his hand slips from my panties, and his other falls from my throat as he pulls away, leaving me with an aching pussy as I try to catch my breath. He raises his fingers to his nose, inhaling deeply as he lets out a satisfied groan. "You smell fucking delicious."

I gape at him. Who the hell is this man, and how does he already have such a fucking hold on me?

He gives me a sly grin as he turns and presses the button on the elevator. My eyes widen at the realization that we hadn't been moving this entire time, but we were just sitting ducks in the elevator when the two escorts could have opened the doors at any time. Could have walked right in and seen what we were doing.

He's left me speechless as near embarrassment warms my face even hotter than before. Stepping back against the wall, he casually laces his fingers with mine as if he didn't just have me pressed against the wall of the elevator, telling me how he wanted to taste and tease me.

Fuck, I shouldn't be this turned on but instead run away from the man whose sharp teeth glint in the light, ready to sink into my skin and tear me apart bite by bite.

The elevator rushes up, and we'll be at the top floor in a matter of moments. The tension in here is so thick that it's nearly suffocating me until the doors slide open, all of it pouring out. I take a deep breath, filling my lungs and trying to calm my nerves as Devin leads us off into the small hallway, taking a few strides to the door and flinging it open. He holds it for me as I pass through the threshold into their apartment. I feel a slight tug in my chest as if I'm being led right back into somewhere I belong. Somewhere safe.

But that's insane, right? It must just be my anxiety or early signs of Stockholm syndrome because I did just let a beast lure me back into their castle, where I'm sure some sort of magic is at play.

"Welcome back, love," he croons, letting the door fall closed behind us, heading straight for the bar cart. "Drink?" he asks casually.

"Um, yes, please."

He watches me with a heated glance over his shoulder, his mask glinting in the light as he turns away. His broad shoulders move and flex, pulling his shirt tight across his back as he makes the drink. The sound of ice clinking against the glass fills the silence.

I look around the apartment with clear eyes this time, noting the simplistic elegance throughout. It screams, *I came from money, but I'm trying not to show it.* My eyes continue across the room until they land on Tony, his face hidden behind his screens, intentionally not looking in my direction or acknowledging us. It's on the tip of my tongue to say something to him, but the words dissipate.

His intent doesn't seem malicious, but it is harsh as he acts like he doesn't like me being in their space. He helped save me from Matt, and I'm sure that wasn't what he thought he was signing up for when he entered that hallway last night. And it probably doesn't help that he got hurt in the process. So, if we're keeping score, that's at least two strikes against me.

I shake off the feeling of rejection that balls up in my chest and turn my attention from him to the TV that shows multiple camera views throughout the club, and its three floors that are open to the public. It's packed again tonight, with people crammed in tight on the dance floor and nearly every booth filled. I watch the masked faces as if I would be able to pick anyone out from here. After last night, I know that I'm being watched and that anyone down there could be the one to take me and force me back to him.

"Here you go, love," Devin says, making me jump as he holds out his hand and offers me my drink. "One whiskey sour, on the house." He gives me a wink as he turns, returning to the cart and pouring two fingers of whiskey into a tumbler.

I take a sip and note that it's light on the whiskey and heavy on the sour. Any thought I had about him trying to get me drunk and take advantage of me tonight dissipates as I take another sip of the nearly virgin drink. A smile tugs at my lips because if only he knew the things that I would let him do to me—drunk or not.

Crossing to the wall of windows, I take in the city line in

front of me. This is the tallest building in this section of town, the skyscrapers towering over the dividing river, causing the setting sun to disappear behind them long before it's truly nightfall. They cloak this district in darkness, bringing out the ones who hide in the shadows, making their deals in either pleasure or pain, life or death.

I feel the heat of a gaze along my exposed back just as Devin steps next to me, a drink now in his hand. He takes a sip, looking out at the skyline. "I grew up on the other side of the river." His voice is low as if he's telling me a dark secret. "And I'm sure you'll be surprised to hear that it's not all it's cracked up to be."

I look up at him, but his eyes continue to stare out the window, lost in thought. "And what brought you over here?" I ask, keeping my voice low, too, like two lovers whispering into the night, their heads sharing the same pillow as they get lost in one another.

There's a long pause, his jaw ticking before he takes another sip. "Tragedy," he says as simply as someone would disclose their favorite color. He turns, fully facing me. His free hand comes up to cup my chin, his thumb caressing my bottom lip. "It's what brought all of us here."

The electricity of his touch prickles along my skin, heat pooling between my legs as he lets his hand glide down to my neck, his thumb moving over my pulse point. The corner of his mouth tics as if he's fighting off a smile when my pulse quickens under his touch. His eyes flash in Tony's direction, his expression unreadable, before he looks back at me. I let my tongue slowly move over my lips and he watches it like a cat would watch a mouse, ready to pounce.

The door clicks and dramatically swings open, making me jump in surprise, my drink almost sloshing over the edge. A woman walks in wearing a sleeveless, sheer, black maxi dress with black heels. You can see her black lace bra and thong through the material of her dress. Her long, Black hair cascades down her back from her high ponytail, and her hips sway as she walks in her black stilettos. Her presence takes over the room, and even Tony looks up from his computer, giving her a nod in welcome.

She saunters up and drops a large envelope onto his desk that lands with a thud. Tony's brow furrows as he looks down at it like it's a bomb waiting to go off. She's shaped like a goddess, her curves almost have me drooling, and I can tell that she knows how to command a room, sending people to their knees.

She throws her hand on her hip and turns so she can look between us and Tony. Her eyes catch on me, and they widen as if she's just discovered buried treasure. She opens her mouth to speak, but before she can say anything, Devin beats her to it. "Tash," he says, his voice low, the deep timbre rumbling through the room as he places his hand on my lower back, "say hello to our new friend, Lena Taylor." She watches me carefully, inspecting every inch as she crosses the room to us. Her blood-red lips turn up into what appears to be a genuine smile, one that meets her eyes.

"Hello, Lena." Her voice is soft and husky. I can only imagine what her dirty, seductive words sound like coming from that sultry voice. She takes my hand and lightly kisses my knuckles, butterflies fluttering in my stomach as she drags her lips on my skin. "I'm Natasha, but my friends and lovers call me Tasha."

I stare at her in a trance but quickly snap out of it and realize that my jaw is nearly hanging onto the floor. What the hell is wrong with me? I snap my mouth shut and swallow the lump that's formed in my throat. "It's a pleasure to meet you, Tasha." The words come out rough, like my throat is coated in sandpaper.

She cuts a look at Devin while still holding my hand. "You didn't tell me *exactly* how stunning she is, you selfish prick."

He chuckles. "I wanted it to be a surprise." His dazzling

smile is almost as bright as hers. "But you can't have her. So you'll have to admire her from afar."

She looks back at me, eyebrow raised. "If you ever get tired of these two cocks, I'll show you a *real* good time." She winks, and I giggle through my closed-lipped smile. Tony huffs from behind his mask, rolling his eyes at Tasha as if he would ever be interested in fucking me. With her free hand, she flips him the bird.

"Tash, you *wound* me," Devin says as he clutches his chest, pretending as though he's going to fall to his knees.

She lets my hand drop, turning her full attention back to Tony, switching from seductress to all business. She perches on his desk, forcing herself into his space. Oddly enough, he doesn't seem to mind and simply moves his things over, allowing her more room. She pushes the envelope across the desk, directly in front of him. "This is from Vince's locker," she says, her voice lowering. "It's obviously his burner since I located his other one in his pants' pocket after his inter-rogation."

Vince. My eyes trail to the spot where he had the shit beat out of him, my mind flashing to the image of his swollen face and dripping blood. The floor shines in the low light, freshly mopped and waxed as if nothing happened the night before.

"What did you find on it?" Devin asks as Tony opens the envelope and dumps the phone onto his desk. He inspects it before plugging it into his computer and doing who knows what with it.

She shrugs. "Tons of messages to three different numbers with things my girls have told me about some of the clientele, along with calls to and from those same numbers." She looks at Tony, whose full attention is on her, hanging on to every word she says, even as he quickly types on his keyboard.

"Which girls?" Devin's voice has an edge to it. I watch Tasha's face become flushed, and she grips the edge of the desk.

"*Don't* you even try to fucking blame them," she spits the words at him.

Tony shifts in his chair, moving his eyes back to his screen, trying to remove himself from the crossfire. Devin crosses his arms, his knuckles going white as he clutches his glass. "I'm not blaming anyone *yet*," he says with lethal calm.

Her eyes are aflame; she reaches down her dress, her finger and thumb sliding between her cleavage. She pulls out a thumb drive, dramatically extends her arm, and drops the plastic clattering against the wood top desk. "You don't get to blame them because *he* fucking bugged their private rooms."

Devin's eyes stare at the USB for a beat, and then he looks at her, his face staying neutral even as his eyes burn. "For how long?"

"There's footage from over six months ago on here." Her lips curl in disgust.

Devin looks to Tony, whose eyes are murderous with rage, as he snatches the thumb drive and shoves it into the large tower of his computer. He starts to type furiously, his large fingers nearly punching every key as their collective rage fills the room.

Devin rolls his shoulders back, cracking his neck and attempting to relax his stance. His effort to come across as unfazed is noble, but the tightening of his jaw gives it all away. The muscles in his crossed arms remain tense as if he's fighting the urge to throw his fist through the wall. "Tony will run the footage and see if it was set to run as a live feed, and if it was, where it was being sent to."

Tasha points a perfectly manicured nail at him. "None of my girls are responsible for this," she growls out. "And I don't want you saying anything to them about it until I can talk to them one-on-one, see if they know anything."

Devin looks down at her, still pointing his finger, his eyes darkening even more. "I want them all questioned and official statements taken." He looks in Tony's direction. "We need to run full diagnostics on their phones to make sure that they aren't communicating with anyone outside of the club and relaying information." He cuts a look back to Tasha. "Everyone is a fucking suspect until proven innocent."

Tasha stands up from the desk, huffing a breath out of her nose like a bull ready to charge, her eyes narrowing on Devin. "Fine, but don't rush me. I don't want any of them getting upset when more information is needed." She cuts a glance at the TV. "Because there's a lot of sharks in the water tonight, circling and waiting to drag their prey under."

Devin's eyes flash to me as if he just remembered that I was standing in the middle of all this, potentially collecting inside information. I catch Tony watching me from the edge of his hood as if I could be the enemy. If I could only get him to understand that I want Matt and all the assholes he's associated with to be taken down just as much as they do.

He looks back to Tasha, whose eyes are on me, gauging my reaction. "Find out what you can and report back as soon as possible. If anyone proves difficult, you need to take them to the basement, and we'll deal with them there." Her eyes and face pale slightly as he continues. "We'll make sure that no other moles are crawling around, and if there are, we'll smoke them right out of the hole they're hiding in."

The tension in the room is thick, and my skin prickles as all eyes fall on me. Tasha closes the distance between us, raising my chin with her blood-red nail, her touch sending heat to my core. Her voice is low as she says, "Don't trust anyone here but the three of us if you value your life." I suck in a breath as she continues. "You are a key player in this fucked up game, whether you want to be or not. Every move you make across the board is being watched." She drops her finger and takes a slow step back, giving me a once-over. "But not just any piece." She looks at Devin and then Tony, who are both watching us. "You're the fucking *Queen* that everyone wants to take." Her eyes soften slightly as she takes in my worried expression.

She turns to leave, not saying another word as she yanks open the door. She gives me one last glance over her shoulder as she saunters out, the door slamming behind her. Both men's gazes nearly burn into my skin, the tension thick from the storm that's brewing around us. They look at me as if they're wolves, and I'm the lamb they can either protect or slaughter, shredding me apart with their razor-sharp teeth.

But I don't want to be a lamb anymore. I don't want to be the image of innocence and stand by as others fight for me. Protect me. No, I want to be a wolf. Sharp, jagged teeth and all.

CHAPTER THIRTEEN

Lena

THE TENSION SETTLES in the room, its presence still suffocating as the minutes tick by. I settle onto the sofa, sipping on my now warm drink, and watch them. Both men are at their desks, seemingly hard at work investigating the bouncer and whatever connections he might have to Obsidian.

Devin steals glances my way now and then, his eyes filled with a mix of curiosity and guilt. He's abandoned the mask that covered his still slightly bruised face. His phone keeps buzzing on the desk with notifications, but he hardly acknowledges it. I can only imagine how Vince betraying them and possibly being a mole has turned the whole club on its head.

Why would someone who's been working here for so long turn their back on it? What was he offered in exchange for information on the club's inner workings and possibly my whereabouts? From the outside looking in, the society that Matt is a part of just looks like a bunch of elite businessmen who come together to rub elbows and show off their partners. It wasn't lost on me that it was always a power play between everyone, and somehow, Matt had busied his way to the top.

I think back through the years, and I could kick my own ass for not seeing the signs that something was amiss. I furrow my brows because I *did* see the signs, and some of his stories didn't add up, but I just chose to ignore them for the sake of my relationship. I thought he was the love of my life and that I wanted to be with him forever. I turned a blind eye to the blood on his knuckles when he would get home late and every other suspicion.

I am so fucking stupid.

The way the other partners looked at me when he brought me around was a mix of pity and disgust. They saw me for the pawn that I was in his game of power and either realized that I didn't even know what part I was in his grand scheme of things or that I was complacent in the fact that he was constantly fucking other women and murdering people when I wasn't there. He really is an evil motherfucker.

I rub at the knot in my chest, trying to ease the tension that threatens to steal my breath entirely. While I wouldn't say I had rose-colored glasses on all the time, it seems like I just chose to close my eyes—and maybe I was just fully complacent. We lived in a beautiful penthouse apartment; he bought me anything I wanted and provided me with an escort to go anywhere I wanted.

He said he loved me and that I was his.

His to control.

I run my thumb over my empty ring finger, the roaring in my ears nearly deafening as memories come flooding back because when things were good, they were really good. He showered me with gifts and took me on vacation to private islands, where we would stay in large beachside villas and were waited on hand and foot by a full staff. He showed me the world while simultaneously showing me off. He would kiss me gently and fuck me hard as if I was the center of *his* world.

I squeeze my eyes shut as the darkness begins to cloud my mind, shifting my memories and reminding me why I ran. Because when it was bad, it was torturous. My cheeks heat as I think about the feeling of his hands on me and the names he would spit at me like venom, diminishing me to a heap of tears on the floor. Kicking me even harder when I was down.

Early on, he would flip the switch—pull me into his arms and beg for my forgiveness—but as the years went on, he would usually leave altogether after a fight. Instead of gathering me in his arms, he would leave expensive gifts or send an expensive dinner as an apology. The gifts would be shoved into the closet, and the food would taste like ash on my tongue as I turned into a shell of myself. He would take me to galas, walking in with me on his arm as the cameras flashed in our direction, capturing his award-winning smile as everyone praised him for being a giving man, all while slowly taking away pieces of me.

I don't even feel the hot tears sliding down my face until a thumb brushes one away. My eyes snap open, meeting Devin's bright blue eyes from where he sits on the coffee table. He watches me curiously. "Where did you go just now, love?" There's a concern in his voice as he catches another tear, this time putting the drop to his lips, as if he's trying to taste my sorrow.

I delicately wipe my face, doing my best not to mess up my makeup any more than I likely have. Bri would kill me if she knew that I was crying about Matt, let alone in front of two very attractive men, one of whom seems extremely interested in me. I sniff. "Just lost in my own head. I'm fine. I promise."

He definitely doesn't buy my lie, seeing right through it. His eyes cut to his desk as it buzzes across the wood before he looks back at me, his eyes full of questions. He stands, huffing, as he crosses back to his desk and snatches up the phone. "This better be good," he bites out to the unsuspecting person on the other end.

He stiffens before turning to the TV, getting close to one of the boxes on the screen. He groans quietly as he scrubs his hand over his face.

"Tell her that he didn't show up for his shift, and we have

no idea where he is." He whips his head to Tony, and I see the flush crawling up his neck. He runs his hand through his hair, gripping it at the roots and tugging it. He lets loose a breath. "Just get her the fuck out of here. Charm her however you need to, and fucking let Chuck know what happened last night because I don't need some fucking rookie snooping around." He hangs up the phone, his eyes flicking to me and then right back to Tony, who's watching him carefully.

Devin's head drops back. "Vince's mother came here looking for him. I guess she thinks she has been stood up for their weekly dinner. We need to make sure that nothing about his disappearance leads back to us and make it look like he skipped town."

Tony holds his gaze but nods before his fingers start flying on the keyboard, doing whatever it is that he does. He leans forward like someone has come out of the screen and is trying to pull him into another world. The light from the screens illuminates his face, making his gray eyes glow. I notice a small scar that cuts through his eyebrow, making him look even more ruggedly handsome. His bright, gray eyes shift to me, and I nearly topple back from the intensity of his gaze, like a tidal wave crashing over me, and I can't decide if I want to let it take me under or not.

After a long, drowning moment, he averts his gaze. My heart is nearly thundering out of my chest and I really can't figure out how his one look has me nearly falling over. I can't be that fucking desperate, can I?

Devin's fingers fly over his phone as he makes his way back to his desk, his jaw tense. He drops the phone onto the desk, lowering himself into his chair. Even when he's stressed, he seems to have this unbothered casualness to him. It's honestly a little unnerving as he props his chin onto his knuckles, lost in thought.

I can't stand the silence anymore and want to see how

much they are willing to tell me. "So, who exactly was Vince? He seemed like something more than just a bouncer."

Devin scoffs, his eyes still distant. "A fucking nuisance who seems to bother me even from Hell."

Hell? "Is he dead?" I ask as my mouth goes dry. "Did you *kill* him?" I try to keep my voice steady, but my voice cracks as the words almost choke me.

The room goes still as they look between each other and me, speaking silently. They're either trying to decide if they're going to tell me the truth or lock me up in this basement that Devin has mentioned multiple times. The muscle in Devin's jaw ticks, his fingers curling around the arm of the chair.

"Not this time," he answers through clenched teeth. "Someone more deserving of the opportunity did, though. He's nothing more than ash in the wind now."

The words are tight, and as much as I want to know who, I swallow down the rest of the words over the lump in my throat, leaving well enough alone. Clearly, this whole situation has them rattled.

Devin suddenly stands, stalking toward me. My body prickles as he towers over me, reaching down and hooking my chin with his finger. He tilts my head back, forcing me to look up at him. He runs his thumb over my bottom lip, and as if on instinct, my tongue darts out, running across the pad of his finger. His eyes light up even more as he gently pushes his thumb past my lips, hooking it over my teeth. Heat pulses through my body as he slowly removes his finger from my mouth. He brushes his knuckles across my face before tucking my hair behind my ear.

I bite my bottom lip, and a feral grin pulls at his mouth. His eyes burn brighter, causing my skin to feel like it's on fire. I release my lip from my teeth as he bends over, resting his hands against the back of the couch, caging me in. He lowers his face to mine, his mouth only a breath away from mine. He drags his tongue over his bottom lip, and I swallow down a whimper that tries to expose how turned on I am.

I mimic the movement, and his eyes drop to my lips. My fingers touch one of the buttons on his shirt, and I feel a pull to him like the moon to the Earth as stars twinkle in his eyes. I want nothing but to stay in his orbit, curl my fingers into his shirt, and pull him to me like gravity. I want our mouths to crash together like the waves in the tide, drowning one another in tongue and teeth.

His breathing deepens as if he's fighting the same urges I am. I can hear the leather of the sofa groan under his grip as if he'll shred it to pieces. Heat curls in my stomach as his eyes linger farther down my body. I lean forward slightly, letting my lips part, and invite him in. He pulls in a breath, as if he's about to dive deep into the waves of our desire, but the sound of a throat clearing halts him.

He growls quietly as he straightens, turning his attention to Tony. My hands tremble, the remnants of the ice in my drink clinking against the glass. I curl both hands around the tumbler, pressing my fingers into the cool glass and doing my best to calm my racing heart.

"What?" Devin snaps at Tony, running his fingers through the hair that fell over his forehead, moving it out of his face. Tony doesn't bother looking at him as he changes the camera view on the screen, blowing up one of the feeds to take up the whole screen. The security feed silently shows three men standing idly next to one of the stages, looking like they're up to no good. They're all dressed in dark jeans, fitted black tees, and basic, black masks.

A few women approach them off the dance floor, but they don't even bother to acknowledge them, sending the now-rejected women slinking back into the crowd. Their heads don't move much, but it's clear that they're scanning the crowd, on the hunt for someone. For me.

I don't recognize them as anyone Matt associates with, but

there are clearly a lot of people working under him and anyone else in Obsidian. Money talks, and it brings out the darkest of people to do the elite's dirty work.

"Send out an alert to keep a close eye on them." Devin's voice is sharp, the command in his tone. Like a sergeant preparing for war, he walks closer to the screen, examining the men closer as Tony zooms in on them.

He pulls his phone out, pressing it a few times before lifting it to his ear. "Tash," he bites out before filling her in. "Send one of the girls their direction and see if we can lure at least one of them off the floor and into a room. They're here for something more than a good time," he adds, his tone harsh. His back is tense as he ends the call, clutching his phone. The veins in his forearms bulge as his other hand curls into a fist.

He looks at Tony who shakes his head disapprovingly. Devin lets out a huff of a breath and drops his head back, looking up at the ceiling. "She's gonna have my fucking balls for that tone, isn't she?"

Tony makes an amused sound, muffled from beneath his mask, and returns to his work.

"Do you know who they are?" I ask, unease replacing the desire in my chest.

Devin turns, his eyes narrowing. "You don't recognize them?"

I look at them again, but nothing rings a bell. "No, why would I?"

He watches me for a moment, as if he's trying to decide if I'm actually telling the truth or not, which makes me uneasy. Just a few moments ago, this man was caging me in, putting his thumb in my mouth, and looking like he was going to devour me whole. Now, he's looking at me as if he wants to lock me up and interrogate me in his mysterious basement.

"Because they've been seen here before with Matt. He seems to keep the same crew around him when he's here."

"Minus the women he fucks," I cut in, anger slicing through me.

His body relaxes slightly at my remark, and the crease between his brows smoothes. "It seems as though that they would be looking for you, love." His words are a little softer this time, but his tone still has an edge to it.

"Why would they be looking for me? How would they know that I was here?"

"It's not like we were discreet when we sent our drivers to pick you up," he says matter-of-factly. "You willingly went to enemy territory. He believes you belong to him," his voice drops lower, "and thinks he can steal you back."

"I don't belong to him. And he can't *steal* me back if I wasn't stolen *from* him in the first place." I lurch forward and slam my glass down on the coffee table, the shaking in my hands working its way over my body as the rage pulses through my veins.

Devin's lips curve up into a devilish smirk as he saunters back to me, his own body pulsing. Leaning down once again to cage me in, his breath is warm against the shell of my ear. "You never belonged to him, love." My pulse is racing, heat flowing through me in a mix of rage and desire as his lips brush against my ear, causing the heat to flood between my legs. His voice is low, a rumble in his chest as he says, "But you are *ours* now."

I grip the edge of the couch as he pulls back, and his lips are once again a breath away. My skin turns hot, and my fingers dig deeper into the couch to ground myself. I should scream at him, telling him I'm not a pet someone owns. I should tell him to fuck off and leave, go back to my apartment, uncork a bottle of wine, and drown myself in trashy reality TV.

But I don't do any of that because he's not the cause of all of this. And even as the rage flows through my veins, it's undoubtedly due to Matt and the way he had me trapped in a gilded cage for so long. Calm rushes over me as he lets out a warm breath, the smell of whiskey and mint flooding my nose. I close my eyes and breathe in his scent. His knuckles brush against the column of my neck before his hand curls around my throat. I lick my lips and press my thighs together. The electricity is buzzing between us, causing my pussy to throb.

It's agonizing to have this man so close to me against my better judgment. My lizard brain screeches at me to grab him and shove my own tongue down his throat. I want to feel his strong hands grip me, feel the sharpness of his teeth rake across my skin. I let out a whimper as the electricity pulses through my clit, needing him to touch me and let me have my release.

His eyes darken as if he's reading my thoughts, and he gently squeezes my throat. His lips are so close that one small move forward would finally bring them together, relieving the tension between us. But once again, a throat clearing breaks our trance, pulling him away from me.

I'm nearly panting like a bitch in heat as Devin stands up slowly, his eyes holding mine. My gaze flicks down to where I'm now eye level with the bulge pressing against the zipper of his pants. My mouth waters as I think about the feeling of it beneath me last night as I writhed against it while he finger-fucked me.

I swear I hear him groan under his breath as he drags himself away from me, a promise in his eyes for more to come. We both put our attention back on the screen, watching as a woman dressed in lingerie and a black lace mask approaches the trio of men.

They do their best to wave her off, but she's persistent. She keeps casting her line until, finally, one of them takes the bait. She links her fingers through his and leads him to a private booth.

They slide in and she immediately straddles him, and it

dawns on me that this is the exact same booth that Matt would bring us to. She runs her hands through his hair, down to his shoulders, and across his pecks. If I didn't know she was sent to seduce him for an interrogation, I would think she was really into him. She's good.

He grabs her waist as she runs her hands farther down to his abs. He whispers something into her ear, and she leans back, nodding her head. She slowly slides off his lap, and they scoot out of the booth.

Her fingers once again laced with his, she leads him around the booths and up the stairs, disappearing behind one of the black, lacquer doors that must lead to private rooms.

Tony flips the camera view to show her walking down the hallway, giggling at something he said before she pulls him into one of the rooms.

I anticipate the camera switching over, but it stays in the same view. My heart races as I wait to see her reemerge, but we're left waiting for what feels like fucking forever.

"What's *happening* in there?" I ask, anxiety rippling through me.

Tony lets out a snort, drawing my attention to them. A devilish grin spreads over Devin's face. "She's playing with her food. A fly caught in our web."

My eyes bounce back and forth between the screen and Devin as I realize this man won't leave tonight alive. The tension in the room grows as we wait for what I assume is a signal from her. Ten minutes pass, then twenty. I worry the corner of my lip as the seconds tick by. After what feels like ages, Devin's phone finally buzzes, popping the bubble of unbearable silence.

"He's out." That devilish grin slaps itself back on Devin's face, easing the tension between his brows.

My anxiety can't take the waiting game anymore as I blurt, "What do we do now?"

His grin widens as he crosses the room to me, holding out a hand. "It's time to remind them *whose* house they're in and why they shouldn't fuck with what's mine."

Lena

THE CLUB IS EVEN MORE PACKED than I realized as Devin and I pass through the center of the dance floor, his fingers interlaced with mine, keeping me close to his back. The crowd parts for him as if he's royalty while he flashes a smile to everyone, putting on a show with his bright gold mask and blue eyes. Men and women both watch him, their curious stares raking over me. My skin heats at the thought of people joining us in the Underground, but I try to push those thoughts away. That seems like too much, and even just thinking about going back down there might be, too.

We finally reach the other side of a set of stairs leading to the next level, where Devin escorts me up like a gentleman, his hand never leaving mine. I can feel the intense gazes of the people in the booths around us as we make our way to the back corner, sliding into a giant U-shaped booth. The red neon lights around it give it a seductive glow but seem to create more shadows to hide us from plain sight.

The music back here is quieter but still loud enough that it will mask our conversation. Even though I can't see anyone, and my mask partially conceals my identity, I still feel like I'm being watched. "Are you sure this is safe?" I ask as a waitress dressed in a fitted corset and a micro skirt approaches us.

She stands at the edge of the booth, keeping her eyes slightly down as Devin answers me. "Other than being in the penthouse, being out in the open like this with me is the safest you'll be. There are eyes and ears everywhere." He gestures for the waitress to approach us as he orders himself a whiskey neat and a glass of white wine for me.

She hurries off, clearly making our order a priority. "You know that's what I'm worried about," I say, thinking about everyone in this club who will continue to watch our every move tonight.

Devin relaxes back and places his hand on my exposed thigh, his thumb tracing circles across my skin, watching people move about. "About the being seen with me or being out in the open?" My cheeks redden as I open my mouth, but he just laughs, the sound like black velvet.

His phone buzzes on the table, but he keeps his eyes on one booth in particular, watching a man who has himself at the perfect angle to look right at us while still being discreet. Devin cocks his head toward me, eyes still on the stranger. "I have a feeling that every member of Obsidian that's here tonight is well aware of who you're with, and I can bet that Matty knows now, too."

I try to swallow around the lump that's formed in my throat, and I feel my body start to tremble as the pressure of the eyes in the room begins to crush me under their weight. I know that I'm technically safe while I'm here, but I'm fucking terrified to make a move without the thought of someone trying to kidnap me. "Why didn't Tony come down with us?" I ask, trying to change the subject from the fact that I'm a sitting duck.

Devin inches his hand up my leg, letting his fingers spread to my inner thigh, causing aching heat to build at my core. "He has a few things to take care of and may join us later. But he's not one for the club scene and tends to make people nervous with his presence." He clocks another man who repositions himself in another booth, eyes now directed toward us. "And right now, love, we want to look like the prey, not the predators."

He watches the room and nonchalantly traces his fingers across my inner thigh, his touch sending heat throughout my body. I shouldn't be this affected by his touch, but it's all I can manage not to straddle his lap right now and put on a free show for everyone here. The pull between us is undeniable. "Is it necessary for you to touch me like this?" I ask, nearly breathless, as my pulse races.

He smirks. "Would you rather me touch you like this?" His hand slides under the slit of my dress, right between my legs, and he cups my pussy. I gasp as his lips curl into a lupine smile. "Oh, Lena, you're already so fucking wet." He leans over, brushing his nose against my jaw, and nips at my ear. Heat floods through me, and I let out a yelp. "And we've only just begun."

"Devin, please," I gasp out as his finger traces along my panty line, making my thighs tremble.

"Beg for me one more time, love, and I'll fuck you right here." He traces his tongue along the shell of my ear. "I'll give them something they can really report on." He brushes his lips against my skin before pulling away, keeping his hand between my legs, and continues to tease me.

The server approaches with our drinks. My pulse quickens more as I try to shift away from his hand so she won't see, but he presses his fingers harder, holding me in place as she sets our glasses on the table. She seems none the wiser as Devin hands her a tightly rolled bill, which she slides between her breasts and gives him a polite smile, but I'm not buying it, considering there's a sex club beneath our feet—not to mention the things I've seen happen on the dance floor here, she definitely knows who's fucking who at every booth.

Devin slides my glass of wine in front of me before he grips his glass and brings the drink to his lips. He takes a sip and makes a show out of licking his lips. My shaking hand grips my wineglass and I take a tentative sip because I am very picky about my wines. It's one of the things that I picked up while being pranced around high society and flying into private wineries. I learned from the top Sommeliers in the world, and while I have no problem throwing back the cheapest tequila in the seediest bar, I'm a total wine snob.

But, holy shit, this is the most delicious wine I've ever tasted. The burst of flavor on my tongue is like mangos and honey, coating my mouth and making me groan at how complex the flavor is.

"What is this?" I ask, the surprise ringing out in my voice. "It's the most delicious wine I've ever had."

He watches me closely as I take another sip. "It's a blend from our private winery in France." He taps on the table, and as if she were waiting in the shadows, the server brings the entire bottle to the table. "I heard through the grapevine that you liked sweet white wine, and I thought I would deliver one of the best I could get my hands on—one of my own creations." He winks.

I smirk at him over the rim of my own glass, mirroring him. "Were you waiting all day to say that line to me, or did it just come to you?"

He chuckles before letting his fingers slip further past my panty line. "I have been waiting all day to do and say a lot of things to you, love. My wittiness is just an added bonus."

I nearly spit out the wine as he circles my entrance. "Devin," I say, careful not to say please because I don't want to try and call him on his bluff about fucking me right in this booth.

He relaxes back, his whiskey in one hand and my pussy in the other. He slowly pushes a finger into me, my breath hitching as he curls it, hitting my G-spot. My head nearly falls backward, and I clamp my mouth shut to stifle a moan. I look around the room because I can feel the eyes that were on us before seeming to be watching more intently. "Devin, they're watching," I say as my fingers curl around his wrist.

He gives me a grin as he continues to play with my pussy. "Let them watch, love." He doesn't give a fuck as he shifts slightly and kisses across my jaw and down my neck. He nips at my pulse point, and a shiver wracks through me as his tongue swirls around the spot. He nips, sucks, and licks across my skin hard enough that I know he's leaving marks. "Lena, your pussy is fucking soaking me, you dirty, dirty girl." He groans against my skin as he adds another finger to his assault.

I slide down in the booth, opening my legs more as the warm buzz of the wine takes over. I take a large drink, finish off the glass, and nearly drop it on the table. He chuckles into my neck as he sets his own drink down on the table, letting his now free hand cup my breast. Hungry eyes from onlookers set my skin on fire as his touch singes me. My nipples harden beneath my dress, aching with need as he pinches one between this thumb and forefinger.

Between my legs, his thumb slides over my clit, and my hips hitch as pleasure rushes through me. "Devin," I whimper as I reach over and palm his hard cock, Devin groaning from the contact. The need to come becomes too much to handle. "What if I said I want you to fuck me in front of all of these people?" I ask with desperation in my voice as his teeth scrape across my skin.

He rasps a breath. "I'd say that none of them will live to see the light of day afterward."

I squirm as the pleasure builds between my legs, tightening my grip on his cock. "But you had me spread for all to see in the Underground," I breathe, cupping his length.

He starts to pump his fingers faster, his thumb hitting my clit with every thrust. "That's not the same as fucking you in front of these pieces of shit who aren't even worthy of having their eyes on you now." He bites my neck hard, and I groan as he swirls his tongue across the spot, soothing the pain. "When I fuck you, Lena, it will not be in the middle of this club." He pumps even faster. "It will be where I can tie you up and use your body in the most diabolical ways of pleasure. I will have you begging to come, and it will be dirty and raw." He slides his hand from my breast, his fingers wrapping around my throat.

"What is this now?" I ask, my breaths coming out erratic as I teeter right on the edge, ready to throw myself over.

"This is me giving you a taste of what's to come," he says, pumping his fingers in time to each word. "And to give these bastards something to talk about." He presses his thumb against my clit, and I see stars as I suck in a raspy breath. Pleasure shoots through me like an electric shock. I bite my bottom lip until the metallic taste of blood fills my mouth as I come. Hard.

His mouth is on mine, lapping up the blood that spills from my bite mark. His tongue invades my mouth as I groan with the final aftershock of my orgasm. He sweeps his tongue through one last time before pulling away. My breaths are heavy as he slips his fingers from between my legs, licking them clean as his eyes stay locked with mine, and letting out a satisfied groan.

"Devin." My voice is low as I run my hands down my dress, attempting to straighten myself up. I tuck a piece of hair behind my ear. "That was…"

"Incredible?" he offers, flashing me a smile as he finishes licking his fingers clean from my cum. "Just wait until I make do with my promises." His gaze slides from mine, scanning the room and smirking as four different men stand up from their booths and leave the area.

Still lounged back, he places his hand back on my thigh, my pussy still pulsing. He picks up his whiskey and throws back the remaining contents before leaning forward and pouring me another glass of wine. I nurse it as we sit in silence, watching the people around us, the music thumping through the space.

It's not long before I see a flash of long, dark hair, and before I can blink, Tasha is sliding into the booth next to me. She grips my chin and looks my face over, her fierce eyes flicking past me to Devin. "Did you just fuck her in front of all these people?" she asks sharply.

Devin shrugs, his fingers pressing into my thigh. "What makes you ask that?" he asks slyly.

She makes a show of taking a deep breath. "Because it smells like sex, and she's covered in bite marks and hickeys." I gasp, pulling my face out of her grip and slapping a hand over my throat. "Oh yeah, *and* fresh bruises from your hand wrapped around her throat."

I look at him, but he just gives me a smirk, as if it's nothing. "Devin," I bite. "What the fuck?"

"That's next, love." He leans in, lightly kissing my cheek.

Tasha pushes his face away with her hand and he looks almost stunned. "Tasha, what the—"

She leans in, interrupting him. "Do you know what you've just done?" she says lowly, but her words have a sharp edge. "Every person in Obsidian either watched you in real-time, or they're seeing it from the videos they were taking of you." The anger in her voice rises. "You are acting like a sex-crazed high schooler, Devin." She quickly slides out of the booth, attempting to block us from view as more eyes flicker our way.

"Don't you have work to do?" he grits out. "We're *enjoying* our evening."

She crosses her arms, pushing her hip out. She's drop-dead gorgeous and extremely lethal in her black mesh corset with roses embroidered just large enough to cover her nipples, paired with a pair of Palazzo pants that make her already long legs look even longer. Her black, strappy pumps look sharp enough to take someone's life.

"I thought you would like to know that you're being summoned to a meeting downstairs." She tosses her long hair over her shoulder, giving me a wink. "But if you're too busy trying to get yourself killed, then I'll just have Tony take care of it."

Devin's eyes flash, giving me an apologetic look. "Tasha, please take Lena back up to the penthouse," he says as he slides around the booth, standing and straightening his clothes, the bulge in his pants is still prominently on display.

I look between them, my eyes narrowing. "No." They both look at me. "Wherever it is that you're going, so am I."

"It's not safe, love," he says, helping me out of the booth. My legs wobble beneath me, my limbs heavy. He watches me for a moment before his gaze flicks to Tasha, her face hardening.

"I think she should be a part of this," Tasha says as she links her arm with mine, standing in solidarity. "I don't think she should be kept in the dark about things that concern her and her safety."

His jaw tics, picking his phone up off the table and shooting off a few texts. He finishes and drops his hand to hang at his side as his other tucks into his pocket. I look him up and down and can only appreciate how handsome of a man he really is. He seems as though he constantly walks a thin line, but being on the edge seems to be his baseline.

He pockets his phone and laces his fingers through mine. "Fine," he grits out, "but if I feel like it's getting to be too much, you're going up to the penthouse with Tasha. Capisce?"

Tasha rolls her eyes, but I hold his gaze as I say, "*I* will decide when and if it's too much. *Capisce?*"

His eyes flare as he looks down at me, his expression heated. I wait to see anger flash, but another emotion seems to take over before he blinks it away.

"Capisce." His voice drops to a dangerously low tone, one

that sends a shiver across my skin. He nods to Tasha who leads the way back across the club to the private elevator. Devin pulls me close to his side, his arm tightening through mine, making it clear that if anyone attempts to take me, they'd have to go through his first.

And even though I have no idea what I'm about to walk into, no matter how terrible it might be, I can't be a weak bystander in this game that Matt's playing.

No. I must be the *Queen*.

CHAPTER FIFTEEN

Lena

THE ELEVATOR DOOR WHOOSHES CLOSED, silencing the thumping bass from the club. The tension in here is thick as the three of us stand in the small space, Tasha and Devin throwing each other death glares as the elevator slowly makes its seemingly slow descent.

I let my eyes drift to Devin as he tries his best to keep that air of coolness about him, hands slipped in his pockets, leaning against the elevator's back wall. He'd have me fooled if I didn't watch the muscles tic in his jaw. It's like he's chewing on the words that are sitting on his tongue, that would express his disagreement with me wanting to go and take part in whatever business he needs to take care of. That if he opens his mouth, his dissatisfaction will all come pouring out.

The ding of the elevator announces our arrival but doesn't pop the bubble of tension that kept us suspended the whole ride. The doors open with Devin striding out, his demeanor all business. Tasha steps forward and holds the elevator door for me. I give her a smile as I follow Devin, her close in tow.

The space off the elevator starkly contrasts with the facade of the rest of the building. It's dimly lit with yellow bulbs, the walls concrete, but where it's chipped exposes dull red bricks. The floor has a slight angle, lowering us even further under the building.

"What is this place?" My voice bounces through the hall, a looming metal door waiting for us at the end of it.

"The basement," Devin gruffs out, his entire demeanor that of a mob man, ready to take down his enemy.

Devin pulls a small fob out of his pocket, the lock beeping before he pushes the large door open. He walks through without a pause. Chivalry is dead down here, apparently.

Passing through the threshold with the door closing behind me, I nearly stop in my tracks. In the middle of the room, underneath a single bulb, is a chair anchored to the floor. The seat is filled with an unconscious, naked man, the same man who they targeted upstairs, with his head hanging down and blood trickling from his temple.

"Looks like he put up a fight," Devin says coolly.

I stare down the man in front of me, and the shadows on the opposite side of the room seem to shift out of the corner of my eye. My head jerks over just as Tony steps into the circle of light. His eyes meet mine with furrowed brows as his gaze shifts to Devin, disapproval evident in his expression.

"She wouldn't take no for an answer," he says, nearly deadpan, as he approaches the man in the chair.

A smirk pulls up the corner of Tasha's lips. "Damn, Destiny wasn't joking when she said she really did a number on this guy." She chuckles lightly as she takes a few steps toward him as Devin looks at her over his shoulder. She shrugs lightly. "She already filled me in before I found you."

"What else did she say?" Devin asks as he wrenches the man's head back, giving his face a once over, before letting it drop back down.

"She said that it was a shame that such a good-looking cock had to go to waste, given the things that his tongue could do while she rode his face."

I choke on my inhaled breath because even though I knew that the woman was luring him in, I didn't imagine that she would fuck him before ultimately luring him to his death.

"Sounds like I don't need to give her a raise if she was already paid that well from this dipshit." Humor filters into Devin's words as Tasha circles the chair, like a shark circling its prey.

"Oh, she's going to get that raise because if this is who I think it is, then you put one of my girls at a *very* big risk tonight." She runs her fingers down his muscular arm as she passes by him.

"And who exactly do you think this *is*?"

She stops in front of him again, gripping his chin and whipping his head side to side. "If I'm correct, and I usually am, this is Cameron Gardner, one of Obsidian's main cronies." Her eyes flick to me. "Matt's right-hand man."

I look at the man again, shaking my head. Not a single feature of him is recognizable. I look up and see that Tony is staring me down, accusation in his eyes as if he's catching me in the act. I feel my face flush as I take a step back, the room turning tense. "I have no idea who this is." My voice shakes. "I've never seen him with Matt before or recognize him from anywhere."

They all look at each other, their bodies relaxing, except for Tony. It's Tony's eyes that continue to swirl with rage and accusation. They narrow as I take a small step back, keeping myself in the shadows, and away from his prying eyes. My body starts to tremble, and I fight the instinct to run. Even though the floors are clean, there's a distinct smell of bleach in the room that says there's been a lot of blood shed down here.

As much as I want to leave, I can't. I don't want them to think that I'm weak and leave me out of things in the future because they think I can't handle it. Apparently, I lived with a mob boss who had no problem killing people right under my nose, so I should be able to handle anything, right?

"Lena," the way Devin says my name sends a shiver up my spine, "you can leave at any time during the interrogation." He looks at me sidelong, the bright light making his mask shine. "It was your decision to come, but you are not required to stay."

He cuts a look to Tasha as if giving her the responsibility to be my babysitter if it comes to that, but no matter how gruesome it might get, I refuse to leave. "I'm staying." My voice is stern as I square my shoulders, and Tasha gives me an approving smile.

She saunters back up to the man, my eyes widening as she straddles him and lowers herself onto his lap. She grabs his face, letting her blood red nails dig into his skin. Titling his face from side to side, she takes in his details, disgust creeping over her face. "Too bad he's such a piece of shit, we could have offered him a job. I really do need more male escorts around here." She looks at Tony, giving him a devilish grin. "The ladies like a big, strong man, don't they, Tony?"

His eyes narrow, and his muscles tense in his crossed arms. He holds her amused gaze for a beat too long. "This is a little poetic of a position, don't you think?" Her voice is filled with the light humor of an inside joke, one he doesn't seem to find funny as he stands stone still, his eyes darkening as she chuckles, waving him off with her delicate hand.

"What are you going to do with him?" I ask as I work to keep my legs from buckling as anxiety courses through my veins.

Devin's eyes cut to mine as he pulls his mask free from his face, laying it down on a small metal rolling table. "Interrogate him. Find out what he knows about Obsidian and who else might be involved." He pulls the metal table closer to him. I gulp as the different instruments of torture gleam in the light. "And maybe I can get some answers of my own," he mutters under his breath.

The sound of a slap cuts through the air, breaking our

trance, both of us looking toward Tasha. The man's head is snapped to the side, Tasha's hand coming back to grip his face again. "Wake up, you piece of shit," she says in a sing-songy voice, bringing her face closer to his. "It's not fun if you're not awake and we're tired of waiting."

"Good God, Tash," Devin says lowly, shaking his head. But I don't miss the amused grin that attempts to pull up the corners of his mouth.

She scrapes her nails down the man's chest, leaving red marks, as she continues to try and rouse him. She slaps him again, his head snapping in the other direction before she reaches between them and grips his dick. Her eyes seem to glimmer as she pulls on his cock, bringing her face next to his ear to whisper, "Wake up, sleepy head."

A moment later, the man groans, flexing his shoulders forward as he tries to adjust his arms that are tied behind his back. His head falls back as she squeezes his hardening cock, her other hand scratching down his chest, leaving lines of blood in their wake.

"Wake up. I've been waiting for you." Her voice is so seductive. He moans again, his head falling to the side, his eyelids fluttering.

"Come on, you're almost there." The smile that takes over her face would have any man running in the opposite direction and has me on edge. "The fun can really start when you wake up."

He starts to try and move his arms and legs, the ropes keeping him tied creak as he forces his eyes open, his lids still heavy. Tasha squeezes his shaft one more time, causing another moan to escape his lips. She lets go of him and pulls herself up to stand over him, a dark, amused look on her face.

This time his eyes fly open, letting out a scream as he yanks on the restraints holding him in place. "What the *fuck?*" he grunts out, his pupils wide with panic. "Let me go, you crazy fucking bitch," he bites out. The chair rattles beneath his weight as he struggles to loosen his bindings and fails miserably.

Tasha's hand comes forward, gripping his throat and squeezing hard enough for him to choke on the next words he was about to say. "You only speak when spoken to, you piece of shit." Her voice is smooth, like a spider's would be if you were caught in her web. "Besides, we have some questions for you."

"I'm not saying *shit*." His voice is strained around her hold, his breaths wheezing.

Devin steps into the light, his hands casually in his pockets as he pulls an ID card out. The man's eyes flick up to his, a glimmer of fear in them. Devin leans down, holding the card up to the man's face, causing his eyes to cross. "How cute for an ex-frat boy to use a fake ID to get into the club." He shoves the ID into the man's mouth before pinching his lips shut. "We all know your name is *not* Matt Chase. So, when I let go, you're going to tell me exactly who you are."

The man's eyes flare with anger and his jaw goes tense. He attempts to wrench his face from Devin's hold, but Tasha's grip keeps him in place. They act as the perfect team, like they have been doing this kind of thing together for years, both playing the part of the bad cop.

Holy shit, what have I gotten myself into?

Devin slips his fingers from the man's lips, wiping them on his pants. He looks disgusted as the man spits the ID out, the card clattering as it hits the floor.

"I'm not telling you shit," he growls and attempts to spit at Devin, but it falls short. Tasha tightens her grip on his throat, her nails digging into his skin, blood welling around them. The man fights harder, looking like a fish floundering on the shore.

"You can make this easier on yourself and die with some dignity left to your name." Devin looks in Tony's direction, his eyes darkening. "Especially since all your fellow Obsidian members will get to see the show later tonight when we send them the video footage."

The man's face pales before he thrashes harder, trying to free his throat from Tasha's iron grip. "Fuck. You," he grits, gasping for breath. Sweat rolls down his face, mixing with the blood that continues to flow from his temple.

"It's a shame we won't get to. Your equipment is *very* impressive." Tasha pouts. Her head whips in Devin's direction. "Oh! Wait! What *if* we lobotomized him and then we could keep him as our pretty pet!" she exclaims. The man thrashes hard, a scream tearing from him.

I feel my face pale at her suggestion and note the bloodlust that fills her eyes.

"Are you sure Nate would appreciate you having a man pet?" Devin teases. All amusement falls from Tasha's face, her eyes darkening as her grip tightens on the man's throat even more. His breathless gags fill the air between them as blood trickles down his neck.

"He has his own pets to deal with." She whips her head away, attention falling back on the man tied up in front of her. She cocks her head to the side before dragging a nail down his forehead and touching the spot at the corner of his eyes. "And all it takes is one quick little tap right here," she murmurs as the man tries to pull his head away, fear filling his eyes.

Tony chuckles as a cruel smile pulls up the corners of Devin's lips. He picks up a pair of leather gloves off the rolling tray and makes a show of tugging them onto his large hands. "We'll see how much we get out of him." Devin picks up a knife from the tray, the large blade glinting in the light. "Or how much is *left* of him."

"You might as well just fucking kill me, you fuck. I'm not telling you shit," the man bites out, his attempts to break free become less and less as his energy depletes, and what I imagine is a concussion takes over.

Devin turns the blade over in his hand, running a leather

gloved finger along the sharp edge. The man's eyes go even wider with panic, his body trembling, as he watches Devin's every move, a bead of sweat rolling down from his temple. Devin runs the blade down the man's face, blood welling in its wake.

"It will be a shame to have to cut up such a handsome face, boss," Tasha says in a pouty voice. She lets her hand slip from his throat, and he sucks in a deep, shaking breath.

Devin grips the man's ear, holding the blade at the base of it. "Agreed, but I promise that we'll send back the pretty parts for his friends." As Devin begins to press the blade into the thin flesh, the man finally breaks his silence.

"Cameron," the man blurts, "Cameron Gardner." He breathes heavily as Devin pulls the blade from his ear.

Devin presses the tip of the blade into the man's cheek, a bead of blood welling beneath the tip. "Who's Cameron Gardner?" he asks, his voice turning even more dangerous.

"I am!" the man screeches. "I'm Cameron Gardner."

Devin looks to Tony and nods. "Good guess, T." He smirks as he turns his attention back to Cameron as he shakes so violently that he rattles the chair. "Now was that so hard?" He slowly pulls the knife away from his face. "Now, tell us where we can find Obsidian and we'll be on our way."

"You'll never find us, you prick," Cameron spits, the words hanging heavy in the room.

Tony takes a step toward the man, but before he can take another, Devin grabs the man's ear, slicing it clean off his head. His scream echoes through the room as Devin throws it at his feet. Bile burns up my throat as the urge to throw up has me slapping a hand over my mouth and stumbling a step back.

"Fucker!" Cameron screams. "You're a fucker!" Blood pours down the side of his head, the spot where his ear was a bright crimson. At the sight of blood, I watch as Devin transforms from the charismatic man who has seemingly swept me off my feet to someone I don't recognize.

Anxiety crawls across my skin like ants as they prod him with questions, blood running from open wounds, his screams filling the silence of his refusal to answer them. I slowly back further into the shadows, my back pressing against the cool wall, steadying me. Nausea roils in my stomach as Devin punches him in the nose, the crunch of it breaking nearly deafening as blood rushes down Cameron's face.

I watch as Tasha stalks around behind him, toying with him, as his head whips back and forth trying to find her. She reaches down and I hear a snapping sound as she breaks one of his fingers that are tied behind him. He throws his head back, a howl ringing out. The sound has me gagging and my knees nearly buckling at the ease that they can inflict pain on him.

Devin chuckles as he lowers his face in front of Cameron's. "Had enough, Cameron?" Devin watches him as Tasha stalks around the chair, waiting for Devin's next move. "If you just answer us, you can put a stop to this."

Cameron hocks and spits a bloody wad of spit at Devin. It splats onto his shoulder, running down his white shirt, leaving a crimson stain. "Fuck. You," he grits out, blood coating his teeth.

Tasha growls as she comes up behind him and grabs under his chin, wrenching his head back and stretching his neck out. Devin stares at the blood on his shirt, a cruel smile pulling at the corners of his mouth. "This was my favorite shirt, you asshole," he says with a quiet calm.

Cameron's haggard breathing is the only sound in the room, but I barely hear it over the roaring in my ears.

Devin weighs the knife in his palm as he breaks the silence. "Well, Cameron, I'll have to say that I'm impressed." Devin's voice is low. "I figured we would have broken you by now.

Your buddies will be proud that you died withholding all their secrets."

Tasha's lips curl into a sly grin as Devin moves around, positioning himself behind Cameron's head. He presses the tip of the blade to his neck, blood welling. "Any last words?"

Time slows as the last five years of lies and deceit come rushing back to me, the knot in my chest pulling so tight that I can barely breathe. The questions I need answers to crawl up my throat, looking for a way out before this chance slips away.

"Wait." My words ring out as I rush from the shadows. They all look at me in shock, Cameron's eyes going wide as if he's seen a ghost. "Don't kill him yet."

Devin's expression is unreadable. I'm not sure if I'm even looking at him or someone else entirely. He looks deranged as he pulls the knife away and steps back. He nods curtly at Tasha, as she loosens her grip, making her way to Devin's side. Cameron gasps and pants, his hair falling over his forehead as his head drops down, his body going limp in the chair.

I approach the chair, and adrenaline pulses through my veins, making me feel weightless. This is my chance to find my own set of answers and give me some closure from my past life, the one that I finally had enough courage to run from. I look the man over and even from behind the blood, I know that I've never seen him before. Another person who lived in Matt's other life, the one he kept me locked away from. My limbs shake, but I stay steady on my feet, not giving this man the satisfaction of seeing me falter.

Cameron's head rises as I ask, "Why does Matt want me back so bad? Why can't he just leave me alone?"

Cameron's eyes widen as he takes me in. He watches me carefully as the realization sets in as to who's in front of him. He laughs darkly, his face changing from pain and panic to a handsome monster who would follow you down a dark alley. "No one takes what belongs to him." Cameron's voice is low, his eyes darkening as he continues. "And he's angry. So fucking angry that you tried to escape him because, you know what, you pathetic little bitch? You fucking can't."

My pulse races, the sound like a train engine speeding down the tracks where I'm frozen in place, standing in the middle of them as his words hit me. "He knows every move you make, with eyes on you everywhere you go, and he won't stop until he has you back. He's been dreaming of ways to punish you for running. For being a fucking whore and sleeping with the first man who showed you any shred of attention like the pathetic little bitch you are." His words hit me like a slap, a small gasp leaving me as he carries on. "He's waiting for the perfect time to pounce, and when he does," his eyes darken more, "he'll tear you and your little boyfriend to fucking shreds."

Tears prick behind my eyes, and I squeeze them shut, trying my best not to look weak. A loud pop rings in my ears and my eyes fly open. Blood and chunks of something splatter across the ground at my feet. My eyes widen and my head slowly floats up from the mess of blood and what I realize is brains, meeting Tony's eyes as he stands behind Cameron's now lifeless body.

His eyes are dark, his hood making them look even darker. His steely grays nearly glow with rage and malice. He takes a slow, deep breath, and puts the gun back into the holster hooked onto his belt. His eyes don't leave mine as he takes a step back, cloaking himself in the shadows like a ghost, as if he were never there.

The loud ringing in my ears quiets as Devin says my name, his voice bringing me back. He cradles my face in his hands, the metallic smell of blood filling my nose from the splatters on his gloves. "Lena, are you okay?" He searches my face, but I continue to look past him, my eyes locked on the man in the shadows. The fire in his eyes only seems to burn brighter, burning into me and heating me to my core.

Hearing Devin's question repeated, I nod my head, eyes

still locked with Tony's. Devin looks over his shoulder, anger rolling off him in waves as he commands the room.

"Cut out his little monologue, make sure you can't see our faces, and send the footage where it needs to go." He turns to Tasha. "You get some rest. The last few days have been a lot. And take tomorrow off."

She nods and heads toward the door. "I'll send down the clean-up crew." She looks between us. "Any parts you want to send personally?"

Devin looks back at Cameron's body, examining what's left. "His eyes and dick. I'm sure they suck each other off enough, they'll know exactly whose it is."

Tasha snorts an amused sound and gives him a lazy two-finger salute. "You got it, boss." She approaches me, her hand cupping around mine and giving it a squeeze. "You did amazing, Lena. Don't let anything that fuck said to you get to your head. You have us now and that's something little Matty didn't bank on." She gives me a kiss on the cheek, a soft smile on her lips as she turns and heads out the door, leaving me with just Devin and Tony.

Tony's turned away, the backlight of his phone glowing around his head. Devin shakes his head and places his hand on my lower back, leading me to the door. "Let's get cleaned up."

I look back at where Tony hides in the shadows, his back still turned, Devin not bothering to say anything to him as we leave. Cameron's words shook me, but they weren't the worst thing that has ever been said to me. Hell, it's not any worse than some of the threatening messages that Matt has been sending me. Do I believe that Matt will do anything to get me back? Yes, I do. But everyone in this room knows that, so I'm not sure what was said that would cause such a visceral reaction from Tony.

Even though his eyes were burning with rage, there was something off about the way he looked at me, as if he was looking at someone else entirely. He appeared out of the shadows after not saying or doing anything before that and point-blank shot a man, one who could have more than likely been broken and answered more of their questions under their torture tactics.

There's something lurking under his hood and mask, something waiting in the water to strike. And I intend to uncover it before it drags me under.

DEVIN

LOUNGED BACK in our private booth, sipping on a whiskey, I casually search the crowd for our target. This one's been on our radar for a while, from a tip that Tony received from an anonymous source on the dark web.

The club is packed tonight, its popularity only grows every week with all the whispers of the Underground. Tasha has worked her ass off to build it up, making a safe space for the taboo. We're not only reaping the financial benefits, but we're seeing an uptick in attendance of some of the elite and powerful from the other side of the river. I'm a little jealous that I didn't think of it myself.

These people like the anonymity with our mask requirement, and I especially like the whisper network that Tasha's girls have created to keep us in the know of everything that happens outside of this building. Even with the upped security from Tony, these fuckers will sing like canaries just to impress a woman as she sucks him off. And who am I to deny them of such a service?

I watch the people as they move about, making note of the targets on my personal list. My skin itches as the monster lurking underneath pushes against me, attempting to rear its head and sink its teeth into those who need to be dealt with. I swirl my whiskey and take a tentative sip as I soothe the beast, reminding it that it will have its chance to feed, all in good time.

Out of the corner of my eye, I catch a small group approaching one of the large booths off to the side. They are not even attempting to disguise their identities with the masks that barely surround their eyes. Even from here, these men in their high-end suits with women hanging on their arms are more than familiar to me than I'd like to admit. My eyes search each face until one stands out from the rest and I home in on him. *Bingo.*

Leaning forward, I rest my elbows on the tabletop, keeping an air of casualness about me as I watch them file into the booth. I make an effort to scan the room for any of their own security who have been planted elsewhere in the club. They're everywhere, but it's obvious who they are with their dead eyes and their placid expressions as they nonchalantly scan the room for any dangers that they might have to take on. Too bad they don't have a clue about me.

This group is laughing and making a show of themselves, clearly wanting to be seen and heard by the rest of the people in this private area. It's how they trick unsuspecting people into their little cult, making them seem like the life of the party, when in reality, they're monsters in disguise.

One monster can usually sniff the other one out in no time and good thing I have a keen sense of smell.

I watch as my main target pulls one of the girls down on his lap, which I can tell is not a normal thing for him to do by her body language. She's rigid, even as she settles onto his lap, her hands unsure of where to land. I look over every curve, and my God, she's a thing of beauty, even with a lace mask covering half of her face. Her amber eyes seem to glow in the disco lights, with her long, brown hair flowing around her, and she looks phenomenal in that black dress. Her long legs come out from the short skirt that rides up just enough, while her full breasts show just enough cleavage for wandering eyes to linger a little too long.

She looks older than the normal barely-of-legal-age women these men bring into the club. If I had to guess, I would say she's right around thirty, just by the way she's carrying herself and most of the other women even acknowledge her. In their eyes, she's probably aged out of being brought into the club with them, but to me, she seems absolutely perfect. While I am a man who can admire a beautiful person, I prefer my partners to be a little more seasoned in life —one just like her.

I clock other sets of eyes that hold their gazes on her a little too long, and I have this feral urge to pluck all of their eyes out for just simply looking at her like she's nothing more than a piece of ass.

I keep my eyes on her, shifting to other members of the group as she stands. She sidesteps around them and heads to the bar. She approaches it and leans over the counter, where the bartender immediately flocks to her.

I can't decide if I should take him to the basement and kill him for looking at her like she's a meal that he wishes to devour or give him an extra tip for noticing a woman like her.

A good bartender like him is hard to come by, so tip it is.

I'm lost in my thoughts when someone steps into my view, blocking her from my sight. "Dev," a feminine voice says in a warning tone. My eyes flick up, and I'm met with the judgmental eyes of Tasha. She stands at the edge of the table, her arms crossed with a very pissed expression on her face. "Quit eye fucking the patrons and do your fucking job."

Leaning over the table, her palms flat against the top, she narrows her eyes at me. I can feel the heat from the eyes around us burning into her as she puts her body on display. I let my lips pull into a smirk. Like they could ever handle a woman like her, one who was trained to eat men like them as a bedtime snack.

"I'm doing my *fucking* job, Tash." I raise my glass of whiskey to her. "And you're blocking my view of my target. So, either sit and watch with me or go pester someone else."

She slides into the booth, giving me a sidelong glance as she makes note of the very rowdy booth that I have my eyes on. She keeps her voice low, shifting her body as if she's making a move on me as she says, "I've been keeping an eye on them, too." She throws her long ponytail over her shoulder in a flirtatious gesture, nodding her toward the bar. "That must be his actual girl with him tonight because she doesn't fit the bill for the other ones he brings in here on a regular basis."

I scan the crowd for her, because she hasn't come back from the bar yet and the crowd has shifted around her. "He must be putting on a front for her because that isn't his usual posse, either. They're far too rowdy."

Tasha scoffs. "Obviously trying to keep up with a double life. I mean, the one woman with the short, dark hair has been straddling that guy all night, shoving her tongue down his throat and throwing back shots between breaths. Definitely not his usual crowd."

I hum in agreement, taking a long sip from my glass, enjoying the burn of the whiskey down my throat. "I could really use a fucking cigarette," I say over the lip of the glass.

"Just go get fucking laid to take the edge off. You know you could have any woman in this room right now." Too bad the one I now have my sights set on is off fucking limits, but I don't bother to interject as she goes on. "You know that shit's bad for you, anyway. Besides, if Tony can quit, so can your ass." She looks around the room, her green eyes dancing in the lights as she runs her hand down my chest, keeping up her facade.

"*Pssh.* He vapes and I consider that fucking cheating," I

tease, taking another sip and letting the liquid sit on my tongue.

Rolling her eyes, she plucks my glass from my hand, taking a delicate sip of the amber liquid. "It's not our fault that you chose to go cold turkey." She slides the glass back toward me on the table. "I can have one of the girls come up and give you something to do with your mouth and hands, and just like that," she snaps her fingers, "you'll forget all about your nicotine addiction. Nothing a little pussy can't fix."

I chuckle as she gives me a knowing smile, her fingers playing with my hair as her eyes move through the room. She's right—I need something to take my mind off things, but I've been too focused on work and keeping my eyes on the people here and one of my favorite flavors isn't currently available. And the last thing I need is a fucking turf war between all these power-hungry assholes and possibly taking the club down with them. Nate, our jet-setting owner, would have my balls if I let that happen.

Tasha pats her hand on my chest. "Let me know if you want to take me up on my offer. I have a few who have been drooling after you and would take the edge off while throwing you over it." She winks and starts sliding out of the booth. Tasha keeps her side of the business clean in a literal sense, and while she employs beautiful girls who get checked every week, I'm not interested when I seem to have my sights set on another woman in the room.

"We'll see, Tash," I say as she leans over, giving me a kiss on the forehead before standing up. She looks over her shoulder and clocks the mystery woman, just as I did. She gives her a once-over, her attention turning back to me.

"Hm, well, just let me know if I need to send anyone your way tonight, before you try to stick your dick into something that doesn't belong to you." She doesn't give me time to respond before she turns and disappears into the crowd.

Pulling out my phone, I shoot Tony a text detailing our target and the current situation of their booth, along with the order to keep our people tight around their booth tonight. I want as many eyes and ears on them, because while I doubt that they know much, people as reckless as them are bound to slip up about something. Knowledge is power and I'm here to make sure that we stay at the top of the food chain.

But I highly doubt we'll learn anything new if he's being rowdy with this atypical group while having his alleged girlfriend here. Men like this know exactly how to play a double life and keep people at arm's length but make them feel like they're the only ones hanging around. If my suspicions are correct, and they usually are, this woman doesn't have a clue what this fucker has been up to around here. And if I'm wrong, then she's just hanging around for the money, because I can't imagine this guy has much else to offer her.

She looks too fucking good for him, anyways, and if I could, I would pull her into a private room and show her what being with a real man is like. While it's unlikely to happen while she's with that tool, it's a fantasy I'm choosing to keep on replay.

Relaxing back into the booth, I cross my ankle over my knee and wave to one of the servers for a refill. I plan on watching them for the rest of the evening and will keep tabs on her every time he brings her back to the club. I would know her anywhere, even from behind her mask. I can already tell this is going to be a long night, and while they're at the top of my list, it's not the only thing I'm concerned about.

It's been a while since I texted Tony, but he finally responds, giving me a thumbs up and letting me know he's been aware of them this entire time. A smirk pulls up my lips because I wouldn't have expected any other type of response from him. I invited him to come with me tonight because he rarely comes down unless it's absolutely necessary, and apparently, he'd rather watch from the comfort of the penthouse. He has an eagle eye when it comes to our seedy clientele, and even though he's a big guy, he has the keen ability to almost disappear in the shadows and not be seen until it's too late for his target.

He prefers to work at his desk, and even though we have the club to watch, I have enrolled his help in my own investigation. He's the only one who I trust with critical information, and he has allegedly been trained enough for the job because every time I question his abilities, he always shows me up.

And even though we're getting roadblocked and hitting dead ends, he's putting in the work to find the answers I'm looking for, and I just wait for the day that every one of my suspicions can be confirmed and I can take down every motherfucker on my list.

As the evening drags on, I'm getting fucking bored, which is never good for someone like me. People tend to get hurt when I'm bored, and tonight will be no different. Laying the phone face down, I signal for one of the girls to head to my booth. Serenity saunters my way, and thankfully, she's one who knows better than to try and flirt with me while I try to give an assignment. Even though Tony and Tasha train every girl in this craft, they conveniently leave out that while I enjoy fucking, I don't fuck my employees, no matter how attractive or good in bed they may be.

The music is loud enough tonight that I don't have to worry about being overheard as I give her instructions to start working the table. Hopefully, she can lure one of these fuckers into a private room, and after she gets off, give us the signal and we'll take over from there.

It's one of my favorite things to bust in from our hidden doors while they're in a vulnerable position. I find joy in their humiliation and pain, and while these men think they're powerful because of their money and status, the true power is holding their lives in my hand and watching the light fade from their eyes as I snuff them out.

Serenity works the table, catching the attention of a few of the men who seem like total fucking dirtbags. It's not lost on me how brave women like Serenity are for putting themselves in front of these dangerous people, but I also know that they love the thrill of the risky game we play and I love the reward of their dutiful efforts.

I scan the booth again and lock eyes with the only woman who has my true attention in this club. The man whose lap she's on is too busy chatting with the man next to him to notice that he has a literal goddess sitting on his lap. If she were on mine, my attention would be on her and fuck all the other people in the room.

She flicks her gaze from mine and checks her phone as if she's trying her hardest to keep her eyes off me. She leans forward, looking down the line of people in the booth, watching the one with the short, dark hair. I tap my fingers on the wood top in front of me, counting the seconds until she looks my way again.

I let my mind wander as I drink her in. I imagine what it would be like to wrap her long hair around my fist and fuck her mouth, tears spilling from her pretty amber eyes. She would look so fucking beautiful kneeling at my feet, my cock in her mouth, her pussy dripping with need. Our gazes lock again and her eyes widen as she watches me, and if I didn't know any better, I'd say she was thinking the same thing.

What a dirty, *dirty* girl.

Movement at the other end of the booth catches my eye and I begrudgingly break eye contact with my newest fixation. Serenity is now leading one of the men from their party to the stairwell, taking him to a private room and out of their sight. Oh, she is *really* good. She throws a look over her shoulder, giving me a knowing smirk, and I know that's her sign that this one must be noteworthy and to be ready for some fun.

I sit back, start the clock, and wait for her signal. Maybe this time, I'll get some of the fucking answers I'm looking for. Until then, I'm going to watch my pretty little amber-eyed goddess squirm under my heated gaze and try to lure her further into my web and eat her alive.

&DEVIN

I STAND RIGHT OUTSIDE of my bathroom, listening to the water run and imagining how it looks cascading down Lena's body. My dick twitches, the need to rush in and fuck her right against the shower wall is almost unbearable. But, as much as I want that, I need to let her have a moment of peace and pull herself back together.

Her pale face on the elevator ride back up here was enough to stop any of my advances in their tracks. Just by her reaction, it's pretty obvious that she never saw any of the carnage that little Matty left in his wake and really was kept under his thumb. And while I'm worried about her, because that is quite the traumatic experience, I'm more worried about Tony.

In the years I've known him, I've only seen him snap once —and it was fucking terrifying. I don't know what that fucker tied to the chair said to set him off, but it burrowed under his skin and really got to him. He's always been able to shut his emotions off, but watching him go nearly lights out is unnerving. Hell, there's more light in his eyes when he lets his own demons take over than what I saw tonight.

A throat clears behind me, and I look to find Tasha's lean

frame blocking the doorway, a duffle bag in her hand. "Quit being a fucking creep, Dev." She throws the duffle on the bed, unzips it, and removes the clothes she brought up to replace Lena's now brain-splattered ones, that have now been properly incinerated. Which is a fucking shame, because that dress was something of wonder on her.

I look back toward the bathroom door, listening for any crying or unsettling sounds coming from the other side. "She's handling it well if that was truly the first person she's ever seen be killed," I say, crossing my arms and pressing my fingers into my skin, lightly pinching just to make sure that I feel something.

Tasha remains silent behind me until I feel her hand on my arm. "She isn't handling it *well.*" I look down at her, and while she doesn't look pissed, she doesn't necessarily seem pleased by tonight's events. "She watched a person be murdered, Dev. And to make matters worse, had brains splattered all over her. She's not like us. So, please, don't be surprised when she falls apart from it. Okay?"

My jaw tenses. "Do you think she'll want to leave?" The question is like ash on my tongue because I just fucking got her here.

Tasha shrugs. "She didn't go running in the other direction after it happened, but she *was* in shock. Just give her time to breathe and process everything." She comes around to stand in front of me, cupping my face in her hands. "What is it about her that's got you and Big T wound so tight?" She reaches up, smoothing my hair back from my face. "I've never seen you two like this. Especially not about a woman."

I relax my jaw as Tasha's hands drop to my arms. I look down and stare at her long, red nails, the exact same color as the blood splattered across my clothes and skin. How do I answer her when I don't even fucking know? I don't know why this woman has been on my radar for over a year other than she is truly a thing of beauty and that I could draw her out of Obsidian and snatch her for myself. And then pin her down and fuck her until she gave away all of their secrets and be done with her.

But now…Now that she's in front of me and I see that she is nothing like the woman I thought she was, I can't figure it out. She has no information to give me and like Tony said, she's more of a liability to the cause.

But I fucking want her.

I take in a deep breath, trying to settle my now racing heart before I answer. "She's innocent in all of this." I look back at her face, expecting a look of disgust or something similar, but instead, she has a small smile on her face.

"From what I can tell, she might be innocent in this, but she's not a damsel in distress like you want to make her out to be." She squeezes my arms, pressing her nails lightly into my skin, but making sure I feel it. "She seems to be struggling with who she really is and what she wants now that she's free of Matt's clutches." Tasha's phone vibrates where she left it on the bed, but doesn't give it a glance, her eyes staying glued to me.

"She spent the last half of her twenties under the thumb of a controlling, abusive, asshole who ended up being a leader in Obsidian." My own phone buzzes in my pocket, but it can wait. "She's an enigma. She *should* be cowering in the corner like a damsel in distress, but instead, she walked into that room with us tonight and never left. She had a man's brains splattered onto her and she never moved. Grown men have run from that room for less action than what she saw tonight."

Tasha closes in and wraps her arms around me, embracing me as she lays her head on my chest. I let my arms relax and pull her to me. She's one of the last things left of my old life, the best thing to be dropped on my doorstep all those years ago, and she has a way of knowing exactly what I need even when I don't have a fucking clue.

We stand there in silence for a beat before she goes on, her low voice vibrating against my chest. "You know, Dev, she can be fucking terrified, but still willing to put herself on the line." She pulls back slightly, watching me as she speaks. "She knows this is bigger than her, but that she's a key player in the game, whether she wants to be or not."

She leans back farther. "But you want to know what I think?" She doesn't give me time to answer. "I think you know that she's not necessarily choosing this path but that she feels like she has to find herself, and you find that fascinating. And she's igniting something in you and Tony that neither of you has felt before."

I scoff. "Tony doesn't—"

She presses her fingers to my lips, cutting off my words. "If you saw the way that Tony looked at her when she stepped out of the shadows and demanded answers from that creep, you would have started that sentence differently."

Her fingers fall away, and I cock my head to the side. "So, what is it that you think she's igniting in us?" My voice is quiet because, for the first time, I'm scared of what her answer might be. What cards might I have shown?

She pats my cheek and pulls herself from our embrace. "Why don't you tell me."

I open my mouth to say something, anything to change the subject, but before I can, the bathroom door creaks open. Steam rolls out, swirling around Lena as she stands in the doorway wrapped only in a towel. The bright bathroom light behind her makes her look angelic. I can't help but look her over, taking her in as she stands there, her damp hair sticking to her skin that's flushed from the hot shower. She looks absolutely radiant.

Her eyes find mine and she goes to take a step into the room but pauses when she sees Tasha. She smiles as if she's seeing an old friend for the first time and a little bit of life was brought back into her. "Oh my God, *please* tell me you found me something to wear so I don't have to put that dress back on."

"That dress is nothing but ashes now, love," I say, but when her eyes cut back on me, they widen in disbelief.

"You…you burned it?" she asks as a look of terror starts to take over her face.

I look at Tasha who is watching her, dumbfounded at the reaction.

"Why would you do that?" Her voice becomes sharper with each word, and her face becomes panicked.

I narrow my eyes at her, trying to understand this reaction from her. "Because it was covered in a man's brain matter, Lena. Why would you want it back?" I ask calmly.

"Because it's not *mine*," she screeches again. She drops her head into her hands and groans. "Bri is going to fucking kill me," she says through her fingers, her voice muffled.

Tasha giggles, actually *giggles*, at Lena. She crosses the room to her and wraps her fingers around Lena's wrists lowering her hands. "Your friend will get over it when a new one shows up at her doorstep in the morning." Lena looks at her, a red flush covering her face. "In fact, I will call the owner of the boutique across town and send over additional pieces." She winks. "For good measure."

Lena's face is priceless as her mouth hangs open and her eyes widen. "I-I can't afford that." Her voice is barely a whisper, embarrassment coating every word.

Tasha cups her face, giving her a kiss on both cheeks. "It's on the house, baby girl." She looks over her shoulder at me. "Besides, I doubt that you'll be made to pay for anything with this guy around." She smirks as she pulls away from Lena, grabbing her hand and leading her to the bed. "Now, as to the matter of clothes for *you*."

Lena's eyes twinkle as she reaches down and picks up a lacy black top. "This is stunning." She lays it down carefully and picks up the dark denim jeans, holding them to her waist. "And just my size." She looks at me in wonderment over her shoulder. "Is this all for me?" she asks as if she's never been given a gift before in her life. Or, one that didn't have strings attached to it, like I'm sure everything did when she was under Matt's roof.

"Of course, love." Lena looks as if she's about to cry as her eyes shine. "And like Tasha said, it's on the house."

Tasha gives her a scandalous look as she pipes in. "I'm sure there's room in the closet next door for you to keep them in if you want." Lena tenses, her head turning slowly, looking from Tasha to me, but doesn't say a word.

Lena seems to have completely frozen in place, her chest not even rising or falling like she's holding her breath. Her cheeks redden a deep crimson, and tears appear in the corner of her eyes. *Shit.* I am not prepared for her to have a breakdown. This is why I have spent years with a man who shows next to no emotions. I have not practiced this level of empathy in a fucking long time.

I just stare as Tasha steps in and picks up the pieces. "It's up to you, baby girl," she says sweetly. Her ability to become a mother figure is a part she plays well. She gently picks up the clothes and duffle bag off the bed and leads her back into the bathroom. The door closes behind them, and I'm left standing alone.

Fuck, could this night get any fucking worse?

And as if on cue, my phone vibrates in my pocket again. I pull it out and am greeted with multiple messages from Tony, each one getting more curt than the last.

TONY

Found shit on the Cameron guy. Get the fuck down here.

TONY

Get the fuck down here.

TONY

Now.

I almost chuckle, because as patient as he may seem on the outside, that man has none. But I see the final message and my heart drops from my chest. I look to the bathroom door and hear the women talking on the other side, their voices light and their giggles turning into actual laughter. Instead of breaking down the door, I type out a quick text to Tasha so she doesn't think I just ditched them.

As much as she wants to be a part of this, I need to get as much information as possible before I actually involve her. She'll more than likely be pissed, and I imagine I'll be in worse trouble from Tasha, but right now, it's about keeping everyone safe.

I stare at the bathroom door again, my body fighting to leave, but I give it another second to see if they'll come out. They don't. My phone vibrates in my hand, knocking me from the trance I was slipping into. My legs are moving and I'm out of the apartment's door in a matter of seconds, closing the door quietly behind me, leaving them with their brief moment of bliss.

I THROW open the door to the basement and am met with the stench of bleach as it infiltrates my nose. The concrete is still damp from where it had been hosed down. Cameron's body is nowhere to be found, and like the rest, he's been properly disposed of, with nothing left but ashes.

I cut across and punch the code to the small office that we keep down here. Tony is at his desk, a wall of screens shining bright in the room, his large body taking up most of the space.

He swings around in his chair, glowering at me. "About *fucking* time," he bites out.

"Sorry, I—" He cuts me off by pulling up CCTV footage from outside of Lena's apartment. I grip his shoulder and lean over him, my eyes glued to the single screen. "What the fuck is going on?" I grit out as panic blooms through my chest.

The street outside Lena's apartment building is surrounded by flashing lights. It seems as though every responder is parked right there, including ladder trucks. Road barricades and yellow tape already block off the street, and the media is posted up as close as they're allowed to get.

EMTs and police officers surround what was once one of our stakeout vehicles, the outlines of two bodies under white sheets at their feet.

My jaw tightens and the sound of my teeth cracking fills my head, along with my pounding pulse. My skin burns from the fire torching through my veins as I take in the smoke that filters from one of the upper floors. "What the *fuck* happened, Tony?"

"Retaliation."

I watch and wonder how many of those responders are wrapped up in Obsidian and how they plan on covering this shit up. "They move quick," I say as I watch them move our men into body bags, seemingly not giving a shit how they handle them. I will make sure to hunt those men down and give them the same treatment.

"Real fucking quick. This happened within an hour of me posting that video to their little corner of the web. If only I could have seen their reactions, but they've managed to keep me blocked from their forums for the most part." He curls his fingers into a fist, lightly hitting it on the desk as he leans in to watch more of the cleanup. "It's almost like they were lying in wait for us to make a move or were waiting for Lena to come around the apartment and grab her."

A pang hits me in the chest at his words. "What about her

friends?" The question is quiet as fear starts to squeeze my throat, nearly choking me. "Where the fuck are they?"

Tony freezes as if he'd completely forgotten about them and starts furiously typing, the screens in front of him moving in a blur as the facial recognition goes to work. I run my hand through my hair and tug on the roots. "They have to be somewhere close," I say as I find myself praying to a God that has never once listened, even when I throw myself down at the altar and beg at his feet.

One screen stops, and I see Bri as she walks around a convenience store on the far end of town, earbuds in her ears and a basket full of miscellaneous goods. I blow out a breath as Tony pulls up his chat, sending messages for someone to pick her up. Responses are almost immediate, and we watch the GPS systems of two of our vehicles head straight there.

The tension in the small room grows to near suffocating as Tony types furiously trying to find Kate, the screens flashing so quickly in front of me that I start to feel motion sick. "She has to fucking be somewhere, goddammit," I bite out, my phone vibrating incessantly in my hand. I hold it up and see the unknown on my screen. My hands tremble slightly as I slide my finger across it to answer, putting it on speakerphone.

I don't say anything as a deep, electronic voice fills the space, causing Tony to jerk around toward me. "You take one of ours." The blood in my veins freeze. "Now we take one of yours."

The call ends, and almost immediately, I receive a new message containing a video. Tony, who has always been hacked into my phone, pulls the messages up onto the screen and presses play. The sight in front of me has bile crawling up my throat.

There, in the middle of a room, similar to our basement, is Kate, tied to a chair. Her head is slumped, but I see the crimson coating her long, blonde hair as blood trickles down. Two men enter the screen, both wearing ski masks, and look straight into the camera, flipping us off. One of them grabs her shoulder and shakes her until I hear a groan from her.

Her head lolls before she slowly lifts it, looking around the room. Her dazed look becomes panicked, and she tries to scream, but those motherfuckers have taped her mouth shut. One of them bends down in front of her and grabs her face, wrenching her head to look at the camera. He points at it with his free hand and gives us a malicious grin as he says, "You have the men on the other side of the camera to thank for this." His taunting has Tony's fist pounding the desk harder, and the screens are starting to shake in front of him, ready to topple over.

"And because we're gentlemen, we don't do to you what they did to our friend Cameron, but the end of this video will be the same as his." She screams, with the muffled sounds of her begging amplified in the microphones.

"No." My voice is no more than a croak, my grip on my hair tightening, nearly ripping it from my scalp. "No!" I scream, the sound deafening in the small room. Tony just stares at the screen, his gray eyes glowing in the screen's light, his body frozen in place.

We watch in horror as the other man in the room steps up and pulls a gun from his side, pressing it to her forehead. I watch as tears roll down her face and her body starts to convulse as she screams and fights the bindings holding her in place. The man looks at the camera and smiles, showing nothing but teeth right before he pulls the trigger and the video goes black.

CHAPTER EIGHTEEN

Lena

I'M numb as I lie in the dark, Bri wrapped in my arms, in my new room in the penthouse. We've laid in this bed together, refusing to be apart for what must be a week. The news of Kate's death brought us both to our knees and I haven't been able to take a full breath since. Bri finally cried herself to sleep tonight, my own well of tears drying out a day ago.

We both figured out to stay out of the news because the fuckers who did this have twisted the story with the media reporting that she set the apartment on fire and then died by suicide. The story is so insane that it's no surprise that people are buying it. Eating it up.

I begged Tony on my knees, nearly laid at his feet, to send the media the video, show them the truth, and let them see the evil in this town. But he just stared at me as Devin scooped me up, explained that it would do no good, and tried to console me as I lost complete control of my emotions and myself. I heard what he said: that the media is corrupt, and someone would intervene and scrub the video, but it wasn't enough for me. Tony is good, but he is only one man in a sea of Obsidian monsters.

While my whole world is shattered, Bri has been hit harder

than me. Bri and I have been friends since we were eighteen years old and were once roommates for years. When I decided to move in with Matt, she put out an ad for a roommate, and Kate came knocking.

She was there for Bri for the last five years, giving her the love that she deserves that I was too caught up in my shit to give her. They lived in that same apartment that is now nothing but ashes. Almost everything they had built, along with some of my things, are now gone.

Devin sent a crew to go through the apartment and find things that were still intact, but there was hardly anything left. There were only a few pieces of jewelry, a casserole dish, and a few pieces of clothing still in the dryer. However, they did manage to find Kate's teddy bear, which she kept on the top shelf of her closet and only took out when she needed to cry or when we watched nostalgic movies together.

He hasn't left Bri's arms since they brought it to us. It still smells of fire because Bri refuses to let them wash it, swearing that it still smells like Kate's perfume and threatening anyone who comes near it.

I keep apologizing, telling her that it's all my fault for what happened. At one point, her crying turned to screaming, telling me to shut the fuck up. That it wasn't my fault, that it was Matt's and she would have her revenge on him for what he's done to the two people she loves the most. My heart aches as I watch her curl into herself, her eyes red-rimmed, and her beautiful face shallow.

I curl myself closer to her, pressing my forehead to hers. The door clicks and soft light fills the room before someone slips in and closes it quietly. A large hand brushes my hair from my face. "Love?" Devin's voice is soft, his warm breath curling around the shell of my ear.

I don't answer because I don't know what to say, and I don't want to let Bri go. I feel the mattress dip as he slides under the duvet, pressing his hard chest to my back. His fingers brush over my arm as he presses his face into the crook of my neck. "I'm sorry," he whispers. His voice seems to crack as the words fill the space between his lips and my skin.

He's been doing this a lot this past week. My numb body flickers to life with the brushing of his hand across my face, tucking my hair behind my ears. Sometimes, he's crawled into bed like now, or he's just stood over me, brushing my hair away and tucking the duvet around me. Other times, he's just a presence in the room.

Those times, I never look because he's been in the chair at my back, and I don't want him to feel guilty for waking me, so I just lie with Bri in silence until he leaves, closing the door so quietly that it's like he wasn't even there.

He rests his hand on my waist, his thumb making small circles on my exposed skin from where my shirt has ridden up. I close my eyes but hear the door click open again, light flooding the room before going dark. I see a figure on Bri's side of the bed and feel the mattress dip as Tasha slides under the sheets. She brushes Bri's hair back, kissing her softly on the cheek, before tucking herself behind her.

"Are they going to be okay?" Devin whispers, his voice filtering past me. "It's been days, and they've barely moved."

I see Tasha raise her head, looking over at him. "Not everyone goes on a killing spree when someone they love dies, you know?" Even at a whisper, her voice is sharp. I feel Devin tense behind me, his fingers twitching against my skin.

I wonder who he lost that was so important to him. The last few days, he's been coming in here and lying with us while he thinks I'm asleep. He whispers to me about how sorry he is and promises to destroy Matt and everyone involved in this disaster. He always says he understands, but when I'm ready, we'll turn this grief into vengeance like him.

"I was here first," Devin finally replies, still in a whisper.

"I didn't know it was a race," she quips back.

I roll my eyes and shift under Devin's arm. "Do you two

mind?" I roll and look between him and Tasha. "Bri finally fell asleep and I promise if you wake her up, she will become a force like you've never seen."

The room falls silent and the tension between them settles as I roll back, pulling Bri closer, and listen to her steady breathing as tears prick behind my eyes. "She's going to be okay, right?" I ask no one in particular. "We are…were the only ones she has…had," I correct myself, the words nearly choking me as reality comes crashing back in heavy waves.

I squeeze my eyes shut, pushing back the swell of tears, as Devin brings himself closer, his warmth enveloping me. "It'll take some time," Tasha answers. "And it'll be very hard, but she has you." She pauses. "And us."

I feel my chest tighten, but this time, it's as if someone has squeezed my heart at the idea of having other people on our side. Having the family we always dreamed of.

"If you guys really love me…" Bri's voice is raspy, her words rough. She turns her head toward me and opens a swollen eye, glaring at us. "You'll either shut the fuck up or get out."

"We'll leave," I say, trying to stifle a giggle. It's the first time in days that she sounded like herself. Devin and Tasha slide out of the bed, leaving me to lean over and give her a kiss on the cheek. "Love you, B," I whisper as she rolls away, pulling the duvet beneath her chin and wiggling further under the covers.

I creep to the doorway that Devin and Tasha have already slipped through. "Hey." Bri's voice catches me right as I'm about to shut the door. Sticking my head back in, I see that she's propped up on her elbow, her red-rimmed eyes looking at me. "I love you so much, Lele." Her voice catches on my name. "Don't worry about me so much, okay? I'll be fine. I promise." She sniffs and then waves me away. "Now get the fuck out and let me sleep in peace. This room has been a fucking revolving door, and I need some alone time away from you people." A soft smile pulls at my lips, and I blow her a kiss, slipping out and closing the door behind me with a soft click.

Devin is already lounging on the sofa with Tasha in the kitchen brewing coffee. They both look at me as I stand in the doorway. I look down at myself and note that I'm only in an over-sized T-shirt of Devin's and a pair of underwear. I touch my hair and it's comparable to a rat's nest that will take some time to get out. My eyes land back on Devin, who is only in a pair of gray sweatpants that, on any other day, would have me drooling like a dog.

How can one man's body be carved to such perfection? It's fucking unfair.

"Can I use your shower?" I tug down the shirt, suddenly self-conscious of my appearance in front of him.

He stands up, the sweatpants hanging low on his hips, the V under his abs is like a neon arrow, and I'm drawn like a moth to a flame. "Let's get you cleaned up, love." He closes the distance between us and takes my hand, leading me to his room. It's clean and pristine, just like the last time I was here well over a week ago.

Flipping on the lights, the crisp, white tiles nearly burn my eyes, proof that I've been in the dark for too many days. He turns on the shower before turning to grab towels out of the massive closet; he sits them on the small stool next to the shower door.

He looks over his shoulder as he reaches in to check the water temperature. "Are you okay?" His brow furrows at me. "It's ready for you."

I tug down the shirt more; my cheeks heat because I don't even want to know what he sees now that I'm in the bright light of this bathroom that illuminates all the grime that covers my body from days of being in that bed. "Thank you." My voice is quiet as I look away from him and step sideways from the door, giving him room to leave.

His finger hooks beneath my chin, forcing my face up toward him. I didn't even hear him cross the large space and my heart thunders in my chest at his sudden touch. His blue eyes are bright, even as they narrow on me. "If you think I'm leaving you, you're sorely mistaken."

I try to look away, but he keeps his hold on my chin as my face grows even hotter. "I'm disgusting and my hair is a mess of knots. I'll be here for a while; you don't need to stay and wait for me."

His nostrils flare as he cocks his head to the side. "I've waited a week for you, what's a while longer?"

My breath hitches because even though I knew he had been checking on me periodically and climbing into bed with us, I didn't think he was actually waiting for *me*. I reach up and touch his face. The last time I looked at it, it was marred with bruises, but they're almost all gone now, with only the slightest tinge of yellow left around his eye. He presses his cheek into my palm, the slight scruff on his chin scraping against my skin, sending a tingle up my arm.

He takes my hand from his face and leads me to the now steaming shower. "Strip," he commands softly and without another thought, I find myself shucking the shirt over my head and letting my panties fall from my body. I step into the shower that's large enough to fit five or more people, the hot water hitting my skin, causing me to moan. This has to be what heaven feels like.

I close my eyes and let the warmth seep into my muscles, relaxing them one by one. I turn to find the shampoo, and instead, I'm met with a hard, chiseled chest. I gasp, my body jerking in surprise, but Devin's hands land on my hips, holding me in place. "Don't fall," he says, tightening his hold.

My hands plant onto his chest and I watch the water cascade down the planes of his muscles. The steam swirls between us, making him look ethereal in the bright light. One of his hands moves from my hip to my cheek, his eyes locked onto me. We stand there in silence, his thumb caressing the side of my face.

He drops his hands and turns, grabbing the bottle of conditioner behind him. "Turn around." His voice is soft as if he's trying not to scare a small animal. I slowly turn as he runs his hands over my tangled hair. "You have quite the mess here, love." He slowly works his fingers through my tangles, careful not to yank on my hair as he loosens them, freeing me of the infernal rat's nest I had created.

After what seems like forever, he rinses my hair with one of the shower wands, running his fingers through my now tangle-free hair. I hear him grab another bottle, this time, gently lathering shampoo onto my head. His deft fingers massage my scalp, causing another moan to fall from my lips. "That feels amazing, Devin."

He says nothing as he rinses the suds out before applying another round of conditioner, twirling it up, and securing it with a claw clip, which makes me wonder how many women he's had in this shower. I shake the thought from my mind and turn toward him and see that he's lathering up a loofah. The body wash smells like eucalyptus and mint as he runs it down my arm in small, circular motions.

"Devin, you don't have to do this." My voice has gained back some of its volume from the soothing steam, but my words are barely above a whisper. Because as much as I feel like I should be doing this myself, I don't want to. I haven't been this pampered by a man...ever.

"I know." His gaze follows the loofah as he works it over my body, cleaning away the days of bed rot. "But I want to do this for you." He looks up at me, his eyes soft and a ghost of a smile on his lips.

A soft smile pulls up on my lips because no man has ever offered to do the work for me. To care for me in this way. I watch as he continues to clean me, turning me around and exfoliating my back before taking the shower wand and rinsing it all away. His touch is gentle, but it sends electricity crackling across my skin. Waking me up.

His arms wrap around my waist from where he stands behind me, his lips barely touching my shoulder. His touch is comforting as he nuzzles into the crook of my neck. My body flares to life at his gentle caress, heat curling low in my abdomen. "Devin," I whisper his name, letting the steam carry my words around to him.

My body is waking up as my heart starts to pick up speed. The ache in my muscles went down the drain along with the soap suds, leaving me feeling fresh for the first time in days. The smell of the mint across my skin reminds me of him, sending my senses into overdrive.

He gently kisses my skin, not pushing me for anything. But right now, I want to be pushed. Pushed up against this wall as he pushes his cock between my now aching core. Pushed over the edge into fucking oblivion. "Please," I whisper, my fingers running down his arm, my nails lightly scraping his skin.

"Lena—" he starts, but I turn in his arms, wrapping mine around his neck.

"Make me forget, Devin." My voice is firm as the heat of the steam mixes with the heat that swirls between my legs. I pull him down to me, our lips a breath apart. "I *need* you."

He doesn't hesitate as his mouth crashes with mine, his tongue slipping into my mouth, sweeping through it. His kiss is hungry as his hand comes up, his fingers weaving into my hair, and he pulls my head back to deepen his kiss. His taste is intoxicating, making me dizzy as heat swirls around me, through me.

He pulls back, leading me against the shower wall. He holds me there at arm's length while I take the time to look down at his body and notice his very large, very erect cock. My hand drifts up as my mouth waters at the sight of him being so turned on, but his hand wraps around my wrist, stopping me. I whimper as he gives me a lopsided grin. "No, love," he breathes. "Tonight is about you."

He drops to his knees in front of me, the water cascading down his shoulders. His hands run up my legs, stopping at the apex of my thighs. His blue eyes burn like the hottest fire as he leans forward, his tongue sliding between my folds, my knees nearly buckling. He grips my calf and hoists one of my legs over his shoulder, opening me up to him. I press my hand against the tile to keep myself steady, watching as his pupils widen and he licks his lips. "Fucking delicious." He looks up at me. "I'm a starved man, Lena, and I am going to devour you like you're my last meal."

He nips at the inside of my thigh, swirling his tongue over the sensitive skin. My head falls back, bumping into the shower wall as my fingers slide into his hair, holding on for dear life. He works his way up to my pussy, once again running his tongue through my folds. I take in a shuddered breath as his tongue swirls around my entrance, teasing me.

"Oh God," I say, my face pointing toward the sky.

He gently sucks my clit between his teeth. I hiss as he swirls his tongue around the sensitive bud. "You can call him all you want, but he doesn't listen. So, from now on, *I* am your god." He buries his face into my pussy, licking and sucking as the heat builds between my legs. "I'm your savior and you're my fucking salvation."

He pushes a finger into me, another moan escaping my lips. "You're so fucking wet for me, Lena," he growls, adding another finger. "I can't wait to bury my cock into this sweet pussy."

"Then do it," I breathe, the challenge in my tone ringing out.

He pumps his fingers faster, my hand gripping his hair, my nails digging into his scalp. "When I fuck you, Lena," his tongue swirls my clit before he continues, "I will have you bound and gagged in my bed." He nips me, the sensation, along with his dirty words, nearly sending me over the edge. "I will fill you up with my cum and have you screaming my name, even though no one will be able to hear you with your mouth stuffed."

I look down at him, my eyes wide as I imagine myself tied up and at his mercy. He fucks me harder with his fingers before curling them, hitting my G-spot just as he sucks on my clit. I see stars and I let loose, screaming his name as I come all over his face and fingers. He continues to pump his fingers and swirl his tongue around my clit as I come down through the aftershocks.

My breathing is heavy as he spears his tongue into me, lapping up my orgasm as if it truly is his last meal. Pulling away, he immediately sticks his fingers in his mouth, making a show of licking them clean. He pulls them out with a pop, his eyes bright. "A fucking five-star meal." He gives me a wild grin, his teeth looking sharper than ever.

He lowers my leg, running his hands up my inner thighs one last time before rising to his feet. His hand grips my chin and he captures my mouth with his, sweeping his tongue across mine, making sure that I taste myself on it. His other hand snakes around my waist, pulling me to him, his hard cock pressing into my stomach. He groans as he deepens the kiss more, letting his teeth scrape across my bottom lip as he pulls back.

I'm breathless as I grip his arms and push him away. His eyes go wide as he takes a step back, flashing with panic as I lower myself to my knees this time. He moans my name as I grip his shaft, precum dripping from the tip. I stick out my tongue, my mouth watering for a taste, but his fingers weave into my hair, gripping it and holding me in place.

"Lena, you don't need—" But instead of listening to him, I pull against his hold and swirl my tongue over the head of his cock. He lets out a long, breathy moan as I continue to tease his tip. His grip loosens on my hair, but he doesn't remove his hand.

I tilt my eyes up, and through the steam, I see his eyes staring down at me, filled with lust and need. I lick my tongue up the underside of his shaft, gripping his balls and giving them a playful squeeze. "Seeing you on your knees, love, is the hottest fucking thing I've ever witnessed." He weaves his hand in my hair, tugging on the strands, sending a jolt right to my pussy. "Even on your knees, you have me at your fucking mercy."

I snake my hand up his thigh, coming around and gripping his ass. The muscles flex underneath my hand, rock hard. I pull him toward me, letting his cock sink deeper into my mouth, pushing against the back of my throat. I pull him back out, lightly scraping my teeth across his velvet skin. "Fuck," he groans, both of his hands bracing the back of my head, slightly rocking his hips.

A smirk pulls at my lips before I pull back, his cock popping from my mouth. He looks down at me, his eyes nearly glazed over with need. "Fuck my mouth, Devin." I dig my nails into his ass, slowly licking the tip, tasting him on my tongue. "Fuck my mouth and come down my throat."

He growls, the grip on my hair tightening. "Are you sure that's what you want?" His eyes darken, still swirling with lust.

I nod, because no words could possibly describe how badly I want this.

"Open your mouth and stick out your tongue." He wrenches my head back and I do what he says. "Tap my thigh twice if it's too much."

It won't be.

He jerks his hips forward, roughly holding my head as his cock slips past my lips, hitting the back of my throat. I keep my eyes on him and watch as the realization hits him as hard as my orgasm did.

Because I don't have a gag reflex.

A Cheshire grin pulls at his lips, his teeth gleaming in the light. "You are such a dirty fucking slut, love." His voice is nearly a growl. "Full of dirty little secrets, and pretty soon, my cum." He slams his cock into my mouth, and another jolt runs to my clit as he slides down my throat.

He doesn't hold back as he fucks me, only pulling out to let just enough oxygen into my lungs. My vision blurs as tears prick my eyes. "So fucking beautiful," he grunts out. "Your mouth was fucking made for me." He thrusts harder, his grip on my hair, pain prickling across my scalp. "Such a good fucking girl taking my cock like this."

I snake my hand between my legs and rub my clit, looking for release as the pressure builds between them, but he yanks my head back. "Hands off," he grits out before returning to his assault on my mouth. I moan as his rhythm becomes erratic. One, two, three more thrusts and he's coming down my throat. His head falls back, and he moans my name as I swallow every last drop, putting the taste of him to memory.

He pulls me to my feet, his grip tight as I loop my arms around his neck. He pulls me in for another kiss, tasting himself and making me lightheaded in the process. He pulls back, scraping his teeth across my bottom lip, nipping it. "I'm going to spread you out on my bed and feast on your pussy until you pass out."

He kisses me hard as I press myself against him, his cock hardening again. He turns off the water, drying me off and wrapping me in a towel. His eyes flick past my head toward the ceiling, but before I can turn, he's scooping me up and carrying me out of the bathroom, straight to his bed. Laying me out just like he promised, ripping the towel from me.

"A meal *and* dessert." He winks as he lowers his head between my legs, fucking me with his fingers and tongue, ravaging me like a wild animal.

And even though we've been alone in here the entire time, I can't shake the feeling that we're being watched.

CHAPTER NINETEEN

DEVIN

THE THOUGHT of Tony hearing her moans makes my cock throb even harder. He'll no doubt be furious about this, but I'm not above falling to my knees, groveling at his feet, and begging for forgiveness. Lena's obviously in a delicate state and I should be the one to encourage her to take it easy, but fuck me, this woman knows what she wants. I can tell she's been starved of a good orgasm, along with an escape from reality, and I'm more than willing to give her both.

My cock aches, ready to explode at any moment, as I stare at her pussy, imagining what it would feel like to have it wrapped around me. Her mouth was like fucking heaven, and to find out she doesn't have a gag reflex makes the possibilities nearly endless with everything I want to do to her. She looked so fucking beautiful on her knees in front of me, my cock between her teeth. Even when I slide it down her throat, she has no idea what kind of control she has over me.

It would be so fucking easy to slide between her legs, right into her dripping pussy, but she's in no state to make the decision to be properly fucked. Not to mention, I will do exactly what I said I would for our first time. I'm a man of my fucking word, even if they're possessive and deranged.

I grip her thighs and pull her closer to me, my tongue devouring her sweet pussy like it's the first time. Her back arches as her body shudders, pressing herself into my face. Her quiet panting has the monster in me wanting to make her scream my name, to play the game and play it fucking dirty.

I watch as she squirms under my touch, my fingers playing her like a fiddle. She sees me as her knight in shining armor when I'm just as much a beast as the ones we're fighting against.

I pump my fingers into her pussy, her need soaking my hand and dripping onto the sheets. Ones that I'm never washing again.

I press two fingers into her and she moans, her hands sinking into my hair, pulling my face even further into her sweet center. If I had to choose a way to die, it would be by suffocating between her legs as I devour her, letting her pussy steal the last breath from my lungs.

Her legs shake as I spear my tongue into her, pressing my thumb to her clit, her hips thrusting for more pressure to her needy cunt.

"On your stomach," I growl, rising to my knees. She looks down her body at me, her pupils dilated as lust swirls around her glowing, amber irises. She rolls onto her stomach, looking over her shoulder at me. "Get on all fours." She rises, her whole body trembling, the inside of her thighs glistening in the low light.

Turning around, I lie flat on my back, my legs hooked over the edge of the bed as I stare up at her, my mouth watering. "Have a seat, love."

Her head drops, looking at me, her impeccable tits nearly blocking her view. She slowly brings herself back, her core hovering right above me. Grabbing her thighs, I lower her onto my face, immediately licking and sucking. She hovers, but I yank her down, forcing her full weight on my face. Now this, this is fucking heaven.

"Devin." Her sweet voice whimpers my name as I fuck my tongue in and out of her. I swirl it around her clit, once again coating my tongue with her sweet desire.

I bring my hand around her ass and slap it hard as I continue to swirl my tongue around her center. She hisses, her ass tensing with the sting, before I rub the sensitive skin, her center relaxing more on my face. If I wasn't wholly consuming her, I would praise her, tell her what a good girl she fucking was, but I don't want to stop.

I open my eyes and look up to see her playing with her nipples, pinching the tight buds between her fingers. Another thing on my list is to fuck those tits and forcing her mouth to be open for every thrust, her tongue licking my cock.

I groan, the sound vibrating up my throat, making her hips buck.

I press my thumb into her as my tongue flicks at her swollen clit, coating it in her cum. Pulling my thumb out, I bring it to her ass, coating her tight hole. She stiffens and stops riding my face. I circle around the hole, pressing my thumb against it. I groan again because she's so fucking tight.

"Devin, I—" she starts, but I refuse to listen. Because if this woman is about to tell me that she's never had her ass filled, I'm going to hunt down every man she's ever been with and drag them back to the basement and show them exactly how they should have been treating her before I end their pathetic lives. How *dare* those fuckers ever deny her any sort of pleasure.

"Relax, love." My voice vibrates through her, and she nearly melts with pleasure on my face. I press my thumb against her hole, going in slowly. She hisses, but once I'm past the knuckle, she relaxes back more.

"Oh my God." Her ass tightens around my thumb as I slowly work it further in. She's fighting against her body, the invasion of my finger in her hole, and the immense pleasure I know she's feeling.

Once she's stretched around me, I wiggle my thumb inside of her, her gasp ringing out as she thrusts her hips.

"Devin." *Fuck*. My dick is so hard that just the sound of my name on her lips has my balls tightening. I might come if she says it in that breathy voice again.

I suck hard on her clit as I press my thumb as deep as it will go, making her cry out. I watch as she pinches her nipples, her hips bucking against me. I don't let up and her whimpering grows louder. I slap her ass with my other hand, her back arching as I do it again, sure to leave my marks across her skin.

"Devin." I could listen to her moan my name until the devil himself drags me to Hell. "I'm going…I'm going to come."

I keep it up, scraping my nails across her ass, causing her hand to drop into my hair, tugging at my scalp. My balls tighten even more as she uses my hair like a horse's rein, riding me like a wild steed, but nowhere near taming me. Her thrusts become erratic, and her pants grow louder as her moans filter through the room. I nip at her sensitive skin and scrape my teeth across her clit, swirling my tongue to smooth the pain to pleasure, keeping up the assault on her pussy until she finally breaks.

Her scream of pleasure fills the room, ringing out as her cum drenches my face. I swirl my tongue around her clit as she comes down from her orgasm, her hip thrusts slowing, keeping up the friction for as long as she can. Her body spasms as I pull my thumb from her ass, my dick twitching at the thought of what it will feel like to stuff her full, my precum leaking down the side of me.

She nearly slumps over as she pulls herself from my face. I lick my lips and taste her, coating my tongue with it. She's become my favorite meal, and I will enjoy it every chance I can.

I sit up and watch her over my shoulder as she turns on

her knees and falls back onto the bed, breathless. Her eyes are filled with lust and contentment. It's the most relaxed she's looked in nearly two weeks.

She looks toward my full erect cock, that's soaked with precum, and licks her lips. I give her a grin but palm myself. "No, love, you need to sleep."

She whimpers as I stand from the bed, going to the bathroom to wash my hands, but keeping her cum on my face. It's like a drug that I can't get enough of it. She looks toward the door as if half expecting someone to walk in, and even though it's unlocked, it remains tightly closed.

Exiting the bathroom, I take in the woman sprawled out on my bed. Her curves were sculpted by a god, and if I knew which one, I'd thank them personally. "You have five minutes to yourself and it's off to bed with you."

Her eyes are already drooping with sleep as she drags herself to the edge of the bed, her feet dropping to the floor. It looks like it takes all her energy to carry herself across the room. "There's a toothbrush on the sink for you. Use whatever you need."

She comes up and wraps her arms around my neck, brushing her lips across mine. She pulls back for a moment before leaning back in, running her tongue across them, a soft moan coming from her.

I grip her ass, pressing my still erect cock against her. "Make a noise like that again," I growl, but she just chuckles, exhaustion causing it to fall heavy from her tongue.

Releasing her, I step back and gesture toward the bathroom door. "The sooner you finish in there, the sooner you can hop back into bed with me."

Her eyes brighten as she steps past me, my hand connecting with her ass, the slap echoing across the tile. "You animal." Her gasp causes my lips to curl into a cruel smile. By her reaction, if she thinks that's rough, she has another thing coming when I can fully get my hands, and dick, on her.

I let her have a moment of privacy, but not too much. I deliberately leave the door cracked open so I can listen to her every move. I prepare the bed, pulling back the sheets so she can find the perfect spot she wants to sleep in. I slide on my boxer briefs to make sure she understands that her resting is far more important than what my cock wants.

Switching off the light, she returns to the bed, sliding in and making herself comfortable. I slide in behind her, curling myself around her, my still hard cock pressing into her back. I have no intention of using him with her anymore tonight, but if he can't fucking calm down, then I'll be forced to take matters into my own hands. Literally.

She groans softly as she presses into me, her ass wiggling against my dick, fucking teasing me. I nip at her shoulder, her yelp making me chuckle. Her body finally relaxes as I pull her closer to me. I smooth her hair from her face, tucking it between us as I nuzzle into her neck. Even though she smells of my body wash, her scent is still intoxicating, making my mouth water.

I snap my fingers, and the lights dim like an artificial sunset until we're in complete darkness.

"Fancy." Her voice is heavy with exhaustion.

"Efficient." I pull her even tighter, lightly kissing every inch of skin I can reach and thinking about the rest that I can't.

She yawns, her hand coming up to cover her mouth. She melts into me, her hand resting on top of mine where it lies across her stomach.

"Hey, Devin?" she whispers into the dark. The way she says my name even as sleep starts to pull her under does something to me that nearly grips my lurking monster by the throat.

"Yes, love?"

"Thank you." The words are simple, but I don't miss the slight catch in her voice.

I give her a squeeze, still peppering her skin with soft kisses. I want to tell her that she will never have to thank me for anything, that what she does to my nearly dead heart, reminding it that there's still something beneath my ribs, is more than I could ever give to her. And I will continue to bathe in the blood of our enemies and burn the world down for her.

But the words lodge in my throat, making it impossible to speak.

Instead, I curl into her, her response a soft sigh as sleep overtakes her. Her breathing steadies, evening out as she drifts off to sleep. Watching her, I let myself mold into her for a while, before begrudgingly pulling myself away, slipping quietly out of the bed.

As much as my body is screaming for me to crawl back under the covers and cover her body with mine, I have work to do. Pulling back on my sweats, I cross to the closet and pull out a T-shirt and a pair of my boxer briefs, laying them on the bench at the end of the bed for her in the morning. While I wouldn't mind her walking around the penthouse naked all day every day, too many people are in and out at the moment. Soon, she will have that luxury of privacy, but for now, seeing her in my clothes makes me nearly feral.

Leaning over the bed, I press a soft kiss on her cheek. I might have imagined it, or the dim light is playing tricks on me, but I could have sworn that her lips tilted into a soft smile. The urge to crawl back in with her is even greater than before. She has me wrapped around her fucking finger.

I take a forced step back, making my way to the door. My hand on the handle, I look over my shoulder at her again. Her breathing is steady as sleep weighs heavily upon her, gently guiding her into dreamland.

Crossing the threshold, I quietly close the door behind me, the latch clicking close. The main living space is dark, the only light coming from the city outside the wall of windows, casting a warm glow on the space.

I don't miss the large, dark figure slouched down in the high back chair. His eyes are hot and hungry, with his legs spread wide, showing off his very hard cock that's pressing against his pants. One hand is clutching the armrest while the other palms his crotch, trying to tame his erection. A smirk tugs at my lips as I stand there, his gaze roving over me and stopping at my waistband.

He's discarded his usual tactical mask, donning a material one printed with the mouth of a skeleton. He's been wearing it around the penthouse at night, worried that someone will see him without something covering his face, especially now that we have two women staying here.

His eyes flicker back up to mine. "What the fuck are you doing?" he growls lowly.

Keeping the smirk on my face, I turn away from him and head toward the kitchen. Coffee will be the only thing keeping me from sliding back into bed with Lena.

My hips are rammed into the edge, hard enough that I know it will fucking bruise. Tony's arm wraps around me, pinning my arms against my sides as his hand wraps around my throat and his fingers press into my pulse point, noting my now thundering heartbeat. His erection presses against my ass as he holds me tight against him, my own dick thickening.

His warm breath filters through the mask on his face, curling around my ear. He inhales deeply, his chest expanding against my back. "You fucking smell like pussy."

I turn my head, my mouth only a breath from his. "Would you like for me to smell like something else?" The words tumble from my lips as my heart gallops in my chest.

He stiffens, but I don't miss how he presses his cock harder against my ass, how easy it would be for him to press me down onto the counter and fuck me. Tony and I have danced a delicate dance for years, sharing plenty of men and women, but we've been careful never to cross that line.

Anger rolls off him. "Wipe that smirk off your fucking face and answer me. What the *fuck* are you doing?"

The growl in his voice vibrates through me, making my dick twitch. Fuck, I'm so fucking hard, and the tension swirling around us makes it damn near impossible to breathe.

"Helping her forget." My voice is breathless as he squeezes my throat, the air almost depleted from my lungs.

"Forget what?" he bites. "Forget that she's a pawn in this sick fucking game that Obsidian is playing? That her life hangs in the balance?"

I look at him sidelong, his grip on my neck holding me in place. "If that's what you think she is, then yes," I wheeze, my vision blurring on the edges as he keeps me on the edge of consciousness.

His other hand slides down my body, gripping my cock through my pants. "You need to learn to fucking control your urges." He squeezes and I gasp, his fingers curling around my windpipe. "They're a fucking hazard to our cause, *Devin*."

"Teach…me…a…lesson," I squeeze the words out around his hand, my limbs starting to tingle.

He squeezes my throat as he grips my cock, completely closing off my windpipe, euphoria taking over. What seems like a lifetime can only be mere seconds before he lets go, making me almost come in my pants.

Gasping, my palms land on the counter, supporting me as I choke on air as it rushes back into my lungs. The dark edges of my vision lighten, the lack of his warm body against mine sending a chill down my spine.

He's halfway across the apartment, heading to his room, when I finally find my voice. "She's going to be the one, you know." I wrap my own fingers around my neck, the skin tender.

He stops with his hand reaching for the handle. He peeks

over his shoulder, his skeleton mask bright in the city lights. "The one, what?" He cocks a brow as he looks me over, his voice rough.

I palm my throbbing cock, my other hand still clutching my throat. "The one to finally break us." His eyes drift down, his fingers curling around the handle as his others curl into a fist. His stony facade cracks right before my eyes.

Without a word, he barges into his room, closing the door behind him with a soft thud.

The whooshing of my veins with every rapid heartbeat is loud in my ears, filling any semblance of silence. Seeing him lose control has my hand sliding past the waistband of my sweats, firmly gripping my cock. I nearly stumble to the same chair that he was in just moments ago, dropping myself down and pulling my throbbing cock out. Precum drips down the side as I slide my hand up and down my shaft, coating myself in my seed.

Biting my knuckles, I stifle a moan as I feel my balls tightening and I pull up my shirt, exposing my abs. That motherfucker knew exactly what he was doing and left me hanging out to dry.

My rhythm falters as heat gathers low and my balls constrict. I drop my head back, biting my cheek until the metallic taste of blood covers my tongue, as I come all over my stomach, stroking myself through the intense orgasm.

I stare up at the skylights in the ceiling, the glow of city lights shining through them, blocking any view of the stars above. I suck in a deep breath and look to Tony's door, flipping it off for being the selfish asshole that he is and not finishing what he fucking started.

CHAPTER TWENTY

Lena

THIS IS the third morning in a row that I've been woken up to Devin devouring me. His tongue flicking over my throbbing clit is what sprung my eyes open. He raises his head from between my legs, his blond locks are tousled, and his blue eyes are bright. "Good morning, love." His voice is still thick from sleep as he gives me a smirk and lowers his head back between my legs.

Gripping my thighs, he pulls me closer, spearing his tongue into me. "Devin," I moan as he replaces his tongue with a finger, curling it to hit my G-spot. With every flick of his tongue on my pulsing clit, he walks me one step closer to the edge before I finally fall over. I reach for the pillow next to me and smother my face in it, smothering the sounds of my release as my thighs squeeze against his skull.

Devin crawls over my body, caging me in as he rips the pillow from my face, closing his mouth over mine. His kiss is deep as I taste myself on his tongue. He pulls back and I look down his body, the only thing between us is his boxer briefs, his cock fully erect with a wet spot. "I need you inside of me," I beg as I rake my nails down his hard chest. And just like the last three mornings, he's ignored me, only to cover my mouth with his.

His fingers float up my side, pushing up his T-shirt, the only thing that I've been wearing, leaving goosebumps in their wake. I moan into his mouth as his thumb brushes over my peaked nipples, the sensitive bud sending a jolt between my legs. I run my hands down his abs, hooking the band of his briefs and pulling them down until his cock springs free. Precum glistens on the tip, making my mouth water.

"Fuck me. *Please.*" It's a quiet plea but an absolute need because even though his tongue and fingers can help me find release, I want him buried inside of me. I want to feel him deep as he takes me stroke for stroke.

He lowers his head to my breast, scraping his teeth across my nipple. My back arches into him, sucking the tender bud into his mouth. "Such a needy girl," he teases before nipping me, a hiss rushing through my teeth. "I love to hear you beg for my cock."

I reach between us, but his hand catches my wrist before I can grip him. He tsks as he brings it back up and presses it to my breast. "Press your tits together," he growls as a drop of precum drips onto my stomach.

I do what he asks and watch as he lifts himself up to yank off his briefs completely, tossing them to the side before sliding up and straddling me, his cock inches from my lips. "Lower your head and hold out your tongue." I stare up at him, my brows furrowing in confusion. His hand wraps around my throat, giving it a light squeeze. "I'm going to fuck your tits, Lena." His voice is smooth, his eyes bright as his thumbs caresses up my jawline. "And I'm going to come all over them and claim them as mine."

I'm panting, my pussy dripping as my clit throbs when he removes his hand, lines himself up, and pushes himself through. His dripping precum gives enough lubrication that it doesn't take much effort. "Lift your head." I raise my head as he leans forward, shoving the pillow beneath it. "Keep your head tilted and that dirty mouth open. Tongue out." I do it just as he pumps his cock between my breasts, his head sliding over my tongue.

He groans as he picks up the pace, his cock hitting my tongue harder and harder with every thrust. "Fuck," he groans, louder this time. His abs constrict right as his rhythm falters. Reaching down, he grips his shaft, pulling his cock from my breasts before coming all over them. Making good on his promise and marking me as his.

He smears his cum across my chest and over my breasts. "A fucking masterpiece." His voice is low as he pinches my nipples, the sharp pain coursing straight to my core, making my clit pulse.

He's playing a game by not fucking me. A game that I know I'll never win until he's ready for me to, and even then, it's on his terms. But, unlike any of my former partners, he's far from selfish. He's made me come more times in the past three days on his tongue and fingers alone than I did in the five years I was with Matt. He was only about taking care of himself and I usually found myself getting myself off long after he either fell asleep or left for a "meeting".

Devin's mouth closes around my clit, sucking on it and pulling me from my thoughts. "Devin," I moan, "we need to get up."

He looks up, his mouth pulled into a devilish grin. "We'll get up when I get you off one more time." He licks up my core, my hips bucking as his tongue flicks my swollen clit. "Just one more snack before breakfast."

He lowers his head and sends me into a frenzy as he makes me come again. He slides from the bed and lifts me, carrying me to shower to reluctantly wash away his cum and the smell of sex.

DEVIN PULLS the bedroom door open, and the mid-morning light nearly blinds me as we step into the living room. "So nice of you to join us." Bri's voice hits me from where she's sitting at the island, her brows furrowed and her arms crossed.

I feel myself pale as I look from her to where Tony sits at his desk, eyes glued to his computer screens, his muscles tense.

Bri stands and crosses the room. She's dressed in black jeans and an off the shoulder crop top tee. Her bad girl style always on display. She reaches me, arms still crossed, and I can feel Devin tense next to me.

"Bri..."

She holds up a hand, shaking her head. "We've been sitting out here listening to you two fuck for the last hour, and while I'm happy that you're finally getting the attention you deserve, only one of us has been enjoying it." She cuts a look in Tony's direction, and I watch his shoulders tense, but he still doesn't look away from his screens.

What the hell is she talking about?

Tony?

She's insane to even suggest such a thing. He obviously loathes the fact that I'm in this apartment, sharing the same air as him. It has him in a constantly shitty mood. He barely looks in my direction, and when he does, his eyes are always darkening as if I'm the fox that was let loose in the hen house. I would have thought that after events that have played out over the last few weeks, he would have finally gotten it through his head that I want Matt gone as much as they do.

Which begs the question, other than for me, why *do* they want Matt gone? I've been so lost in grief and Devin's distractions that I haven't thought about why they are so hellbent on taking down Obsidian when it's nearly half their clientele. Their influence runs deep in the club, and while it seems to be a place of neutral power, there's a lot of blackmail and bribes happening, both in and out of this building.

"I want to leave." Bri's voice cuts through my thoughts, pulling me back into reality, her words slamming into me.

"Leave?" The word makes my mouth dry. "Bri, I'm sorry, we'll…"

Devin steps between us, looking down at her. "It's not safe for you to leave." He steps closer to Bri, doing his best to intimidate her, but she's not one to fall for those kinds of tactics. "We're not losing anyone else."

She pokes her finger into his chest, her face flushing as her anger rises. "I'm not your fucking prisoner." Her words are sharp, her grief falling into anger.

Devin looks at where her finger is poking him before cutting his gaze back to hers. He leans down, their faces merely inches apart. "No, but you can be, and it won't be as luxurious as what you have now." His words seem to slap her, her mouth hanging slack as she stares at him, face paling at the promise in his tone. "So don't push me, Brianna, or you will get your wish to leave this apartment, but not in the way you want."

"*What* is going on in *here?*" Tasha's voice purrs as she leans against the doorway. She's dressed in an immaculate maroon pantsuit, with nothing under the jacket, showing off her perfect cleavage in a way that only she could pull off. Her heels now click on the floor as she crosses into the kitchen. She looks stunning like always and I don't miss the way that Bri shifts in her presence, as if she's in the presence of royalty and not sure if she should bow at her feet or kiss her.

She pulls Bri away and steps in her place, staring right up at Devin as he towers over her. "Because I know that you're not threatening a woman. Let alone a guest in *our* house."

Devin straightens, his body stiffening at her accusation. "No," he bites out. "I was explaining to her how—"

Tasha grabs his jaw, halting his words. "I heard enough, *Dev*."

She looks behind her at Bri, who is now standing a few feet away, her hands balled into fists at her side. "She will come live with me." She turns back to Devin, her eyes glittering. "The sexual tension in this place is suffocating." Winking, she drops her hand from his face, her anger dissipating right before our eyes.

I look between her and Devin, waiting for more retorts, but the room is nothing but silence for a beat.

"Can I really stay with you?" Bri's voice is full of wonder as she steps toward Tasha.

Tasha holds Devin's gaze, a silent conversation finishing between them before she turns on her heel and faces Bri. "Of course, I have an extra room with an ensuite that would be perfect for you. And it's on prime real estate."

"That would be amazing." She bounces on the balls of her feet like a little girl. "I can't wait to get the hell out of this building. Where do you live?" She claps her hands in front of her and presses them to her chest.

Tasha tilts her head down, looking straight at the floor. "Not far."

Bri looks down and groans, covering her face with her hand. "You mean you fucking live here, too?" Her hand slides down, her arm dropping at her side. "I didn't know when I came to stay here that I was moving into a fucking cult compound." She throws her arms up. "What's next, I'm gonna have to drink the Kool-Aid or sleep with the leader?"

Devin tenses, but a laugh fills the room. *My* laugh. I throw my head back, the laughter spills from my lips, vibrating my throat and tickling my tongue. I slap a hand to my mouth trying to quiet my outburst, but I feel a large hand wrap around my wrist and remove it. Devin's eyes are bright as he takes me in, cupping my face. "That was beautiful." He's nearly whispering as he leans down, kissing the corner of my mouth.

I look past him and see Bri smiling, a true smile on her face, one that I haven't seen in weeks. Devin turns toward her. "Say something like that again." The wonderment in his eyes and the command to Bri has another laugh bubbling over. He watches me closely as the laugh fades away, leaving a small smile on my face. "A symphony." He kisses the other corner of my mouth before pulling away.

I hear Tony's chair shift, and I see that he's looking at me, his gray eyes dark under his hood. But for the first time since I got here, there seems to be a little bit of light glimmering in the shadows. He blinks and it's gone, right back to the dark expression he wears day to day.

"Want me to show you your new digs?" Tasha's voice rings out, looping her arm with Bri's. "It's a whole floor down, and thanks to soundproofing, we'll never have to hear anything that goes on above or below us." She winks at me before turning and leading Bri to the door.

"Oh, and don't forget about the show tonight," she says over her shoulder to Devin. She turns her body in Tony's direction, looking him up and down. "And fucking dress appropriately. There *is* a dress code, and it applies to *everyone*." She stares down her nose at him before he turns his attention away from her and back on his computer.

She smirks and is almost through the door when Devin calls out to her, "Oh, I didn't forget." He steps back, pulling me into his side. "And a little birdie told me that Nate is coming into town tonight and he *rarely* misses a show."

She drops Bri's arm and turns, a look of panic flashing across her face, but in a blink, it's gone. She raises her chin and flips her hair over her shoulder nonchalantly. "The more the merrier, I suppose."

She steps through the threshold, Bri on her heels, and lets the door slam closed behind her.

I look up at him. "Who is Nate?" I ask curiously. He must be someone important to have flustered Tasha like that.

Devin shrugs as he leads me to the island. "Just the owner."

I halt my steps, yanking his arm. "The owner is coming here. *Tonight*? Why?"

Devin grins as he turns, opening the fridge and pulling out ingredients to make breakfast. "I may have tipped him off about Tasha's show tonight." Facing me, he says, "And I felt like it might be time to let him know what's truly going on. He's been asking a lot of fucking questions lately."

I cock my head to the side. "He doesn't know anything about what's been happening here? Where has he been this whole time?"

He lays out strips of bacon into the hot pan, the sizzling sound filling the room. "He's the only heir to a real estate mongrel who keeled over unexpectedly, and now he must run the family business. Flying across the world and checking in on the properties and investments. Rubbing elbows with other billionaires." He watches me. "He doesn't have time to worry about the organized crime happening here when we're taking care of it and intentionally leaving him out of the loop."

"What's his name? Would I have heard of him?"

"Nate Bennett, the President and CEO of Bennett Enterprises. He's the charming 'Billionaire Heir' as the media likes to call him."

Devin sounds nearly exhausted after that long winded title introduction, but I'm curious about a man who jets across the world and owns a club in a place like this. Though, I do recall the headlines of when he took over, his dazzling smile, and his rich boy aura in every tabloid photo. Devin cracks eggs into a bowl, whisking them before adding salt and pepper. "So, what are you going to tell him?" I ask. "Won't he be upset that you didn't tell him before now?"

He sits down the bowl and walks around the island, turning me in my seat. He puts his hands on the countertop, caging me in. "You're asking a lot of questions about another man, love. Should I be worried?" His tone is teasing, but there's an edge to it. "Because outside of this apartment, I don't fucking share."

I gulp, but he pulls back and laughs before I can say anything. "Enough about Nate, you'll meet him sooner or later." He's back at the stove, flipping the bacon. "Tonight's show has a dress code and Tasha is having an outfit delivered for you to wear. Nothing but the best for you."

I cock my head to the side. "What show are we going to? Who will be there?" Faces of the men that Matt would keep around flash through my mind. Who else is he connected to that could give him an opportunity to watch for me?

Removing the bacon from the pan, he plates it before moving on to omelets. "It's invite only and that's Tasha's responsibility to hand pick her guests from a closely curated list. Anyone who's anyone could be there tonight. For the right price."

I feel the anxiety crawling across my skin. What if Matt got to people who were once allies and Tasha doesn't know? I could be a sitting duck and if anything goes wrong, who knows what will happen.

Sprinkling cheese into the pan, he flips the egg mixture, keeping them fluffy. "And don't worry." He looks up, clearly sensing my unease. "Security will be at its tightest in the Underground tonight."

He slides the giant omelet and bacon in front of me, and I inhale the delicious scent. It's my new favorite breakfast, especially since I wasn't one to eat breakfast. It's usually nothing more than a granola bar or a smoothie. Matt was always on me about watching my figure, and I'm now realizing what I was missing out on.

Someone knocks on the door, causing Tony to rise. He's there in what seems like a few steps, wrenching the door open. A young woman stands there, staring back at him, holding a garment bag and a shiny, black gift bag. She's dressed in tight jeans and a corset top, her heels a minimum of 6" tall. Even with that extra height, she barely meets Tony's chest. She raises her arms as if she's presenting a crown to a queen. "For Miss Taylor," she says sweetly. "Compliments of Tasha."

She stays put until Tony pulls his wallet out of his back pocket, hands her a bill, and then takes the bags from her. She smiles, shoves the money into her back pocket, and saunters away back to the elevator.

Tony lets the door fall closed, holding the items like they're going to bite his hand off. I slide from the barstool, Tony's eyes watching my every move like he's tracking his prey, as I cross to where he's standing next to the door. I hold out my arms, but he doesn't move. His gray eyes look down at me and I feel heat curl in my abdomen as his gaze slowly moves down my body, taking in every inch of me as if he's looking down the nose of his enemy. Sizing me up.

I reach out for the clothes in his hands. "Thank you, Tony." My voice comes out quieter than I anticipated, but it's like he doesn't even notice I said anything. My hands hover over the bags dangling from his hand, and I'm unsure if I should take them or hold out my arms. He seems to be frozen, his eyes going icy under his hood.

I admire his ability to completely shut off his emotions from everyone, but I just wish that he would give me something to make me feel like he doesn't hate me. My fingers lightly brush against his as they curl around the garment bag. His free hand comes up and grips my wrist, yanking me toward him.

I'm almost flush against his chest, the only thing between

us is the bags. He lowers his head, his mask inches from my face as he watches me, waiting for my reaction. What he doesn't know is that I've been handled worse than this for just breathing wrong. Accidentally touching someone who knowingly considers me their enemy is more of a reason for this reaction.

"*T.*" Devin's voice is a warning, but he doesn't seem to move because Tony's eyes never leave mine.

I don't move and just let him hold me in place. I listen to his steady breathing that filters through his mask, noting the small scar that's cut through his eyebrow. The sweet scent of his vape mixed with his skin's clean scent rushes up my nose with every breath I take. I fight the urge to reach up and touch the ridges of his mask, but unless I want to make this situation worse, I keep my free arm at my side.

"T, let her go." Devin's voice seems closer, but not by much. I let Tony keep me in his grip, his fingers feeling my racing pulse as his touch burns through my skin right into my veins. Electricity wraps around my body, tiny jolts shooting right to my core. The heat in his eyes matches the heat curling in my abdomen.

The seconds tick by as we stand there, just looking at one another. I wonder what he's thinking and whether it's the same dirty thoughts that I've been having as I wait for him to burst through the doors while Devin's head is between my legs, wanting to join us. *Or* maybe he's figuring out a way to kill me and make it look like an accident. The latter seems to be the more plausible choice.

He sucks in a deep breath before he uncurls his fingers from around my wrist, taking a full step back, his arm still extended toward me. He loosens his grip on the bags, and I slide them from his hand, bringing them into my chest. Taking me in one more time, he huffs out a breath and is gone, the front door slamming closed behind him as he leaves in a hurry.

I continue to stare at where he was just standing, as if I had just seen a ghost. Devin's arm encircles my waist, pulling me against his hard chest. "Are you okay, love?" His warm breath curls around the shell of my ear as his other arm comes around my waist, both squeezing me.

I look over my shoulder at him, my face hot. "Why does he hate me so fucking much?" It's nearly a sob as the words tumble from my lips. He loosens his grip on my waist, letting me turn to him. Burying my face in his chest, my words are muffled. "I don't want him to hate me because I was in love with a monster."

Devin's hand strokes through my hair as he comforts me, tears gathering in my eyes. "He doesn't hate you." He wraps his arms tightly around me, hugging me even more to him. "He's complicated and seems to have the ability to project that onto other people. He'll come around, eventually. One way or another." He guides my head back, closing his mouth over mine, and smothering my doubts with a deep kiss.

CHAPTER TWENTY-ONE

Tony

"WHAT IN THE actual fuck were you doing up there?" Devin's voice rings into my ear after he snuck up on me and ripped my headphones from my head.

He's lucky that I didn't react to his hostile move and accidentally killed him. I fucking hate it when people touch me or my things, and he nearly crossed the line. It's why I'm always in control when I'm fucking someone—usually from behind or with their hands bound to where they can't reach for me. There have been very few times that I've let anyone have control and I learned my fucking lesson.

"She *touched* me."

Devin raises a brow at me. "That's it? You yanked her even closer to you because she *touched* you?"

This motherfucker needs to mind his own fucking business. He thinks that just because his sociopathic ass has been able to figure people out enough over the years that he can read me thoroughly. And even though we can have near silent conversations because we've existed in the same setting for years, he has no idea what kind of thoughts still plague my mind.

"Fucking leave," I say gruffly, putting my headphones back

on my head to drown out his bullshit. I turn back and squat down, curling my fingers around the hex bar.

"She thinks you hate her, you know." His flat tone burrows under my skin.

I don't look over my shoulder, refusing to see what kind of expression he has on his face. "Maybe I do." I lift the bar, focusing on my reps and waiting for him to get the fucking hint that I don't want to talk and leave.

The gym is on the fourth floor of the club. It's on a private floor but offers some employees access to extra rooms if they're here late, a few hot tubs, and a gym. Some staff stay here permanently in curated apartments, preferring to be closed off from the rest of the world like we are, but mostly, it's an empty floor.

This gym, however, is my private gym. Only a few have the right access to let themselves in. *Apparently*, I need to remove Devin from the list or block him while I'm in here if he's going to interrupt me like this. Invade my fucking space.

I can still sense him behind me, my skin burning from where I know he's staring at me. I continue to ignore him because eventually he will leave, and if he doesn't, then I'll fucking throw him out on his ass. Our relationship might be complicated, but we have, for the most part, figured out our boundaries.

My music cuts from my headphones and I drop the weights to my feet. *Motherfucker*. I turn and see that he's holding my phone in his hand, screen out to show that my music is paused. His eyes are narrowed on me, the heat in his gaze burning across my exposed skin as he takes me in. I'm only in gym shorts and a cut off tee, my hood and mask left in my gym bag, leaving my expressions out in the open.

"Put the fucking phone down and I won't cut your hand off for touching what's *mine*." My breaths are heavy from the weights, but my heart is thundering as if I just ran for miles.

Devin smirks at me. This motherfucker doesn't take

anything I say seriously, and even though he holds a lot of power in this place, he has no idea what I'm truly capable of. He only knows the bits and pieces I've fed him through the years to shut him the fuck up. To silence his nagging questions.

Is he my only real friend in the world? Basically. Do I want to throw him from the rooftop when he's being a cocky little bastard and getting on my last fucking nerve? Absolutely.

"You're being insufferable." He rolls his eyes, curling his fingers around my phone and holding it at his side. "You don't think I can't see right through that fucking mask you hide behind all the time?"

I step over the hex bar toward him, my fingers curling into fists at my side. "You don't know fucking shit, *pretty boy*." I close the distance between us, our chests nearly touching as I look down my nose at him. "Now get the fuck out."

He nudges forward and warmth fills my chest as he presses against me. "So, you think I'm pretty?"

I suck in a breath through my nose, because he's pushing my limits, and he fucking knows it. "Fuck you," I bite.

"Would you like to do it with or without Lena?"

I growl in response, the sound like rumbling thunder. I'm ready to unleash on him, but he doesn't fucking shut up. "Admit it, Tony, she's getting under your skin, and you don't know what to do about it. You hide behind your fucking computer and watch what's unfolding instead of stepping the fuck up and getting in on it." He presses his chest harder to mine, our noses brushing as he sucks the breath from my lungs. "And I know you fucking want in on it. I see the way you look at her. At *us*."

I grip his neck that he has extended right in front of me, his Adam's apple bobbing each time he swallows. Wrapping my fingers around his throat, it bobs against my palm. "Shut the fuck up," I enunciate each word, attempting to use the intimidation tactics that I already know never work on him.

"Make me, *big guy*." He snaps his teeth, showing them off as I squeeze tighter, careful not to crush his windpipe. His eyes bulge slightly, but he doesn't let his smile falter as he enjoys the pain I inflict on him.

Goddamn masochist.

I walk him backward a few feet until he's pressed against the wall, my body pushing against his to hold him in place. I feel his cock harden, pressing against mine. I ignore the heat curling in my abdomen, anger still circulating through my veins.

"Admit it," he says, breathless. "You like the way we look together and you can't fucking stand it." I squeeze tighter, cutting off his ability to say anything else. His face reddens and I try to steady my breathing, but all I can smell is his scent of whiskey and mint, making me lightheaded.

This motherfucker is on the verge of making me lose it. I was trained within an inch of my life to maintain control, and if I lost it, then I more than likely lost my life. I was stripped bare and broken before I was rebuilt into the soulless machine that I am now.

I refuse to let anyone else break me, and the few fucking times I've lost it has been in the presence of him and Lena. I refuse to have anyone be a weakness, and keeping my distance from them ensures that no one will ever use them as bargaining chips and bring me to my knees, that it will keep them safe from the monsters that lurk in the shadows. From the snakes waiting to strike.

The light begins to fade from Devin's bright blue eyes as he starts to slip into unconsciousness, that smile still plastered onto his fucking face like he's enjoying this dance with death. Pulling my hand from his throat, he sucks in a breath, choking as air fills his lungs before sliding to the floor. He massages his throat while looking up at me, the light filtering back into his eyes as his breathing regulates.

"You know, T, either you really are a fucking sadist, or

you're just playing hard to get, leaving me hard not once, but twice in twenty-four hours." He chuckles, but there's an edge to his words, one that I've never heard directed at me.

I roll my eyes, ignoring the knot tightening in my chest as I see him heaped on the floor, flushed and gripping his hard cock. I refuse to play into his little mind games. It might fucking work on the people he torments for information, but it doesn't work on me. He thinks he knows what makes me tick, but you can't figure out what's inside of someone if they're just a shell of who they used to be.

"We're done here," I grit through my teeth as the knot in my chest tightens even more. "Now, for the last time, get the fuck out."

He stands, brushing off his clothes and once again looks me over. Thank fuck I'm wearing my compression shorts under my workout shorts, otherwise, he might just see what my domineering tendencies do to me. What *he* does to me.

"Be ready to go to the Underground by nine sharp, or Tasha will have your balls." He moves toward the door, resting his hand on the handle. "Oh, and T," he looks over his shoulder, his eyes as bright as ever, "make sure you zoom in next time; that camera is not at the best angle."

I swallow around the lump that suddenly forms in my throat as he yanks the door open, leaving me in stunned silence.

My phone vibrates on the floor, and I almost ignore it, but something tells me to check it out. The screen is bright, and a message from an unknown number appears on the screen. I narrow my eyes as I slide the phone open.

UNKNOWN

You can hide in your little club all you want, motherfucker, but we're always watching.

I stare at the message, the sound of my pulse rushing in my ears filling the silence, my mind kicking into overdrive.

Who the *fuck* has my fucking number? I have ensured that all of ours have been scrubbed from the internet, and I have systems in place to stay on top of that. Plus, none of the staff has a real number for me, just a random one that connects to my closed network app.

So, that leads to the question of who fucking leaked it? Or has someone hacked into our system and found it? I need to go up and trace it as soon as possible, but I can't let Devin see that this is the third message I've gotten in the last several days that's making threats. And of course, they're all dead ends sent from a fucking burner.

I need to stop getting distracted by the sharks that are circling closer to us. I need to have my head in the game and be ready to fight back, not fucking sitting and waiting to be ripped to shreds.

CHAPTER TWENTY-TWO

Lena

"YOU LOOK LIKE A FUCKING SMOKE SHOW." Bri's hand connects with my ass, a loud smack echoing in Tasha's massive bathroom. Squealing, I laugh, swatting her away, but she grabs my ass. "Bitch, are you not wearing any panties?" She rubs her hand over my now stinging cheek. "Damn, you are *ready* to get fucked tonight."

Rolling my eyes, I look at myself in her full-length mirror. Tasha really outdid herself with this dress. It's a soft, black satin that comes halfway down my thighs, accentuating my hips, with a slit that makes it nearly impossible to wear panties. The front comes down to a V, stopping just past my breasts. The width of the straps tapers off as they come over my shoulders, the thin straps crisscross down my open back and stop right above my ass. I almost died when I picked up the black, strappy heels and saw the glossy, red bottoms. The mask she had left for me was black lace with silver threading, making it shine.

I shoot her a look. "For whatever reason, Devin hasn't fucked me yet and I can't for the life of me figure out why." I lean forward, triple-checking my makeup. "I can't decide if he's waiting for the right time or if he actually doesn't want to fuck me but has just been giving me petty orgasms."

He seemed wildly distracted after Tony's little outburst and suggested I come down to Tasha's to get ready. That he had business to deal with before the fun that was planned for the evening. I almost insisted that I go with him because I had a feeling it had to do with me, but the look on his face gave me pause, and I didn't push any further.

I catch Tasha leaning against the bathroom doorframe, a smug look on her face. "Is that what you really think?" She stands, heels clicking as she comes up and rakes her fingers through my curls. "You think that man is only tongue fucking you because he feels *sorry* for you?" She laughs, the sound bouncing off the tiles. "You really were gaslit *and* brainwashed for all those years to think that a woman like you wouldn't have every man in this club ready to stick his dick into you the first chance he got. Devin might not be conventional, but he always has a reason for his actions."

Bri narrows her eyes slightly as if she's ready to take offense for me, but I just shake my head. She's right, I was fucking brainwashed into thinking that I would never survive in this world without *him*. That no other man actually wanted *me*, they just wanted the power that I was connected to.

Tasha turns her attention to Bri, looking her up and down. "You look like you're about to make a killing tonight, B." A smile pulls at her lips at the use of her nickname. It's such a simple letter, but she only lets her closest friends use it. While Tasha can't ever replace Kate, I can tell she's stepping in and keeping my best friend from spiraling further into the black hole she was falling into. And I don't think I'll ever be able to repay her for giving Bri another person to lean on.

Bri really does look killer in her black jean shorts with fishnets that lead down to her Doc Marten boots—that could do some real damage to anyone who crosses her. Her shirt is a tight-fitting crop top, showing off her pierced navel. Of course, she's not wearing a bra, as usual, and her pierced nipples are the real accessory to her outfit, their little sun-shaped hoops pushing through the fabric. Her maroon lips and black eyeliner finish off the look as her short, black hair shines in the light. "I always make a killing when I'm slinging drinks. They won't know what hit them," she winks, giving her slyest smile.

We've both been party girls, but where I was tamed when I was thrown into Matt's high tower, she continues to keep up with the twenty-year-olds, nearly drinking them under the table at the ripe age of thirty-one. She even held a keg stand for over six minutes before finally having them let her down because she kicked everyone's ass at that party. Kate would try so hard to calm her down, worried she would get arrested for starting a drunken brawl with the wrong person, but she didn't succeed any more than I did.

I've bailed my friend out a few times, even when I was with Matt, which didn't help her case when I invited her to go to things with his posse. She would try her hardest to intentionally piss him off by fucking at least two of his men when they were supposed to be working. I wonder if anyone in the world could ever tame her or be the gasoline that ignites her fire, making her burn even hotter.

Bri looks Tasha up and down in sleek black jeans with a lace corset that bares every inch of skin beneath it, her nipples barely covered by the delicate lace and boning. "Is that what you're wearing to your show tonight?" she asks, a slight purr in her voice.

Tasha grins, her eyes flashing at me. "Oh no, babe, this is just my daytime outfit. My show outfit is in my dressing room." She winks at her. "Maybe I'll let you see it later."

Bri's cheeks seem to flush, and she giggles like a schoolgirl. Seeing her come alive around Tasha, whether it's platonic or something more, makes my heart swell. I know I haven't been a very good friend these past few days, and I also know that everyone grieves differently. But, seeing her come back to her old self in the last day has been a breath of fresh air, even if she has been more of a spitfire than ever before. A phoenix rising from the ashes.

With time to kill, Tasha pours us each a glass of wine and we sit back in her living room, taking a moment to just breathe. I see Bri's face as it dawns on me that the last time there were three of us in the same room, it was Kate in place of Tasha. My heart seems to shrivel back and ache as I think about her and how I could have done more to protect her. Tears prick my eyes, but I do my best to blink them back, not trying to kill the mood.

Tasha is filling Bri in on the inner workings of the bartenders on staff as I pull up the news app on my phone. Curiosity has gotten the best of me because it's been almost two weeks since I last looked at it, my stomach churning at the thought of the article that was filled with lies about what happened to Kate and the cover up that Obsidian orchestrated about her death. I swallow the lump in my throat and scroll through the top headlines.

I slow my scrolling as a headline catches my eye:

Anonymous Donor Contributes $250,000 to Safe Haven in Memory of Drew Green

I read the article; my eyes widen as I take in each word.

In a heartwarming display of generosity, Safe Haven, a local domestic violence shelter, announced today that it has received a significant gift of $250,000 from an anonymous donor. The donation to the Drew Green Endowment Fund honors the memory of Drew Green, a beloved community member known for his commitment to helping those in need.

The picture next to the headline shows a handsome man with soft green eyes, a dazzling smile, and cropped blond hair.

His features strike me as familiar, but I heard all about it at a party with some of Matt's business partners, and I know that this was a huge story whenever he was found dead in his home.

The endowment fund was established to provide ongoing support for the shelter's programs and services, which assist individuals and families affected by domestic violence. Safe Haven has been a vital resource in the community, offering safe refuge, counseling, and empowerment resources for survivors. The anonymous donor, who chose to remain unnamed, expressed admiration for Safe Haven's work and wanted to ensure that Drew Green's impact on the community would be remembered.
Safe Haven plans to host an event in the coming weeks to honor Drew Green's memory on the anniversary of his death and celebrate the generous donation, inviting community members to participate and learn more about the shelter's work.

Bri's face is next to mine, reading the article over my shoulder. "Oh, I remember when he died. It was all over the news and so fucking tragic." She points to his photo as I scroll back to the top. "It was so sad that he took his own life all because he didn't win the election for mayor."

The phone is yanked from my hand, a disgusted look pulling at Tasha's face. "Do you really believe everything you read? Especially this fucking garbage?" She scrolls on my phone, her eyes moving quickly over each line. Her face softens, whispering something to herself before she hands me back my phone, crossing her arms.

"Did you know him?" Bri asks, looking down at the photo of him still on the screen.

She stares at us. "You really don't recognize him?" She cocks her head to the side, looking between us. *"Seriously?"*

Bri and I look at one another, trying to find the answer between us. "If we recognized him, would we be asking?" Bri retorts, her hackles rising as she rests her hand on my arm.

She looks at me, rolling her eyes. "You look at his near identical face every fucking day."

My eyes widen as I look at Bri, her mouth slackening as the realization hits us both. "Oh my God," I say quietly. "That's Devin's brother."

Tasha shakes her head, breathing heavily out her nose. "It's a good thing you two are pretty."

Bri rounds the sofa, sitting back down next to me. "It's so sad how he took his own life," she repeats. "It's hard enough knowing that Kate was murdered in cold blood, I can't even imagine how Devin feels."

Tasha sits back in her chair, leaning forward to rest her elbows on her knees. "Who says that he wasn't killed in cold blood, too?" Her words are quiet, but there's a sharpness to them that cuts through the bullshit in the article.

Bri shrugs. "Why would they lie about that shit?"

"Because it was a cover-up by the same motherfuckers who come into this club night after night, and we're doing everything we can to prove it." The words are like a whip snapping at us. I stiffen and I hear Bri suck in a sharp breath. The fire in Tasha's eyes burns bright. "Drew was a wonderful man who was working to change this piece of shit city."

She leans back, picking up her glass of wine off the side table and swirling it. She closes her eyes, seeming to fall back into her memories. "He saved me from my previous life and brought me here, knowing that I would thrive in this environment with Devin and his promised protection. Drew was very passionate about protecting women and working to support people who found themselves in situations they felt trapped in." She opens her eyes, shining bright with tears as she looks right at me. Her eyes nearly burn through me as she looks right into my soul, the one that was nearly taken from me by the devil himself.

"Once Devin got involved, the men who hurt me and others like me didn't stand a chance. Some of them were permanently removed from this Earth to rot in the worst corners of Hell, while he chose to keep others alive to suffer, rotting in a cell, begging for death. Drew looked the other way, knowing that what his brother was doing would leave a mark on the city and he was hopeful it would deter others and make a change."

Taking a sip of wine, she clears her throat. Her eyes still shine with tears, and she doesn't bother to dab them away, letting one fall freely down her cheek. "Drew was the golden child to his parents. Smart, talented, good-looking, and an upstanding citizen." She sighs. "While Devin was less than desirable to his parents and trying to work through his socio-pathic tendencies. He would fight constantly, his bloodlust typically getting the better of him. He was arrested once for participating in an illegal underground fight club, but his parents managed to scrub that from his record." Another tear falls, this one she wipes away, sniffing quietly.

"What really happened to him? To Drew?" The question comes out quietly, my heart aching for her and Devin at such a big loss in both of their lives.

She looks at me, the tears in her eyes evaporating as rage burns through them. "He was running for mayor and was favored to win, but you see, he was actively being recruited into Obsidian. They liked the idea of someone so popular with the people having a position of power and the influence they thought they could have with him." Her eyes flash, nose flaring. "However, he was actively turning the tables and exposing them as the crooks they really were. People started asking questions about some of the other powerful people, and then suddenly, the election flipped, and he was found dead from what they were calling suicide the next morning."

She takes another sip, her hand trembling slightly before she sits it back on the table. She grips the armrests of the chair, her spine stiff. "Devin and I called bullshit on the whole thing the minute the story broke and have been working diligently to prove that he was murdered by Obsidian. Tony was recruited for the cause after we…after he joined the team." She looks out the large wall of windows, identical to the ones in the penthouse. "I think the worst part is that Devin's father blamed him for Drew's death."

Bri gasps. "That's fucked," she bites out. "He *clearly* had nothing to do with it." She leans forward, her wine nearly spilling over the edge of the glass.

"It gets fucking better." Tasha's eyes stay glued on the windows, taking in the lights from the cityscape. "Devin went to visit him prior to the funeral to discuss any of Drew's last wishes from his will, and the fucker sat right there in a drunken stupor and told Devin that it should have been him. That Drew was what the world needed, and Devin was only a bloodstain on society."

My heart nearly shatters at the thought of any parent saying something so heinous to their only living child. Yes, it sounds like Devin was quite the handful and maybe didn't make the best decisions when he was a kid, but he clearly has the same stances as his brother did. He just chooses to take a less-than-noble route to dealing with things.

"That's fucking terrible." Bri leans back against the couch, seeming to curl in on herself. "I hope he fucking killed that bastard."

Tasha sighs deeply, this time looking at Bri. "Unfortunately, he only got one good swing in before his father's security threw him out. But he hasn't seen or spoken to his father since then and is seemingly better off going no contact."

"What about his mother?" The question bubbles over my lips, because surely, she has kept in contact with her only living child.

The scoff that Tasha makes is answer enough. "She's a *noble wife* who stands by her husband, not caring to cut ties with Dev." The same kind of wife that Matt would have expected me to be.

Laying my hand over my heart, I can almost feel it cracking as I think about how his own mother turned her back on him in such a tragic time. Leaving him to grieve alone.

"But he had you, right?" Bri looks at her longingly, as if she is aching for her to have her, too.

"We have each other, and our friendship has only gotten stronger as we've fought to honor his memory and uncover the truth with as much cold hard proof we can gather." She grabs the stem of her wineglass, swirling it before downing the rest. She licks her lips, savoring every drop.

"Who does he think did it?" My mind flashes to Matt, and while I used to believe that he would never commit such a crime, knowing what I know about him now, I wouldn't put it past him. However, he wasn't one to ever really get his hands dirty; if he was involved, someone else did the bidding for him.

"Whoever it is," she says darkly, "will suffer a long and terrible death."

CHAPTER TWENTY-THREE

DEVIN'S EYES turn ravenous and he looks at me like I imagine the Big Bad Wolf looks at Little Red Riding Hood if she was trapped in an elevator with him. He looks hot as fuck in his cream shirt with the buttons undone, showing off his chiseled chest and his fitted, navy blazer, cutting in to accentuate his trim waist. He's had me pulled to his chest, running his hands up and down my arms, leaving goosebumps in his wake. He presses his warm lips to the crook of my neck before nipping me, a whimper slipping through my parted lips.

However, my eyes are glued to Tony as he takes in every move we make from the other side of the elevator. He watches us with a sniper's precision. This is the most attention he's given me since I was whisked away to the penthouse weeks ago. I drink him in as he stands before us in charcoal dress pants and a black shirt, unbuttoned in the same fashion as Devin's, showing off his massive, muscular chest. His shirt sleeves are already rolled up to his elbows, his snake tattoo on full display along with the rest of his sleeve on his other arm, as he flexes his corded muscles, adjusting his sleeves.

The energy between the two of them is charged, and the

way they are watching each other intently has me a little on edge. It's like I'm a rabbit trapped between two rabid dogs, their maws dripping as they snap their teeth, ready to devour one another.

I want to prod at what's changed since Tony stormed out and Devin left me at Tasha's, but I decide that maybe it's for the better if I just let it be. Whatever it is, I'm not going to let it get in the way of what I hope will be a fun evening.

We never step foot into the actual dance club. Instead, we bypass it with the private elevator and step off into a dimly lit hallway, the sconces making me feel like I'm traveling through a castle corridor. At the end of the hall is a black, metal door with a security guard standing outside, his leather mask covering his whole head, with only his eyes showing, and a closed zipper across his mouth. He turns, the door beeping before he pushes it open, nodding as we pass through.

My heart thunders in my chest, electricity crawling across my skin as we step into a large lounge area. The space is filled with lounge couches, high-back chairs, settees, and a few curved booths along the walls. The lighting is dim and precariously arranged, so each seating area is cloaked in shadows, obscuring identities from the rest of the room. Soft music plays throughout the room, overlapping the sound of quiet moans, creating a sensual symphony.

We cut to the left, coming face to face with another security guard donning the same full mask as the first one. He unclips the maroon, velvet rope, letting us pass to start our ascent up a metal spiral staircase. Devin leads with Tony at my heels. The heat from their bodies swirls around me, their scents intoxicating. I grip the railing because falling right now would be the least attractive thing I've ever done as I'm sandwiched between these two incredibly hot men.

At the top of the landing, it opens onto a balcony with a large, curved booth facing out over a railing. We're not too high up, but we sit at a near perfect view to take in the entire stage that's positioned below. I look over the edge and see all the people who were once cloaked in shadows now on full display from above. I gasp and step back, bumping into a hard chest behind me, just as Devin runs his hands down my arm.

"Welcome to our private balcony." His hand runs over my collarbone before lightly wrapping around my throat, sending a shiver across my skin.

"I'm sure the people you've brought up here adore it." The words tumble from my lips. Am I *jealous*? I can't possibly be jealous of them bringing people into a private booth in their club before they met me. Don't be a fucking bitch, Lena.

Devin's chuckle is dark, his fingers tightening on my throat. His other hand caresses up and down my arm, goosebumps forming with each pass. "What if I told you that you're the first person we've ever brought up here?" I try to turn my head, but his grip holds me in place, his mouth right next to my ear. "We take VIP status *very* seriously around here, love." His breath is warm against my skin. He plants a soft kiss just below my ear, humming as he works his way down my neck to my shoulder. The feeling of his mouth on my skin makes me weak in the knees.

A throat clears behind us, and I feel Devin's smile against my skin. "I think it's time we take our seats." He loosens his grip on my throat, stepping away. I turn to be met with his outstretched hand. Sliding my fingers into his palm, he leads me to the booth, guiding me around the low table, right to the middle. He lowers himself next to me, lounging back and making himself comfortable.

Tony remains standing watching as a server steps onto the balcony, a tray of drinks already in her hand. Her lace mask is a deep maroon. She's wearing a matching lingerie set with her blonde hair pulled up into a high pony. She gives me a genuine smile, handing me a glass of white wine before placing Devin's whiskey into his waiting hand. She sets another glass of amber liquid on the low table, which I'm assuming is for Tony.

She turns to leave just as Tony holds up a rolled bill. She gently plucks it from his hand, careful not to touch him. She nods at him, but he gives her nothing in return before she exits the balcony. He catches me watching him, his gray eyes turning near molten as the lights dim around us, darkening his expression.

Devin places his free hand on my thigh, his thumb making circles over my exposed skin. Tony lowers himself next to me, careful to give enough space between us. But to my surprise, he stretches his arm across the back of the booth. I can feel his fingers twitch against my hair, and as much as I want to lower my head back and let him rake his fingers through my strands, I keep my head upright, practicing my self-control.

Heat curls in my lower abdomen, and I do my best not to show how nervous I am about tonight. It doesn't help that their presence is so large it's suffocating, the lack of oxygen making my head swim. The tickle of desire begins to crawl across my skin, and the urge to touch them, claim them as mine, is almost too much.

Devin leans in again, his lips brushing the shell of my ear. "We are perfectly positioned to see the whole show, and no one can see us." His fingers move up my thigh, a jolt pulses through my clit. I place my hand over his and his fingers flex, pressing into my skin as he looks at me sidelong, a smirk curling up the one side of his mouth. His golden mask glints in the soft light, his eyes looking to where my hand covers his and licks his lips.

The lights dim to near darkness, a crimson glow making the room look as though we didn't just step into the Underground, but right into the Underworld. Warm spotlights turn on and point to the stage at the front of the room, Tasha already in the center of it.

My mouth drops open as I take in her stunning form. She's wearing a black leather body suit that gleams in the light, making it look like liquid night painted across her body. Fishnets cover the skin between the bottom of her bodysuit to the top of her black, leather thigh-high boots. Her creamy skin is a stunning contrast to the dark fabrics.

Her long, black hair is pulled back into a high ponytail, showing off a thick, black choker. She looks like a queen of the night as she sits in the dark, high-back chair resembling a throne on one side of the stage.

She snaps her fingers, the sound echoing in the silent space, signaling for two women to walk out from behind a curtain on the left side of the stage. One woman has a bob of light, silvery hair that shines bright in the warm lighting. The other has red hair, high on her head, in a ponytail that looks like flames cascading down her back.

They turn simultaneously toward the audience, their faces adorned with a black mask shaped into bunny ears jutting up past their heads. The only clothing covering their bodies is the matching black bras, with satin bows replacing the cups, barely hiding their nipples and panties. Heat curls through me as I take in the women and as Devin's fingers inch even closer to my core.

Tasha snaps her fingers again, and the girls immediately widen their stance, exposing their pussies in their crotchless panties. I let out a quiet gasp as Devin slides his fingers along my inner thigh, sending a jolt of electricity to my own throbbing clit. As if on instinct, I widen my legs slightly, allowing him more access if he wants it. He teases me by tracing a figure eight on the sensitive skin of my inner thigh.

Tasha gracefully stands from her throne and starts to circle the women, running her fingers along their shoulders like a predator sizing up her prey. She saunters back to her throne, pulls something from a black box that I didn't notice was there before, and approaches the silver-haired woman, her lips pulled up into a lupine grin.

Out of a bag, she pulls a ball gag. From behind, she lowers it in front of the woman's face, letting her bite on it, before buckling it tight around her head. Tasha drops down onto one knee and pulls more things out of the bag. She runs her fingers down the back of the woman's leg, starting at her ass, and then buckles cuffs onto the woman's ankles, repeating the process for the other leg.

I squirm in my seat watching something that's usually so private be on display for a room full of people. Devin's fingers dig into my thigh, holding me in place. I catch him looking over my head to Tony, who's intently watching Devin's hand from the edge of his hood, his expression unreadable.

I try to focus on the show in front of us, but their gazes bear into me, making it almost impossible. I watch as the women obey every command Tasha gives, the sound of her heels clicking on the stage floor makes my heart race. Sometime during the last few minutes, a padded bench has been rolled out onto the stage, giving the scene a whole new element.

The silver-haired woman lies across the bench with her back to the audience, her hips over the edge and her ass in plain view. Tasha secures her wrists to the side so her arms are out in front of her, kissing the top of the woman's hands. "Such a good little slut, aren't you?" Her voice is low and velvety but echoes through the room as if she has a microphone in her hand.

Tasha comes around and widens the woman's stance, producing a metal bar from the underside of the bench where she secures it to the cuffs on the woman's ankles. The woman's pussy is wide for everyone in the audience to see, glistening in the stage light with how turned on she is.

Tasha runs her fingers through the woman's slit, opening her up for the audience to see while simultaneously squeezing the woman's ass. A slap rings out from the impact of Tasha's palm against her skin, her moan muffled by the ball gag. "Such a good girl," Tasha croons, gently rubbing the now red spot. "Now, wait here, and I'll be back soon." She slaps her ass again, this time letting the sting linger on her skin.

Tasha crosses the stage to her throne and lowers herself onto the seat, her long legs going wide, snapping her fingers. The redhead crosses to her and drops on her knees before her like a commoner bowing to their queen. Tasha's smile is warm but almost wolfish at the woman in front of her. Her admiration shines at the show they're putting on together, but her dominatrix side plots all the ways she would inflict pain and pleasure on her.

She reaches between her own legs and starts to unbutton the body suit, the snap of each button like a staccato note ringing out in the room. She folds back the fabric, exposing her pussy, and casually starts to play with herself, teasing the woman on her knees and everyone in the room.

"You would like some of this, wouldn't you, you little slut?" she asks the woman kneeling in front of her. My mouth begins to water while Devin's hand starts to drift even closer to my center.

"Yes, mistress." The woman's voice was soft, but firm, knowing exactly how she wants this scene to play out, but not daring to cross a line with her dominatrix. "Please let me lick your pussy."

Tasha's laugh is light as she relaxes back on her throne, beckoning her with a crooked finger. "Lap me up like the little bitch you are."

The woman leans forward and begins devouring Tasha's pussy, her head eyes fluttering shut from the pleasure. Tasha grips the woman's hair and then clamps her thighs around her head, holding her in place.

Tasha moans, her pleasure building, causing the air in the room to become electric with other moans echoing throughout the room. I lean forward slightly, Devin's fingers gripping into my skin. I give him a sidelong glance, but his eyes are forward, intently watching the show as his fingers finally brush against my center. I let out a whimper as he growls, "Goddammit, Lena. You aren't wearing any fucking panties." I give him a devilish grin as I lean back, letting my legs spread wider.

He slides his fingertip up my slit, another whimper crawling up my throat as my pussy throbs for attention. "I should take you down there right now and punish you in front of everyone for coming in here with no fucking panties on. *Goddamn.*"

I gasp, trying to face Devin, fear and desire heating my skin at the thought of being on stage in front of all these people, being fucked in ways I couldn't imagine. Tony's fingers twitch behind my head, heat radiating from his hand. There's so much electricity swirling in the booth that it could set the whole place on fire.

Tasha loosens her hold on the woman's head and gently pulls her away. Panting, she leans forward to run her knuckles down the woman's face, cupping her chin and praising her.

She reaches over the armrest, blindly rummaging through the box, pulling something else out, a lupine grin on her face. She stands, steadying herself as her long, flawless legs step into a strap-on, the black silicone of the cock shining in the lights.

Sidestepping the woman still on her knees, her heels click delicately across the stage as she comes up behind the woman still strapped to the bench.

She runs her hand through the woman's pussy and lightly plays with her entrance, her same smile playing across her face. The woman lets out another moan from around her ball gag, trying to shove her hips back to gain more friction.

Tasha slaps the woman hard on the ass, the woman's groan is almost guttural in response. "Oh no, no, no. You will keep that tight little pussy still because only good girls get to come. Isn't that right?"

The woman's hips are still in response, and her "Yes, mistress" is muffled from around her gag.

Tasha rubs her hand across the woman's ass where she slapped it, the woman relaxing under her touch. "We'll just see if you've been a good enough girl to get to come in front of everyone tonight. Won't we?"

Devin's fingers are getting closer to my clit, and I feel the heat rising in my core. "You hear that, love? Only good girls get to come." My inner thighs are slick, and my pussy is throbbing from desire. I glance down to see that Tony is palming his cock through his pants, and I cut my gaze back to the stage, trying my best to focus on the erotic show in front of me because the sight of Tony touching himself has me on edge, desire coursing through my veins, the show affecting him as much as it's affecting me.

It's as if I'm fighting against someone as they're pulling on my wrist to reach over and lay my hand on his, to feel his length beneath my palm. He obviously loathes my existence and is only entertaining Devin by being here. The best sex I've ever had is when I was hate fucking Matt, the rage burning through my veins when he would let me on top and I could grind my clit against him. I bet Tony's hate fucking would put mine to shame.

"Go ahead, touch him." Devin's whisper surprises me, his velvety voice making my pussy even wetter as my eyes widen at his words. "Touch him, and I'll touch you like the dirty little slut you want to be tonight."

My hand trembles as I move it in Tony's direction but at the last moment, I chicken out and drop it to his leg instead of placing my hand on his. His muscles tense under my touch and I hear him let out a low growl. I keep my head facing forward but cut my eyes to see him gripping his cock even harder than before. Even through his pants, I can see just how fucking big he is, and my mouth starts watering even more.

I move my hand slowly up his thigh, his growl turning into a soft rumble as Devin pushes his fingers between my folds, his finger hovering at my entrance as he waits for my next move. I gasp, my eyes widening as pleasure pulses through me. I spread my legs more, allowing him more access and nearly begging for him to finger fuck me. He doesn't hesitate as he continues to caress his fingers against my sensitive center, teasing me and driving me wild.

The sound of skin slapping against skin echoes throughout the room, the tension rising with the sounds of erratic breathing and a symphony of quiet moans from the crowd. "What a good little slut you are, taking my cock like this. Do you want to come?" Tasha slaps the woman's ass. "Do you?" The woman is so turned on that her muffles come out as screeches around the gag.

Tasha pulls out, the tip of the dildo resting against the woman's pussy and snaps her fingers. The other woman, who was left on her knees, stands, clasping her hands together in front of her, her eyes down. Even though she's been waiting, stone still moves with grace across the stage. "Yes, mistress?"

"Lie on your back at her feet." She points to the floor, her command the same velvety soft voice. It warms the room but is domineering enough that even I want to go and submit to her.

Crossing the stage, she gracefully lies down on her back, anticipation coursing through my veins at the debauchery unfolding in front of us. Her wrist cuffs are attached to the bar that's between the other woman's ankles, connecting them.

Tasha circles the two women, heading to her box, pulling out a black wand vibrator, strapping it to the woman's thigh, and positioning it against her pussy, her moans of pleasure growing louder.

"I'm going to eat your pretty pussy until you scream," she

says as she slaps the ass of the woman bent over the bench, a muffled moan emitting from her, "and I'm going to sit on your face," she gracefully lowers herself to her knees over the woman on the floor, Tasha's center hovering just above her face, who's already panting from the vibrator, "until you make *me* come."

Tasha lowers herself to the woman's face as she grabs the other woman's hips, leaning into her center, her tongue licking her from bottom to top, swirling around the woman's clit.

I squirm in my seat, my own clit throbbing as I watch them move in tandem. This is the hottest thing I've ever seen, all while sitting between two incredibly hot men, the tension between us choking me.

"I'm getting jealous of how intently you're watching them, love. It's almost as if you want to join in on their fun and not mine." Devin's voice is low, feral. Like a beast waiting to devour his next meal. His fingers continue to glide over my center, his middle finger teasing my entrance as he leans in. "Mm, and you're so fucking wet." I look at him, but he's still staring ahead, giving Tasha his attention. "Eyes on the show, love, or you won't be allowed to the after show."

He slows his teasing finger, and I groan in frustration. I don't have a fucking clue what the after show is, but if it's nearly as hot as this, then I don't want to fucking miss it.

Turning my head and keeping my eyes on the stage, I watch the women and imagine myself being sucked and fucked like them, imagining my own threesome with Devin and Tony. The gentle touch of his fingers on my skin. The heat from Tony's hand resting behind my head, with his other still gripping his bulge. It's going to send me over the edge sooner rather than later. I move my hand up even further, Tony's muscles tense even more under my touch they're almost vibrating.

Devin's challenge echoes in my mind, and I'm only a few inches from where Tony's hand lies, and I can't help but imagine what his cock feels like under my fingers. As if he can read my mind, he lets out a soft growl, the sound filtering through the slits of his mask. I stiffen as I feel a phantom, almost fleeting touch against my hair.

Liquid heat is pooling between my legs, soaking Devin's hand as his fingers continue to circle around my center, my mouth going dry as I try to keep my panting quiet.

To add to my growing desire, I watch as the women on stage come undone, their orgasms hitting in unison. They continue to fuck each other through their pleasure until finally, Tasha slowly lifts herself from the woman's face, turning toward the crowd. Their bodies glisten with sweat and cum in the stage lighting, looking even more beautiful than they did before.

Tasha releases the women from their restraints, helping them to their feet. She cups each woman's face, giving each one a passionate kiss. Taking their hands in hers, they face the room together, pleasure and pride on their faces. She escorts the girls to the edge of the stage, allowing them to join others in the crowd, the room filling with polite applause.

Tasha gently claps her hands together. "Now that we have you all turned on, please, feel free to imagine it's *us* that you're fucking. Enjoy your evening, sinners." Her smile is wide and devilish as she looks up and winks directly at the private balcony.

The lights on stage go down, casting the room into a dim, red glow as the music gently goes up. No one moves from their seats as they begin to indulge in their own pleasures, the room getting hotter by the second.

I look between the men, the current running hot between us. The pleasure is building even more between my legs from Devin's touch, and I want nothing but for him to sink his fingers, or better yet, his cock, into my throbbing pussy. "What now?" I ask as the desire in my voice becomes undeniable.

Devin's thumb pushes into my clit, and I gasp, wanting to

come right then, but he pulls his hand away, casually standing up.

That motherfucker.

"Come, love." He holds his hand out for me. My fingers curl around his as he pulls me to my feet with the same hand he had between my legs, making sure to thread his fingers through mine, spreading my need across my skin. "Let me show you to our *private* suite."

CHAPTER TWENTY-FOUR

Lena

DEVIN LEADS me out of the booth, pulling a velvet curtain aside to reveal a hidden door directly behind us. The sound of the group orgies heightens below us, making my skin heat. We slip through the door, the room dark as we enter. The door closes and we're standing in total darkness before neon lights power up, making the room glow crimson.

The room is spacious. In the seating area sits a black leather sofa and two black leather chairs, similar to the ones in their apartment. A large black, stone fireplace fills the wall next to the seating area with a large painting of Persephone, holding a pomegranate, on the mantle. On the other side of the room, there's a four-poster bed with black satin sheets pulled back as if it's waiting for someone to crawl into it.

The room is pristine, and it doesn't seem as though it's been used in a while. Or at all. And if I'm the first one they've allegedly brought to the private balcony, then that means I'm the first brought to this room. But do I really believe them?

I'm standing in a private suite in the middle of a sex club, with the two men who run the place, power pulsing from them with every heartbeat. I can only imagine that they've had their fair share of partners, and while I'm no saint, my sex life has been the equivalent of cinnamon.

The cruel voice in my head repeatedly tells me that I'm just another woman who will be kept safe until they catch Matt. Then they'll cut me loose, letting me back into the world to fend for myself. That fucking terrifies me as the jealousy bites me, envious poison coursing through my veins, making the edges of my vision turn red, matching the glow of the room.

I walk to the portrait of Persephone, noting that she has no real facial features, only simple brush strokes. This denies her any of her defining features and gives the looker the chance to put any face on a goddess-like body. Clever. "A private suite, huh?" I ask as I run my fingers along the stone mantle, the low fire warming my legs.

"One of them," Devin answers from where he leans against the doorframe, watching me with a predatory stare as I move around the room, taking in the sleek, modern decor.

"So," I turn to them, my vision flaring, "how many people have you fucked in these suites?" Jealousy coats my words as the thought of being brought to a room where they have fucked countless people, and that I could be just another notch on the proverbial headboard seeps into my mind.

Both of their eyes darken, Devin's words just as dark. "Jealousy doesn't suit you, love. And like I said, it's our *private* suite, no other guests are allowed in here." He throws the words like a knife, landing in the wall next to my head. I try to spot the lie, catch them in the act, and prove that I'm not as blind as they might think I am.

"So, you mean to tell me that you've never brought *anyone* to this room? That you've never *fucked* anyone in this room? Not a *single* person?" My voice is dripping with disbelief, eyes narrowing at them.

I don't know why I care so fucking much, but I do. I really fucking care, because this is turning into something more than just a promise of protection and being lost in a haze of lustful orgasms. Whatever this is, it's easy, and it's breathing life back into me, filling my lungs with more than just air.

Devin's head cocks to the side, his gaze sweeping over me as he takes me in. I wait for him to call me a child and throw me to the curb because my jealousy is about to ruin everything that's been building between us over the last few weeks. "You're the first person we've ever brought to this room, Lena."

I keep my eyes narrowed as I turn toward the bed. I sway my hips, my designer heels clicking on the hardwood floor as I cross the room to sit on the edge of the bed. I brush my fingers over the cool, soft sheets. "Then where have you been fucking people all this time? Just your apartment?"

Devin's on me in a blink, his hands planting firmly on the mattress, caging me in. His gaze is hot as he leans in, our breaths mingling. "Do you want us to fuck other people, love?" My eyes widen at the fierceness in his voice. "Do you want to *watch* us fuck other people?" He leans in more and I lean back, my elbows propped on the mattress as the heat in his gaze burns me to my core. "Because we can do whatever *you* fucking want."

His words startle me, and he clocks the shock on my face, feeding into it and not backing down as he degrades my childish outburst. "We've never brought anyone to our private rooms and no one else is allowed to use them." I see movement behind Devin as Tony takes a seat in one of the high back chairs, watching us with his intense gaze. "So, would you prefer that we warm the bed up with someone? Give you a sneak peek of what I'm capable of. Do you want me to push your face down and smother you in their cum, letting you smell their desire as I fuck you within an inch of your life? Because I can do all of that and *more*."

I gasp, the breath getting lodged in my throat as he brings his knee onto the bed, pushing it between my legs. My elbows sink further into the mattress, dipping from his weight as he hovers over me. I look past his intense stare, his dark, silvery mask making him look even more devilish, to Tony. He lowered himself into one of the chairs that faces the bed, letting his legs fall wide, his fingers curing into the armrests as he grips them tightly.

"Look at me," Devin grits out, my eyes snapping back to him. His weight presses into the mattress, the heat between my legs growing hotter at his command. "Tell me what *you* want, Lena. Tell me *your* darkest desires. Let me show you the monster lurking under my skin. The one that's been waiting to come out and eat you alive. To consume you bite by bite. To drag you to Hell and make you his queen."

My body trembles as he nudges his knee further up, pressing it to my center, the pressure causing me to hold my breath. "I-I don't know," I gasp out, digging my fingers into the sheets, trying to hold on as I begin to spiral out of control.

"I think you do." He lowers himself, his mouth now next to my ear. His hand comes up to palm my breast, flicking my peaked nipple, eliciting a moan from me. "I think you want to be a dirty little slut for me. For *us*." He pulls back. "Don't you?"

I open my mouth to speak, but nothing comes out, the words shriveling up and turning to ash. My tongue feels heavy, and my mouth goes dry. What do I want? Of course, I want him. *Them*. I've been begging for Devin to fill me with his cock, stretch me, and fuck me into oblivion for weeks. I want him to make me his with more than just his tongue and fingers. I want him to drag me to Hell, burn me, and show me the monster that so desperately wants to consume me.

My eyes flicker to Tony and since he refuses to touch me, I want him to watch, letting his gray eyes burn into my skin as he gets off to me being used by Devin.

Is it insane of me to want them both? At the same time?

The questions burn into my mind, and I squeeze my eyes

shut for a long blink, the dark desires creeping out of the corners of my mind, ready to be let out into the light. The same desires that I was shamed for having and was forced to lock away and ensure that they never saw the light of day. I had to be obedient and couldn't wander from the straight and narrow path that was laid out for me. Such nefarious thoughts couldn't leak, or it would ruin the perfect image that had been curated for me. The one that was so suffocating that it drained the life from me and nearly killed me.

But even as Devin pushes me, cages me in, and holds me down, I can finally breathe. I can take a deep breath and fill my lungs with the desires that I've been deprived of for so long. I can get lost in the darkness with them and maybe find myself again.

I open my eyes, Devin's intense gaze watching me. "Well, love?" He presses his knee firmly into my center, stoking the flames of my desire as the heat rolls from him. "The decision is all *yours*."

"I—" This is it. This is the chance for me to finally take my life and desires into my own hands. To hand myself over, but on my terms. And whether I come out on the other side unscathed or crash and burn, it's worth it. I take a deep breath and take the leap, diving head first. "I want you to *fuck* me, Devin. Fuck me like I'm *yours*."

His eyes widen as the corners of his mouth pull up into a devilish grin. "Oh, Lena. That's the thing." His voice is low, and it feels like the room's lights have dimmed, the shadows creeping in on us. "You're already *mine*."

I suck in a desperate breath as his mouth crashes with mine, pulling me under. I grind my center against his knee, moaning as my pussy throbs in need of friction. He slows his kiss, and from the corner of his mouth, he says, "Such a dirty girl. So fucking horny for me."

His words have me pulling his face back to mine, our tongues gliding over each other as he pulls himself up on the bed, caging me in. He pulls away from our kiss, lifting himself upright onto his knees. "Scoot up to the headboard."

I drag myself up the mattress, laying my head on the soft pillows as he slides off the bed and kneels at the foot. The room is deafeningly silent except for the sound of a drawer sliding open and Devin's satisfied hum.

Climbing back on the bed, he stops at my feet, looking up at me. "Just like I promised, I'm going to cuff you and tie you to the bed, love, and you're going to let me. Understood?" My skin prickles as excitement and desire courses through my body. I nod, his eyes lighting up as he runs his fingers down my leg. He delicately wraps a cuff around my ankle, the sensation of his fingers across my skin making me flinch with anticipation as he repeats the process on my other leg.

"Tell me your safe word." His voice is husky, and I note his cock bulging in his pants, already as turned on as I am. My heart is pounding in my chest at the thought of submitting to someone again, giving myself over completely. The show tonight showed me that even during the roughest moments of sex, the Dom and sub relationship is one of trust and compassion, with the Dom taking care of their sub and letting them live out their desires. Something that I was deprived of for five years and craved like forbidden fruit.

"Torch," I blurt out the first word that comes to mind. The torch, or better yet, the *flame*, that's been kindling, burning, between us. Like the fire in Tony's eyes as he watches us from across the room. Like the heat between my legs as I think about what he might do to me.

"*Torch*," he repeats, rolling the word across his tongue, tasting it. "Interesting."

He moves on the bed to my right side, wrapping the cuff around my wrist before securing it to a ring on the end of a short chain link coming from the headboard. I feel my face reddening as he gently runs his fingers down the inside of my arm, goosebumps forming over my skin.

He climbs back off the bed and slowly makes his way around to the other side, his gait nothing short of predatory. I see Tony still sitting in the chair, massaging his bulge, as he watches Devin move around the room. The dim lights and glow of the fire make him look like a dark, masked king seated upon his throne. His gaze is as hot as the flames that blaze next to him.

Devin sinks onto the mattress, putting the cuff on my other wrist before securing me to the headboard. I give my wrists a tug which makes Devin's face curl into that wolfish smile that has heat pooling between my legs. "You're not going *anywhere*, love. You're *mine*."

He begins to unbutton his shirt, exposing more of his skin. "*My* whore." He undoes another button. "*My* slut." Another button. "*My* angel." His eyes soften as he undoes another button. "*Our* salvation."

He slides the shirt off, fully exposing his chest and chiseled abs. He reaches over and runs his fingers down my cheek, neck, and chest, letting his fingers trace the deep V of my dress. "Such a dirty girl to wear such a slutty thing in public tonight *and* with no fucking panties." He continues down my body, his fingers tracing the slit in the skirt as I clench my thighs together, searching for friction.

"Ah, ah, ah." He wags his finger at me, his eyes glinting. "Keep those legs open so I can feel how wet your pussy is for me." He slides my skirt up, exposing my center and my slickened thighs.

I hear Tony groan from across the room and I raise my head to see him lounged back, palming his fully erect cock. I hear a click, then feel a cold metal against my hip. I stiffen just as Devin cuts the slit of my skirt up past my navel, exposing me even more.

He cups my center, humming in satisfaction. "Such a perfect pussy. So wet for me already and we've only just begun." He removes his hand and carefully bends my knee, planting my foot on the bed and raking his nails up my calf. A groan breaks free from my lips at the sensation.

He centers himself between my legs, running his fingers across my skin, bending my other knee up before lowering between them, slowly running his tongue through me. My back arches as he surges me higher when he swirls around my clit.

I'm lost in the movements of his mouth against me, his tongue and teeth sending me into a haze of ecstasy. I lift my hips and try to grind against him to the rhythm of his tongue, my cries of pleasure echoing the room. The build-up is almost too much. "I'm—" I grind my pussy against his mouth as my desperate, pleading whimpers hang in the air. "I'm going to come." He sucks my clit and rakes his teeth across the sensitive nerve, sending me over the edge.

My orgasm crashes over me like a massive wave of pleasure. My words, cries, and sounds are stuck in my throat as I try to breathe, starbursts filling my vision. His tongue gently swirls around my clit as I ride it out. He pulls away, grinning, his face glistening with my cum. His eyes are bright from behind the mask that still sits on his face. "Such a good girl." He looks behind him to Tony before turning back, his fingers running down the inside of my thighs.

I look up, still panting, and see Tony fisting his cock, desire swirling in his gaze. The flickering fire makes his gray eyes molten. I watch as he rubs his thumb over the head of his length, his precum coating his skin. My mouth waters at the sight of his large cock that is engorged in his hand, the tip turning a tinge of purple.

Devin slides off the end of the bed, slowly undoing his belt and letting his pants fall to the floor, followed by his boxer briefs. He pumps his hand slowly over his hard, thick length while his eyes rove over my body. "So beautiful, all tied up with your cum soaking the sheets." He stalks around the bed, still pumping his hand over his cock. Anticipation rushes through me at the thought of what he will feel like as he fucks me for the first time and how he'll stuff me full of his cock and cum.

He reaches the head of the bed, over me, and unclips the cuffs. "Head toward the foot of the bed, on your stomach, and keep your arms in front of you." Without hesitation, I flip myself down to the foot of the bed, keeping my arms outstretched as Devin pulls chains out from under the mattress, clipping my cuffs to the rings on the end, holding me in place.

"Such a good girl." My legs clench together at his praise, the words sending a pulse right to my clit. The bed dips under his weight as he comes behind me, sliding between my legs. Lifting my hips, he slaps my ass, the contact stinging my skin, causing me to cry out. He hums as he gently rubs over the tender spot before slapping it again. I cry out, this time his name tumbling from my lips, the mix of pain and pleasure sending me into overdrive.

"Oh, Lena," he croons, "I could listen to you scream my name all night." He pulls my hips up higher, and I feel the head of his cock pressing against my entrance, already stretching me. "Oh, baby, I can't wait for this needy pussy to choke my cock." His filthy words have me trying to shove my hips back, but he slaps my ass again and I bury my face into the mattress. He slaps the other cheek; this time the pain is sharper. "Eyes up, love." He smooths his hand over my skin before his fingers trace up my back and grip my hair, jerking my face up. "I want you to keep your eyes on Tony while I fuck you." Tony's eyes are dark under his hood, his hand gripping the base of his cock as he watches Devin grip my ass, his thumb playing around my hole.

Devin leans over, his cock sliding between my folds, hitting my clit, as he kisses my shoulder blades, his fingers still tangled in my hair in a tight grip. "Let's play a little game, shall we?" His lips trace back down my back. "Let's see who comes first.

Loser gets their mouth fucked by the winner." I gasp and see Tony's eyes harden as he gives his shaft a hard squeeze.

I open my mouth to protest just as Devin slams his cock into me. It fills me and I cry out as he continues to pound into me. His fingers snake across my lower abdomen before landing on my clit. He presses against the sensitive spot and sparks fill my vision. I moan as he works my clit, pressing down and moving his fingers in delicious circles. My hands grip the sheets as I fight against the orgasm and the chains, desperately trying not to come first.

I feel a warm wetness on my ass as Devin loosens his hold on my hair, his thumb against my hole, a hiss passing between my teeth from the intrusion. That motherfucker is cheating.

I watch as Tony matches Devin's rhythm, his eyes boring into mine, his cock shining with his beads of precum as they spill down his shaft. I can hear him panting through his mask, his breathing matching mine as we build up to our climax. Devin lets out a rough moan behind me, his rhythm going erratic before falling back into time.

Just as I think I can hold out, he pulls his hand from between my legs and smacks my ass, pushing his thumb deeper into my ass, and I fall off the edge. I moan, shoving my hips back, the corners of my vision blurry as the waves of pleasure crash over me. I ride it out as Devin slows his rhythm to let me breathe, the side of my face pressed into the mattress.

"Well, love, it looks like you lost." From the corner of my eye, I see Tony stiffen. "Looks like it's between me and you, T," he says, amused.

They both start to pick up the pace, matching their thrusts, Devin into my pussy and Tony into his hand. Devin's cock is hitting that deep spot and it's driving me wild as I sit on the edge of another orgasm. I squeeze Devin's cock, my walls contracting. "Devin, *please.*"

His hips pound into me harder before his hips buck and he

lets out a growl, followed by a deep, bellowing moan. His fingers dig into my skin as his cum fills me. I feel my walls contract around him, my greedy pussy taking every last drop. "Yes, love, choke my cock. Take all of me." His thrusts slow before he stops, holding his cock in place. "*Fuck, Lena.*" My walls contract as he grabs my ass, smacking it again. "I'll take your ass next time and you'll get off just as hard." I melt at the thought of his cock penetrating my ass, his chuckle soft as he pulls out.

I look up and Tony is roughly pumping his hand around his cock, his eyes starting to roll back into his head as his balls constrict. "Come for us, T." Devin's voice is rough, his grip on my ass near bruising. "We want to see you come."

Just as the words leave Devin's lips, a snarl rips from behind Tony's mask as his cum covers the front of his shirt in streaks. His hips twitch as his head falls back against the chair, his breathing erratic as he thrusts into his hand, until he finally settles, his breaths heavy.

"Well, love, you know what this means, don't you?" I try to look behind me as Devin slides off the bed, coming around to undo my cuffs. "You're *all* Tony's for the next round."

I watch as emotion flashes across Tony's face, one that I can't catch within the shadows of his hood. He gruffly gets up and grabs a towel from a shelf, quickly cleaning himself up and buttoning his pants. Without another glance, he storms out the door, music filling the space before the door swiftly shuts, leaving Devin and me in deafening silence.

CHAPTER TWENTY-FIVE

Lena

IT'S BEEN over a week since the night of Tasha's show, where Devin gave me one of the best orgasms of my life, and Tony has barely looked in my direction. Even behind his mask and hood, I can tell he's tense. I thought that we would have made a breakthrough after the intense and insanely erotic moment that we all shared, but it's obvious that I was wrong. He's been working nonstop, and when he's not doing that, he just disappears without a trace for hours on end.

Devin has been working just as hard, trying to keep up with the club's demands, not to mention the fact that another employee was uncovered as a mole working for Obsidian.

And while he's been fucking me every chance he gets, I can tell it's to pleasure me and take the edge off for him. Anytime I try to protest and demand that he rest, I somehow end up with his cock in my mouth, his cum pouring down my throat, so he doesn't have to hear it from me. However brutal it can be as his hard cock hits the back of my throat, drool pouring out of my open mouth, it still sends me over the edge every time.

I've been spending more evenings in the club at the bar with Bri. She is the happiest I've seen her in a long time and completely in her element. She's been working alongside Rodrigo, one of the other bartenders who's been training her. She raves about him, and they've become pretty close over the past week, and if he wasn't in a committed relationship with his long-time boyfriend, I'm sure she would have already fucked him in his apartment on the fourth floor by now.

Tonight, I'm dancing and trying to shake the feeling of being watched. And even though Devin and Tony are nowhere to be seen, there are plain-dressed security guards who have been tasked with watching me and cameras in every direction, watching my every move. But it's more than that. It's an intense stare, one that has the hair on the back of my neck standing on end. I feel like a fawn who's about to be cornered by a wolf and eaten alive. I shake my head because it's just paranoia getting the best of me, and I let my body get lost in the music.

I feel a hand wrap around my waist and another grip my hip. I stiffen and see that it's a man with dark hair in a plain, black mask. I let the stranger pull me against him and I grind my ass into him, his cock hardening beneath me. It's a dangerous game, one this man doesn't know he's playing, but it's fucking worth it if it gives me a chance to let loose. And I'm banking on Devin getting off on punishing me for letting another man touch me. He groans into my ear, the rumble from his chest vibrating through my back as I sway my hips to the music.

He nuzzles his face into the crook of my neck, kissing the bare skin, and the distinct feeling of being watched intensifies. I let the mix of fear and excitement roil through me as the song switches and the man lets his hand skim down my thigh, the other up to my breast, palming it and lightly squeezing.

I've never been this free before, even before Matt when Bri and I would show our tits for shots and fuck frat boys in the bathroom at house parties off-campus. Or that time when I was momentarily sleeping with my boss in his office when we were "working late" at my first job out of college. I always wanted to live on the edge, but I've never let myself get so daring that it would put another person's life in danger and right now, that's exactly what I'm doing. I know he has a target on his back, and I don't care; the thrill is fucking hot. The image of him being tied up in the basement as Devin tortures him and fucks me after he's done, blood still coating his hands, has my pussy clenching.

Fuck, what is fucking wrong with me?

"Wanna get out of here, baby?" The man's voice rumbles into my ear, pulling me from my thoughts as his teeth graze my earlobe. I don't answer and just keep swaying my hips, letting his large hands caress me.

The weight of the unknown gaze starts to press down on me, and I can feel an anxious knot tying in my chest. I look up to the balcony and see the empty spot where Devin will occasionally watch me while I hang out at the bar with Bri. A tinge of panic lands on my chest, mixing with the already knotting anxiety as the danger in the room closes in on me.

I pull away and give him a smile, knowing that I probably sealed his fate once Devin sees the security footage of this man groping me. I let the crowd pull us apart like a wave, just as his hand reaches out, trying to grip my arm, but I slip away into the sea of people. I push through the crowd, the music and people laughing, singing, and the sound of public fucking fills my ears. It's like I'm seeing the club through a new lens.

It's dirty, filthy, and fucking dangerous. I take in the dark eyes as I pass by, men who are just as dangerous as Devin and Tony letting their sharp gazes rove over me, ones that have probably been sent in to watch me and possibly take me, but even though they're a danger to me, these aren't the eyes that I still feel on me. It's as if I'm being watched from all directions and I try to look around, expecting someone to come out from the crowd, but everyone is ensnared in their own debauchery.

When Devin asked me about my darkest desires, this was

the one on the tip of my tongue. To be *hunted*. But this has seemingly become too real and for it to actually be unfolding before me has me near panicked.

My phone vibrates in my pocket, and I pull it out. A message from an unknown number. My heart thunders, rattling my chest harder than the bass that pumps through the club, and I swallow around a lump in my throat. I slide it open to read the message that sets off my fight or flight instinct.

UNKNOWN

Don't let me catch you.

Nausea rolls through me and I'm suddenly burning up. I look around, trying not to panic. I turn to head back toward Bri, but I catch the man who I left hanging on the dance floor making his way in my direction, determination in his eyes.

I need to get off the floor, away from that guy, and most of all—I need to fucking catch my breath. The feeling of eyes on me is even heavier than before as I work my way through the crowd, heading to the other side of the dance floor. Finally stepping out of the mass of people, I am greeted by the same doorway that started all of this.

I slip through the threshold into the dim hallway, the air cooler and the music dampened, giving me the chance to think. Leaning against the cool wall, I take a deep breath with a hand on my chest, trying to untie the knot that continues to tighten.

I look between the doors and see that all but two are occupied tonight. The red lights stick out like a sore thumb on the black wall. I pull my hair up from my neck, letting the cool air hit it and drying the sweat that threatens to drip down my back. Smoothing my hands over my dress, I straighten from the wall. Out of the corner of my eye, I see a shift in the shadows by the door. I blink, but it can't be anything more than my eyes adjusting to the dim light and my mask pressing into my face.

I pull my phone out and check it again.

Nothing new, thank fuck.

I'm sure that Devin is too engrossed in his work to make note of my little escapade. Hopefully, he won't see it until that man is long gone and has at least had a chance to flee.

Out of the corner of my eye, I see that the shadows seem to move again and I stiffen as the feeling of a heated gaze blazes across my skin. Turning my head slowly, I see a giant figure blocking the doorway. His hood hides his eyes, ones that I know are a sharp gray, his mask covering any expression on his face.

I freeze, keeping my eyes glued to him. It feels as though the heat radiating from him is pure rage. He's never pursued me on his own like this, and I fully expected Devin to find me tonight, whisking me away to the basement to deal with the man I teased him with.

The knot in my chest pulls even tighter as adrenaline courses through my veins, my thundering heart and rapid breaths giving me away. I'm not afraid of Tony, but I also haven't been alone with him. And right now, I can't tell if he wants to fuck me, kill me, or both.

He takes a step into the hallway, sliding the door shut behind him, closing us off from the rest of the club. "T-Tony." His name barely makes it off my tongue as I look at a man who doesn't think twice about blowing a man's brains out, point blank.

He doesn't speak. He just stands there, watching me, letting the tension build between us. Goosebumps pebble across my arms and my hair stands on end at the nape of my neck. He's watching me like a predator does prey. "D-does Devin know you're in here with m-me?" I try to keep my words steady, but of course, I fail miserably and look like a fucking coward as my limbs begin to shake. I don't think he would hurt me, but I didn't think Matt would, either, and we saw how that turned out.

Tony is pure power and rage. A quiet rage that would scare the shit out of anyone on the receiving end of it, but I'm not scared...*I'm excited.*

I know now that his piercing gray eyes have been watching me all night, not Devin's or anyone from Obsidian.

"You let another man touch you." His voice is rough, and it pricks across my skin like the tip of a knife, dripping with violence. His first words to me are an accusation that I can't deny. I did what I did tonight, hoping to get a rise out of Devin, who has been too distracted this past week. I wanted to walk the line and give myself a thrill.

I stammer, words jumbling in my throat as he takes a slow step closer. His hands curl at his sides, my mind screaming at me to run, but my body keeps me planted like the traitor it is. "You sent that text, didn't you?" I finally force the words out, but they seem to fall before they ever reach him, his expression never changing.

I take a clumsy step back, my hip bumping into a door handle. I lean against it and curl my fingers around it as he closes the distance between us. Heat rolls off him, his heady scent filling my nose as he moves down the hall.

"Tony, *please*," I plead, but he keeps moving toward me. His steps are slow, like that of a killer in a horror movie as they chase their victims and toy with them. "*Stop*, Tony." The words come out choked, fear filtering through my words as it nearly sputters from my throat.

I wrench open the door and rush inside, slamming it closed and locking it. Taking a step back, I watch the handle, waiting for it to move in his attempt to enter the room, but it stays still. I back up further into the room until the backs of my legs bump into the bed that's bolted to the floor in the middle of the room.

I lower myself to the mattress, keeping my eyes on the door, waiting for the monster of a man to burst through. The fact that these doors are controlled by his computer system puts me even more on edge because he could more than likely unlock it at any time.

The room is deafeningly quiet, with the soundproofing working a little too well. I sit on the bed and slowly relax as the minutes tick by, the window of Tony busting through the door closing. I go to pull out my phone and text Devin, but it's not on me anymore. "Shit," I mutter because that means I dropped it in the hall, and Tony more than likely has it. Probably snooping through it to see if I'm still connected with Matt. He'll be pleasantly surprised to see that all the messages are one-sided but might also be pissed that I haven't told them about the newest string of threats that he's been sending me. I'm not even sure how he got my new number, but no matter how many times I block him, he always finds a way through.

I rise to my feet, taking in the room around me as I walk the perimeter. A massive, black, lacquer dresser takes up almost one whole wall of the room. Sitting on top is a tiny Bluetooth radio. I click the top button, and it comes to life, filling the room with low, seductive music. The beats match the thump of my heart and could even match the steady rhythm of a hard fucking.

Pulling open the large top drawer, my eyes widen as I look at a sea of leather. Everything you could imagine, from full head masks, chokers, cuffs, and pieces I've never even seen before. I pick up the pieces and feel the soft, supple leather under my fingers before dropping it back into the drawer.

Sliding it closed with a soft thump, I move on to the next drawer, this one filled with toys of every shape and size. Vibrators, butt plugs, nipple clamps, dildos, and blindfolds. I feel the heat of desire curl in my abdomen, and I think about all the pain and pleasure these items would bring. Tasha knows what she's doing to keep people turned on and satisfied, playing out their kinks, and returning to these rooms night after night.

The feeling of being watched shivers over my skin again. I examine the door over my shoulder, but it remains closed. I pull a wand vibrator out of the drawer and turn it on. The buzzing sound fills the room and vibrates down my arm before I click it off and place it on the dresser.

Working my way through the dresser, I pull out vibrators, plugs, and different toys. This dresser alone is filled to the brim with any fantasy you could imagine, and if I'm going to be stuck in here for a while, then I might as well use my time to find new ways to pleasure myself.

I do live above a sex club, now, and it seems like this kind of exploration is firmly encouraged.

I look at the array of toys laid out on the dresser and pick up the vibrator wand again. Turning up the music, I walk over and lie on the bed. Sliding my dress up to my hips, I slide my panties off, dropping them to the floor next to the bed, and turn on the toy.

On the lowest setting, I slide it between my folds, the buzz sending a sudden jolt through my core. Closing my eyes, I let out a soft moan and get lost in my pleasure.

My heart thunders in my ears as my pulse quickens, my body heating as pressure builds between my legs. I switch the settings, find a pulse that builds, and then cuts off, edging myself and toeing the line of release. Another moan leaps from my lips when the hairs stand up along my arms.

I ignore the feeling of being watched because I would hear someone open the door, and keep going as liquid heat pools between my legs, slicking my inner thighs. I'm lost in the moment, my eyes closed; the only sound I can hear is my racing heart in my ears and the buzzing of the vibrator in my hand. I'm so close to coming that my thighs are shaking. I dig my feet into the mattress, lift my hips and press the vibrator hard to my aching clit.

Stars burst behind my eyelids as pleasure rolls over me and I come. *Hard.* I let out a loud moan and ride the toy until my overstimulated clit aches, the aftershocks pulsing through me.

Clicking the vibrator off, I come down from my orgasm, my heavy breaths filling the silence.

Wait. *Silence?* Where the fuck is the music?

Just as my eyes pop open, a hand curls around my throat, pressing on my windpipe, cutting off my air. I try to scream, but nothing comes out as the hand cuts off my vocal cords. My eyes focus in the low light, and a hooded man stands over me, his shadowed eyes and slitted mask looking down on me.

I scratch at his large, veiny hand, trying to get him to loosen his grip as the air seeps from my lungs, but he holds it in place. Holds *me* in place. How could I be so stupid to think he wouldn't find a way in here? He practically owns the place and is likely the one who installed the security systems in this room and throughout the entire building. I'm a fucking idiot who was more interested in getting off than watching the fucking door as a predator waited to grab me in my most vulnerable moment.

He grabs my wrist, forcing it above my head, followed by the other one, and by his look alone, I know better than to move them. My breaths come out short, my vision turning fuzzy. With his free hand, he undoes his belt, pulling it free from the loops of his pants. As if he's done it a thousand times before, he lets the buckle drop over the leather before he reaches up and loops them over my hands, tightening and securing it around my wrist. The leather digs into my skin, just tight enough to be uncomfortable and keep me on edge.

He's watching me, his gray eyes dark and swirling with intense emotions. I try to say something around his hold, but it's nearly impossible to even take a breath. His free hand brushes my hair from my face, wiping a rogue tear away. "You let a stranger touch you," he bites out, the words breathy through his mask, echoing what he said in the hall. His voice is deep and rough, matching him and sounding exactly like I imagined. The edges of his words are sharp like a knife, holding them at your throat, ready to cut and watch you bleed out.

"And then you come in here and touch yourself to the thought of *him*? Getting off while in *my* club to the thought of another man's cock pressed against you?" My eyes widen at his harsh words, and I shake my head, moving it as much as I can under his hold. He tightens his fingers around the column of my neck, my traitorous body reacting to it with my pussy dripping even more than it was earlier.

His hold on me is strong, pressing hard enough that he will leave a mark, one that I'm sure Devin won't miss. "What were you thinking about, then?" His free hand brushes over my cheek, trailing his fingers down to my breast, palming it, squeezing it so tightly it almost hurts, eliciting a breathless gasp from me. "Whose cock were you imagining?"

He's fucking pissed, the rage rolling off him in waves that are nearly drowning me. "Y-yours," I rasp out, my voice barely audible around his hold as his palm presses down more.

He pinches my nipple between his thumb and forefinger, twisting it so hard that I try to cry out, but am left with a quiet whoosh of air. "So, you're a lying little slut, then?" His harsh words, mixed with the assault on my sensitive nipples, have me panting as I shake my head again. His calloused hand continues down my body, brushing over my hip and then roughly cupping my pussy.

I'm exposed to him, and as fucked up as it is, this is exactly what I've imagined in every wet dream I've had of him. He's nothing more than a shadow, but his glowing gray eyes are unmistakable. He takes me right to the edge every time before my eyes fly open, and I'm left panting and my pussy aching, hand between my legs. No amount of masturbating can take the edge off after those dreams and I have to rely on Devin to curb my cravings.

He lets out a quiet, approving groan, his eyes burning

brighter. "So fucking wet, aren't you? Fucking dripping for me."

I let out a whimper as his fingers caress over my aching pussy, middle finger swirling around my entrance, teasing me. My clit throbs with desire like I didn't just get off moments ago, and I try to adjust my hips so his fingers will hit the right spot. He pauses his movements, his gray eyes roving over my body, the heat from his gaze melting me. "Don't you fucking move unless I tell you to. And keep those hands over your head or I'll remove them, just like we're going to remove the hands of the fucker who dared to touch you."

Heat flares between my legs as my heart races. I knew there was a chance that he was in danger, but I didn't expect that they'd already have him in their custody, and more than likely already beaten to a pulp. I shouldn't be this fucking turned on by the thought of this man being possessive enough of me to do such a thing. And this doesn't seem like the same Tony Fox who could barely stand to share the same air as me not even a few hours ago. It's as if he's giving me a glimpse of his true self from behind his mask.

His eyes cut to the dresser, and he chuckles. The dark sound crawls across my skin, encircling me like his hand at my throat. "You want to play, *baby*?" He lets go of my throat, peeling his fingers off my neck one by one as if we were fused together, his steely gaze keeping me frozen in place. His next sentence sends a mix of fear and desire through me, right down to my throbbing pussy.

"Then let's fucking *play*."

CHAPTER TWENTY-SIX

Tony

WATCHING her dance with that stranger nearly sent me over the fucking edge. The way she allowed his fucking hands to grope her like she was his was fucking bullshit. He's currently tied up in the basement, my men grabbing him before he could get near her after we caught him trying to hunt her down. We'll find out shortly if he's with Obsidian, but even if he's not, he doesn't get to touch what isn't his and live to see another day.

I've been watching her for days as she lets herself get more and more comfortable in the club. The sharks that have been circling her have been closing in, coming up from the depths, and we've been taking them out one by one. Hook, line, and sinker. The way that she's willingly putting herself out there as fucking bait has me seeing red. She fucking knows what she's doing and the implications of it.

The thing is, though, I think she gets off on being followed. *Hunted.*

I've taken this little hidden kink and have amplified it for her this week. I watched the way she would look around the club, the feeling of my gaze on her, and trying to pinpoint where the feeling was coming from. She doesn't know that I learned a long time ago how to keep hidden in the shadows, and I can choose if I want someone to know if they're being watched.

A game of cat and mouse that I never lose.

This little game of mine would drive my targets to the edge of paranoia, where they would get reckless and make my job easier. Some nearly went insane until they finally came out of hiding or ended their own pathetic lives. It's a skill that is not normally successfully done by a man as large as I am, but when you're threatened within an inch of your life every day, and failure means you die, well, you learn to master said skill. No matter what it takes.

Looking down at this woman, who I could snap in half if I wanted to, has my cock throbbing. She's flushed, her thighs and pussy slick with her cum, her delicate arms above her head with my belt digging in and already leaving marks as she presses against the binding.

She's almost fucking perfect.

The only thing missing is my cum mixed with hers, my marks across her skin. I press my fingers harder, making sure that her soft skin will bruise under my touch. My snake tattoo looks at her like it's ready to strike, to sink its teeth into her and fill her with poison. *My poison.*

Devin has coddled her and has been treating her like a fucking damsel, one who was locked away in a tower. When I suspect that she knows exactly what she's doing, luring Obsidian out by being on the club's main floor for multiple nights in a row. She's fucking clever and while I don't think she knows all the rules, she's a key player in this game.

Devin has been pushing me to cross the line with her, with him. But if he's not careful, I will fucking break her, and it won't be pretty.

But the way she's looking at me right now, she's practically begging for it. She wants me to shatter her piece by piece, cracking her open, and letting the dark parts of her show before I haphazardly put her back together. She's trembling under my touch, but not in fear. No, I would be able to smell her fear from a mile away, just like I can smell her arousal that has soaked the sheets beneath her. She's drenched in desire.

Devin thinks he's been rough with her for the past week, but he doesn't know what rough with her can be. She's not delicate like he tries to make her. Because in front of me is a woman who fought to free herself, ripping the claws of a monster from her skin one by one until he no longer had a hold on her. A woman who took a risk and ran on nearly bloody feet, who has fought for herself not only the last few months but all the years that she was in that fucker's grasp. She was a caged bird and now that her wings have stretched, she's attempting to fly.

I've listened to him devour her and I know that she's been begging for more. She wants it harder. Faster. *Rougher.*

She wants *me*.

And the night that I watched him fuck her was when I realized that she was no different than me.

A fucking masochist.

The torment between her legs reminds her that she's alive, and I'm sure that's how she survived for so long under Matt's grasp, just submitting and letting him fuck her until he was satisfied and then keeping her head down. I know because I used the same tactics while I was being held prisoner. When I had to learn to play the game to stay alive.

I saw it in her eyes that night, that she wanted me to get up and fuck her until she wasn't breathing. I saw the disappointment in her eyes as I came in my own hand and not in her beautiful pussy. I think Devin had a flicker of disappointment, but it was fleeting, and he had to play his little game to take back control.

I couldn't fucking handle it, the disappointment, because I hadn't ever come that hard in my own hand while watching other people fuck until I started watching them. I have used my voyeurism as an escape tactic, and unless I had the overwhelming urge to dominate someone myself, I found my own satisfaction in watching people in the Underground. Lately, I haven't needed to, because I have taken my kink to new heights, watching from the corners of my own apartment.

It's sick and twisted, and it hasn't been helping my urges, but seeing her being wholly degraded by him and pushed over the edge multiple times had a part of me that I had locked away years ago banging on its cell door. Rattling its cage.

I palm my cock. All I want to do is sink my dick right into her sweet pussy, but I hold back because I'm fucking furious, and if I try to fuck her now…Well, I'll do more harm than good.

I know she could sense me watching her as she let that fucking piece of shit touch her, grind on her, feel her up. She was fucking with me, and whether she knows it or not, she'll have his blood on her hands after I let Devin loose, letting him cut off every finger from the man who grazed her skin.

She may think I'm the crazy, brooding one, ready to blow a man's brains out for running his mouth, and she's right—but Devin's not much different from his own bloodlust. He has his own pent-up rage and deep-seated Daddy issues. She hasn't seen fucking anything yet.

I let my finger slide through her folds, her breath hitching as I circle my finger around her hole. Goddamn she's so fucking wet, it makes my mouth water. One of these days I'm going to fucking devour her pussy, fuck her with my tongue, and let her drown me in her cum.

One. Of. These. Days.

I inch my finger in and start pumping it in and out, eventually adding another finger as she stretches for me. Her own hands curl into a fist, tensing above her head as she moans into the open room, her eyes fluttering shut. I want to shove all her holes full of the toys that she laid out for herself, but I don't want to sacrifice the chance to feel her against my skin.

To fuck her with my fingers and let her come all over my hand before I sink my throbbing cock into her needy pussy.

"Eyes on me," I bite out and her eyes fly open, looking at me with dilated pupils as my hand wraps back around her throat, roughly pressing my fingers into her skin.

My two fingers pump in and out, and with each thrust, I let my thumb press into her clit. Her thighs are shaking as she soaks the sheets beneath her. Her needy cunt squeezes my fingers and I imagine it being my cock.

She moans my name, and I love the way it sounds as it pours from her lips. "Say it again," I spit, my cock twitching behind the zipper of my pants, ready to sink into her tight cunt. I tighten my grip on her throat, feeling her pulse quicken as it pounds against the pads of my fingers.

"Tony," she breathes. Her voice is thick and seductive, like a siren trying to lure me into the sea.

"Again." My voice gets harsher as her legs start to shake, her orgasm building as her walls clench my fingers with every thrust, her breaths quickening.

I press on her clit, and her hips buck as she screams my name, her pussy holding my fingers in a death grip as she soaks my hand and the sheets.

Fucking perfection.

This woman has burrowed herself under my skin and infected me. I knew it from the moment I saw her that she would cause me trouble, but like the soldier I am, I pushed all of that down and carried on into battle. She was nothing more than a civilian, and I was there to take down the chaos that was ensuing around her. I didn't plan on stepping on a bomb and watching as my chest blew open, letting everything I'd been suppressing for weeks out.

She's now mixed into the narrative of my nightmares, ones where she's just out of reach as the whole building collapses, rubble covering her delicate body, and before I can get to her, I'm ripped away. The nightmares have plagued me for years, but since she's shown up, they've only gotten worse, and my ability to sleep has receded more and more.

She's driving me closer and closer to the edge of insanity as my addiction to her becomes harder to ignore.

She grinds her hips, and I slow my rhythm, letting her waves of pleasure crash over her. I watch her eyes roll back into her head as the aftershocks pulse through her. Her body relaxes slightly after each one.

Reluctantly, I remove my fingers from her pussy, my hand coated in her cum. I want nothing but to taste her on my tongue, but my mask stays in place because only those closest to me get to see what's underneath, and I can count those people on one hand. It's a privilege hard-earned, and she's not ready for the virus underneath to infect her.

Instead, I reach up and wipe my cum-coated finger across her lips. She gasps at my touch, opening her mouth as I shove my fingers in. "Suck," I command, and without a second thought, I feel her soft tongue go between my fingers and clean herself from me. "Such a fucking good girl," I praise as I pull my fingers from her mouth, releasing them with a pop.

She's breathless and flushed, her cum smeared across her lips as the red marks from my fingers shine on her neck. The sight makes my dick twitch, and I can feel the precum soaking my underwear, threatening to expose me. "So fucking beautiful with my handprint wrapped around your pretty little throat like a necklace of blood rubies." I run my knuckles across her throat, and I feel her swallow deeply, her throat constricting.

Her eyes are wide as I grip her waist and turn her onto her stomach, yanking her hips back with one hand, her glorious ass ready to be spread and stuffed with the butt plug she had picked out for herself. I pull it from my pocket and pump it into her pussy, coating it with her cum. I slap her ass, the sound echoing in the room, and she cries out. I smooth my palm over the skin, knowing that she likes it in rapid succession.

Smack. Smack. Smack.

My handprints welt her skin, and they look just as perfect as I knew they would as her cum drips down her thighs. I spread her cheeks and press the plug against her hole, and she tenses. "Relax, baby. I'm going to stuff all your holes and fucking make you *mine*."

The last word nearly comes out a growl, but she relaxes, and I easily slide the plug in. She groans as I press the little button on it to turn it on, the vibrator coming to life. Her ass cheeks clench and she attempts to muffle her moans into the mattress. I smirk as I pick her panties off the floor that are still soaked from her dripping cunt.

I come around the side of the bed, the panties balled in my hand. "Look at me." She turns her head, her eyes bright as the vibrator goes to work on her ass. "Open that dirty little mouth, baby." She eyes my hand, and a sliver of panic flickers across her face as if I would actually hurt her.

She has no idea what I would do.

Like the good little girl she is, she obliges. I stuff the panties in, making sure that she can taste herself. "If you know what's good for you, you will keep those in your fucking mouth, or I'll find a way to keep them there."

Her eyes widen as I step away, and her whimper follows me back around the bed. Kicking off my boots, I nearly rip off my pants and boxer briefs, my cock springing free with precum dripping from the tip. I step up behind her, slapping her pussy and she jumps, letting out a muffled yelp as I line myself up with her entrance, gripping her hip. I ease myself into her, doing my best to go slow, but the sound of her moaning has me shamelessly thrusting myself into her. Her pussy clenches around my cock as I hit her deep with short thrusts.

Fuck, she feels like fucking heaven.

I pound into her, turning up the speed of the vibrator stuffed into her ass. Her knuckles are white as she grips the sheets even harder, the muffled sounds she's making almost animalistic. It's so fucking sexy watching her come undone like this. Only the people I pay willingly take me as I fuck them like this, but she's taking me like she was made for me.

"You're taking me so fucking good, baby." I let each word match my thrust. "Such a slut for my cock, aren't you?" She responds with a moan, pushing her hips back and meeting me with each thrust. Oh, she really is fucking made for me. The only thing we're missing is Devin, and I don't think that it will be difficult to convince him for next time, because there will be a next time.

And another.

And *another*.

My balls tighten and I feel a tingle in my lower back as I pound harder into her. I pick up her vibrator from the bed and reach around, turning it on to its highest setting and pressing it roughly against her swollen clit. She screams, her inner walls choking my cock. "That's it, baby, come for me. Come all over my cock before I fill your needy cunt." Her hips falter, her breaths coming through her nose even more labored as she clenches my cock and screams around her panties, falling over the edge.

I drop the vibrator, the buzzing sound muffled against the sheets as I pound into her. My hips stutter, my orgasm hitting me as a growl tears from my throat. I fill her with my cum, thrusting through my own aftershocks before reluctantly pulling out. My cum drips down her thighs and I catch it with my fingers, pressing it back into her. She's panting as I take a step back to admire the masterpiece I made.

She's a mess. A fucking *beautiful* mess.

Her makeup is smeared across her face, our cum dripping, her panties soaked with her spit, and her ass in the air with the plug that I have yet to shut off. Her skin is covered with my red marks, to remind her that while she's her own woman, no one else but *us* gets to touch her.

Grabbing my phone from my pants, I snap photos of her on the bed while she looks right at me. A smile pulls at my lips, and I know that this one meets my eyes as her own widen, taking me in as if she's truly seeing me for the first time.

I have images of her getting licked and sucked by Devin. Hell, I even have images from the other night when he finally manned up and fucked her. But this, this is my own masterpiece that I will keep locked away and admire in the darkest hours of the night.

I pull the plug from her ass and deposit the toys into the cleaning bin that is in every room. She keeps her ass in the air, like the good girl she is, as I come around and unbind her hands. I pull the belt away and see the angry red marks that mar her skin.

I let another smile pull at my mouth because those won't be going away for some time, and I can't wait to see the look on Devin's face when he notices them. I watch her hands to see what she does, but she keeps them curled into the sheets, not moving. It's like she understands that I don't like to be touched, but right now, I want her to defy me. Reach up and brush her fingers across my skin. What the fuck is that about?

Pulling the panties from her mouth, she sucks in a breath and licks her lips. She lifts herself up on all fours, her eyes still on me, dropping to my cock that is getting hard again by the way she's looking at it.

At *me*.

That can't be fucking right. People don't look at me like the way she is. They look at me as someone to fear or to get fucked by. She's looking at me as if she could wrap herself around me like a snake and suffocate me, sinking her fangs into my chest and ripping out my heart. Swallowing it whole.

And the fucked up part? I would let her.

I pull her phone from my pocket and drop it on the bed,

letting it bounce on the mattress. She turns to face me, eyeing her phone as her screen lights up, showing her sunset lock screen. Her brow raises and it's obvious that she knows I went through it.

One of my points of rage is that she's been receiving threatening messages and has yet to tell us. Every number they come from has already been disconnected and registered under dead or nonexistent people. Devin is going to lose his fucking mind when he finds out.

I redress, taking my time as I slowly feed my belt through the loops, my cock twitching at the image of her bound with it. Yanking on my boots, I make sure to go even slower as I tighten the laces like the good soldier I am. I've been watching her out of the corner of my eye this entire time, and she hasn't moved a muscle or said a word. Instead, she's been watching me curiously, like a cat would watch a bird. Or a snake.

I eye the door that's hidden at the back of the room, the one I so cleverly let myself in with. She follows my gaze, narrows hers at the door, and then back at me. Well, there's another secret that she's in on now. I'll either have to keep her or kill her.

She finally moves as she scoots to the end of the bed, sliding off, she gracefully stands on her feet. She adjusts her dress that doesn't even come close to covering the sheen of cum that coats the inside of her thighs. Her brows furrow as she looks around before her head slowly floats back in my direction, her eyes locking onto my pants pocket. The same pocket that her panties are now in.

I let my gaze roam over her, the urge to bend her over and fuck her again has the tension in the room building, and I can see in her eyes that she's thinking the same thing. I broke my own rule by following her into this room, knocked down my own fucking wall, and let her waltz right in.

There's no going back now.

I fixate on the red marks across the column of her neck, some of them already darkening into bruises, and even with the best makeup, will be hard to conceal. Devin will have a fucking field day with that.

Sliding my phone back out, I fire off the video footage of what just went down right to Devin's phone. Dangling the carrot. He's going to be chomping at the bit for her to get back to the apartment and have his way with her to even the score. The cameras here are on a secure line that only we can access and only check if something provokes an investigation.

I move to the back door, pushing it open to the back hallway. "Let's go," I say, my voice rougher than before.

Reaching down, she grabs her heels, taking tentative steps to the door. "Where are we going?" She peeks around the doorframe, looking down the hall warily.

"Either you come willingly, or I will throw you over my shoulder like a fucking caveman and make you." Her skin flushes at my threat and she gulps, the new bruises on her neck coming to life. My hands itch. I want her to fucking push back. I want her to show me her bratty side so I can carry her back to my room, throw her onto the bed, and let Devin hear *me* fuck her this time. Unfortunately, she doesn't and takes another tentative step into the narrow hallway, the door closing behind her.

"Does Devin know?" I cut a look at her, a smitten look on her face. This little fucking vixen.

"Maybe," I gruff out, thankful for my mask as it conceals the shit eating grin plastered on my face.

She quietly snorts a laugh, catching on to the game we're playing, pulling her gaze from me. "Will he be upset?"

I cross my arms, my fingers twitching to touch the bruises that grow darker with every breath she takes. "I *highly* doubt it." Dropping my arms, fighting every urge that pulses through my body, I start down the hallway. I feel my phone vibrate in my pocket, my grin growing wider at what response I could have possibly received. "What he will be upset about is that you've been withholding text messages from us. Text messages that threaten your life and ours."

She stops and stares at me, all lust draining from her as her body stiffens. I don't know why she's acting so surprised, because it couldn't have been more obvious that I was going to go through her phone. Check every message thread. Download every nude that she had saved in her secret album. Or maybe it's the fact that she's still thrumming from her orgasm, and I just threw a bucket of cold water over her. Ruining this pleasant moment between us.

I turn and plant my hand on the wall, letting myself tower over her as she backs against the wall. "A punishment might be in store. In fact, I might encourage it."

Her face pales and she stammers, the words a jumbled mess on her tongue as she tries to explain herself, but her senseless blabbering is lost on me. My hand drifts up and I let my fingers curl into her hair, roughly gripping it as I pull her head back. Her breath mingles with mine, the smell of her pussy still on her lips as she licks them, still tasting herself.

The image of that tongue licking up and down my cock sends heat flaring through me. I nearly moan at the thought as heat swirls in her eyes, any fear she had of me burned away with the wildfire in her eyes. I pull away because if I don't get moving, I will have her face pressed against the wall while I fuck her from behind.

And I truly hope she's ready for whatever punishment Devin is planning for her, but for now, she's *mine*. Which will drive him to near insanity and royally piss him off, something I thoroughly enjoy doing every chance I get. And maybe if I'm lucky, I'll be punished, too, because after years of living with him, I'm a fucking glutton for it.

CHAPTER TWENTY-SEVEN

Lena

MY EYES FLUTTER OPEN, and I'm met with darkness. The curtains of Tony's room are completely blacked out and my sense of time is hazy. Sitting up, I let my eyes adjust to the dark, and it seems like I'm alone in his giant bed, which is the size of a small island, surrounded by a sea of black satin sheets. I didn't peg him as a man who appreciated the finer things, but he continues to surprise me. Like last night, instead of taking me to my room or back to Devin's, he brought me to his.

He put me in the shower and watched me through the clear glass from where he leaned against the doorframe. As soon as I was out, he was on me, pressing me against the wall, forcing my palms to stay flat, holding my head against it and fucked me, pulling out just to make a mess of me again, coming all over my lower back and ass.

Like I was nothing more than a rag doll, he threw me over his shoulder and carried me out to the bed, where he forced me onto the mattress face down. Using his cum as lube, he took my ass, his huge cock stuffing me full. It was painful bliss, the kind that I wouldn't mind relishing in for the rest of my life. I will walk the edge and wait for him to push me over again and again.

Dragging me back into the shower, he cleaned me up, making sure to take care of every inch. His touch was delicate, so much so that my eyes grew heavy, and before I knew it, I was dried off, in bed, and drifting off to sleep. Dreaming of two dark figures as they hunted me down, making chase.

Tony's rough and unapologetic. And for a man of little words, the ones he does say are some of the dirtiest I've ever heard. It makes me wonder who he was before he came to the club. Before Devin. It's the way his eyes change, the light filtering in and out of them as he turns into a shell of himself before snapping back to reality. But he still manages to be careful with me when it matters, and he seems thoughtful in everything he does. The way he treats the staff and Tasha shows that even behind his hard, masked shell, there's a caring soul.

The lock on the door clicks, and Tony slides in, quick to close it behind him and lock it once again. He's clearly making sure that Devin stays out, which, from my understanding, could be a bad thing for both of us, especially since Tony sent the video of us in the private room. According to Tony, Devin's taken to bloodlust to calm himself down while he waits for us to come out.

His room is about the size of my first apartment with Bri, which was spacious even for the two of us. He has a full desk, a seating area, his fireplace, and this giant fucking bed, and he still has room to put more furniture if he so chooses. His walk-in closet off the bathroom is massive, and his shower could fit five people, just like Devin's. Their rooms are similar in size, but their styles couldn't be more different.

Where Devin's room is filled with light, neutral colors, his bathroom is bright with white tiles, and Tony's is dark, with black tiles, black bedding, and dark flooring.

Both their styles are sleek and minimalistic, and the details in their rooms clearly give away just how different they are. Devin prefers to cover the walls with high-end art, showing that he came from money and enjoys finer things, spreading himself throughout the apartment.

While Tony is high tech, his computer setup is extremely impressive, with a large screen mounted on the wall. He's even installed neon lights around the room and under the bed, which give off the same vibes as the lighting in the Underground. It was so sexy when he powered them on, the red glow making his gray eyes look monstrous.

He's carrying canvas totes and headed toward the large desk area of his room. He maneuvers around before opening one of the cabinets on the wall. No, not a cabinet, but a full-sized fucking refrigerator.

He unloads groceries from the cloth bags and quietly closes the refrigerator door, cutting off the dim light. He turns and I catch his eyes, freezing him in place.

"Is that a refrigerator?" The disbelief drips from my words, but I shouldn't be surprised that he installed a full-sized refrigerator in his room. This man nearly has this place set up like a fucking bunker and enjoys his privacy. But I swear I see a twinkle of amusement in his eye, or it could just be a reflection from the glow of the neon lights as he brings them up, the room glowing. He chuckles, actually chuckles. "There's a microwave in the cabinet next to it, if you're interested."

All I can do is shake my head and scoff. "Who *are* you, Tony Fox?" It's posed with a joking tone, but it's a question I've been dying to ask over the past few weeks. There are things about him that just don't seem to add up and no one can seem to answer for me.

I hardly know anything about him, and he'd rather keep me at arm's length than let me in. I try my hardest not to compare it to the way that Matt kept me in the dark, but the cruel voices in my mind seem to remind me that I have a type. Dangerous and full of fucking secrets.

He watches me curiously as if he can see right through me, reading me. "It's not important." He says the words lowly, as if it's a whisper in the wind. "But what *is* important is that you know that I'm not like *him*."

His words knock the breath from me, because now I wonder if he can read minds or if I am just that predictable. "I never said you were."

He takes a few steps around the desk, the open space now the only thing between us. "You didn't have to. It's written all over your face."

Shit. I've never been good at hiding anything, so of course a man like him could see right through the dark and read my face. "If you're not him, then who *exactly* are you?" I tap my chin with my pointer finger. "Who is the man behind the mask?"

He takes a slow step toward me, his footfall heavy as it hits the floor. "Who said it's a man behind the mask?" He curls and uncurls his hands at his sides. "What if I told you, it was a monster? One that you let crawl into your bed, right between your legs."

Sliding myself over to the edge of the bed, I hook my legs over the mattress, letting them dangle just about the floor. My legs are bare, and the only thing covering my body is Tony's oversized T-shirt, one he insisted I wear after our shower. "Then I'd say I'd want to see for myself." He flexes his hands again as I stand, the cool floor under my feet. My steps are slow as I move toward him, letting the tension build between us. "I know what monsters look like now, and from what I can see, you don't share a single resemblance."

"You've only met one kind of monster, the kind that are *born* that way. Some of us were made into one." My breath catches and my feet freeze in place. He watches me carefully, assessing my reaction. A reaction that is once again written all over my face.

I relax my shoulders and continue to close the distance

between us. "I don't care what kind of monster you think you are, Tony. I'm not afraid of you."

He takes a step toward me, heat radiating off his massive body in waves, heating my skin. "You fucking should be," he nearly growls, the words a rumble in his chest.

"Maybe." I shrug. "But Belle fell in love with the Beast, didn't she? And look how that turned out for her."

He cocks his head to the side, narrowing his eyes at me. "He turned back into a man at the end, but I'm cursed to be like this forever." He takes another step, electricity crackling between us. "Is that what you fucking want? Half of a man?"

I close the distance, our bodies inches from each other as I look up at him. My hand floats up and I let it hover over his chest, unsure of what he might do if I touch him. "I'll take whatever you give me, Tony."

His breath hitches and his steely gray eyes dilate as if he just took a hit of his favorite drug. His hand comes up and wraps slowly around mine, finger by finger, before pressing it to his chest. His heart thunders under my palm and I feel the hard muscles that he has hiding under his tight, black tee. We stand like this for a moment before he takes a step, leading me back toward the bed.

He lets go of my hand and bends, removing his boots and kicking them under the bed, in bachelor fashion. He lowers onto the mattress, sliding himself up to the headboard to sit against it. I watch him curiously because this feels like some kind of trap, but he reaches out a hand, and any doubts I have about his feelings for me come crashing down. The wall that's been between us coming down once and for all.

I take his rough, calloused hand, letting it scrape against my palm. He pulls me onto the bed, where I straddle his lap, my exposed pussy sitting right on his black, tactical pants.

I let my hands drop to my thighs, unsure of what he wants me to do. I'm worried about pushing him too hard, something that Devin told me not to do because Tony's fuse is short, and his patience is thin. But right now, the man that Devin described is not the man in front of me.

My hands hover on his chest, my fingertips brushing against the fabric of his shirt. He takes a sharp breath as I lay my palms flat against his pecks, a quiet growl rumbling through him. His heart is still racing, even though he gives off this unnatural air of calm. Resting his hands on my waist, his fingers press into me, holding me in place.

He wants me here.

I trace the edge of his hood with my finger, feeling his cropped haircut underneath. I hear him take a sharp breath as I move my finger up slightly, but I never hear him exhale. I lean in and brush my lips over the scar that cuts through his eyebrow, my fingers inching further under his hood, feeling the longer hairs on top of his head.

He tenses up, and I hear another quiet growl, causing me to freeze. "I'm…I'm sorry." I let my hands drop down to his shoulders as I lean back to look at him. "I didn't mean—"

He presses his finger to my lips, silencing me. "This wouldn't be happening if I didn't want it to, baby. Keep going."

I hold still, even as his hand pulls away from my mouth and I watch in awe as his fingers curl around the black fabric of his hood, pulling it back and putting himself on display. Even with a short cut on top and the sides blended into a fade, his hair is dark brown with wisps of silver all over, looking like a dusting of starlight against a stark night sky. Small, black diamonds glint from his pierced ears.

I take a quick breath in at the sight of all the scars across the right side of his scalp that disappear into the slightly longer hair on top. I slowly reach up, giving him time to stop me if he wants to, and let my fingers trace over them. I explore every raised scar, following each one like lines on a map.

Even though his skin is marred, he's even more handsome

than I could have imagined— with his mask still covering the bottom half of his face.

"We don't have to do this," I say quietly, my voice making him tense up. "It doesn't change anything."

I watch as emotions swirl in his eyes, his brows furrowing as he considers my words. I attempt to slide back to give him some room, but his hands fly to my waist, once again holding me in place. "*Stay*," he breathes. The single word alone would have stopped me in my tracks, even without his shaking hands, his fingers tightening their hold on me to near bruising. It's a rough, almost raw command that sounds like it has been ages since he said it.

I trace my finger along the strap of his mask, watching as his eyes widen with what looks like fear. My heart aches at the thought that even this simple touch has him on edge and that whatever happened in his past life has made him so afraid to show me what's under his mask, that he's physically shaking.

My fingers trace the ridges of his mask as I listen to his sharp and heavy breathing that filters through the grates of his mask. My fingers stop at the clip on the side, dancing over it, but before I can press it, his hand shoots up and grips my wrist. I let out a startled gasp as his fingers tighten their hold.

Tony holds my gaze, wariness in his eyes. We're frozen in this moment as I wait for him to decide if we're going to cross this line because when we do, there's no turning back. He will have laid it all out there, bearing all his scars to me.

His shaking hands remain on my wrists, gently pressing his fingers into my skin, the heat of his touch sinking into my veins, warming me all over. He uncurls his fingers, letting them fall away one by one. He closes his eyes and breathes deeply as my finger presses into the clip until it clicks free. The strap loosens as I unclip the other side, pulling it away and finally revealing the man behind the mask.

His lips are full, and I fight the urge to press mine on them immediately, pushing my tongue past them and tasting him.

His skin is smooth, except for the jagged scar that cuts up from his chin, across his lips, and across his cheek. A battle scar that looks as though it had been poorly stitched on the field to have healed like this. It poses too many questions about who he was before he came here, ones I'm not sure I'll ever have the courage to ask.

He's so ruggedly handsome that it's not fair to the world for him to hide his face. But, then again, I might be selfish enough to relish the fact that I'm one of the only people who knows what he looks like, that I don't have to share it with the rest of the world. He's the one who would follow me in the shadows, whether to protect me or hunt me down like the monster he claims to be. I'll take him either way.

I gently run my finger across his soft lips, his warm breath filtering through. "Tony," I breathe. His eyes stay closed, and his body relaxes. I cup his face and lower my mouth onto his. I trace my tongue across his still-closed lips, begging for him to let me through; the need to taste him almost unbearable.

I pull my face back, the subtle feeling of rejection growing in my chest as his now open, gray eyes take in my face, looking for something in my expression. I sit back, his hard cock still pressed against my center, and take in the man sitting in front of me, a dozen questions sitting on my tongue.

I let them sit there, waiting for the perfect moment to open the dam and let them through, but they evaporate as his hands run up my thighs, pushing up his shirt to expose my bare pussy. I untuck his shirt and start pulling it up. He grips the hem, leaning forward, pulling it and his hood off.

I take in his broad chest, peppered with tiny scars. My fingers trace the muscles down to his belt, running them along the top of his pants. His fingers press into my skin as he breathes my name. I don't hesitate as I crash my mouth into his, and this time, he opens for me, letting me taste him, sweet from the nicotine of his vape.

He grips the back of my neck, deepening his kiss, and

sucks the air from my lungs as he leans forward. I mirror his hand and grip his neck as he stiffens under me. My thumb brushes over a giant scar at the base of his neck and as I pull back, I see his eyes have gone blank.

Clearly another thing from his past that was concealed beneath his hood, and while I could poke and prod, demand to know what happened, find out who fucking did this to him…I don't. He has never once asked me about anything in my life, and while I know he has looked up every detail, if it wasn't for my connection with Matt, I actually doubt that he would have.

He pretended not to listen as I bared my soul, but I know he heard every word and noted every detail of my shitty life. He hates the bastard as much as I do. I know he kept his distance for so long to protect himself and those he cares about from falling into the hands of people like Matt. Like I so unknowingly did.

I brush my thumb over the thick scar tissue at the base of his neck and across other small scars that push out from the edges, trying to smooth the skin and his pain away. I gently kiss the scar that cuts through his handsome face. "I don't care about your scars, Tony," I whisper against his skin. The words seem to curl around him, relaxing his muscles one by one. I continue to run my thumb over the scar. "I only care about the man…or better yet, the monster, beneath them."

Brushing my other hand through his hair, I let my fingers get tangled in it, gripping it at the scalp. I guide his head back, slanting my mouth on his and eliciting a groan from him as we go to war with our tongues and teeth.

I grind my core against his hard cock, letting the zipper area of his pants press into my clit. I want nothing more than to explore this man and let my tongue soothe over every scar. His hands push up my shirt again as he runs his hands up my sides, a shiver skittering across my skin. His thumbs caress the sensitive skin under my breast before he palms them.

I hold the shirt up as he squeezes my budding nipples between his fingers, causing me to gasp. "I can't wait to taste more of you." He bends down, pressing my tits together to run his tongue across my nipples, my head falling back as I grip his hair. "I've been waiting for so long to devour every inch of you." He scrapes his teeth across my skin, nipping and sucking at my breasts, my desire flooding between my legs.

I reach between us, undo his belt, and unbutton his pants. I slowly pull down the zipper, letting each click echo through the room. He watches my hand tease him as I run my fingers under the waistband of his boxer briefs before he meets my gaze, his eyes dark and hungry. I give him a sly smirk before I grip his dick. "I want your monster to fuck me, Tony." I lean in as his eyes darken even more. "Show me what you've been hiding under that mask of yours." I press my thumb onto the head of his cock, smearing his precum. "Make me fucking *scream*."

CHAPTER TWENTY-EIGHT

Tony

WRENCHING HER OFF MY LAP, I toss her onto the bed. If it's the monster she wants, it's the monster she'll get. Mine and Devin's monsters are not even remotely the same, and she's about to find out just how different we really are.

I slide off the bed, yanking my knife out of my pocket and curling my fingers around it before shucking my pants off. Her eyes widen as I stand there, my cock dripping with precum. I grab her ankle and pull her to me, my shirt riding up, obstructing my view of her perfect fucking body. "This fucking shirt has to go."

Flipping open the blade, I catch the hem with the tip and slice through it like butter. She gasps as it flays open, showing off her perfect tits and body. I run the blade lightly across her skin and she whimpers. "Be a good girl and lie still." I run the blade across her hip, then down her inner thigh that shines from her soaking pussy.

I push open her legs, the smell of her desire turning me fucking feral as my knife hovers over her smooth skin. I press it harder against her and she hisses as blood wells around the blade. I smirk when her hiss turns into a moan as my free hand cups her pussy, letting her soak my fingers as I run them through her slit.

I will mark her and make her fucking *mine*.

She says she doesn't care about my scars, but I certainly care about hers, *especially* the ones I intend to leave across her perfect skin.

I lower myself to my knees, running my tongue over the nick on her thigh, the metallic taste of blood hitting my taste buds as I lick up toward her center.

God fucking dammit. She's like nothing I've ever tasted before, and I will never go without her again. This is what I've been fucking missing out on and I could kick my stubborn ass for waiting so long to take her. And her moans are all the more sweeter from this side of the door. No wonder Devin never wanted to leave his fucking room, because I may keep her all to myself. And I like the thought of him on his knees, begging from under the door to come in while I fuck her so hard that they can hear her screaming my name all the way from the club.

I press the blade against her other thigh, marking her in the same spot. Her gasps and whimpers are so sweet, I could listen to them all night as I carve her up and eat her piece by piece. I lap every drop of blood like the sick puppy I am. I wait for it to be too much for her to ask me to stop, but she never does. Instead, she surprises me.

"*Mark me*, Tony. I want them to know I'm just as much yours as Devin's." The words aren't a plea. No, they're a sharp command, like a queen giving out orders on the battlefield. It makes my cock go hard and my head spin as desire crashes over me, sucking the air from my lungs.

I straighten from between her legs and see her propped up on her elbows, watching me, eyes burning hot with need. I could ask her if she's sure, but I don't need to. The look on her face, along with her dripping pussy, is confirmation that it's exactly what she wants.

I lay my hand across her thigh, pressing her leg down. I look up and see she's nearly panting with anticipation. Fuck, this woman is more of a masochist than I could have ever imagined she would be. I press the tip of the knife to her sensitive skin, just far enough down from her pussy that if she wears a short skirt or shorts, everyone will see it. I let the blade glide over her skin, the line thin and just deep enough to scar. Her moan is low and vibrates through her body just as I slide the blade the other way, completing my brand on her.

Her blood wells and drips down her thigh, leaving beautiful drops of crimson on the sheets. I wipe my thumb through the small lines and press the pad to my tongue, tasting her very life. "Tell me who you belong to." I press my thumb against the skin right next to the now brandished '*T*' on her thigh.

"You," she says, the word a panting breath.

I slap her thigh, her back arching and a small scream escapes her lips. "Tell me the *name* of who you fucking belong to, or I'll mark every inch of your skin, so you'll never fucking forget."

She rises into her elbows again, her eyes fluttering, her breaths shallow. "I belong to *you*," she licks her lips slowly, dropping her chin as her next words drip across my skin like honey, thick and sensual, "Tony Fox."

A growl rumbles through my chest as the knife falls from my fingers, clattering as it hits the floor. This fucking woman. She has no fucking clue what she's doing to me as she lies here in front of me and infiltrates all my defenses. She has pulled them down brick by brick and forged through even before the dust settled.

I want to hate her for it, make her pay for what she's done to me. The feelings she has filled me, an empty shell, with. It should be hate that's coursing through my veins, as that's the only real emotion I've felt in what seems like two lifetimes, but it's different. It's *more*.

It simultaneously tames the monster in me but riles him up at the same time, reminding him how starved he is. How we must devour those who are a threat to us but also devour those who will fill us. Even with her, I'm still half starved, my monster fed but not completely satisfied. We will revisit that later. For now, she is the main course, and I fully intend to eat my fill.

I grip her hips, press my fingers into her soft skin, and drag her dripping center back to my mouth. Hooking her legs over my shoulders, I unleash the monster that's been pressing against my skin all night. If she thinks that he will go easy on her, she has another thing coming. Because he's never gone easy on anyone.

Not even me.

"I'm going to fucking ruin you, Lena," I say into her center. "Whatever happened behind that door with Devin won't hold a candle to what I intend to do to you." I suck her clit into my mouth, scraping my teeth across the sensitive bud, and I feel her nearly come out of her skin as a yelp fills the room. "But not tonight. No, tonight, I will make everything about you."

She moans, and I note the goosebumps that rise across her skin from the effects of my words. I slide her legs from my shoulders and stand, licking her from my lips. She watches me, her body trembling as I slide on the bed next to her. Grabbing her, I pull her on top of me, her hands planted on my chest, legs straddling my stomach. Her hair cascades down, creating a curtain around us, smelling like a field of lilacs.

I grip her ass, holding her in place, and she gives me a sly grin. One that I've never seen on her face before and one I never want to leave. "Tony, what are you doing?" Her voice is soft and skitters across my skin as her nose brushes mine. "Didn't I tell you I wanted you to be rough? Didn't you say you were going to *ruin* me?"

My fingers drift up her back to rest on the back of her

neck. Inhaling her scent, I bring her head closer to mine. "Torture is meant to be slow and agonizing, baby." My voice is a rough whisper, just as my mouth crashes with hers, kissing her deeply. I could live behind this curtain with her until my last breath. I want to keep her from this fucked up world we've already endured enough of, because she is far too precious to me to let anyone even look at her.

I would never be able to do that. She needs to thrive in this world. I am the Hades to her Persephone, with Devin being the link between our worlds. He's just the right amount of sunlight for her and darkness for me. The knot in my chest seems to loosen at this realization, one that I've been refusing to see all this time. I was too busy being blinded by his light and charisma to notice that he prowls the dark corners of the world just as much as I do. And that maybe, even though Lena is the light, she loves to see the shadows it can create and let us wreak havoc in them.

Our fucking queen. The only one who can bring us to our knees. The one I would crawl through the flames for and not even notice as it melts my skin from my bones.

She grinds her pussy against my abs, searching for friction that I refuse to let her find right now. Still gripping her ass, I drag her up my body, planting her center right onto my face. "Grab the headboard," I murmur as I lick up her center. She moans my name as I swirl my tongue around her swollen clit, her pleasure building. But, if she thinks that she's going to get off just because she's sitting on my face, she couldn't be more wrong.

I lap her up, careful not to stimulate one area for too long. Every time I move my tongue, she growls in frustration. It's music to my ears to hear her suffer through my edging. It'll be that much more rewarding for the both of us when I finally let her come.

Her thighs start to shake and at the last second, before she can find release, I throw her off me, her body bouncing on the mattress. She yells my name, but I just lick her from my lips as I stand and make my way to my dresser. If it's rough she wants, it's rough she'll get.

I grab the black, leather bag from inside the top drawer, filled with some of my favorite things. I turn and see her on her knees, running her fingers over her breasts like a fucking brat who knows better. Her face is flushed, and she's still breathing heavily, her eyes darkening as they fill with desire.

Smirking, I cross the room and dump the contents onto the bed. The flush that had just filled her face vanishes as she takes in the toys that are scattered in front of her.

Twirling my finger, I gesture for her to turn around. "Hands on the headboard, like I fucking told you." She complies, but not without a scoff, dramatically planting her hands firmly on the top of the headboard. Fucking *brat*.

I take a moment to stare at her ass, already speckled with red marks and bruises from my harsh grip. Fucking *beautiful*.

I curl my fingers around the ball gag, running it across my palm and squeezing it. "As much as I love to hear you scream my name, muffling them seems to be my favorite." Lowering the gag in front of her face, I press it to her lips. "Open wide, baby." She opens her mouth, the ball gag filling it, as I buckle it around her head.

Next up is the blindfold. "Lights out," I say, as I lower the mask over her face, her body shivering at my touch as I run my hands over her skin. Her small tremors of anticipation as my fingers brush over her make me even harder. I've fucked my fair share of women, ones who chased after me until I finally gave in, but I've never had one anticipate my touch so much.

She doesn't have a fucking clue what she does to me.

I scrape my nails down her calf and buckle a cuff around her ankle, doing the same with her other leg. Her muffled whimpers are music to my ears as I make her wait on pins and needles for my next moves.

I cup her breast with my hand, playing with her budded nipple, eliciting a surprised gasp from her. Goosebumps crawl across her skin, her head falling back with a moan as I adorn her with nipple clamps. My cock twitches at her every reaction, making this just as tortuous for me as it is for her.

I can hear her begging behind her gag, her pleas barely making it past the rubber ball secured in her mouth. "That's it, baby, fucking beg for me. Beg like the dirty little slut you are."

Cuffing each wrist slowly, I watch as her fingers tighten around the wood of the headboard, her muscles twitching with each caress of my fingers up her arm. "I hope you're flexible, baby because this is where I mold you to exactly how I want you." My words are deep, but I barely hear them over the thundering of my pulse in my ears.

I'm *excited*. I have a beautiful woman in my bed willing to give herself to me. To take me exactly for who I am, and not ask any questions, even though I know it's killing her not to, and I'm fucking excited. It's like unwrapping a gift on Christmas morning and it is exactly what you wanted.

I guide her back away from the headboard, just far enough that I can bend her over. With her ass in the air, her arms slide under her body, lining her wrists up with her ankles. I clip them together, keeping her in place. "Such a good girl, letting me bend you until you nearly break." I slap her ass, and she lets out a muffled cry, the sound running straight to my already throbbing cock. "Your ass looks so good, so fucking perfect with my marks across your skin." I slap the other cheek, her body twitching, but this time instead of a cry, it's a moan.

Perfection.

Grabbing the butt plug, I slide it between her legs and pump it into her cunt, letting her arousal coat every inch of it. She lets out a soft sound, one of relaxed pleasure. I'll have to do something about that and keep her guessing all night.

Removing the plug, I use my free hand and spread her cheeks, causing her to stiffen, a soft whimper pushing past the gag.

"Relax, baby. I intend to fill every one of your holes and fuck you until you pass out." I press the plug against her tight hole and watch as she tries to relax. I slide it in, her arousal easily the best lube, and she lets out a guttural moan just as I turn it on, the small vibrator coming to life. I'll buy stock in these fucking things if only to hear her make that sound for the rest of my life.

Sliding my hand between her legs, my pointer finger circles her entrance and I groan. "Goddammit, Lena, you're so fucking wet." Slowly pumping it in and out, I'm careful not to touch her swollen, sensitive clit. I add in another digit, building on her torture, her moans of pleasure getting louder.

The mattress sinks under my weight as I position myself behind her, taking in the view of her ass and pussy on display for me. I have her at the perfect angle that my secure camera feed will let me watch this moment back whenever I want. And to broadcast it on the living room TV, just to fuck with Devin. He's not the only one who's trained in torture.

I line up my cock to her entrance, her hips rocking back, trying to take me. My palm connects with her ass, the smack ringing out, causing her hips to jerk away and a muffled yelp. "Don't be a greedy little slut, Lena. It will only make me draw this out even longer." I bend down and sink my teeth into the flushed skin of her ass, taking a bite like it's the most delicious apple. Her scream turns to a groan as the metallic taste of her blood fills my mouth.

Fuck, she takes the pain better than I could have ever imagined. If I believed in a god, I would be thanking them for dropping this angel right into my life.

I pull back and see my teeth marks, two curved rows, pressed into her ass. "I could just eat you alive, baby, bite by bite." I swirl my tongue over the marks, wiping away the small swells of blood. She won't get out of here without a mark from me on every part of her body. I don't care how long it takes, I will make sure everyone, including Devin, knows that she's just as much mine as she is his.

I rake my cock up her center and across her clit, applying just enough pressure. Her body shudders as her desire drips all over me, coating me in it. I slide back, lining myself up again and sinking just the tip into her. Her walls attempt to grip me, but I keep myself just far enough out that they can't pull me in. "Do you want this cock, baby?" My voice is rough and I see her nodding her head, her unintelligible muffles pleading for me. "How bad do you want it? Come on, tell me?" I taunt and tease her as she tries her fucking hardest to tell me around the gag, her spit running down her face onto the sheets.

"What's that? You *don't* want my cock?" I hear the panic rise in her voice as if I would ever actually take it away from her. I want this just as much as she does, if not fucking more, but torture is torture. Just as she tries to rock her hips back, I slam my cock into her all the way to the hilt. Her pussy tightens around my cock, and I let out my own groan as I hold still in her, keeping her right where I want her. "Such a good fucking girl, taking my entire cock."

Gripping her hips, letting my fingers bruise her skin, I pull back out and slam into her again, the sound of her cries already has my balls tightening up. "Fuck. Your pussy was made for me." I find my rhythm, and just by the way she feels, I already know that when I do come, I will come *hard*.

I slow my rhythm slightly and reach down, picking up the last toy in my arsenal: the black wand vibrator. "Do you want to come, baby?" I turn it on to the highest setting because I want her to come hard and come fast. I want her to continue to walk the line of her pleasure and my inflicted pain.

Nodding her head, I place the wand directly on her clit, making her jump. Her moans are a symphony as she starts to rock her hips, creating even more friction. "That's it, baby. I want to watch you come undone and scream my name." Her pussy clenches around my cock as I pump in and out of her, her pleasure rising until she's falling over the edge. She screams my name and even muffled, it's a beautiful sound as she comes hard on the wand.

I throw it on the bed, grip both of her hips and pound myself into her, my cock thickening as she clenches around me. "Yes, baby, choke my cock with that sweet pussy." The words are gruff as my balls tighten even more and the warm tingle works up my spine. I slam myself into her as I come hard, filling her with my cum. I pull out slightly, letting my cum seep out and down her legs, painting her like a prize winning portrait with my seed.

I pick up the still vibrating wand, and I hear her whimper as I hover it over her swollen clit. "I said it would be torturous, baby, and I'm a man of my word." I press the vibrator against her, and she sobs as she instantly orgasms, her pussy clenching around my semi hard cock. "What's that, baby? You want me to fuck your ass now?" Her sobs of pain and pleasure are making me hard again.

I lean over her and peck soft kisses along her spine, her body nearly spasming beneath me as I hold the vibrator against her center. I see tears running down her face from under her mask, mixing with the drool that's pooling on the sheets. I can't wait to look back on this video, because she's never been more beautiful than she is being filled with my cum and coming completely undone at my touch.

I pull out from her pussy, my cock gleaming from the mix of our cum, and pull the plug from her ass. I throw both the plug and the vibrator over my shoulder, a mess I'll clean up later. Raising myself up, I slap her ass, marking her all over again as I line myself up with her hole. "You're stretched and ready for me, baby. I'm going to fill you up with my cum all over again."

I press myself against her as she wiggles her ass against my tip, clearly begging for it. Fuck, I love the way she wants me. I press into, filling her inch by inch, my cock twitching as it begs for more of her.

She groans as I keep pushing in. "Such a good little slut, taking my cock so perfectly in your ass." I grip her hips and yank her back onto me all the way to the hilt. "Fuck, baby, you're going to make me come again in no time."

I don't waste any more time and pound into her, our cum the perfect lube for me to take her ass over and over. She moans with every thrust, and it gets me going even more, because the next time I take her, I'm going to take that little mouth and fuck down her throat. She will be mine and mine only until I'm ready to share with Devin again, and who knows how long that will be. I can't wait to see his face when he sees the marks I've left on her—and I can't wait to give him ones to match.

These two are *mine*. Fucking mine and no one else's. I might be a recluse in my nature, my past driving me away from anyone who remotely showed me any compassion, but I want to come out to the world with them and only them. This delicate game that Devin and I have been playing for years is over, and he doesn't have to question the rules anymore.

I lose myself in her and before I know it, I'm coming and filling her up, my monster coming to the surface and roaring through the room. I pull out and let my cum coat her even more, the sight being something to behold. If I could keep her just like this, I fucking would.

Sliding from the bed, I take her in, a perfect mess of cum, blood, and saliva wrapped up with a bow on my bed. I step out of the way to make sure that the camera can capture her perfectly before I finally release her. Unclipping her restraints, she keeps in her position like the good little girl she is.

Removing her blindfold, she blinks the tears away that have collected on her lashes. The look on her face is one that I don't think I've seen yet. Contentment. She looks completely satisfied and that damn near makes me hard again. Unbuckling the gag, she licks her lips and flexes her jaw, still staying in the same position until I lift her under her arms and bring her up onto her knees.

Raising her chin, I lower my mouth to hers, my tongue pushing through to hers. Her hands are warm against my chest as she lets her nails dig into my muscles. My teeth scrape against her bottom lip as I pull back, gripping her chin. "Tell me who you belong to." My voice is thick, my words rough.

"And what would you do if I said Devin?"

Oh, you fucking little tease.

"Then I'd have to do everything all over again until you get the answer right."

She smirks as she wraps her arms around my neck, pulling me back to her. "I think we might be able to find the answer in the shower, but you might just have to fuck it out of me."

A growl rips through me as I grab her hips, yanking her to me, her legs wrap around my waist as I hoist her up. I walk her to the shower as she licks and sucks at my neck, my cock hardening again. "Lena, I will fuck this dirty mouth for as long as it takes until you get it right."

I take the time to clean us up, making sure that she's okay to do more, even though she runs her hands over me and grips my cock at the base. I let her press me against the wall and touch me from head to toe, something I've rarely let anyone do. She's brought back a part of me that I had thought had long since died in my previous life, a small part of who I used to be.

I let her explore me as the water washes away the soap on our skin, asking me about my scars and tattoos as she lets me fuck her. I don't even bother shutting the shower door, because I don't want Devin to miss out on the sounds that she's about to make as she chokes on my cock.

CHAPTER TWENTY-NINE

DEVIN

He fucked her *without* me, that motherfucker.

And now, he's had her locked away in his room for two days. *Two fucking days*. I know he's been watching for me on the cameras and only leaving when he knows I can't be in the penthouse. He's playing dirty and fuck me if that's not fucking hot.

Weeks. He's been a brooding asshole about her for fucking *weeks*, and then suddenly, he's skipping over the niceties and jumping right to fucking her. And the icing on the cake is him sending me the videos of the dirty things they've done. That's all I've been jacking off to while I listen to them endlessly fuck behind his locked door. If I weren't so fucking turned on by the whole idea of them finally being together, I would kill him. So instead, I'm taking my frustrations out on the man who chose to touch what didn't belong to him.

I would normally go a little easier on unsuspecting assholes who are just looking to get laid, but not only did he touch the wrong woman, he's also on the wrong side of this war. According to Tony, he'd been here watching her on the dance floor, waiting for a chance to strike like a fucking snake in the grass. And how do we like our snakes? *Dead.*

His blood drips from the stump where his hand used to be as it dangles at his side. The smell of burned flesh fills the room from where I cauterized it after I sawed it off and he passed out like the pussy he is.

I look over my handiwork, looking at the box of body parts that will be shipped out to one of the top members of Obsidian. An ear, his hand, an eye, and I'm just waiting for him to wake back up so I can take his dick and then end this little game. I feel bad for the assistant of the man we're sending it to, who will most likely be the one to open the box, but she knew what she was signing up for when she started working for him over eight years ago. And I'm sure she's well aware of his nefarious acts since she started fucking him seven years ago, his wife seeming to turn a blind eye to his affair and staying married to the bastard.

It makes me even more pissed at the thought that Lena was the innocent one whose shitty fiancé was out fucking who knows who and getting away with it almost the same. This guy in front of me didn't stand a chance when my bloodlust took over and all I could see was Matt's fucking face. No one hurts Lena and gets away with it, especially not now that Tony and I have both claimed her.

She's *ours.*

Whether she understands what that means or not, no one will lay a hand on her again unless it's us, and only for her pleasure. My dick hardens as I think of the fascination on her face when I took her down to the Underground all those weeks ago. I can't wait to take her down there again, tie her up, and fuck her until sunrise. All while the other members watch, their own scenes playing out around us.

I press the button that raises the new chair that I had installed to make these torture sessions a little more fun and let it flatten out like a table. I lower the hose that is hanging from the ceiling and spray him with ice cold water. He sputters and gags as I shoot it right at his mouth, and his remaining eye flies open.

"Good, you're awake." I deadpan. He whimpers, one of the few sounds he can make after I took out his tongue. He wasn't giving me the answers I wanted and was calling me every name in the book like the tough guy he is, so he fucking lost the privilege to speak to me at all. His head lolls, his blood loss showing as he struggles against his bindings, his handless arm flailing. Well shit, I guess I should have strapped it back down before I woke him up. Oh well, I do love a challenge when dismembering body parts. "One last little gift for your friends and then I'll see you in Hell."

His screams echo, making me even harder as I undo his pants, flopping his extremely underwhelming, flaccid penis out. Lena would have been extremely disappointed if she had seen it, even if you didn't compare it to Tony and me. "Well, well, it seems we have a small guy in our presence." I flick out the blade of my favorite knife, allowing this moment to be a little poetic for me as I press the tip of the blade to the base of his cock. "No matter the size, it'll still be a big surprise for your friend."

The blade slices through like butter, silencing his screams as he passes out again. Blood pools between his legs, cascading over the edge like a waterfall and spilling to the floor. I throw the now dismembered dick into the box, blood splattering against the plastic bag that lines it, and grin. An early Christmas present, for sure.

The color drains from his body, and his blood loss is almost too much as he starts to fade. I imagine if he still had his tongue, he would be begging for death. But even as his reaper, I wouldn't be bothered to answer.

Instead of slicing his throat, I just leave him there to bleed out. I'll give it some time and then I'll send a message to the cleanup crew. They'll have a fucking hay day with this one.

It takes a special kind of person to clean up a dead body, but they're just fucked up enough for the job. It doesn't hurt that I pay them more for every cleanup than they would make in a month or two, so they definitely don't complain when there's more than one body. The higher the body count from me, the bigger the payout for them.

I'm happy and they're happy. We're the perfect team of miscreants.

Peeling my gloves from my hands, I drop them in the biohazard bin before going to wash off my knife. I stare at the door on the far side of the room, the need to pull another body from our dungeon prison choking me. But, unfortunately, there's no time for another one tonight. They'll just have to wait their turn.

I think about all the scum on the other side of that door, the ones who attempted to lure my brother into their fucking little club and then turned on him because he didn't follow their rules. He didn't let the darkness of the world seep into his sunny disposition but instead used it to swoon the people of this godforsaken city to side with him instead of the crime lords. He was everything good in this world and those fuckers snuffed him out. Plucked him like a flower from the garden to then smash it beneath their shit-stained boots.

We were completely different in so many ways, but even as my older brother, he never looked down on me, even when I was being a complete asshole. For those formative years of my life, he was the only one who could calm my urges and help me find other ways to cope. He kept me from getting locked up or sent off to a boarding school and showed me what love could look like from another person. Something neither one of our parents offered me once I started showing my tendencies and I was no longer cut from the same cloth.

He convinced Nate's father to bring me on as the guy who could make this club into something more than a seedy hangout for thugs and low-grade criminals. I focused all of my pent-up energy on making Masquerave a destination and hot spot for the elite members of society who wanted a place off their beaten path and out of the limelight. I found that working eighteen-to-twenty-hour workdays and fucking whoever smiled in my direction was the best way to spend my pent-up energy.

I built an empire and made a name for myself while making my brother proud. When I lost him, my heart turned a little blacker and the last sliver of my morals went out the fucking window. The last thing he gave before he died was Tasha, who later brought in Tony. The top floors of this club became the home to our band of misfits, and we made a life out of controlling the chaos that came through these doors with whatever means necessary.

Now we have Lena, along with Bri, who seem as though they can match our level of derangement or at least accept it. Something that the people of high society claim they could never do, even though they act the same way, just in fine clothes and fast cars. Which, I made sure to supplement for myself and not bother with a dime of my father's dirty fucking money.

The last time that fucker ever bothered to speak to me was on the night that Drew died, and he finally told me exactly how he felt about me. I was damn near breaking; I remember the press against my skin as my monster tried to rip through my armor and devour my father whole. It was my mother's voice that took him down a notch, until she asked me to leave, saying hardly anything but telling me enough to know that she would pick my father over me every fucking time.

Keeping up my brother's legacy by protecting those who need it and forcing the fucks of this city to remember him is the least I can do until we finally take them down, exposing them all for who they really fucking are. I don't believe in angels, but I do believe that Lena was placed in my life to fuel the fire in me and keep me going to find out what happened to Drew. Even if he would have genuinely lost that election, he would have done it with grace and still challenged the fuck who falsely won every single day.

I haven't gotten all the answers I've been looking for from the men who sit in the cells down here, who Tony has scrubbed from existence, or has them on the national missing person's list to make it seem like they've run. It's the only way to keep the direct target off our backs. Most of what they tell me I already know. A few new names here and there, but for the most part, they're just fucking criminals who have done heinous crimes and deserve some vigilante justice from us.

In the years since I started this manhunt, I have only had two mistaken identities set up by Obsidian to throw us off their trail. Those two were not only compensated but now work for us full time and get a thrill out of dragging pieces of shit down here and locking them away.

Just more vigilante shit.

Wiping my knife off on the only clean towel in the space, I pocket it and tell myself it's time to leave, not letting the voice in my head convince me to drag another man out and dissect him like a frog in science class. Instead, I let the pressure continue to build under my skin like I'm a shaken can of soda. I intend to use this energy on two people who have finally crossed the line with each other and complete our little love triangle.

"Having fun?" I whip around, flipping the blade of my knife open, ready to tear down whoever snuck up on me, but almost instantly relax.

I grin as Nate steps out of the shadows, looking as much like the heir of a billionaire as one can. "Always. Care to join me?"

His lips kick up, showing me the same handsome smile that the tabloids catch at all his fancy gatherings. He looks down at his expensive suit. Armani, his favorite designer. "Not in this suit." He steps more into the light. "Maybe next time, though."

I laugh, because we both know he would never dirty his hands in such a literal way. Nate might be a good man at heart, but he knows a lot of dirty people who can do his bidding for him. For example, me. Except, he's never had to blackmail me, as I've always been a willing participant in this kind of debauchery.

"I've been looking for you for the last two days." He narrows his eyes to me. "Where have you fucking been?" He's yet to look toward the body of the man who's slowly bleeding out on the chair fifteen feet away—blood and gore are not really his thing. Shame, I think he'd be really good at it if he took the time to practice.

Crossing my arms, I give him a smirk. "Well, you have to look other places than between Tasha's legs." I point my finger to the ceiling. "And you're a whole floor off."

A deep red flushes up his neck, because he might be able to fool the world with his good image, but I know exactly what his kinks are and *who* he exclusively does them with when he's in town. "Fuck you." He looks away from me as the man in the chair starts wheezing. "Dev…" he starts.

I wave him off. "He's almost there, just a few more minutes."

Nate slowly turns his head back to me, the color draining from his face at the sight of the blood. He clears his throat, taking a big step away from the blood that's pooling on the floor. "If I didn't know you, Dev, I would be fucking terrified to be in a room with you."

Flipping the blade in my hand, he watches it, his eyes following it up and down. "I would never hurt *you*, Nate, but you should probably still be afraid. I'm a fucking lunatic."

He chuckles. He knows all too well how true that is, given the things I've done to people like the sorry fuck strapped to the chair. "So, I heard that you have a new lady in the house."

He gives me a smirk. "Does she know what you're down here doing or are you letting her think you're a good guy?"

Shrugging, I keep flipping the knife, the blade gleaming in the bright light with every pass. "She's too busy fucking Tony at the moment to care what I'm doing, but she's seemingly aware of my proclivities."

He stiffens and his eyes go wide as the words sink in. "And you're not pissed that she's with Tony?"

Am I pissed? Yes, but not for the reasons he might think. I'm pissed that he's locked me out and won't let me be part of the fun. I'm also pissed that it took him so long to stop being a stubborn motherfucker about her. Now, if only he'll stop being one about me, because if he's in the room the next time I fuck Lena, I won't be able to control myself and have to take him too.

"As long as she doesn't stop fucking me, what do I care?" I give him a Cheshire grin. "And if I'm lucky, maybe I'll get them both." I give him an exaggerated wink and turn toward the bathroom, ready to scrub the blood and gore off me.

Nate just shakes his head, his own smile on his face. Even when we were roommates in college, he never judged me for who I fucked or fucked with. The only time he ever said anything was when I left the door open to fuck the RA; Nate walked in on us while I was balls deep in his ass. He called me a motherfucker and slammed the door shut, letting me finish what I started, but he never mentioned it afterward. To which, we silently agreed that I would lock the fucking door from then on out.

Of course, other than seeing your roommate's bare ass, there's nothing like a good round of trauma bonding over shitty fathers to bring two guys close together, not giving a shit who they're fucking.

What he doesn't know is that I put a kid in the hospital by hitting him with my car when he called Nate a homophobic slur, all because people thought we were sleeping together since we stayed roommates for all four years and we're obviously close. Whether he ever came out or not, I don't take lightly to someone disrespecting the people I care about. The guy's lucky that he only ended up in a body cast and not a casket like I was going for.

"How long are you in town for this time?" I ask as I pull open the bathroom door, flipping on the light. While I'm down here, I might as well clean up and wash off the blood from that pathetic worm.

He comes up and leans against the doorframe. He's slightly taller than me, his shoulders a little broader as he crowds the doorway. "I think I might stick around for a little longer than normal." He's using his boardroom voice, which tells me that he's hiding something.

I cut a glance over my shoulder as I turn the shower on, the pressure of the water blasts from the shower head, the pipes squealing. "This doesn't have anything to do with the fact that Vinny is no longer in the picture, does it?" It's a dick move on my part to ask, and even though he is one of my only true friends in this world, I'm still a nosey bastard.

He leans harder into the doorframe, the wood creaking, taking my bait. "That fuck was a waste of space." He crosses his arms, his fingers curled into fists that are tucked under his forearms. "He deserved every last thing that she did to him."

Interesting. "Did she tell you about it?"

He furrows his brows, a flicker of confusion going across his face. "No, *you* sent it to me, you fucking asshole. Don't you remember or were you too lost in bloodlust?"

Motherfucking Tony. I'm going to fucking kill him for continuing to fuck with Nate, even after I distinctly asked him to stop after he almost killed him last time. Tony *will* be getting punished for that one way or another.

However pissed I am at Tony, I don't let it show. Instead, I kick up the corner of my mouth, playing it cool. "It was definitely the bloodlust. I'm sorry I got caught up and you had to see that."

His eyes flick away and go a little distant. "Don't be sorry, it's just a little reminder of how ruthless she can be." His voice is low, but I don't miss the look of wonder on his face as his hand flexes. This bastard has no fucking clue that what she did was mild, but here it is, making him hard. And what a day it'll be when he finds out just *how* ruthless she can be when it's someone she cares about. Actually—I hope he doesn't have to find out and can live in blissful ignorance about the woman he shares a bed with, no matter how unconventional and messy their relationship may be.

Shaking his head, his eyes clear, bringing him back to reality. Steam starts to fill the space, water droplets already forming on the tiles. I shuck off my clothes and step into the stream of hot water, watching as the blood mixes with it as it flows down my body, swirling down the drain.

"Let's plan dinner tomorrow, Dev. For all of us."

The water burns across my skin, the loofah making it raw as I scrub away any evidence of tonight. "Your treat," I tease, but he just hums in agreement. "But I only want to order in, we're not leaving until the dust settles and we have more intel on who we're targeting. I'm not putting anyone else in danger."

The glass of the shower doors has fogged, but I can still see as he shifts uncomfortably. The thing about Nate is that unlike me, he doesn't want to know shit about what goes down in the club—unless it's Tasha going down on him. Disclosing anything to him makes him feel like a liability. He continues on as the out-of-touch owner who occasionally graces us with his presence to "check in" and "see how things are going". It's all bullshit, and we know it.

"I'll have it catered to the penthouse at seven on the dot." The glow of his phone bounces off his face, making him look angelic through the steamed glass. "Any special requests?"

I don't even hesitate with my answer. "Lena likes sushi, so order all the fish in the fucking sea. Spare no fucking expense."

He chuckles and I can see him typing away as I scrub my hair before dunking my head under the stream of water. "Tasha enjoys it, too. And from what I hear, Brianna does, as well." I smirk because I'm sure the only reason he gets by with calling Bri by her full name is the simple fact that he's technically her boss—and Tasha's one and only booty call.

He falls silent for a beat. "You love them, don't you?"

His words wrap around me, squeezing the air from my lungs. I suddenly feel dizzy and find myself bracing my hand against the cool tile wall. I'm invested, obviously…but *love*? Is that what this aching feeling in my chest is? Is it the buildup of all these years of sidelong glances and tense moments with Tony, plus these last few weeks with Lena, and what I'm feeling is the equivalent of love for any other person?

Wiping the steam away from the glass, I look at Nate. His normally fierce green eyes, the kind that would bring anyone to their knees if they so much as looked at him wrong, have gone soft. His frame is enough to intimidate in a room full of powerful people and still look like an heir in his suit jacket. He's entirely too handsome for his own fucking good with his sharp jaw and his dirty blond hair is always cut into a nice fade with longer hair on top, which is mussed and currently hanging over his forehead like he can't keep his hands out of it.

It's obvious why Tasha would be so smitten with him. Hell, even I find myself crushing on him from time to time with his god like body and devilish good looks.

I watch him as the steam slowly clouds the glass again, but he doesn't move, allowing me time to think through his question. Wiping away the fog once more, I look him in the eyes. "I would die for them and if that's love…then I guess I do."

His face stays neutral, never showing any judgment, as it

always has when I come to confess something so deep and dark to him. Saying those words out loud solidifies everything that has been swirling inside of me for so long. And if told to the wrong person could be considered a weapon of mass destruction.

He nods in acknowledgment but says no more on the subject. Because what else is there to say to a sociopath when they make a declaration like that?

He drops his gaze to his phone and lightly clears his throat. "I'm heading back up to my apartment." A smile tugs at my lips, one I know he can't see through the steam as I turn up the heat on the water. He's not fucking fooling me. That apartment is right across the hall from Tasha's; we both know he's not staying in it. Unless they've moved over there now that Bri is her new roommate. Something that I'll have to investigate a little further for my own research. "I'll see you tomorrow night, Dev."

His body moves out of the doorway. "Great, and after dinner, we can have a good old-fashioned orgy, like one big happy family," I tease. He groans, my joke landing exactly how I wanted it to, but he doesn't say another word before he disappears out the door, leaving me alone with my thoughts.

I stand in the silence for a while longer, my face under the showerhead. I let the pressured water fill my mouth and nose, clearing the voice from my head and the pressure against my skin. Once it's finally settled, I cut the water and towel off.

I slide into my gray joggers, leaving my chest bare, and slip into my spare pair of shoes, not wanting to track blood through the entire building. I blink as the elevator door closes in front of me and I pull up the video, watching Lena take Tony's rough fucking like the dirty little slut she is. She never wavered, even as he held her down, bound her, and fucked her senseless. She really is a fucking queen.

After Tony's text that they were waiting for me, and for me to get my ass up to the apartment, they better be ready.

Because tonight, I'm letting *my* monster loose and taking a bite out of both of them. I'm going to make them pay for locking me out for days.

The elevator slides open, and I stop the video, sliding my phone into my pocket as I exit. I open the penthouse door and am greeted with silent darkness. I check Lena's room first, but it's dark too, with no one to be found. Next up is Tony's room, which is also empty.

What the fuck?

My heart thunders in my chest as a ripple of anxiety thrums through me. Where the fuck are they? If Tony has stolen her away, I will hunt him down and incinerate him but be careful to remove his dick to keep for myself. Fuck whatever feelings that are infecting me with him, he'll be a dead man for fucking with me like this.

Running my hand through my hair, I grip my roots, yanking hard enough to rip some strands out. My eyes scan the space, taking in every detail. Have they even been in here or…My door, it's not all the way shut, and even though I trust Tony with my fucking life, we *never* leave our doors ajar and disrupt our unspoken privacy rule.

I slip out of my shoes, my footsteps silent on the hardwood floors as I stalk toward the room. It's pitch black inside and a thrill runs up my spine, pulling a grin up at the corners of my mouth. Someone is in here, and whether it's them or an intruder, it's going to be a fun night.

My fingers curl around the door, pushing it open enough for me to slip inside. I stand next to it, ready to make an escape if I need to, and inhale quietly as I let my eyes adjust to the dark, familiar smells lingering in the air. Oh, they're playing a little game of hide and seek, are they? Our bedrooms are as big as some people's full-sized apartments, so there's plenty of room to hide here.

I approach the bed first, the most obvious place they'd be. The covers of my Alaskan King bed have been pulled back, but it's empty. I turn toward the sitting area, and as I approach, that's when I see a figure sitting in one of the black, leather chairs, its high back hiding them. The shadows around them seem to move, and I catch the sweet scent of a vape.

Delicious.

"If I'd known we were playing a game, I would have drawn it out a little longer," I quip, but there's no answer from the figure in the chair. I stand there, waiting for something, and just as I'm about to close the distance, a delicate hand snakes around my body, running over my abs.

I stay still as Lena runs her fingers over each muscle, tracing along the waistband of my sweats. "Isn't it *always* a game with you?" Her voice is thick with lust, and immediately, all the blood rushes to my cock, making it turn achingly hard and causing my head to spin.

The fireplace comes to life along with the red neon lights that line the baseboards, illuminating the room and matching the vibes of the Underground. The crimson glow turns Tony's gray eyes fiery as he sits low in the chair, legs spread wide, already palming his hard cock. And *holy shit*, he's not wearing his hood or either one of his masks.

These two worked together and lured me right into their trap. How *fucking* hot is that?

"Well, now that you two are *well* acquainted, we can finally play by *my* rules." I see the glow reflect off of Tony's teeth as he viciously smiles at us.

Lena's hand slips under my waistband, her fingernail lightly tracing my length, causing me to let out a soft moan. "Playing dirty tonight, are we, love?" She runs her nails of her other hand down my back, pressing hard enough to leave marks, running her tongue over them, easing the pain.

"I am learning from the best." She wraps her arms around my waist, leading me backward toward the bed. She turns me to where I'm facing it, and I don't miss the array of toys already laid out on the bench at the foot. She comes around me, trailing a finger as she goes like one of the dancers as they round their poles. I see she's been picking up on their cues during her time down in the club.

I finally get my eyes on her, taking her in for the first time in days, and I almost howl at the fucking moon like a wolf. She stands before me in her little black heels, in a black, leather bra with shiny silver zippers up each cup, when unzipped, would expose each of her perfect, pink nipples. Her panties are a strappy, black leather number that lies perfectly across her skin. Each thin strap just waiting to be snapped by my teeth.

Wait. Holy shit, they're fucking *crotchless*, giving me the choice of whether I want them on her or stuffed in her mouth for me to get later. And I don't miss the way that her pussy is already dripping, glistening in the firelight as if I've missed out on some foreplay. I can't complain about the little numbers that Tasha has been filling her dresser with. Her taste is fucking impeccable, and I'll need to make sure she gets a bonus for this.

I follow the curves of her body up and see the leather choker around her neck, a small O-ring in the front, just waiting to be clipped to something. And I *will* find something to secure her to and fuck her doggy style as she whimpers and whines like a little bitch, taking me hard and fast.

Fuck, I can't wait to use her like the little sex toy she's presenting to be. The sweet woman who showed up at my club is not the woman who is standing in front of me now. No, *this* woman has fully embraced the new life she was thrown into and has wholly given herself to her dark desires. Whether she realizes it or not, she's powerful, a force like no other, and has both Tony and me by the fucking balls.

I give her my darkest smile, one that visibly sends a shiver across her skin as I look over to Tony, whose fiery eyes are still burning into me *and* Lena.

"Let the fucking games begin."

CHAPTER THIRTY

Lena

DEVIN'S LIPS crash into mine as his hand wraps around my throat, squeezing just enough to give me a rush. I run my nails down his forearm before reaching up to run my hands across his chest and down his abs, because I can't get enough of him after all these days. He grips my wrist, pulling his mouth from mine and tsking. "Not so fast, love." He steps back and keeps me at arm's length. "I want this to be slow and *painful*."

I gulp around the lump that's formed in my throat, his palm adding more pressure. I take in his still damp hair, knowing that he must have just showered off the blood of one of his victims and his bloodlust is still pulsing through him. He's a hunter who has a need to kill, and right now, I'm the main target of his destruction.

Disregarding his words, I reach up and lightly cup his bulge, giving it a playful squeeze. A moan of pleasure escapes his lips. "You dirty, *dirty* girl." His eyes light up, flicking past me where Tony is seated before coming right back and drinking me in. "How should I make you pay for the games you've been playing tonight? Hm?" Leaning down, he nips at my jaw, his teeth scraping against my skin, sending a jolt between my legs.

He pauses and slowly pulls back, his eyes locked on my neck. He crooks a finger under my chin, lifting it and exposing the column of my throat. "What the fuck is *this?*" His eyes darken as he looks at the speckles of dark bruises across my throat, ones that Tony brandished into my skin over the last couple of days, not to mention the initial carved into my skin and the teeth marks he left behind. That will be a surprise for later. He leans his head down, looking at them closer. "Well, this just won't fucking do."

His eyes turn in Tony's direction again, this time, it's Devin flashing his perfect teeth. Turning his head back, he bites down on my neck. I let out a choked scream as he sucks roughly on my already sensitive skin. I grip his wrist for support as I lean into his assault on my skin, relishing in the pain. He bites and sucks down my neck, across my collarbone, and to my breast. His free hand reaches around to my lower back, roughly pressing my hips to him, his hard erection against my stomach.

He pulls back, his pupils wide as he looks over his handi-work. "*Now,*" he growls. "Everyone will know *exactly* who you belong to."

I look at Tony, who is watching us with hungry eyes. "And who exactly is it that I belong to?" I plant my hands on his chest, his finger hooking through the O-ring.

"*Us,*" he purrs as he gently swirls his tongue across my hot skin. "And *only* us."

His hand slides down to my ass, grabbing it and yanking me hard against him, his hot breath at my ear. "Tonight, you're our little slut to do whatever we want with. And what I want is to see you straddle and ride Tony. I want to see what you two have been up to these past few days *without me.*" A jolt pulses down to my clit as he unhooks his finger and steps away. His gaze lowers to Tony's. "It's *my* turn to watch until I'm satisfied with what I see."

Tony growls as his massive body rises from the chair, his

long legs closing the distance in only a few steps. His large hand grabs my face, wrenching my head back as his mouth slants against mine. We moan in unison as his tongue slips past my lips, my teeth nipping at him, the taste of his vape coating my tongue.

His other hand slides down and cups under my ass as he begins to lift me. In one move, I'm off the ground and I wrap my legs around his waist, our kiss never breaking. He carries me to the bed, letting me fall onto the mattress.

Towering over me, he looks at me like I'm his next meal. Pulling his shirt over his head, he exposes his torso. The tattoos on his arms flex as he bends down, wrenching off his boots and stepping out of his pants. He stands gloriously naked in front of me like he has the last few days, but this time seems different as he looks in Devin's direction with a fire in his eyes. Their connection with one another is undeniable.

He's taken over Tony's seat, the fire making his blond hair look like wild flames as he spreads his legs wide. "I want to watch you fuck her." His words are smooth, but there's an edge to them like he's barely able to hold himself back. "Give me a show I'll never forget."

Tony reaches out and grabs my ankle, yanking me toward the edge of the bed. His cock is huge, precum nearly dripping from the tip as he drops to his knees without a word and begins to devour my pussy. My legs are thrown over his massive shoulders as his fingers dig into my hips, keeping me pressed to his face. His tongue spears into me before coming up to swirl around my throbbing clit.

I'm propped up on my elbows and I moan as my head drops back. He's gotten so good at eating me out over the last few days that my thighs are already quivering, the pulsing ache of his brandished 'T' on my skin reminding me of what he's capable of and who I belong to. Body and soul.

He scrapes his teeth across the bundle of nerves before sucking it into his mouth. I let out a deep groan, the sound nearly animalistic as he takes me closer to the edge. I run my fingers into his short hair, gripping it at the base. He growls against my pussy as my pleas tumble from my mouth, begging him to let me come.

"*Don't* you do it, Tony." Devin's voice thunders through the room, halting Tony's tongue mid-lick. "Don't you fucking let her come. She hasn't proven that she's been a good girl yet."

I whimper as Tony pulls away, a malicious grin on his face as my hand slips from his hair, listening to Devin's command. Leaving me with my legs spread and my pussy throbbing, Tony stands and moves to where the toys are laid out on the bench. He casually pumps his hand over his cock, the large vein on the underside already pulsing, precum continuing to drip, splattering onto the floor.

The tension between us grows thick as Devin's heated gaze watches us from across the room. "Now I see why you like this so much, Tony. It's almost the perfect angle, except…"

I raise my head, my brows furrowing in confusion as I look between them, because I have a feeling that he's not just talking about the fact that he's mimicking when Tony watched us fuck in the private room. My eyes drift to Tony at the end of the bed, looking as if he's about to throttle Devin.

I open my mouth to ask what he's talking about, but I feel Devin's hot gaze on my center, and I hear his growl before he's on me, his fingers pressing into the tender skin of my thigh, a hiss pushing through my teeth. "What *the fuck* is this?" His words are hot with rage as he lowers his face to the bright red letter before whipping his head in Tony's direction. "You *motherfucker*."

Devin rises and closes the distance on him, but before he can make any closer, Tony has his hand wrapped around Devin's throat. "You get to show your claim in the light, in front of everyone," he growls, "so I left my own, for us in the dark." He yanks Devin to his chest, looking down his nose at him. "But don't you worry, you'll get the same one to match."

Devin's eyes darken, his hand drifting toward Tony's cock between them, but before he can lay a finger on him, Tony pushes him away. "Now, go sit like a *good boy* and watch the show you've been dying to see." Tony's words cause Devin's lips to curl, flashing him a lupine grin, ready to gobble us whole, before walking backward to his chair, not taking his eyes off us.

Tony slides back onto the bed, dragging me with him. He's abandoned all thoughts of the toys on the bench as he pumps his hand up and down his cock, coating it in precum. I can't help but lick my lips at the sight and I catch his grin. "Take a taste, baby. You know you want to."

I don't even hesitate as I move to straddle his legs and lower my lips to the tip of his cock, mindful of making sure that Devin sees every motion. Swirling my tongue across his head, I tease him as his hand weaves through my hair, keeping his grip loose for now. I take him deep, letting his moans of pleasure help me find my rhythm. His cock lengthens down my throat, his grip on my hair tightening, gently forcing my head up and down as he murmurs about me being a good girl and how good I look with his cock down my throat, throwing my praise kink into overdrive.

He pulls my head up, his cock popping from my mouth, a string of saliva connecting my lips to his tip. I let my gaze drift to Devin who is looking as though he is about to jump out of the chair, his nonchalant façade cracking right before my eyes. He's gripping the arm of the chair so tightly that the vein in his hand is popping out. He's resting his chin on his fist, but I see how tense his jaw is. And if I didn't know better, I'd think I could hear his teeth grinding.

Tony hooks his finger under my chin, forcing my gaze back to him. "Eyes on me, baby." He leads me up his body, and I sit on his hard cock, grinding my pussy against it. His large hands grip my hips, guiding me back and forth up his length, coating it with my desire as my hands rest on his chest.

"I'm going to fuck you nice and slow, not only to torture you but to make him wait even longer to have you." The smile on Tony's face is one I've never seen before. His eyes are light, and the smirk is playful, but his gaze never leaves mine, as if Devin isn't even in the room.

"I'm on top, so it's my turn to fuck *you*." The words are a rasp as the taste of him still sits on my tongue.

He chuckles darkly as I lift myself off him just enough to reach between us and grip his length, lining him up with my entrance. "Then fuck me, baby. Show him what he's missing." Tony winks as his eyes finally cut to Devin, but only for a moment before he's back to watching me, giving me his undivided attention.

I lower myself slowly onto his cock, taking him inch by inch. He fills me and my walls contract around him as I let out a sigh. It's strange to be this tame with him, especially with Devin in the room, but this new side of Tony is refreshing. This side of him has put enough trust in me to take control and lead him right over the edge as he has me time and time again.

I clench my walls and start to move my hips in a figure eight motion, my clit rubbing against him, the friction already building. He doesn't dare move even as I scrape my nails across his chest and let my hand creep up to his throat. My palm rests against his Adam's apple and I feel it bob as he swallows deeply. "You want to choke me, baby?" His voice vibrates up my arm. "Then choke me and hold my life in your hands." I hear Devin groan as I let my fingers tighten on Tony's throat.

"Fuck," Devin rasps as I hear him shift in the chair, creaking under his weight like it's ready to shatter from all the pressure in the room. "Choke him for me, love." His voice is tight as if a hand is wrapped around *his* throat, and I tighten my hold on Tony, giving them both what they want.

"Show them who *I* belong to." Tony's voice is low around

my hand, his eyes darkening as he presses his neck further into my hand. "I want you to make me come, baby."

I squeeze and his groan vibrates into my chest. I speed up my hips, the friction turning delicious as I walk on the edge, almost tumbling over. He reaches up a hand and pinches my nipple, pushing me right over with ease. My head drops back, and I speed up my movements, tightening my grip even more on his throat. I grind into him as the waves of pleasure wash over me until I can finally slow my movements, the stars in my eyes clearing.

I look back at him and see his face has turned deep red, my hold choking the air from his lungs. Wrenching my hand away, I let out a gasp as panic races through me. "Tony!" I can't believe he let me do that and he didn't bother to do anything about it. He growls as he sucks in a breath and reaches around me, roughly grabbing my ass. He hoists me up his cock and slams me back down in one fluid motion. I am barely able to breathe his name as he slams me down, his motions getting rougher each time.

For the first time tonight, his eyes aren't on me. Instead, they're on Devin, burning bright like the flames roaring in the fireplace. He slows his motion, holding me in place on his cock, not even allowing me to wiggle my hips.

He lifts me and turns me away from him, seating me back onto him as he shifts to the edge of the bed. "It's time to come and play, Dev," he croons, as he puts one hand on my throat, the other palming my breast, squeezing it hard.

Devin slowly rises from the chair, his limbs stiff as he kicks off his shoes, his pants dropping to the floor. His cock is hard, and the tip leaks with precum as he prowls across the room like an animal on the hunt, ready to devour its prey. "Open up that filthy mouth, love, and let me slide down that pretty throat of yours."

I slowly open my mouth and stick out my tongue, his cock sliding into my mouth, immediately going against the back of my throat. I flick my tongue across the underside, just the way he likes it, before sucking him in more. He grabs my hair, holding himself steady as he pumps in and out of my mouth, his eyes burning into mine. Tony starts to rock me back and forth on his cock, his hand dropping from my throat to between my legs, pressing his fingers against my clit.

A moan crawls up my throat around Devin's cock, and he tightens his hold on my hair as he growls, "Do that again, love, and I'll be coming down your throat in no time."

Tony pauses his movements, his other hand coming to grip Devin's cock just as he pulls it out from my mouth. Devin freezes at the touch, his eyes flicking from mine to Tony's hand, his snake tattoo looking like it's ready to strike. "No coming." Tony's voice is gruff. "Not until *I* say so."

The room tenses slightly as I watch the men square off, their dominant personalities on the verge of clashing, two titans at war with one another. Tony shifts beneath me and lifts me from him, sitting me on the bed as he stands, his chest almost heaving. "Go on, Devin, fuck her. I know you're dying to."

Devin steps up to Tony, their chests nearly touching, the temperature in the room rising so much it has me panting. Tony's hand wraps around the column of Devin's throat just as Devin's fingers curl around Tony's shaft, his thumb pressing against the head of his cock. Both men groan at each other's touch and watching them like this has heat flooding between my legs.

I always sensed something between them and knew there was more there than just long-time friends and roommates, but this makes it real. And they're both mine, just as much as they're about to make themselves to each other. I let my hand drift between my legs and circle my own clit, because seeing them this way has my pussy pulsing with need.

"Maybe, I'm ready to finally fuck *you*, Tony." Devin's eyes shift to mine, his pupils blown out with desire. "Maybe, I'm ready to fuck *both* of you." He leans in and kisses Tony on the neck, sucking his skin into his mouth, scraping his teeth across the column of his throat. Tony's hand shifts around to the back of his neck, pulling his face away far enough to slant his mouth over Devin's. Their kiss is deep, unleashing years of pent-up tension and finally finding exploding like a volcano, their heat filling the room. It's so hot that I can barely contain myself from moaning as the pleasure builds between my legs.

Devin pulls away, dropping to his knees, and stares at Tony's cock, licking his lips. "Maybe, I'm ready to cross the line that we've been toeing at for years." He wraps his fingers around Tony's cock, running his thumb over the tip. "The one that we've been trying to pretend isn't there." Tony's eyes stare down at him, the expression on his face unreadable as he takes in the man at his feet.

"I've been starved, Tony, and I can't wait to taste you. Eat you alive." He grips Tony at the base and starts to suck him, his tongue swirling around the tip of his cock before he takes him deep. The men are coming undone right in front of me, their moans of pleasure muting my whimper as I let my fingers take me over the edge. I moan as my orgasm hits and the room goes silent. I know that I just made a critical mistake and I'm in very real danger.

"Well, T"—Devin slowly rises to his feet, licking his lips and keeping his hand wrapped around Tony's shaft, both their eyes on me now—"looks like we're going to have to show our dirty little slut what happens when there are two monsters in the room. Two very hungry monsters who are ready to *eat*."

CHAPTER THIRTY-ONE

DEVIN

THE HOTTEST FUCKING thing is Lena getting off to Tony and me in the heat of the moment, but I can't have her thinking she can just finger-fuck herself right in front of us, not when there are two perfectly good mouths to eat her and cocks waiting to stuff her full. Leaving Tony where he stands, the taste of his cock still on my tongue, I stalk toward Lena, my eyes narrowing on her. Her eyes are wide with guilt as she braces her hands behind her on the bed. Good, because she knows that while I will let her walk over me in her heels and grip my cock in her hand, she, in no way, is allowed to get off without one of us.

She should never have to orgasm alone again.

My fingers wrap around her ankle, yanking her across the bed right to me, as she lets out a tiny yelp. "Devin, I—" I cut off her words by slapping my hand over her mouth, pressing my fingers into her cheek.

"No talking for you tonight, love, only fucking." I slowly unzip one of the zippers on her bra, her perfect, pink nipple peeking out, peaked, and waiting for me. I lower my mouth and nip at the bud, her head falling back as a muffled whimper presses against my hand, just before I swirl my tongue over it. I do the same with the other side, making sure to taste every inch of her. This lingerie is something that I want to keep for her to wear in the Underground, so I need to be very careful not to destroy it and buy more of it.

I press her into the mattress, spreading her legs wide and sliding my cock through her center, her cum coating me from tip to hilt. She moans my name as I press my tip to her entrance. The days of her being locked away in Tony's room were torturous, where I was forced to masturbate to the sound of their orgasms through the fucking door and take my frustrations out on the fuckers in the basement. Now, I'm going to take all of this pent-up energy and use it on both of them.

"Fucking mine." My words are gruff as I slam my cock into her, her back arching as she grips my biceps, digging her nails into my skin. My name mixes with her moans of pleasure, the soft whimpers unraveling me as her walls tighten with every thrust.

Large fingers run up my back and grip the nape of my neck. Tony's chest presses against me, his cock rubbing against my ass as lips brush against my shoulder before he sinks his teeth into my skin. "Ah, *fuck*," I groan as his approving growl rumbles through my back.

His teeth sink deeper into my skin, the pain making my cock thicken as I pick up my rhythm, pounding even harder into Lena. Tony's tongue runs over the broken skin, lapping up the swells of blood. "One to match," he says as his hand runs over my ass, the sound of his palm connecting to my skin like the crack of flogger tendrils.

Between the pain at my neck and the pleasure of my cock as I slam in and out of Lena's pussy, my balls begin to tighten, my name becoming a chant from her lips. My rhythm falters, and just when I'm about to come, my hips are jerked back, my cock pulled from her, and my orgasm ripped from me.

"What the fuck?" I growl as Tony yanks me to him, his hand sliding around my neck, pressing me against him. His cock is

hard against my ass and I'm nearly salivating at the thought of him plowing into me. I've been waiting for too fucking long.

"You're letting her off the hook too easily." His grin is malicious. "It's time we show her what we do to bad girls who can't wait their fucking turn."

Fuck, he's right. She has me so wrapped around her finger and so horny after days without either one of them, that I'm giving in to myself too soon. I've been so lost in my bloodlust, getting off to my own destruction, that I've lost control. Even as my dick throbs from the edging, I want to give them all of me, every last bit of me that's left after being a shattered man for so long.

He steps around me, Lena's eyes widening as he stands over her, his sharp gray eyes glaring down at her. "Tony," she breathes, relaxing her legs and letting them hang over the bed.

He climbs onto the bed, sliding up to the headboard, his legs spread wide as he strokes his cock, motioning for her to come to him. She crawls across the bed, her ass in the air, and that's when I notice the teeth marks that will be a permanent addition to her ass. I touch the space between my neck, the skin tender and throbbing. So, that's what he meant by Lena and I matching. That sadistic fucker.

My hand connects with the opposite ass cheek, and she nearly falls forward, a choked sound coming from her. Looking over her shoulder, I see the surprise on her face, her eyes wide. I slap her ass again and again as her cries ring out, her desire dripping from her pussy. "You like that, don't you, love? You like the pain."

Her teeth scrape her lips, but before she can do anything else, Tony grips her hair, yanking her head right to his cock. "Open wide," he gruffs out, wrapping his hand tighter into her hair as he wastes no time fucking her mouth; her staccato moans music to my ears.

Tony's eyes shift between us as I position myself behind Lena, slamming my dick into her tight, soaking wet pussy. She groans, and I watch as it turns Tony feral, his cock going deeper down her throat, choking off her sounds of pleasure.

We find a rhythm, our eyes locking as I reach down and run my fingers lightly along his leg, his muscles tensing under my touch. He brings Lena's head up, her ribs expanding with each deep breath she sucks in. I slow my rhythm as he shifts out from under her, sliding off the bed.

He walks behind me, his large body looming, the heat radiating off him in waves, ready to drown me. He runs his hands down my back, over my ass, and down my thighs, letting his nails scrape along my skin. It's just deep enough to leave a mark, but not enough to break the skin. Even though he's already left his teeth marks, ones I will make sure scar over, I want to be left with every mark he inflicts.

My body is craving the pain I know he can cause and my heart races with anticipation of what he's going to do next. He's so unpredictable with his hard exterior, but his possessive nature is nearly as strong as mine. He wants to mark and claim both Lena and me just as badly as I want to with them.

I feel him step away, a chill running up my spine as I keep thrusting deep into Lena, her moans coming out clipped each time I take her to the hilt. She's so loud and lost in her pleasure that I don't hear what he's doing. I thrust back and am met with his fingers running along my ass, the feeling of cool lube coating my skin faltering my rhythm.

His hand comes around my body, the sound of a vibrator clicking on as he says, "Hold this to your clit, baby, and don't you dare take it off until I fucking say so." He has it at a high speed already and she whimpers as her hand blindly takes it from him, the sound muffling as she puts it between her legs. Her hips hitch back onto my cock and she's already gripping the sheets with her other hand, panting as it vibrates her core.

Fuck, it's so hot when he talks like that. When he takes control and soullessly makes his demands.

He leans into me, the tip of his cock pressing at my ass. He licks and sucks along my neck, his hand weaving into my hair as he roughly tilts my head back, exposing more of my throat. His tongue flicks at my ear before he drags it down my jaw, causing a shiver to run up my spine. "You taste so good, Dev, I could devour both of you *right now*." His low voice has my balls tightening. "But once we do this, there's no going back."

His words swirl around me, making me lightheaded. "Once we do this," I start, "I never want to go back. I want this, here, now, and forever. I've waited fucking long enough."

He growls as he lines his cock up and presses it into my hole, a hiss pressing against the back of my teeth as he stakes his claim on me, the lube helping him slide in with ease. "Fuck, Dev," he growls. "This is your last chance to back out."

"Take me, T," are the only words I can manage before he slides into me further, forcing me deeper into Lena. Sparks fly between us as we find our rhythm. I've been in threesomes and orgies, having taken my fair share of men and women as I navigated my way through my kinks. But this? This is a whole new kink that I'll never be able to shake, one that I'll beg on my knees for. That I'll sell my soul for.

Tony attempted to give me an out, but I know he never intended to let me have one. He's giving me exactly what I've wanted this whole time while giving me so much more. I'm claiming Lena while being claimed by Tony, our bodies working in tandem as if they were made for each other. Made by the devil himself, ready to watch us fucking burn.

Lena falls over the edge, our names sounding as sweet as honey on her tongue. She keeps the vibrator in place, her pussy clenching around my cock as my balls tighten further. "I'm going to come, Lena," I grit out. "I'm going to fill you with my cum." I slap her ass, and she orgasms again, this time sobbing as the pleasure becomes too much for her.

"Devin," she cries, her body trembling beneath mine as Tony picks up his pace.

His breath is warm at the shell of my ear. "Fill her up, let her pussy milk every last drop of your cum." His words take me over the edge, and I slam into Lena, coming hard into her as I grip her hips.

Tony's rough thrusts keep me coming in and out of Lena, my cum running down her thighs, coating her skin. He tightens his hold on my hair, yanking me back and nipping at my neck.

He holds my head steady as his thrusts become erratic. "I'm going to fill your ass with my cum. Claim you. Own you. Make you *mine*." My own cock twitches as he thrusts into me *hard*, his length thickening.

"Devin," he growls, letting his hips twitch against me as his orgasm washes over him, his teeth sinking into my shoulder. He pulls out and I feel the warmth of his cum sliding down between my legs. I reach around and take the vibrator from Lena's hand. She nearly sobs in relief, her body trembling as the shockwaves of her orgasms wrack through her.

"If either one of you thinks we're done, you're fucking wrong." Tony strides to the bathroom, looking over his shoulder before going in. "Fucking *stay*." He eyes me as if I would run out the door the moment he steps out of the room, but I just give him a satisfied grin. I haven't left after all this time, and I don't intend to now.

As Tony cleans himself up, I run my hands over Lena's legs, massaging her calves. "You take our cocks so well, love," I croon, smoothing my hand over her skin, her muscles relaxing beneath my touch.

She looks over her shoulder, her face streaked with tears, but she still gives me a smile that's borderline feline. "Like you said, I was made for you two." She wiggles her ass at me, and I give it a playful slap. She's blossoming. The most beautiful flower in a field of weeds, her petals unfolding, basking in the light after being forced to live in the dark for so long.

She giggles and lifts her hips, inviting me to dive back in for a quickie before Tony returns. Such a bad girl. But before I can make a move, I catch Tony as he leans against the doorframe, watching every move. His body is packed with muscle, his time in the gym giving him the body of a god. His skin speckled with scars, with my favorite shining on his thigh from that faithful night all those years ago.

His snake tattoo looks as though it's about to slither off his skin and down the doorframe, his muscles flexing beneath the dark ink of both arms like he's fighting off one of his dark urges. He watches us with a heated gaze, his cock hardening again as he runs his hand down his abs.

"Back for more?" I ask, making a show of running my hands over Lena's legs, circling my finger around his bite mark, tapping my finger on every tender spot. "We've been waiting patiently for you." Lena raises herself up on her elbows, giving him the same sly smile she gave me. Her long hair is mussed and her skin is flushed, giving her a glow that shines as bright as the fire roaring across the room.

A deep growl rumbles through Tony as he straightens from the doorframe. He crosses the room, stopping at the end of the bed where the toys are lined up on the bench. His eyes are bright as he contemplates all the ways he wants to inflict pain and build up our pleasure.

I watch him closely, taking in his face, and can't figure out why he's so insistent on hiding it from the rest of the world. He's handsome in a tortured way, the only way I would ever want him to be. His scarred face shows that it would take a whole fucking lot to kill him and take him away from us.

In just this short time, he's given so much of himself, so much more than he would ever let anyone else see. I don't know as much as I would like about his past, but this is the most open he's ever been with anyone, and to see him coming undone and then taking control has my inner monster pressing against my skin, wanting to come out and play. Even on the days I let him out for the insatiable bloodlust, he still hasn't been satisfied, and while I can tame him for a while, I really don't know if he ever will be.

But I feel like that's about to change by the look in Tony's eyes as he looks over Lena, her body sprawled on the bed beneath me, still trying to steady her breathing. Her thighs are slick with cum, the teeth marks Tony left behind are bright red against her skin, and those crotchless panties are about to be ripped from her to give full access to her ass. Fuck trying to save them; I could buy her as many as I want and shred them just the same.

I slide off the bed from her as Tony steps up, a flogger gripped in his large, veiny hand. He runs his free hand over her, slapping his fingers on the teeth marks, her fingers curling into the sheets as she tries to quiet the hiss that slides between her teeth. "My marks are so perfect on you, baby, branding you as mine." He runs the leather tendrils down the back of her legs, her skin prickling with goosebumps. Without saying a word, she shifts, pushing her ass up in the air, giving him the perfect angle, telling me that they've done something like this before over the past few days.

If only I could see what all they did. It drives me fucking insane that I was left out of the fun.

Tony cuts his gaze to me and holds out the flogger, giving me a wink. I let my fingers brush against him as I curl my fingers around the handle, his eyes flicking down to where I let my touch linger. I want to run my hands over every inch of him, taking in every hard ridge of his muscles, and feel every raised scar.

He steps up to me and cups the back of my head, pressing his lips to mine, his tongue sliding between my lips. His teeth scrape against my lower lip, nipping at it, drawing blood. This man has no idea how long I've been fucking waiting for him to finally get the fuck over himself and lean into who he really is.

A *challenge*.

A perfect *match*.

A beautiful *monster*.

Lena's watching us, a smile on her lips as she takes us in. Her features are soft, and I can see her healing even more right before our eyes. The wounds across her heart stitching themselves closed. The woman who ended up in our clutches weeks ago is not the same one in front of us now. Letting her stay and believing in her was the best decision I've made in my shitty life and I can't imagine going on without her. I will never let anyone touch her, and the only pain she'll ever feel is the kind that will send her over the edge with pleasure.

Stepping up to the edge of the bed, I let the tendrils of leather tease across her skin. She arches her back, sticking her ass out even more, inviting me to take it piece by piece. "You're our little whore, aren't you, love? Taking whatever you can get from us?"

Still looking over her shoulder, she bats those long lashes at me. "I'm only a whore for the two of you." Her voice is low and husky. Sultry enough to send a rush of heat to my cock and for Tony to groan behind me. "Go ahead. Take what you want, boys."

Her words wrap around my wrist, and without another thought, I let the flogger come down on her ass, the leather whooshing through the air and snapping across her skin. "Oh fuck," she moans, gripping the sheets around her. *"More."* Flicking my wrist, I let out three more good hits, giving her exactly what she wants. "Fuck, Devin. *Fuck.*"

She lets out a whimper as I continue to flick the flogger across her ass, creating delicate red lines on her perfect skin. I smooth my hand over them, an approving sound vibrating up her throat. "We're going to show everyone who you belong to." I flick the tendrils over her again, her moans growing louder as the marks crisscross on her skin. "This ass." *Snap.* "This pussy." *Snap.* "You." *Snap.* "Fucking *ours.*" Her screams of pain turn into deep moans of pleasure with every snap of the flogger, making my cock so hard that it's pulsing, the tip turning purple as the blood rushes to my head.

I slide my fingers through her slit. "Goddamn, love, you're still so fucking wet. Our cum is dripping from your perfect pussy." I press a finger into her, crooking it and hitting her G-spot. "So horny for us. So fucking needy."

Tony steps up, the blade of his knife glinting as he slides the metal against her skin, under the band of her panties. She gasps as he slices through the fabric, then again on the other side. It falls away, curling like ribbons atop a present. Exposing her tight ass, he wads them up and holds them to her lips. "You know the drill, baby." I watch in wonder as he presses the panties into her mouth, taking extra care to make sure she can taste herself from them.

Fuck me, she really will do anything for us.

Tony steps back, a grin pulling at his lips, before he moves to the end of the bed, grabbing the leather binds, and slowly securing her wrists. "Bound and gagged, just like you like it, baby." He smooths her hair away from her face and kisses the top of her head. The gentle gesture makes my balls tighten, wanting some of that tender, loving care for my fucking self.

She's panting as I drop the flogger to the floor. Reaching over to the bench, I grab a black plug adorned with a shiny black gem that will look perfect in her. I press it into her pussy, her walls clenching around it as I pump it slowly in and out of her, soaking it with the mix of our cum.

I pull the plug from her pussy and spread the cheeks of her ass. She gasps as I lightly press the plug to her tight hole, giving her a warning before I press it further into her ass, moaning around the panties stuffed in her mouth until it's fully inserted. The shiny, black jewel sparkles in the light. "That's such a good girl, letting us fill you up one hole at a time." I slap her ass and smooth over the tender spot. "Fucking good girl."

Bending over her, I pepper kisses along her spine, feeling

her relax under my touch. She truly is everything I've ever wanted in a woman and has opened the floodgates to feelings I've never felt before. Ones I didn't know I could feel or even existed. I don't want this night to end, and if I could, I would keep them locked in here with me until we took our last breaths.

"On the bed, Devin." Tony barks the words out, pulling me back to reality.

Normally, I would fight him for giving me such a harsh command, but I'm curious what he has in store for me. I slide onto the bed on the other side of Lena, resting my head on the down pillow, and running my hand up and down my abs. Tony effortlessly picks Lena up, her muffled yelp making me chuckle as he places her on my lap. Her center rests on my thickened cock, her desire already coating it.

"Fuck her. *Now.*"

I grip her waist, and she lifts herself up, my free hand lining my cock up to her entrance as she sinks down onto me, taking me inch by inch. Tony pulls her arms behind her, binding her wrists together again. He presses her down, forcing her chest to mine as she continues to move up and down on my cock, never stopping.

He watches her ass, his eyes gleaming like the devil who just bargained for someone's soul. He climbs up on the bed, grabbing her ass with one hand, the other pulling the plug from her. She moans as he takes a small bottle of lube and coats his cock, his hand roughly running up and down his shaft.

He presses against her, holding her cheeks apart. Her inner walls clench around my cock as he glides into her, her muffled sounds vibrating against my skin. "Good girl, baby. Fuck, you feel so *fucking* good."

He finds his rhythm, holding her ass up with one hand, allowing me to fuck up into her, and gripping her bound wrists with the other. "Every hole is full, baby. So fucking full."

Together, we take her. She looks so beautiful as she finds her pleasure, my fingers pressing against her swollen clit as she sucks shallow breaths through her nose, looking so beautiful at our mercy. Her eyes roll back into her head as she comes, her body spasming as the tremors rock through her.

Watching Tony take her ass has my balls tightening, that familiar tingle crawling up my spine. "I'm going to come, baby," I say to neither one in particular, my thrusts turning erratic.

"We're coming together," Tony grunts, speeding up his thrusts. "We're going to fill you up, Lena."

Her muffled pleas have me walking the line as she begs for us to come. "Tony," I bite out. "Tony, *fuck*."

My orgasm crashes over me just as Tony roars, Lena's body shuddering between us as we ride out our release. The sound of our heavy breaths fills the silence. Lena presses her cheek to my chest, looking up at me as tears glisten in her eyes and track down her face, panties still stuffed into her mouth. I go to remove them and hear a low growl from Tony and drop my hand to her back, a chuckle bubbling from my lips at how easily I've fallen into taking orders from him.

Fucking asshole.

He swiftly undoes the bindings on her wrists, her arms falling around her body and landing on my chest. "Look at me, baby," he says darkly. She drops her chin to look at him and I smooth over her hair, kissing the top of her head. He runs his thumb along her bottom lip, her mouth popping open as he removes her panties. She sucks in a quiet breath, her eyes fluttering at him.

His eyes flash with satisfaction as he runs his knuckles down her cheek. He looks at her with such admiration that it's clear she stole his heart the moment she walked into the penthouse, whether he admits it or not. The trust that they've already put in each other curls around my heart and squeezes it, pumping it back to life.

"You know"—I look at him over her head—"I wanted to keep those for when we debut in the Underground, but you just had to go and cut them off of her."

Tony rolls his eyes, closing his fingers around the fabric, hiding it from sight. "I'm pretty sure we can fucking afford a new pair...or twenty." He rises from the bed, once again moving toward the bathroom. "Besides, I want more leather when we show her off in the Underground. Make a fucking statement. Remind all those assholes who's really in charge around here."

He's more into this than I ever imagined he would be. He's never wanted to show himself in the Underground, let alone be out in the open. Tasha and I have begged him for years to be a Dom and that he would never have to show his face, but he's always shut us down by either ignoring us or threatening my life if I asked him again. The challenge always made me press more, sometimes leading him to rough me up, leaving me bruised, panting, and hard as fuck. Some would call that a death sentence, but I call it a kink.

I look down at Lena and catch her looking between Tony and me, curiosity written all over her face as if she's still trying to figure us out after all these weeks. And as much as we're willing to give to her, I don't know if she'll ever have us completely figured out because there are things even I don't know about myself. And Tony is locked up tight. Not even the best PIs could track down any information on him, so what we know is all he's willing to tell.

"What's the matter, love?" I cup her cheek, her eyes bright and tear lined, my own doubts starting to creep in. "Did we hurt you? Was this too much?" My heart rate picks up, because what if we did? We were fucking rough with her, leaving marks and drawing blood like fucking animals.

Her hand wipes away the tear that tries to escape and she sniffs, stopping Tony in his tracks. He looks over his shoulder, his eyes wide with what looks like fear swirling in them and his hard jaw set. He doesn't move, just watches us as she shudders in a breath, emotion swirling in her eyes.

"No, it's not that." She lets out a choked laugh, wiping another tear as it tracks down her face. "I just have never been treated like this before and never thought I would be. I thought I would be trapped in my terrible fucking life forever. That the only pleasure I would find would be the kind I would have to do for myself, alone, for the rest of my life."

Pulling her up to me, I tilt her chin, kissing her deeply. I pull back, keeping her chin tilted toward me, and look her over. Goddamn, she's fucking beautiful. "You're ours, Lena, and we would never let anything happen to you. I know this isn't conventional, but it's *real*, you know that, right?"

Tony continues to watch from across the room, his hands clenched at his side like he's caught and doesn't know what to do. Lena looks at him, her eyes warming, before turning her attention back to me and giving me a soft smile. "I don't want conventional." She runs her fingers down my jaw. "I only want *this*. Whatever this is with the two of you is everything I've ever wanted, that I didn't know I needed."

"You don't want to run the other direction screaming?" I ask as I hold Tony's gaze, his body shifting toward us, waiting on bated breath for her answer.

"I thought about it." I stiffen at her words and feel the air turn thick as Tony faces us. "But I figured you wouldn't let me get far, and it's much more fun to be here than anywhere else. And while I like the chase, I never want to be anywhere else but right here." She looks between us, her smile coming up and meeting her eyes. "With both of you."

I exhale the breath I didn't know I was holding and let out a chuckle to match the smile that's plastered on her face. "I think that was the smartest move you could make for our sanity and yours, love." I kiss her softly, the tension in the room disappearing. "Because we like the chase too, and we are very, *very* good at finding our targets."

Tony finally shifts away, the tension that was rolling off him dissipating as he disappears through the bathroom doorway. He turns the shower on and gives off the vibe that we were expected to join him. Lena slides off the bed, her feet padding toward the bathroom, disappearing through the doorway. She is so eager for us.

What the fuck did I do to deserve them? For the first time in years, I actually feel happy, and somehow, I feel like that even in an alternate universe, one where Drew was still alive, and my own father hadn't wished me dead, I would still end up here. With them. They are the ones I would be destined to find in each and every life because they're who I'm supposed to be with.

It's both exhilarating and fucking terrifying. Because at any time, they could change their minds and decide that I'm the complete opposite of what they want and need. And that my father's sentiments weren't far off about me being a fucking lunatic and impossible to love. That I was nothing more than a mistake brought into this world, and if he had it his way, I would have never existed to begin with.

But even with those words weighing on my mind, no matter how hard I try to let them go, a part of me knows that they will never leave. They're as invested in this as I am, and I believe they would die for me as I would for them.

Like the insane fool I am, I believe they love me the way I love them. It's a wild concept to think about because this could be nothing more than a physical attraction, and I'm playing a delicate game, but if it were, Tony would have moved on to his next fuck buddy by now. Not giving this a second thought and forcing us to continue our game, but he's more than enough of the truth that I need to know that this isn't a dream.

A chuckle pulls me from my thoughts, and my monster rises from his haunches, pushing against my skin to get the fuck up and get in there, making sure they don't get to have all the fun without me *again*. My head spins as I rise to my feet, my body weightless as I float to the bathroom to see Tony caging her body against the shower wall, nipping at her neck as his hand cups her breast.

I slip into the shower, pressing my body to Tony's backside, letting him feel my rising cock against him. The steam rises around us, and for what seems like the millionth time tonight, I slip into a euphoric state, getting lost in this dream that is now my life. The two have fucking ruined me and I don't ever want to be the same again.

CHAPTER THIRTY-TWO

Tony

MY COCK HAS FINALLY DRIED up for the night after I fucked them both again. Devin and I rounded out the night by taking turns eating Lena out as the steam of the shower swirled around us, feasting on her until she was begging us to stop, tears streaming down her face as her pleasure became too much. I love it when she fucking begs.

I have never felt so fucking alive. So *free*. So much like the part of myself that was stripped away from me.

We managed to step out satiated and clean before falling into bed. I'm pressed against Lena's back, her legs tangling with mine, while Devin is curled into the front of her, our naked bodies meshing together.

Lena's breathing has evened out, and she has fallen into a deep sleep, her body fully relaxed. Devin's eyes are closed, but even though he's a sociopath and can trick most of the people around him, he can't fool me. I can tell he's awake and waiting for me to do or say something. Always ready to pounce.

I don't say anything as I try to close my eyes and drift off for some much needed sleep, but he breaks the silence, not able to keep up his charade. "I meant what I said, T. I don't want to go back to what we were before tonight." He opens his eyes, meeting mine, the glow of the fireplace setting his blue eyes ablaze. His voice is soft but serious, making his intentions clear. "This, right here, is it for me."

There's an ache in my chest like someone is squeezing my heart as I look him over. The bright red bite mark shines out from his skin, bruises peppering the column of his neck and across his chest, showing off every mark I gave him. I smooth my hand over Lena's hair before reaching over and hooking his chin, holding his gaze. "Are you sure? Because I can walk. Pretend that none of this ever happened and let you have her. Have the happiness you deserve."

The look on his face is like I slapped him. His brow furrows and his lips pop open as if he's waiting for the words to come out. My words stung, but I need to know the truth, and sometimes the truth can hurt. I haven't given my heart to anyone, yet somehow, they both managed to rip open my chest and take it. It's in their hands, and if I can manage to get away with minimal scarring, then I will leave with the small scrap of dignity I have left.

"Are you that fucking dense, Tony?" Devin's whisper is harsh as he grips my wrist. "Do you really think I would have gone this far with you or let you have her for days if I didn't think that this was it? That you were part of this equation? For a computer genius, you're acting really fucking stupid right now." He pulls my fingers from his chin and runs his lips over them before scraping his teeth across my knuckles. "You don't get to walk away now."

I push my knuckles against his teeth, letting them cut into my skin. "And you're not worried about what the public will say? What they'll think of us if we come out together?" Every insecurity that had been beaten out of me seems to come flooding back. I feel as though I'm a teenager again and realize that I not only liked girls, but I also found myself looking sidelong in the locker room at a few boys.

Unsure and fucking lost.

Devin sucks my fingers into his mouth, biting them. I don't even bother trying to yank them back before he pulls them out, sliding his tongue across them before he releases me. "I don't give a flying fuck what anyone thinks about us. Especially not what they think about me." He runs his fingers through Lena's hair. "The only person I would have even bothered to care what he thought is long dead, and I know he wouldn't have batted a fucking eye about it."

Drew. Of course, he would only care what Drew thought. And from what I've read about the man and the stories I've heard from Devin and Tasha, he would have celebrated the fact that his brother has found happiness. I'm not worried about his parents trying to wreck anything, because they can go fuck themselves. They're estranged for a fucking reason, and he's built this life without them. Made a name for himself without using the Green name to get him where he is now.

However, he has a public persona, and being in a polyamorous relationship could be detrimental to the club. But, judging by the look on his face, he really doesn't fucking care.

"We manage a sex club, T." His voice is softer now; his statement is as if he can read my mind and see the doubt on my face. "Taboo is what we're about, and while this isn't the path I imagined for myself, it's the right one for me. For *us*. One thing that I'm going to make sure that the whole world knows is that Devin Green is in love with Lena Taylor *and* Tony Fox. And if anyone lays a finger on either one of you, it'll be the last thing that they touch before they die a cruel death."

The pressure in my chest releases as I chuckle. This deranged man has me by the heart and the balls. "I guess you're right." I look down at Lena, her features relaxed and her breathing deep and steady. Her head barely hit the pillow before she was out. A freight train could come through and I doubt that she would wake up. "I embraced the fuckery that is

Masquerave all those years ago, letting you slide the knife right into me, forcing me to bleed for this place, so what's any different now?"

He smiles, a genuine one. "That's the spirit."

Both of our gazes fall on Lena, letting silence fall over us for a beat. "Do you really think she's all in? Or do you think she was lost in the moment?"

He leans down and kisses her forehead, pressing his head to hers. "I don't think she would be in this bed with us if she weren't." He breathes her in. "But I would let her walk if she wanted to, even if it killed me. Because I would never want her to think she's a prisoner like she was with that Obsidian motherfucker."

His voice breaks, as if it's a real possibility that she could wake up tomorrow and decide that she has had her fun but only wants to stick around for our protection and nothing else. And just like him, I would give her that, but I know it would break me. The voice in my head, the one who spoke unimaginable cruelties while their hands beat me down and broke me, tells me that I am nothing more than a body to fuck. That she could never want a man like me. But looking at her now, at how her body is pressed into mine, relaxed and at peace, my heart tells me that she would never want to leave.

"She won't leave." My words are nothing more than a whisper as I bend down and kiss her cheek. "And neither will we." I stretch over and brush my lips across Devin's stubbled jaw.

All of this doesn't seem real, but like I'm living in a dreamscape that I'll wake from at any moment. But the way he reaches across Lena to brush his fingers across my skin tells me just how real this is. The only thing darkening this moment of bliss is the ever lingering threat of Obsidian.

"This is bigger than all three of us," I say, trying to shift the subject from the matters of our hearts to the reality of the situation that has been laid out in front of us. "We can have these fun romps, Dev, but none of us are safe until we take down Obsidian. The bliss is only a façade to mask the real danger lurking around."

His brow furrows as he cups Lena's face, running his thumb over her cheek. I grab her waist, keeping her flush to me, my cock instantly hardening at her ass pushing against it. I rest my face into the crook of her neck, giving her a soft kiss. She quietly moans in her sleep, and in unison, Devin and I groan at the sound.

"I will do whatever it takes to keep her safe." I look up at her and watch him as his eyes go distant, thinking through every possibility. "I will take down whoever I need to in order to keep us all together."

I grip his shoulder, his eyes immediately snapping to mine. "And so will I, Dev." I flex my fingers, squeezing the hard muscle in his arm. "We'll do whatever it takes. *Together.*"

He nods and I let my hand drop back to Lena's waist, rubbing my thumb across her skin. I could get used to sharing a bed with both of them. If I had the choice, I would never let any of us leave this penthouse, protecting them at all costs.

"Have you found anything else on them?" Devin keeps his voice down, making sure not to wake Lena.

"Not shit." I huff out a breath. "Most of their communications have gone dark or any traces of them on the dark web go cold in a matter of a few hours. They're playing the game well."

Devin growls as his frustration fills the space between us. I reach over and run my thumb over his furrowed brow, trying to smooth it over. "I'm working on it, Dev. I have our best team going around the clock, searching in every corner, and cutting off the head of every snake they can."

His eyes cut up to mine, softening. "I know, T." He takes a shaky breath. "You know I'm fucking impatient, and I just want us to be able to move on, start our lives together. Take a fucking break."

I look down at Lena, my mind reeling, trying to work everything out, but exhaustion begins to cloud my mind. "Let's sleep on it and see what we can come up with tomorrow, okay?"

Devin narrows his eyes on me, and I can tell he doesn't like that answer, but we're both exhausted, and there's no fucking way that we're going to find anything at this moment. We're only spinning our wheels.

I stare him down, letting my expression convey my silent thoughts and not budging. He groans, rolling his eyes, a yawn escaping from him. "*Fine*. We'll get some sleep and then revisit in the morning." He shifts farther down into the bed, nuzzling his face into Lena's. "You win, you motherfucker."

I chuckle and curl into Lena, breathing her in as I let sleep take me under, falling right into the darkness that plagues my mind.

I'M JOLTED AWAKE, my body coated in sweat as I try to take in my surroundings. The room is pitch black, with only the low light of a single bulb from under the door.

No. Not here. Not now.

The thud of boots echoes from the other side of the door before they come to a sudden stop. The tension in the air presses down on me, stealing the breath from my lungs and the only sound is my thundering heart.

The quiet jingle of keys floats through the crack as one slides into the lock, forcing the deadbolt. The door swings open, thudding against the wall, as a large figure blocks the hallway's light, standing there in silence.

I stare, unmoving from the cot that I'm in, working to steady my breathing and not to give away the fear that's coursing through my veins. But I know he can smell it, that he's watching me like the predator, ready to kill his prey.

In a blink, he's on me, wrenching me from the bed by the nape of my neck. Once I'm on my feet, he shoves a bag over my head, cloaking me in complete darkness. He yanks my arms behind, slapping handcuffs on each wrist, the cold metal biting into my skin as he fastens them too tight. He shoves me forward, causing me to stumble, but I know if I fall, I won't be able to walk for a week from the beating he would give me for being weak.

I'm blindly led down the long hallway, the sound of muffled cries filtering through the metal doors. My body starts to tremble, but I fight it off, not wanting to show an ounce of weakness as I'm being led into the depths of Hell.

The man stays silent as the sound of another metal door opening fills the long hallway. The smell of bleach fills my nose as I'm shoved to my knees, my bones cracking as I hit the concrete floor. The bag is yanked from my head, bright lights blinding me, filling my vision with stars. When my vision finally adjusts, I suck in a breath as a pair of glowing snake eyes stares back at me.

A scream lodges in my throat as I sit up, my eyes flying open as I wake up from one of the nightmares that have plagued me for far too long. I heave in a deep breath, look around, see the dim glow of the fire across the room, and feel the warmth of Lena's body pressing against me. She and Devin are fast asleep, curled into one another, lost in a deep sleep as my heart pounds in my chest.

I scrub my face with my hand, anxiety prickling at my skin, as my muscles strain, beckoning me to run. To fight.

You're fucking fine, Tony. You're in your bed, safe. Not back at that fucking makeshift prison.

You're home.

As if she can sense my stress, Lena's hand reaches behind her and touches my bare thigh. Her fingers are warm against my clammy skin, and she lets out a deep sigh, as if touching me has put her at peace. Curling my fingers around her hand, I give it a squeeze, letting her subconscious know that I'm safe —that I'll be okay eventually.

I sink back down under the covers, curling myself into her and keeping her pressed against me. I press my face into her hair that's spread across the pillow and let her scent envelop me. It was only just a dream, and this is my reality.

Even if the dreams continue to plague me until I leave this world and am greeted at Hell's gates, I have nothing to be afraid of anymore. Not with them by my side.

I force my eyes close and listen to her steady breathing, feeling Devin's warm breath on my face as I let sleep pull me back under, where this time, I dream of the Underground and just how I would show them off to the seedy underbelly of this city. Show them what's *mine*.

CHAPTER THIRTY-THREE

Lena

INCESSANT BUZZING from the nightstand pulls me from my deep sleep. My eyes flutter open to the dim light that filters around the curtains in Devin's room. I shift, but it's nearly impossible since I'm wedged between two massive men. Our legs entangled together, their arms draping over me, making us one.

This last week of fucking has me exhausted but fully recharged at the same time. The way that I have more than peeked behind the curtain of these men has shown me that while they are the same in so many ways, they are wildly different. I have never fallen so hard or so fast for anyone, let alone two people. They bring out different parts of me that I either didn't know I had, or I had locked away a long time ago. The way Tony has claimed me in the shadows shines just as bright as Devin has claimed me in front of other people. Both of their marks are left on my skin and my scarred heart.

I attempt to untangle our limbs, my muscles and skin are blissfully sore, but being the light sleepers they are, they both tighten their holds, clamping me in place. Staring up at the ceiling, I let out a heavy sigh. "You two have to let me go. I can't stay in this bed forever."

Devin nuzzles his face further into the crook of my neck, his breath warm against my skin, his words muffled. "See, that's where you're wrong, love. We will *never* let you go."

Tony chuckles into my ear, shifting himself against me, his cock already hard against my ass as he pulls me closer to him, running a hand over his bite mark, the sting jolting through me. I wiggle myself loose from his grip, just enough to reach past Devin to the nightstand. His lips graze over my nipple, and for a moment, I completely forgot that I'm naked. This shouldn't surprise me as much as it does, considering this is their favorite way for me to be now that we've torn down each other's walls.

Naked and ready to be fucked at a moment's notice.

I gasp at the feel of his warm tongue as it flicks at the now peaked bud, before pulling back and settling between them. My eyes go wide as I take in the time. "Fuck, it's 3:45," I gasp out, scrolling through my messages from Bri and Tasha in our group chat.

Devin rolls onto his back, scrubbing his face with his hand. "Well, fuck." He pulls himself up, leaning against the headboard, grabbing his phone off the nightstand. "I don't think I've slept this long in years."

Tony rolls away from me, grabbing his phone, the screen illuminating the annoyed look on his face. While annoyed, he actually looks rested. They both do. I guess sex for days on end will finally expel enough energy to make men like them sleep.

His brow starts furrowing the more he looks through his phone. He sits up and quickly gets out of bed. I watch his naked body as he moves through the room, his semi-hard cock already making my mouth water just as he slides his boxer briefs over his toned ass. This should show just how sex crazed these men have made me because seeing them fuck each other, along with fucking me in every position they can contort me to, is the hottest thing I've ever witnessed. I always thought

I was a one-man kind of woman, but they've changed my perspective on everything I thought I knew about myself.

"What's up, T?" Devin asks, looking up from his phone with furrowed brows.

"Just some things I need to look into." His clipped, gruff tone doesn't mask the wariness in his words.

Sitting up, I pull the sheet up with me. "Is everything okay?" My heart starts to race, anxiety crawling over my skin. "You two are kind of freaking me out."

"Everything's fine, love," Devin says as he cups my chin in his hand. He pulls me in for a soft kiss, his tongue sweeping into my mouth, meeting my quiet moan with his. "Absolutely nothing to worry about."

He pulls away and looks over at Tony who is leaning against the bedroom doorway, the muscles of his bare body tense as he types away on his phone. He looks over his shoulder, his eyes flashing to Devin as he starts a quiet conversation that only they can have. The tension in the room builds up, but not in the way it has been for the last few days with them. Devin slides out of bed, throwing on his boxer briefs, striding out of the room.

Tony is already at his computer, his fingers flying over the keys as Devin takes a seat at his desk, his mouse clicking rapidly. The light filtering through the main living space is dull as I look out the wall of windows and see a storm creeping over the city.

"Is there anything I can help with?" I ask, standing in the middle of the room, unsure of what to do.

"No, baby," Tony gruffs. "We can handle it." His voice is tight, nearly dismissive. The Tony who I have shared a bed with, has exited the room, and he's all business again, closing himself off as he works.

While I may have been naïve for years with Matt, believing his lies and coverups, I can tell when they're hiding the whole truth from me. There's obviously something wrong, because a crane couldn't have lifted them from that bed before they checked their phones, and they practically sprinted out of it like it was on fire.

I propose a test to see if it's nothing or if I should be worried. Still wrapped in the sheet, I make my way to the kitchen to brew some coffee. They're so enamored in their work that when I let the sheet fall to the floor, neither of them even looks over at me. *Bastards.*

Making their coffees, I deliver them, still in the nude, delicately placing each of their cups on their respective desks and making a show of it. And not even a narrow glance my way. I scoff and Devin immediately picks up his mug, sipping on the coffee. "Delicious, love. Thank you." I roll my eyes because that is definitely a man's way of trying to appease his woman without actually acknowledging her. I'll fucking show them. If they can play games with me, then I can play the same games with them.

I pull out Devin's chair and straddle him. His eyes flash with annoyance before he takes in my naked body. He groans as I lean back, grinding my center against his cock and cupping my breasts. Playing with my nipples, I arch my back as his hands land on my hips, keeping me in place on his lap. "I take back what I said about the coffee, *this* is delicious."

He leans down, taking my nipple between his teeth, nipping at me. I gasp and giggle as he swirls his tongue around the peaked bud. His hands move up my body, and we're just getting started when Tony clears his throat, causing Devin to jerk his head up, all lust leaving his eyes.

"I hate to interrupt because I would much rather be doing that, but we need to look at something." Tony's serious tone snaps me out of my horny daze, and I turn to look at him.

Devin's hand replaces mine on my breast, a devilish grin on his face. "Oh, I have something for us to look at, T." He chuckles as he kisses my chest.

"I'm serious, Devin." I pull back, Devin's head once again

coming up to meet Tony's gaze. "We have multiple cars that have been in the parking lot since early last night. The cameras show people exiting them at various times, but no one has come back for them."

I cock my head to the side, trying to think with the logical side of my brain, even as Devin mindlessly traces his fingers across my skin, clearly lost in the thought, too. "Maybe they left with someone or took an Uber and haven't been back for their car. It's a nightclub, you know?" I try to tease him, but my efforts are lost on him.

Tony keeps typing, the screen zooming in on each car. "Normally, I wouldn't be this alarmed, but I ran all of the plates, and they came back with fake registrations." He furrows his brow. "And there's one in every row, evenly spaced in the parking lot, going diagonal across it."

"So, it was intentional," Devin says. His fingers fall from my skin as he stares at the shot of the entire parking lot. "They wanted us to notice." Tony nods, his hand rubbing against his stubbled jaw.

"But why? What does it mean?" I stand up and cross the room, pulling the sheet back around me. This is no time to be naked and trying to seduce these men when Obsidian is playing one of their games. No, Matt is playing one of *his* games to try and fuck with me. The unknown texts have sent a very clear message that I can hide in my tower, but eventually, I will need to come down.

"Have you talked to Tasha?" Devin asks. "Has she noticed anything?"

Tony pulls up his phone. "I sent her a message, but I haven't heard back. Which is odd, because she's the one who gave me the heads up. She's usually up and going by now and wouldn't leave me hanging like this."

This is all so strange. I check my phone again, noting the time on the group chat, and the last message I received from either her or Bri was around 2:00 a.m. I know my best friend, and if she hadn't heard from me in over 12 hours, she would have kicked this door down herself and had these men by the balls.

The prickle of anxiety crawls across my skin as I send a message to them, marking as delivered. As soon as the message is sent, Bri's name pops up on my phone. I quickly answer her call, because the timing is just too weird and my instincts are screaming that something is terribly wrong. "Hey, B. Is everything okay?"

My heart drops as I hear whimpering and a sob as it crackles through the phone. "Lena. *Help me.*"

I clutch the phone and spin toward the guys. "Bri? Where are you?" Both of their heads jerk toward me, their eyes wide with concern.

I can hear her crying, her words choked. "They have me. I don't know where I am, please help me."

I drop the sheet and run toward my room as Tony calls out my name. "B, we're going to find you. Stay with me, okay?" I yank on sweats and a T-shirt, the phone wedged between my ear and shoulder as I listen to her quiet whimpers. She lets out a scream, and I jump, almost dropping the phone.

"B!" I scream just as the call disconnects. I repeatedly say Bri's name, panic rising up my throat and nausea roiling through me. My pleas turn into screams as both men crowd the doorway. "Lena?" Devin's voice is sharp as his hands land on my shoulders, spinning me to him. "Talk to me. Tell me what happened." Devin's words are muffled as the sound of my racing pulse rushes through my ears.

"They have her. They have Bri." I shove my feet into a pair of black tennis shoes. "We have to help her. We have to go *now*."

"Lena," Tony breathes. "I'm running the tracker on her phone to get an exact location. We need to wait for it—"

I cut him off, my vision blurring on the edges from the

anxiety that is now biting at my skin like an army of fire ants. "There's no fucking time. We have to go." I screech the words as I rush past them, heading for the door. "I'm not losing another person I love to that fucking monster."

"Lena, wait." Devin grabs my elbow, yanking me to his chest.

I wrench my arm from his grip, anger coursing through me. "Aren't you listening to me? They *have* her!" My chest rises and falls rapidly, my anger only growing hotter. "If you won't fucking come with me, then I'll just go on my own."

Tony emerges from his room, dressed in his usual attire, and throws clothes at Devin. "Get dressed," he grits out. "It's honing in now and we can start heading across town."

Devin hurriedly dresses as Tony almost wrenches the door from its hinges, eyes on his phone in his other hand. "You're not fucking going *anywhere* on your own. You will only be safe with *us*." He cuts a look at Devin. "But she's right; we need to go now because they like to work quickly."

And even though they never let me see the footage of Kate, I can only imagine the look of pain and despair on her face right before they pulled the trigger, taking a piece of me right with it. I refuse to let Bri have the same fate.

We file out, riding the elevator down to the garage. My body thrums with adrenaline, ready to take down anyone who gets in my way. The doors open to the garage, and both men exit, walking in separate directions, leaving me standing right outside the elevator, panicked and confused.

"Where the fuck are you going?" Devin's voice echoes across the garage just as Tony wrenches open the door of an old, white Honda Civic. "We're not fucking taking that fucking piece of shit."

Tony turns, eyes turning molten gray. "It's too old to have any tracking devices, so they won't see us coming, and you know I souped it up. It's *fast*."

Devin rolls his eyes and lets out a growl as he yanks open

the door of the large, blacked out SUV. "Tony, that thing won't make it across town, and we don't have time for this. Get the fuck in and we'll discuss that fucking piece of shit later."

"Devin, just because you fucking think that you know what's best doesn't mean—"

I scream, the sound bouncing across the concrete, silencing them. "I don't have time for this fucking shit. Tony, get in the car, and let's fucking go. Bri's life is in danger." I run toward Devin and yank open the back door, sliding in on the driver's side.

Tony stands frozen as Devin walks around the vehicle in long strides, putting himself into the passenger's seat. I hear the door to the Civic slam, echoing through the garage as Tony's boots pound against the ground.

His massive body takes over the driver's seat, angrily slamming the door shut. He throws the vehicle into reverse and whips it out of the spot, gaining speed as we travel through the garage. The door is barely open as he flies through it. The air in the vehicle is thick, suffocating me as we pull out onto the street.

The sky has just opened up and the rain is coming down in sheets, making it hard to see even as the wipers move as fast as they can. Tony speeds through the streets with precision, even as the car attempts to hydroplane multiple times as he flies through every intersection. I grip the handle on the door and hold on for dear life as Tony races through town.

"Hurry, Tony. *Please*," I plead. He hits the gas to speed up because even though I don't know exactly where we're going, he has honed in on it, his GPS guiding us. We make several turns, swerving in and out of vehicles that all feel like they are watching our every move. I can't shake the feeling that somewhere, someone has eyes on us. But, just like Tony, I'm sure they can see us on CCTV, lying in wait for us to barge in.

The rain comes down harder, thunder rumbling the car.

My heart races as we approach an intersection. The green on the stoplight is nothing more than a blurred speck of light through the rain-splattered windshield. The engine revs as Tony accelerates, making sure we make it through the light before it changes.

I close my eyes, trying to think of anything else, but the idea that Bri is in the clutches of the same person who abused me and killed our friend because he fucking won't let me go rushes through me. They have turned to such violence because he can't stand the fact that I got away and I'm happy. Genuinely happy for the first time in years. That my life has changed for the better since I took the chance and found myself in the arms of not one, but two men who would burn the world down for me.

Even in this time of crisis, I have never felt more safe and secure than when I'm with them. I believe them when they say that they won't let anything happen to me as long as they're alive. And I feel a pang in my chest knowing that I would tear down the world for them, too. For the new family that I've found inside the club. And in the name of this new life, we're going to take down the fucker who's trying to take all of that away from me.

We slide through the intersection and just as we pass under the stoplight, I catch headlights as they come up on my window. The vehicle seems to go deafeningly silent, the world slowing around me. A crunching sound fills the cab, pain prickling across my skin like shattered glass. I grip the handle with all my strength as my body becomes weightless. A scream bubbles up my throat but is cut off as the gravity of the world falls on me, and everything suddenly goes black.

EPILOGUE

THE DOOR SWINGS OPEN. The same apartment that I have walked through a million times, that has always welcomed me, feels off. My eyes skim across the space and it's obvious that it was left in a hurry. I suck in a shuddering breath as I rush in, my heels clicking on the floor. Thunder rattles the wall of windows as the rain hammers against the glass, blurring the lights of the city.

"What are we doing here, Tasha?" Nate's voice is low, filled with annoyance. "We should be at the fucking hospital."

I give him a fleeting glance as I take a seat at Tony's computer. "Go then. You don't need to be here." I keep my voice smooth, mirroring the one I use when I'm forced to talk to the same pieces of shit that I know did this. "This is something that I need to do."

His eyes darken, giving me a look that I've seen from him, but never directed toward me. "There are other ways that we can help them besides snooping on Anthony's computer." He looks around the apartment, his eyes narrowing like a detective looking for clues.

"Or you could just board your private jet and fly somewhere safe since that's where you prefer to spend your time."

His head whips toward me with such ferocity you would have thought I had punched him with my impressive right hook. But even as he opens his mouth to object, I push on. "Plus, I wouldn't want your golden boy status to be tarnished. I can see the headlines now if you're seen with me outside of these walls."

His mouth hangs open as if the words that were on his tongue became too heavy and have fallen to the ground at his feet. His eyes widen before he snaps his lips shut. His fingers curl tightly around the phone, his large hands nearly crushing it to pieces. "Tasha, I—" he grits out before I raise my hand up to cut him off.

"I don't have time for this discussion, Nate," I say as I try to navigate Tony's *very* cryptic computer. "Right now, *this* is more important."

I click on the icon that Tony damn near burned into my memory, my heart thundering in my ears louder than the storm raging outside. I feel Nate close the space between us, heat radiating off him as he bends over, looking at the screen over my shoulder.

He watches quietly, even as the tension grows between us, as I go through each step just as Tony showed me all those years ago. His deep, gruff voice fills my head, giving me step by step instructions, the same instructions he made me repeat back to him until I could recite it in my sleep. It was one of the few times that he truly opened up to me, giving me a glimpse into his fucked up past and the steps he took to ensure that it didn't catch up to him. A glimpse that neither one of us ever spoke of again.

The only person who knows more is Devin, and he will take those parts of Tony to his grave, never letting them see the light of day.

The keys click under my fingers as I type in the first of the security codes. It opens a new screen, and I just stare at the words in a foreign language that I haven't seen written before, because Tony's simulation was in English.

Is it fucking German? What the fuck is it?

"Swedish?" Nate's breath is warm against the shell of my ear, sending goosebumps across my skin. He leans in closer, his chest pressing against me. "This is an offshore bank account." He reaches for the mouse, but I lay my hand over it before he can touch it, stopping him in his tracks. His eyes cut to mine; his words borderline accusatory. "Why did he give you access to a bank account? What the fuck is this about, Tasha? I want some fucking answers."

Ignoring him, I put my focus back on the screen because I don't really have an answer for him. I have a million questions that I could have asked, that I *should* have asked when Tony first sat me down and gave me this one thing to do in a situation like the one we're currently in.

I can hear his voice and picture us in this exact spot as he said, "*If anything ever happens to me and Devin, this is what you need to do. Someone will come and help.*"

I feel the prickle of tears behind my eyes as I squeeze them shut. Stay the fuck together, Natasha. You can't lose it now, not when the guys need you the most. When *Lena* needs you.

I suck in a deep breath, Nate's presence suffocating me as I click the word *Överföra*. It's the only word on the page that I recognize from Tony's instructions. It brings me to a page full of words that I don't know and don't have time to look up. However, I am extremely familiar with the little box in which you put your monetary amount. I type in the first set of numbers, 9204, and click the button next to it.

Given what the simulation said, the screen refreshes, the box now blank with the words Överföringen slutförd or transfer completed. I check my phone, but the only thing new on the screen is a few messages from my girls downstairs. I place the phone down face up in case a message comes from whoever is supposed to be on the other end. Tony's tech intelligence makes the government's own defenses look weak, and he's *incredibly* thorough. The way he has rooted himself in the darkest parts of the internet is terrifying, and the less I know about it, the better. I don't know how long to wait until the next step, but I will give it a few minutes.

"What is the significance of 9204?" Nate's voice has softened, but I can still hear the agitation in it as he breathes down my neck. Why did I fucking let him come with me?

"I-I don't really know." His eyes are still glued to the screen as I take him in. He really is a handsome man with his sharp jawline, dirty blond hair, and deep blue eyes. Not bright like Devin's, but dark like the depths of the ocean. I look at his large hand that's planted on the table, his fingers spread wide as he supports himself, leaning over me even more. I think about the way those hands have felt against my skin and fight the urge to lay mine across it, to soak up his warmth.

Instead, I turn my attention back to the screen and type in the second set of numbers: *9003*, repeating the same process as before. The screen refreshes, and I sit back, letting it stay open for a few more minutes just in case.

Nate looks back at me. "What did this do?"

I can see the wariness in his eyes, and I already know he's not going to like my answer. "I already told you that I don't know."

He leans in. "You mean to tell me that Anthony sat you down, told you to do this in an emergency, not letting you in on anything more, and you're okay with that?" His eyes darken. "You have put too much trust into someone who keeps everyone at arm's length and has next to no morals. This could be a part of some plan he's had all along. We don't know anything about his past or who he could have been involved with, and yet you just sent out some fucking beacon?"

Yes.

It's the only word I can form, but I let it die on my tongue. I don't have to answer him about anything, because while I am still in the dark about a lot of things with Tony, he also doesn't know everything about me. Only Drew does, and those secrets died with him, the ones he promised to take with him to his grave, and unfortunately, he did too soon.

Nate's eyes flash with the lightning before they darken again. He stands up quickly and spins the chair toward him, nearly giving me whiplash. His body cages me in as he leans back down, his nose grazing mine.

His breathing is deep and rabid, and his mouth is gritted, showing his teeth. His breath is hot on my face as if he's breathing fire. "I want some fucking answers, Tasha. What is the fucking purpose of this? Who the fuck did you send out a message to?"

My spine is rod straight, and the tears that I fought back earlier are pushing against my eyes, burning them. I can feel my entire body vibrating as adrenaline and fear run through me. "I did *exactly* what he told me to do, Nate." I push down the sob that's trying to climb up my throat. "He told me that if anything happened to them, I was supposed to come here and do this. I don't know who or what is on the other end, but I did what I was supposed to do."

The arms of the chair creak in his grip. My heart roars loudly in my ears as I take Nate in. He looks angry and confused and is barely holding it together, but he doesn't take his eyes off me. "What else has he told you to do? I didn't think you listened to the commands of men anymore. Or have you fallen back into your old ways?"

His words are like arrows that were launched through his gritted teeth, and they snap me out of my panic-induced stupor. My hands fly up and shove at his chest, but his hands only tighten on the arms of the chair. He yanks it closer to him, making it impossible for me to escape him. "Did he tell you his little secrets before or after you fucked him, *Natasha*?" he growls out.

His words awaken the cruel street rat that I have kept

locked away, rattling in her cage until I let her out. It's been years since I let a man corner me and then speak to me like this. My hand connects with his face, and the smack echoes up into the high ceiling. The impact causes his head to snap to the side, and his hair falls across his forehead.

He takes a few deep breaths before he pushes himself up, straightening himself to his full height. His fingers hover over the now red mark across his face, blood welling from the scratches of my nails. I push the chair back from him before standing on my own wobbling legs. The tension in the room is thick because I don't know what to do right now even as his breathing slows. I fight against my flight response and stand my ground. He's never spoken like this to me before, and I've only seen images of his father on the internet, but right now, he's never looked more like him.

He finally looks at me, his eyes wide with shock as he takes me in. I swallow around the lump in my throat and let him be the first one to speak. "Tash, I—" He steps toward me, but I don't allow him to close the distance between us, and I step back. I refuse to cower away, and instead, keep my head held high. "Tash, I'm sorry." He runs a hand through his hair, pushing the strands out of his face before yanking on them. "I just…I don't know what to do."

I watch as his anger transforms into fear. He attempts to blink away tears, but one escapes, running down his cheek to his jaw. I understand his fear because I would be devastated if I were to lose anyone in our circle. I haven't let it sink in that Devin and Tony are fighting for their lives while we're here transferring money to an offshore bank account, hoping that whoever is on the other end answers the call. I can see why Nate would think that this is a waste of time, but Tony was adamant that this had to be done if anything happened to them and not to tell anyone about it.

It's not lost on me that Devin is Nate's best friend. They have leaned on each other well before I ever came around, and while I have never really let myself get too close to other people, I let these men in. Devin never treated me as the street rat I was but encouraged my deviant ways and helped me become the powerful woman I am now. They both showed me that I am more than just a few holes to be fucked by slimy men, but that I'm an intelligent woman whose opinions matter.

I see the pain in Nate's eyes as his shoulders silently slump, his hand coming up to wipe away another tear that mixes with the blood welling on his face. I feel a tug in my heart, and I take a step toward him. He doesn't move as I close the distance. I let my hand float up to his chest, his heart thundering under my palm. "He's going to be okay," I whisper. "He has to be. They *both* have to be."

I look into Nate's eyes, the emotions swirling through them, nearly drowning both of us. His hand slips to my waist, gently pulling me toward him. He presses his forehead to mine as his other hand tucks loose strands of my hair behind my ear, his touch burning my skin.

I close my eyes as our hearts thunder in time with each other. "What do we do now?" he asks, his deep voice going rough and breaking the silence.

I pull back. "Well, as their emergency contact, I should probably head to the hospital just in case Devin tries to torch the place to the ground. Apparently, he's already tried to escape, and they had to sedate him again."

The corner of his mouth twitches. "Of fucking course he would need to be sedated." His gaze flicks to the computer. "What about Anthony?"

I pull in a deep breath, letting my hand fall from his chest as I run it through my hair. "He's, uh, still in surgery." I stare at his desk, my heart sinking in my chest. "He lost a lot of blood and he's fighting for his life right now."

"And what of Lena?" he asks, barely above a whisper.

I gulp as bile rises up my throat. "I have our best people

looking for her." I press my hand to my chest, trying to ease the knot that's tightening, threatening to steal my breath. "But they've hidden their tracks, and they're blindly looking everywhere within a fifty-mile radius." And the one who could uncover them is just doing what he can to stay alive.

A hole rips open in my chest as the reality of the situation finally hits me. Her piece of shit ex-fiancé stopped at nothing to get her, and I know that the guys will stop at nothing to get her back if they make it out of the hospital alive.

Nate's fingers brush my jaw before he lifts my chin to look up at him, sending a jolt through me. His eyes are burning bright, and I can feel the heat burning through me. "We need to go," he rasps, his emotions almost choking him. Dropping his hand, he pulls out his phone and begins sending messages as he moves toward the door.

He's nearly in the hallway before my legs start moving as I work around the apartment, prepping it to be empty for a while. The knot in my chest tightens, stealing my breath as I turn off the lights. I don't know when or if my friends will be back in the apartment, but after all they've done for me, I will do everything I can for them. They deserve to come out on the other side, let the world see them for who they are, and let them be happy.

All three of them.

It's not a conventional love, not even close, but seeing them open up over the last few weeks has been like watching the first flower of spring rise from the snow. I've watched the shadows around Tony lighten, his eyes brighten. Lena has started to accept her dark desires, while both have accepted Devin and his demons. They don't shy away when they step out into the light, showing off the darkest parts of him. It's the way that Lena reaches out a hand and walks side by side with them that squeezes my heart and lets me know that true love does exist in this god forsaken world.

I only hope that someday, someone will do the same for me.

Leaning against the open door, Nate waits for me. His brow is furrowed as he stares down at his phone, his fingers flying across the screen. I imagine that he's working to pull favors with his string of contacts, both in and out of the city.

He's just as stressed as I am and wants to find whoever did this. He might not be one to get his hands dirty, but I am. I will have no problem strapping every single motherfucker involved to the table and slicing their balls from their bodies. I will make them pay for the damage that they've caused in my fucking home. To my family.

My phone rings and I'm met with the hospital's number as it moves across my screen. As I answer it, my heart leaps into my throat, jamming the phone to my ear. "Hello?"

"Natasha?" The nurse's tone is clipped. "We need you to come down here. It's urgent."

My stomach drops and nausea rolls through me. "Is-is everything okay?" I can feel Nate's eyes on me as my body starts to tremble.

"There have been some major changes to Mr. Fox's status, and unfortunately, we have had to put Mr. Green in a medically induced coma. Please come as soon as you can to get their affairs in order."

I press my hand to my mouth to stifle a sob. My vision begins to tunnel as my knees wobble, threatening to go out from under me. The nurse's voice fades as a high-pitched whistle fills my ears. If Tony doesn't make it, Devin will run down the path of destruction to find Lena and will sooner give up his own life than be without them.

He's made that point very clear on more than one occasion.

A large, warm hand grips my shoulder, and I can hear my name cut through the noise. "Tasha?" My phone is pulled from my grip as I fight to get myself out of my head. I'm met with deep blue eyes as my vision clears onto Nate's handsome face. "Tasha, we need to go." He wraps an arm around my shoulders and moves us toward the door.

My heart thunders in my chest, making my ribs vibrate with every beat. I can hear the murmur of Nate's voice as we pass the threshold, my feet carrying me toward the elevator as his arm slips from my shoulders. He pauses behind me, giving the apartment a once-over before gripping the door handle. The elevator doors whoosh open, and my legs are still unsteady as I step in.

Nate's eyes are down on his phone, his attention caught between whoever he's messaging and me as he pulls the door behind him. The roaring in my ears has softened, and just as the door is about to shut, a ding sounds from inside the apartment.

ACKNOWLEDGMENTS

What a fucking journey, y'all.

This book wouldn't be here without the push and pull of the people who believed in me the most and inspired me to write it based entirely on a bit—one that we clearly became *very* committed to. It's a labor of love and it is a little piece of me that I have always wanted to share with the world. I hope you loved it as much as I loved writing it.

First and foremost, a massive thank you to Kayla M., whose incredible insights helped shape this novel from the very begin- ning. Your creativity and support are invaluable in bringing the world of Masquerave to life.

A special thank you to Hannah G. Scheffer-Wentz and Zee of English Proper Editing. Your meticulous attention to detail and dedication as editors have truly polished this book into some- thing I'm proud of. Your comments gave me life and made the process of editing that much easier. We're bound for life.

To Courtney, my amazing PA, thank you for keeping me organized and on track during the final publishing push. You truly helped make the impossible tasks possible, and I'm forever grateful for our nearly lifelong friendship. In the spirit of The Click Five, we're gonna have a good day.

I want to thank my commissioned artist, Giovanna, for bringing my characters to life with her beautiful art style. You have laid the groundwork for how I want people to envision this world and these characters. There is no better place to showcase your talent than to have your incredible art featured prominently at the very front of this book.

Thank you to Designs by Charly for the breathtaking cover design—your work is stunning, and you turned my vision into

reality in the most beautiful way. I have many books planned for this world, and now there's only one person I want to create all my covers with. I'll let you guess who.

Thank you to Brianna for making the interior look absolutely incredible. You're now officially part of the team and will continue to receive long-winded voice notes from me for every project.

To my Mooses—Kristen, Stephanie, Ashlee, and Kim—thank you for being some of the best humans. Can you believe that what began as a joke to help us survive the workday, evolved into a whole-ass book? Without your friendship, humor, and support, I wouldn't have made it to the finish line.

To Olivia, the ultimate pusher—thank you for always encour- aging me to keep going, even when my imposter syndrome doubled down. Your belief in me propelled this book forward and occasionally saved me from drowning in self-doubt. If a straight, white guy can do it, so can we.

To the real Tony Fox, thank you for having such a badass name that was impossible to ignore and for always being an upstanding guy. Your legacy will live on in this story forever.

To my ex, who served as the inspiration for the antagonist — thanks for being a shitty human, the villain in everyone's story, and for providing the perfect source material. (You truly did me a favor.)

To my Beta readers, Courtney, Christina, Amy, and Anna, thank you for your honesty, dedication, and invaluable input as dark romance readers. Your feedback helped make this book what it is today.

Thank you to my ARC and PR Teams for reading, sharing, and helping me spread the word. Your feedback and support were essential to this book's success and helped me shape my career as a writer and author.

To my parents, thank you for nurturing my creativity and always supporting my wild imagination. Even though I will never let you read this book (for your own good), if you do,

you'd probably look back and question all your parenting choices.

Lastly, to Casey, my endlessly devoted husband, who has stood by me through it all for the past 15 years and has supported this wild writing journey, thank you for being my rock and my biggest cheerleader. I couldn't have made it without you. I love you.

ABOUT THE AUTHOR

KL Hill has always been a maladaptive daydreamer with a boundless imagination, often lost in the wild stories she dreams up. While this is her debut publication, it's far from the first story she's wanted to share with the world, and certainly isn't her last.

If you enjoy her work, subscribe to her Substack for weekly updates and access to exclusive serial chapters, sneak peeks, and art commissions for her latest projects.

KL Hill calls Indiana home, where she lives with her husband, various pets—including cats, dogs, chickens, and racing pigeons—and, of course, her never-ending stream of stories.

SUBSCRIBE TO KL HILL'S SUBSTACK

amazon.com/author/klhillauthor
instagram.com/klhill_author

facebook.com/klhillions
goodreads.com/klhillauthor
threads.net/@klhill_author

www.ingramcontent.com/pod-product-compliance
Lightning Source LLC
Chambersburg PA
CBHW021402310726
48971CB00005B/1171